USA TODAY and *Wall Street Journal* bestselling author **Janice Lynn** has a Master's in Nursing from Vanderbilt University and works as a nurse practitioner in a family practice. She lives in the southern United States with her Prince Charming, their children, their Maltese named Halo, and a lot of unnamed dust bunnies that have moved in since she started her writing career. Readers can visit Janice via her website at janicelynn.net.

Susan Carlisle's love affair with books began when she made a bad grade in mathematics. Not allowed to watch TV until the grade had improved, she filled her time with books. Turning her love of reading into a love for writing romance, she now pens hot medicals. She loves castles, travelling, afternoon tea, reading voraciously and hearing from her readers. Join her newsletter at SusanCarlisle.com.

HEART DOCTOR'S SUMMER REUNION

JANICE LYNN

WEDDING DATE WITH HER BEST FRIEND

SUSAN CARLISLE

MILLS & BOON

First published in Great Britain 2023
by Mills & Boon, an imprint of HarperCollins*Publishers* Ltd,
1 London Bridge Street, London, SE1 9GF

www.harpercollins.co.uk

HarperCollins*Publishers* Macken House, 39/40 Mayor Street Upper, Dublin 1, D01 C9W8, Ireland

ISBN: 978-0-263-30616-3

08/23

This book is produced from independently certified FSC™ paper to ensure responsible forest management.
For more information visit: www.harpercollins.co.uk/green.

Printed and Bound in the UK using 100% Renewable Electricity at CPI Group (UK) Ltd, Croydon, CR0 4YY

HEART DOCTOR'S SUMMER REUNION

JANICE LYNN

MILLS & BOON

With love to my grandmother, Janie Green,
who broke her foot last summer and inspired this story.

CHAPTER ONE

FLIPPING ON THE LIGHT, Dr. Charlotte Fairwell breathed in the familiar surroundings of her grandmother's South Carolina home, a plethora of comfort, art and bright colors that all told of the sea.

Walking to the kitchen island, Lottie ran her fingers over a smooth piece of bird-shaped driftwood that her grandmother had twisted rusted wire around and mounted on a pedestal. Lottie had visited last year over the Christmas holidays, but her grandmother's artwork was constantly in flux, and she wanted to wander through the house to reconnect with every nook and cranny of the two-story home. Her red-eye flight out of Boston that morning was taking its toll, though. She'd shower, then sleep. With Gram in the hospital, the next few days weren't going to be easy.

Placing her suitcase in the room she'd claimed during the summer she'd spent with Gram when she was eighteen years old, Lottie stripped off her clothes. The en suite bathroom was as uniquely decorated as the rest of the house with its colorful decor. Nothing matched, yet it all blended in a way that somehow fit. Just like Gram.

The tension in her shoulders relaxed beneath the shower's hot water. Gram was going to be fine. Yes, she'd shattered her foot and ankle in multiple places—how had she done that with a simple fall?—but she would heal and be back to combing the islands for "treasure" that she repurposed into artwork. Everything would be fine.

Wet hair brushed back and body wrapped in a towel, quite possibly one she'd used as a teen as her earth child grandmother wasn't one for replacing anything that had remaining life, Lottie headed toward the kitchen, planning to search for something to appease her growling belly. Other than the pretzels on the plane that morning, she hadn't eaten. Gram wasn't much of a cook, but always kept a generous supply of the salted caramel, chocolate and the pecan candies that were her weakness. A weakness Lottie had inherited.

Click.

She hugged the towel tighter. Had that been the front door's lock turning, then opening?

Sweat broke out on Lottie's skin. Someone was in her grandmother's house! Had the hire-car driver who'd driven her from the hospital in Beaufort to Fripp Island returned and jimmied the lock to let himself in? She hadn't gotten a bad vibe, but one never knew.

Too bad she hadn't picked up Maritime, Gram's dog, from her neighbor's. A sixty-pound dog being in the house might have caused the intruder to reconsider.

Trying to quietly retrace her steps down the hallway to her room to dig a can of pepper spray from her purse, Lottie bumped into a metal canister that held a variety of colorful glass bottles Gram had rescued from the sea and poked over a large driftwood piece's roots and branches. Clang! She grabbed at the bottles, loosening her towel, which took immediate precedence. In her efforts to grasp the fabric, she hit Gram's piece again. Metal, wood and glass crashed onto the tile. Clackety-clank-clank! Glass shattered about her feet.

So much for whoever was in the house not knowing she was there.

Intending to make a run for her pepper spray, Lottie took a step. A sharp shard sliced deep into her bare foot. "Ouch!"

She couldn't suppress the excruciated cry or the tears that prickled her eyes.

Ignore the pain. Get to your purse.

She'd barely taken two hobbling steps when the hall light flicked on and a ghost from her past stepped into the hallway.

At Jackie Dunlap's request, Lincoln Thomas stopped by her place to ready the house for what would hopefully only be a few days of sitting empty. Unfortunately, he suspected she'd be away from her beloved Fripp longer than she'd claimed during her call. Then again, Jackie was just stubborn enough that it wouldn't surprise him if she'd found a way home that very evening.

Hearing movement in the hallway, then the loud crashing of Jackie's art piece onto the floor, had him pausing long enough inside the foyer to grab a sea-weathered oar from where Jackie had hung it. It wasn't much of a weapon but would still deliver a good whack. Crime was rare on Fripp, but word of Jackie's hospitalization may have gotten out. Had someone broken into her home with plans to search out easily removed valuables while the house sat unattended?

Oar at the ready, Linc mentally prepared himself for whatever was about to happen. Rounding the corner, he saw the one thing—the one person—he could never fully be prepared to face even though he'd imagined seeing her again hundreds of times over the past twelve years.

"Lottie." Saying her name out loud had his heart hammering even faster. Maybe he'd rounded the corner and he'd been the one hit in the head. His was certainly spinning enough he'd believe something had hit him. Outside of his dreams, he hadn't set eyes on Lottie Fairwell since he'd been nineteen and so in love with her that he'd barely been able to think for how his heart had pounded when near her. His heart was pounding crazy right now.

Lottie!

"Linc!" Green gaze wide, eyeing his still raised weapon, she hugged the towel, which barely covered her midsection.

"What are you doing here?" they asked in unison.

Not that Linc couldn't guess. She'd returned because of her grandmother's fall. Jackie hadn't mentioned Lottie's return when she'd asked him to check her place. Had she known her only grandchild was home? He'd thought it was odd that she hadn't asked her next-door neighbor, who'd taken Jackie's Carolina dog home with her the night before, to ready the house, but he'd agreed to go by as soon as he'd finished sanding the bathroom walls he'd spackled earlier that week in his dream house. Well, he was working to transform it into his dream house.

Lottie was on Fripp.

Linc fought to keep his eyes on her face rather than the body that had haunted his dreams for over a decade. Maybe one's first love always set the bar by which to measure all others. Either way, he'd gotten over that nonsense years ago. It was just the adrenaline rush of not knowing who was in the house that had his heart slamming against his rib cage.

But that didn't keep his insides from stirring at the fact that, except for the flimsy towel, Lottie was naked and less than ten feet from him. How was that supposed to not resurrect memories? Her toned body had filled out a little with age but was otherwise just as he recalled. Although a busy cardiologist in Boston, she obviously took time to stay in shape. With her wet blond hair combed back from her makeup-free face, she looked much as she had the summer they'd spent every spare second together. The summer they'd fallen madly in love with one another. Summer love. Teen love. Real and yet, not.

"Linc, I— Am I imagining that you're here?" Shifting her weight, she grimaced, as if in pain, then arched her right foot, its nails painted bubblegum-pink, and balanced on her toes.

"You're cut." Guilt hit that he'd been so stunned at seeing her that he'd missed what should have been obvious.

Taking in the blood trickling onto the floor, she lifted her gaze back to his. A pleading emotion shone in the green depths of her eyes for the briefest second before they went blank. Her lids closed and, skin losing all color, her body went lax.

"Lottie!"

"You always were one for dramatics, but I never expected you to fall into my arms first thing."

Lottie recognized the voice. It was one she'd never forget. How could she when it belonged to Linc? Her sweet, sweet Linc, with whom she'd spent hours exploring Fripp the summer before she'd left for university.

She hadn't heard his voice outside of her dreams in more than a decade. The events of the past twenty-four hours swirled through her consciousness. Gram had broken her foot and was in the hospital. Lottie had flown to South Carolina and was in Fripp. A noise had startled her. Had she fallen and hit her head and because of where she was, where she'd spent that magical summer prior to her leaving for university and his working a construction job on the island, her brain was filling in that Linc was there?

No, she hadn't fallen. Strong arms wrapped around her, carried her. Linc's arms. Eyes still closed because they were too heavy to open, she breathed in. Her senses exploded as he filled her nostrils. He smelled the same, all spice, sea and man. With his teasing tone mixed with concern, he sounded the same. He'd always teased her, made her laugh at herself and the world. He felt the same, too. *Better*. His boyish nineteen-year-old body had filled out, his chest thicker, his shoulders broader, his arms stronger. Lottie swallowed the lump forming in her throat. How long had it been since she'd been so aware of a man? Brian certainly didn't elicit such strong responses from her senses. Not that he'd tried in eons. These days they felt more like friends than a couple.

"I'll give you a little slack since that's a nasty cut on your foot," Linc continued. "But I'm positive there's some rule that doctors aren't allowed to pass out at the sight of blood."

Her throbbing foot registered. She'd stepped on broken glass. Heat flooded Lottie's face. She was never opening her eyes. She was practically naked and in Linc Thomas's arms within seconds of seeing him. Some things never changed. It sure hadn't taken him long to have his way with her that summer. Or had it been her who'd had her way with him? The specifics blurred, just that they'd been young, healthy and in love. That their relationship had been so physical had seemed a natural progression of the sweet nothings they whispered to each other. Linc had been her first and she'd never regretted that, not even after they'd ended things. Or maybe she had wished she'd never known what it felt like to be with Linc so she wouldn't have such high expectations and could possibly move forward with her relationship with Brian without wishing she could describe his kisses as more than just so-so.

"I think I recognize this towel," Linc continued. "It looks like the one we used to take to Pritchard's with us and that the wind caught that time. I had to wade out into the water to retrieve it, remember?"

There had been nothing so-so about the kisses she'd gotten that day. Goose bumps prickled her skin as she recalled lying on a blanket with Linc, the ocean playing a song just for them and their bodies dappled with moonlight. With his fevered kisses and gentle touch, he'd coaxed her body to the ultimate in pleasure. Whispering his affections, he'd promised to love her forever. But by forever, he'd clearly meant only until summer's end.

"Ah, there's some color in those lovely high-boned cheeks of yours." His tone was teasing, as if he knew she was conscious and purposely keeping her eyes closed. Did he also know where her mind had gone? That part of her wanted to beat her fists against his chest that he'd ended things, that when she'd thought she might die from missing him, he'd ignored her heartfelt voice mail declaring her love and desire to come back to him? Saying that she was willing to go to university close to wherever his next construction job took him?

"I was beginning to wonder if you were going to come to on your own," he continued, his arms strong around her, "or if I was going to have to do mouth-to-mouth to wake you."

Face hot, she opened her eyes, looking into the bluest eyes she'd ever seen. Eyes that seemed to look right through to her very soul. She'd once bared all she was to him, which hadn't been difficult since he'd always known what she was thinking, anyway. The way his eyes sparkled had her wondering if he still had that power. Did he know her body had instantly come alive at his nearness? Did he have any idea how many nights she'd cried herself to sleep because he'd said it was better for them to end things rather than try to maintain a long-distance relationship and end up tainting their perfect summer together?

Why didn't you call me back?

"No mouth-to-mouth." She wished she could bury her face in his chest rather than reveal to him whatever it was he saw in her gaze.

As those all-seeing eyes continued to search hers, one corner of his mouth hiked up. "Too bad."

Seriously? Anger and frustration hit.

"Put me down!" She put a hand protectively over the towel to make sure it didn't slip. Why was he still holding her? Why was he even there?

More and more senses popped to life as the feel of his arms against her bare legs registered, as the once tightly tucked towel now rode up her hips. If there had been anyone else in the room, they'd have gotten an eyeful.

"So that you can bleed on Jackie's floor?" Shaking his head, he set her on the kitchen countertop.

Lottie kept her arms tightly around herself, making sure the towel stayed in place as she crossed her legs to try to decrease how exposed she felt. Why hadn't she wrapped two or three of the things around her? Or better yet, gotten dressed? Then again, she hadn't known she was going to be face-to-face with anyone, much less her past.

Linc examined the bottom of her foot. His blue eyes, fringed with dark lashes, lifted. For the briefest of moments, it struck her that his eyes no longer held the adoration that they had in the past when he'd always gazed upon her with passionate love. Deep loss hit. Ridiculous. It's been over for twelve years. She did not expect Linc to gaze upon her with adoration—but the fact that he wasn't was doing odd things to her that felt akin to grief, as though she'd lost something precious. Bringing up things she'd grieved long ago and gotten over, moved on from.

"You aren't going to like this," he warned, still holding her foot, "but I need to clean off the blood to see if there's glass in there."

Yeah, he was right. She wasn't going to like that. Nor did she like that her brain was more aware of his strong, yet gentle fingers holding her foot than it was of the glass that was definitely still in there.

"I can do it," she insisted, feeling more and more self-conscious. She'd imagined seeing Linc again more times than she could count. They'd bump into each other. He'd see the accomplished cardiologist she'd become, that she'd moved on and had a great life, and he'd realize how wrong he'd been to let her go. Not once in those imaginings had she been soaking wet, wrapped in a towel and bleeding while he looked like hunky male perfection.

"Letting me would be easier."

True, and yet, nothing had ever been further from the truth. Nothing about Linc was easy. Not the way he held her, not the way his eyes no longer held affection, not the way he sounded so immune to her presence, when she was so off-kilter.

"Turn so that I can rinse off your foot in the sink," he requested. "And hang on to your towel."

No worries there. Lottie clung to the towel for dear life as she scooted to where she could drop her foot into the ceramic basin. Linc flipped on the faucet, then checked to make sure the temp was okay. When satisfied, he took the nozzle, sprayed her foot and gently cleansed away the blood.

Watching him, a hundred emotions hit. This was Linc. The young man who had been her first love. Her first lover. Her first heartbreak. Linc.

"I'm sorry you're having to do this. I really could have." Sitting on the kitchen countertop with her foot in the sink, wearing only a towel, was about as awkward a reunion as she could imagine.

"It's not a big deal." He shrugged as if it truly wasn't. He'd clearly forgotten her long ago, writing off what they'd shared as summer love that had been wonderful, but never meant to last.

His fingernail scraped over the glass, sending a sharp pain all the way up her leg.

"Ow." She jerked free from his grasp.

"Sorry. I didn't mean to hurt you."

But you did. Hating her thoughts, she closed her eyes, counted to ten, then opened them to find that he was watching her.

"You okay?"

No. Yes.

"Fine."

"Good. There for a second I thought you were about to black out again." Reaching into a nearby drawer, he pulled out a dish towel. He gently wrapped the fabric around her foot to prevent blood from dripping, taking care not to put any pressure over the area with the glass so as not to push it deeper. Moving to the cabinet that contained Gram's odds and ends, he rummaged until he found her first aid kit, which had been buried beneath boxes. He removed gauze and alcohol pads. "I need tweezers to get the glass from your foot. It's deep, but I can see it and can hopefully grab hold without having to dig it out. I can't imagine Jackie not having at least one pair in her art supplies. I'm going to go look. I'll disinfect them prior to removing your friend, there."

He obviously wasn't going to leave until he'd extracted the glass.

"There are tweezers in my makeup bag in my bathroom. They're inside a little travel kit."

His brow arched. "Is it okay if I get them?"

Realizing he was asking permission to go into her private bathroom, Lottie nodded. It wasn't as if it made sense to tell him no. She had glass in her foot. He was planning to remove it. No matter how many mind games her head was playing, it was really nothing more than Linc being helpful the same as he'd have done if she was a complete stranger.

When he returned, he didn't comment, just lifted her foot and after a few failed attempts that had Lottie gritting her teeth and clenching her fists, he pulled out a chunk of glass.

"There. Got it." He placed the tweezers and offending blue glass on the countertop, then pressed gauze to the wound. "Hold that while I find an adhesive bandage. There weren't any in the first aid kit."

"Gram's forever nicking her fingers while working on a project and keeps them out. They're—" She paused as he searched the cluttered built-in desk to one side of the kitchen. "You remember where she keeps them."

Opening one of the bandage strips, he placed it across her cut, then applied pressure to the area with his thumb. "I remember a lot of things."

Her heart thudded to a halt, then jerked hard. "I, uh, that's good."

His gaze locked with hers; he lifted his brow. "Is it, Lottie?"

Why did she get the impression he wasn't referring to where her grandmother stored things?

He glanced back at where he held her foot. "You'll be a little sore, but you should be good as new within a few days."

"Thank you."

"I should be thanking you for the glimpse at my past."

Heat flooded her face, and she adjusted the towel, making sure not to uncover her top while trying to fully hide her bottom as she crossed her arms over her chest. "A gentleman wouldn't look."

"I actually meant—" He shook his head, then losing his serious expression, he chuckled. "That wasn't what I meant, but don't sweat your terry cloth fashion statement, Lottie. It's nothing I haven't seen before."

More heat infused her cheeks.

"That was a long time ago." She hadn't expected to see Linc while in Fripp. Not once over the years since her preuniversity summer had their paths crossed. Originally from northern Florida, he'd only been on Fripp for his job. Yet, she never came back without wondering what it would be like to see him again.

Ha, who was she kidding? It didn't take visiting Fripp to make her wonder about Linc.

"Yep. It was." His gaze stayed locked with hers, almost as if he was searching for the girl she'd once been, the one who'd run into his waiting arms and showered him with kisses with complete abandon. Maybe it was that pure happiness she'd felt that summer, her world had been right, carefree, that had made them seem so perfect. So much had changed since then that it was no wonder her psyche clung to that summer as the happiest she'd ever been.

"But, like I said—" Linc's thumb eased its pressure against her foot "—I remember a lot of things."

Linc certainly hadn't forgotten Lottie. Not that he hadn't tried. He had. Especially in the months following when she'd first left South Carolina. Sometimes, he thought he'd gone a little crazy during that time. Maybe he had, especially after her phone call. But she'd been an upper middle class young woman about to leave to start school at Harvard, and he'd been nothing more than a poor kid working a construction job to help put himself through community college. He hadn't needed her mother to point out those stark differences to him.

Memories had his jaw clenching and he fought sighing. Things had worked out as they should have, though. He and Lottie had both gone on to become the people they were meant to be. Her a cardiologist as she and her parents had wanted. And, although he hadn't known at that time that it was what he wanted for his future, he loved being a physical therapist. Ending things and leaving them ended had been the right thing. But holding Lottie, feeling her skin against his again after so much time, even under such innocent circumstances, was blurring the lines of the present and the past.

"This isn't the first time I've removed something from your foot."

She bit into her lower lip.

"We'd been walking on the beach," he continued, letting the past wash over him, "and you stepped on a shell, crushing it. A piece stuck in your foot."

"I really need to learn to wear shoes, eh?" She stared down at where he held her foot. "You carried me piggyback to Gram's. I could have walked, but you wouldn't let me."

"She wasn't home. You thanked me with a kiss." More than a kiss. Much, much more.

A strangled noise came from deep in her throat. "I wouldn't expect a repeat of that."

Was she remembering how they'd ended up in her room, in that bed that flooded him with memories when he'd gone after her tweezers earlier? He'd made love to her, told her his dreams, felt her cup his face as she told him how being with him was like living a fantasy.

Being on Fripp that summer had been a fantasy. Unfortunately, they'd both had to return to reality. Lottie's reality hadn't included someone like him. Everyone had known that except her.

"No kiss?" Why was he pushing? Teasing her? He didn't want or expect a kiss of gratitude from Lottie, or anything more. "Good thing I wasn't."

Linc refocused on her foot. Lifting his thumb, he was glad to see she hadn't bled through the bandage. "Looks as if you've stopped bleeding. My work here is done." How mundane they sounded. Then again, why wouldn't they? Picking up the used gauze and tape, he tossed them into the trash bin beneath the cabinet.

"How is it that you know where everything is located in Gram's home?" Lottie asked from where she still sat on the counter.

Jackie mentioned Lottie to him from time to time. Did she not do the same with her granddaughter? Telling Lottie that he now lived on Fripp? That she'd invited him over multiple times since he'd become her neighbor and vice versa?

"It's not as if she's rearranged things since we were teens. Despite being such a creative person, she's also very much a creature of habit."

Studying him, she frowned. "That's true. I guess what I'm really wondering is why are you here, Linc? In my grandmother's house?"

"She asked me to come by to make sure everything was locked and okay for her to be away for a few days." His explanation contorted her face. "It's a bit confusing to me, too, since you're here, which she failed to mention. I'm guessing she didn't give you a heads-up, either?"

Lottie's forehead crinkled. "Gram sent you here? Why would she do that?"

He shrugged. "I assumed it was because she knew I wouldn't mind stopping by since I'd either be home or go by here on my way home."

Her eyes widened. "Home? You live on Fripp?"

She looked incredulous. Did she still think him the poor construction worker he'd been at nineteen? That she'd been the only one to obtain her dreams? Granted, her dreams had stayed on track and his ambitions had changed. But he liked his life and was proud of what he'd achieved, both in construction and as a physical therapist.

"I bought the old McMahon place when it was put up for sale this spring." His bid hadn't been the highest, but the McMahons had accepted anyway as the higher bidders wanted to tear down the house to build a much larger, modern structure and the family hadn't wanted that to happen to their late mother's place.

"I can't believe you live on Fripp in the house I always loved." Still sitting on the countertop with her thighs crossed, she hugged the towel tighter over her chest. "For that matter, I can't believe you're here and that I'm not imagining you."

Leaning against the kitchen island, he eyed her. "Why would you imagine me here, Lottie?"

Had she thought of him over the years? Of course, she had. He'd been her first. If nothing else, that would always set him apart from any lover she'd had since. Fingers curling into his palms, he recognized he had no right to feel the jealousy that punched him at the thought of anyone touching what had once been his.

And to think he'd thought he was going to do a quick walk-through at Jackie's place, then get back to working on his bathroom remodel. Nothing so mundane as that when Lottie Fairwell had returned.

Her lashes lowered, hooding her green eyes. "I, uh, you know."

Pretending a calm he didn't feel, he shook his head. "I don't. Tell me."

Her cheeks pinkened. "No matter. I don't know why I even said that. Just poor word choice. Anyway, thank you for coming by to check on Gram's house, but there's no need. I'm here."

"For how long?"

"I'm not sure." Concern etched itself onto her lovely features and remorse hit at the circumstances that had triggered her return. "As long as Gram needs me and that I can manage away from work. That's not a problem, is it?"

A thousand problems. More.

"Why would that be a problem? Whether or not you're in Fripp makes no difference to me, Lottie." Only, it did. Knowing Lottie was on Fripp, that she was so close, had every nerve ending in his body short-circuiting. "Since you're here and can keep an eye on things for Jackie, I'll head home."

Indecision shone in her green depths. "I… It was good to see you, Linc. Unexpected, but good."

"Uh, yeah, it was good to see you, too."

"I'd walk you to the door, but I'm afraid of just how much you'd see if I attempt to get down."

Running his gaze over her bare shoulders, arms and legs, realizing that if she slid off the counter, the towel likely would shift to reveal the curve of her thighs, maybe more, Linc swallowed and pushed himself away from the kitchen island. "I'll let myself out. Welcome back to Fripp, Lottie."

"Just temporarily, though," she reminded him.

Yet another thing he hadn't forgotten.

For Lottie, Fripp had never been anything more than an escape from reality.

A wise man would keep that in mind.

CHAPTER TWO

"ANYTHING INTERESTING HAPPEN last night?" Gram asked within seconds of Lottie's arrival at Beaufort Hospital the following morning.

Any doubt that her grandmother hadn't purposely sent Linc dissipated.

"You shouldn't have done that." Keeping her weight mostly off her right foot, Lottie kissed her grandmother's cheek. Although not enough to make her limp, her foot had been sore when she'd cleaned the area and put a fresh adhesive bandage over it that morning.

"Done what?" Gram's eyes, so similar to Lottie's, sparkled as she blinked innocently. As if. Lottie doubted her grandmother had ever been innocent, and that had played a huge role in why Lottie's mother had guarded all interaction she'd had with Gram. Vivien had protested Lottie's decision to spend that summer with her grandmother, but Lottie had longed to know the grandmother she'd only seen a few times.

She narrowed her gaze at the woman she loved with all her heart. "You know exactly what. Shame on you."

"Oh, that." Gram chuckled. "To be fair, I'd planned to ask Linc to go by before you got home."

"In South Carolina, you mean? Not home."

"You always said Fripp felt like home." Gram's brow lifted. "Has that changed?"

Placing her oversize purse next to the more comfortable appearing visitor chair of the two in the room, Lottie sat down. Being cautious so as not to alert Gram of her injury, she angled her foot to where her weight balanced on the back of her heel. "Let's just say that having you in the hospital is messing with my sense of homecoming."

"Yours and mine both." Gram gave her a sly look. "Did Linc tell you that he's my neighbor?"

Trying to appear nonchalant, Lottie pulled out her laptop from her bag. "He mentioned he'd bought the McMahon house. Good for him."

"He's only been there a few months and is restoring the place. Jean had been sick for so long that the house had run down while sitting mostly empty over the past couple of years." Gram's forehead squished with thought. "Before that, she tended to stay in just a few rooms so didn't notice how neglect was affecting the house."

"I recall you mentioning a few years back that she'd moved in with her son. I was sorry to hear that she had died last year. I know you'd been neighbors for decades." Lottie had never been able to decide if the two women were anything more than frenemies as they continually bickered and were rivals at everything they did, but Gram had been truly saddened when she told Lottie the news.

"Our card club hasn't been the same since she got sick. She and Gerty were the only ones who could beat me and Mary. Who would have thought that winning all the time would be so boring?" Gram rearranged the white top sheet covering her. "I was glad when her family sold her place to Linc. Apparently, he'd been looking for a while and his real estate agent contacted him the moment it went on the market."

His purchase hadn't been a random, spur of the moment impulse, but something he'd thought out. Duh, it's a house. An expensive house. Of course, he'd had to plan for its purchase.

At her grandmother's expectant look, she said, "It's always been a beautiful place."

"But in need of a lot of TLC, which Linc's giving the ole girl. Although he hired contractor friends to help with the outside, he's doing most of the work himself. It's looking great. He's a very talented young man."

Gram had no idea.

Lottie fought to keep her cheeks from heating. No way would her grandmother miss that telltale sign that Lottie was affected by her ramblings about Linc. Why had Gram not mentioned him a single time? She must have been busting on the inside knowing she was setting Lottie up to come face-to-face with him. Unlike Lottie's mother, Gram had adored Linc.

"I like your new piece, Gram. Is it commissioned or will it be going to the gallery in Charleston?"

Her grandmother's expression said she knew Lottie had purposely changed the subject away from Linc, but she acquiesced. Probably because Lottie had changed it to her art. Gram's true passion was her artwork, and few things took precedence over that.

"It's just something I've been working on, but maybe I will send it to Charleston. They've been asking me to get them more pieces." Gesturing to where she lay in the bed, she frowned. "I really don't have time for being laid up like this. Terrible timing."

"Is there ever a good time for fractures, Gram?" Lottie's

question earned a scowl, but before Gram spouted a come-back, someone knocked on the hospital room door. Both women glanced that way. Carrying a beautiful flower ar-rangement, Linc walked into the room. All the oxygen took a hiatus, leaving Lottie light-headed. She hadn't imagined how hunky grown-up Linc was. The man was hot.

He smiled at Gram. "Good morning, Jackie."

What he wore registered. Navy scrubs that fit just right everywhere except his biceps. There they appeared not too tight for comfort, but a little snug. He'd always had a body well-honed from work. Those arms and how easily he'd scooped her up the night before attested that hadn't changed. Lottie bit into her lower lip. Her gaze dropped to his ID badge. Lincoln Thomas, PT, DPT. He'd gone to physical therapy school and gotten a doctorate degree? When had he decided to pursue patient care? Then again, had she ex-pected him to be the same person now that he'd been back then? Of course, he'd grown, changed, just as she had. Re-calling how gentle he'd been with her foot, she admitted she could see him working with patients and being very good at what he did. Still, the different career path he'd taken was a shocker.

Eyeing the flowers he held, her grandmother's face lit. "Linc! We were just talking about you. Are those flowers for my beautiful granddaughter? They're gorgeous." Lot-tie's face caught fire. "The blue moons, chicories, cornflow-ers and phlox mixed in with spartina grass and dried palm fronds in that shell-covered vase makes me think of the sea."

Linc just grinned and placed the flowers on the tray table. "You know you're my best girl, Jackie. I thought you'd like the colors."

Gram beamed. "It's like having a bit of the island here with me."

"I'm impressed. It's the perfect arrangement for Gram."

"I thought so. How's your foot?"

"Fine," Lottie and her grandmother answered at the same time. Lottie grimaced.

Gram frowned. "What happened to your foot?"

Lottie wrinkled her nose at Linc. "You just had to tell on me, didn't you?"

Not looking the slightest repentant, he shrugged. "I figured you had already told her all the drama she caused. You didn't think you could replace those bottles and her not know the difference?"

"What bottles?" Gram's gaze bounced back and forth between them. "What happened that's my fault?"

"I knocked your bottles off the large hallway piece." She narrowed her gaze at her grandmother. "For the record, I refuse to take blame for the break as, had you mentioned that you'd asked Linc to stop by, I wouldn't have been frightened to hear someone."

A tiny bit of remorse flickered. "I'm sorry that you were frightened. Now, what happened to your foot?"

"I cut my foot on a glass shard. Linc got the glass out." Wondering at her giddiness that he was near, she glanced his way. "Thanks again."

"You're welcome. Sore?"

"A little. It only hurts when I step down. Thanks for asking." Listen to them sounding all polite with Gram as their avid audience. The surface might be mundane politeness, but peel away that layer and kinetic energy threatened to burst free. She didn't like the Richter-scale worthy rumbling in her chest, though. It was completely normal to feel shaky when one reconnected with their first love, right?

"No problem." Had his voice sounded a little shaky, too?

Or had Lottie imagined that? Either way, he turned toward Gram. "I hear you're going to surgery in the morning."

"Gram!" Lottie frowned. "You didn't tell me you were scheduled for surgery."

"You didn't ask," she said matter-of-factly, as if Lottie should have known to do so. "Nor had I a chance to tell you, not with us talking about how excited you were to see Linc last night."

Heaven help her.

"You were excited to see me?" Amusement laced his words to where she knew he was well aware of what Gram was doing.

"That's not what we were talking about." She avoided looking toward him for fear her eyes might reveal that she had been excited and that his teasing tone pinged a whole lot of feel-good memories. "Um—" she cleared her throat "—Gram, tell me what the surgeon said."

Gram was still looking back and forth between Lottie and Linc. "He's going to pin me back together like one of my pieces of art. He's worried that with my heel having multiple fractures that if he doesn't pin it together like some type of jigsaw puzzle that it'll refracture when I put weight on it. It's not going to be able to bear weight for at least four weeks, maybe longer. Four weeks of no walking, maybe not even with crutches." She frowned. "What would using crutches hurt?"

"He's afraid that you'd end up putting weight on your foot by accident," Linc suggested from where he stood next to Gram's bed. He spoke to Gram, but Lottie could feel his gaze still on *her*. "He doesn't want your recovery to have a setback."

Gram patted his hand. "Enough about my surgery. Let's

talk about my house. Everything looked good when you stopped by last night?"

"Yeah, everything looked just as I remembered."

Why did Lottie think he wasn't talking about the house?

"There was no need for Linc to come by last night, Gram." There. She sounded halfway composed.

Her grandmother wore a "duh" expression. "Of course, there was. Much better for you and Linc to bump into each other for the first time in the privacy of my house rather than here. Don't you agree, Linc?"

Lottie hadn't thought of it that way, but Gram had a point.

"Well?" Gram asked.

Lottie met Linc's gaze, and he chuckled. "Don't look at me. She's your grandmother. I'm just a neighbor."

"And a good one," Gram said. "You'll keep an eye on Ole Bessie? Stop by and make sure Lottie's okay?"

Lottie shook her head. "I'm thirty years old and haven't needed anyone to stop by to check on me in years."

"Maybe not, but I'll rest better knowing Linc's keeping an eye on you and my house." Gram's shoulders sagged, and a rather pitiful look come over her face.

Linc smiled at Jackie's nickname for her house, Ole Bessie, named after a beloved childhood dog.

"No worries, Jackie. You just focus on getting well. I'll keep an eye on your place and on Lottie while you're away. Anything in particular you want me to watch for?"

Delighted by his response, Gram's eyes sparkled. "Just make sure my two girls are taken care of."

The following morning, Gram wasn't nearly as perky as the day before, and she told Lottie her surgery had been postponed. During the night, her blood pressure had dropped, and her nurse had had to call Dr. Collins. They'd made medication tweaks. Although still a little lower than her baseline, her pressure had improved. Thank goodness.

Dr. Collins checked on Gram, but she was still pale and irritable.

"I'm not taking you into surgery this afternoon, but I'm ordering more labs." Empathy showed on Dr. Collins's face. "If you behave, we'll get you in the operating room in the morning to put your foot back together."

Jackie gave him an unhappy, squinty-eyed look. "Isn't that what you said yesterday?"

He held her gaze. "If you want out of this place, then don't give the nurse a reason to wake me up during the night, again."

Her grandmother didn't seem amused. "Fine. Surgery tomorrow, then home. But you'd better not change your mind again."

"Don't give me a reason to."

Gram mumbled something under her breath.

After Dr. Collins had left the room, Gram sighed. "He's just delaying my surgery for kicks."

"I'm sure that's his reason," Lottie agreed, causing Gram to cut her gaze toward her.

"Aren't you full of sass today?"

Lottie leaned over and kissed her grandmother's cheek. "I can't help myself. It's my genetics."

Whether the kiss or the comment, Gram grinned and relaxed against her pillow. "That it is. Lucky girl. How's my house?"

"I haven't torn it down yet."

Gram frowned. "Bite your tongue. How about my baby?"

"Maritime is fine." She'd picked up the blasted dog from the neighbor's the night before and dropped him off that morning. "The house is fine, Gram. They're both waiting on you to come home when you're back on your feet."

Gram's gaze narrowed. "Did Linc come by?"

"The house?" Lottie shook her head. "Not since when you forgot to let him know I was home. Why would he come by?"

"You know why he'd come by. To check on you like I asked him."

"I know you're matchmaking, Gram, but don't, okay? You know I'm in a relationship with Brian." Things were complicated enough without her grandmother's interference. Lottie took a deep breath. "You always did like Linc."

"So did you."

"Yes," she agreed, knowing there was no reason to deny it. She'd liked him right up until they'd said their goodbyes and he'd meant his. "He was a great guy."

"He still is," Gram mused, looking thoughtful. "Your first love."

"But not my grown-up love," Lottie reminded her. A vision of her mother telling her those very words flashed through her mind. She'd been miserable with missing Linc, had confessed to her mother that she was transferring to a medical school in South Carolina. Vivien had been aghast at the thought, telling her she was not throwing her future away on a silly summer love.

Linc had been a summer love, her first love, her first everything. No doubt that was why she felt so connected to him, why seeing him again had her so off-kilter. If he'd answered her call all those years ago, would she have been able to win him back? To convince him that what they'd had was more than a summer fling? Or would she have been making the biggest mistake of her life by throwing away all of her other dreams to chase after her heart's desire?

If he'd really loved her, he'd have returned her call. He hadn't. Her mother had been right to beg her not to throw her life away on a man who expected her to make all the concessions.

Lottie had loved Linc so much that she'd have dug ditches if it meant being with him, but she'd never meant that much to him. She'd thought she had, but she'd been so naive...

"If thinking about that doctor guy puts that look on your face," Gram said, interrupting her thoughts, "then I was wrong about him."

Guilt hit and Lottie fought hard to keep it from showing. "I'm both shocked that you admitted you were wrong and curious as to exactly what you're wrong about."

"I never believed you loved the doctor. When I'm wrong, I admit it." Gram fluffed her pillow, then settled back against it. "I promise to be nicer if our paths cross again."

Lottie's gaze shifted to her grandmother's. "That would be good. Brian doesn't think you like him."

Gram shrugged. "I don't dislike him."

"He's a good man." Everyone told her how lucky she was that they were a couple. Her roommate, Camilla, went on and on about how crazy Lottie was to have not already married him. Lottie's mother had wanted nothing more than for Brian to be her son-in-law. "You'd like Brian if you gave him a chance."

Gram shook her head. "Doubtful. He convinced you to stay in Boston rather than practice in South Carolina. You do realize that just because your mother approved of him doesn't mean you have to stay with him, don't you? Staying with him won't bring her back."

Lottie's throat tightened at Gram's blunt words. "Mom isn't why I'm with Brian, Gram. Nor is he why I stayed in Boston. I had an amazing job offer at the hospital to be a part of a great team that's making a difference to so many cardiac patients. Brian is only part of my life in Boston."

A small part, she realized. When not working, she had her friends and usually when she and Brian were together, it was as part of group events or with Camilla. Maybe that's why he felt more like a friend than her significant other these days. It had been eons since they'd spent any quality time together as a couple, and she couldn't recall the last time they'd done more than a quick kiss goodbye or hello.

Why had Brian's kisses never set her on fire the way a nineteen-year-old young man's had?

"I said I was wrong too soon," Gram said, interrupting her thoughts again. "Your normal look when we discuss the doctor is back."

Curiosity got the better of Lottie. "What look is that?"

"Resignation."

"Here. I thought you could use this."

Leaning back in the chair she occupied in the operating room waiting area, Lottie glanced up to see Linc holding out a coffee cup. A wooden stir stick stuck up through the lid. Today, he wore perfectly fitting black scrubs and his hospital ID badge. His hair looked a little ruffled, as if he'd run his fingers through the sun-kissed brown locks a few times.

Every time Gram's door had opened the day before, Lottie's heart had done an anticipatory quiver that had been followed by disappointment when it hadn't been Linc. He hadn't come by but had called Gram to tell her he wasn't working and had previous plans with a couple of friends helping him hang Sheetrock so wouldn't be making the drive to Beaufort for a visit.

"Thanks." She took the coffee before her fingers reached up to see if his hair was as soft as her memory believed.

Twelve years, and yet if she closed her eyes, she could see everything from that long-ago summer, could hear the sounds, smell the scents. Probably because the memory of him had never been far from her consciousness.

Popping the lid, she lifted the cup to breathe in the strong brew's aroma. Her stomach growled in appreciation. She'd been too nervous to eat. Maybe she still was, but having the coffee in hand provided a momentary distraction from the fact that Gram was in surgery and Linc had just sat down in the chair opposite from hers.

"Want these?" Reaching into his scrubs pocket, he pulled out a single sugar and creamer. Just how she liked her coffee.

Taking his offering, she eyed him. "Is it a coincidence that you brought one sugar and one creamer, or did you re-member that's how I liked my coffee?"

"Coincidence."

Lottie didn't believe him. Then again, with the grin on his face, had he meant for her to?

He watched her tear open the sugar packet. "Any word yet?"

Pouring the contents into her cup, she shook her head. "I was hoping that's why you were here, to give me an update."

"Sorry. I've been with patients all morning. Other than swinging by the cafeteria to grab your coffee, I came straight here from the therapy room."

She lifted the cup to take a tentative sip of the hot liquid, realized she hadn't put in her creamer, and wasn't sure if it was his being there or nervousness over waiting to hear about Gram's surgery that had her so discombobulated. "Gram's surgeon didn't foresee any complications, but this waiting is killing me."

The only other time she'd been in a waiting area in a nondoctor role had been when she'd gotten the call about her parents' wreck. That hadn't ended well. No wonder she was a bundle of nerves.

"Gram's going to be okay." Was she talking to Linc or reassuring herself? "It's just surgery to repair her foot."

"Waiting is never easy, but especially not when you're used to being on the other side of medicine." Linc's gaze held kindness, as if he knew, and yet, he couldn't. Although he'd caused the first, he hadn't been there either time her heart had broken.

Knowing she had to get her thoughts away from the past before it pulled her down a hole she rarely let herself fall into, she took a deep breath. "You're right. I'm usually the one delivering news of how a procedure went, rather than being the concerned family member. Maybe that's why I feel as if I should be doing something rather than just sitting here waiting and waiting and waiting."

One corner of Linc's mouth lifted. "Patience was never one of your virtues."

Pouring in the creamer, she stirred the steaming mixture. "I was eighteen when you knew me. How many eighteen-year-olds are patient?"

"Good point." He chuckled softly. "Back then we were ready to tackle the world."

"Or at least a whole lot of school." She took another appreciative sip of the coffee. A small sip because the refreshing brew scalded her tongue a little. "Speaking of which, how did you end up in physical therapy? I had thought you were going into construction and planning to start your own company."

Watching as she blew on the coffee to try to cool it, he shrugged. "I thought that, too. When I went back to school that fall, I continued with my business classes and worked construction part-time. I enjoy building, still do, but I realized I wanted to do something more directly hands-on to help people. A coworker got hurt and was with a therapist when I visited. I remember thinking how amazing it must feel to help someone rediscover the things most of us take for granted, such as walking or being able to reach into the kitchen cabinet. I was hooked and knew therapy was what I was meant to do."

His passion for his job came through. He'd once talked just as passionately about someday owning his own construction company and building affordable housing complexes in big cities. Over the years she'd imagined him on construction crews, sometimes as the manager, sometimes being the laborer swinging a hammer. He'd changed his mind about her. Why hadn't she ever considered that he might have changed his mind about his career, too?

Biting into her lip, her gaze lowered to his ID badge. "You work exclusively for the hospital?"

He nodded. "Since moving back to the area, I'm here three days a week. More when covering for someone. I've no complaints. The pay is good, decent benefits and I'm part of a great team."

"What do you do the other four days?" Heat warmed her cheeks. "Sorry. I'm being nosy, aren't I? What you do on your own time is none of my business. Forget I asked."

He shrugged. "It's not a problem. Currently, I'm working on my house and enjoying life."

Lottie worked five, six and sometimes seven days a week. Week after week. She could cut back, she supposed, but there was always so much to be done that rearranging her schedule seemed impossible. Even now, guilt plagued her that Brian and her colleagues were having to cover her patients. When he'd called the night before, they'd talked for less than a minute, with Brian stating he had to go as he was still at the hospital but had wanted to say hi before it got any later. Or maybe it had been because Maritime had gone nuts with her barking when the phone had rung.

Whether she wanted to or not, she couldn't keep from comparing the two men. Handsome and always impeccably put together, Brian had dark hair, dark eyes, and pale skin that rarely saw the light of day. Linc was a relaxed blue-eyed hunk who loved being outdoors. Looking at him, Lottie couldn't help but wonder if it had been more than wanting to finish her residency and focusing on her career that had held her back from agreeing to marry Brian.

"Is there anyone special in your life?" The question had popped into Lottie's head several times since he'd startled her at Gram's. He didn't wear a wedding band and Gram must think he was single, but was he involved? Her stomach twisted. Why did the thought of there being someone special in his life make her belly hurt?

"You don't have to answer if you don't want to," she added, swallowing the knot forming in her throat. "That was me being nosy about something that's none of my business. I can't seem to help myself."

"It's okay. Ask whatever you want, Lottie. We're old friends catching up, so it's not a big deal, right?"

She supposed that was one way of looking at it, but he didn't answer her question. Did that mean there was someone special? What was she thinking? There was someone special in her life. Someone her parents had wanted her to someday marry. No other man could ever hold that honor. The one in front of her held the distinction of being the one person her mother had begged her to forget.

"To answer your question, there hasn't been anyone special for a while." His gaze bore into hers. "How about you? Is there someone in Boston waiting on you to come home?"

Was Brian waiting on her to come home? Maybe. More likely that, outside of work, he hadn't missed her since they typically only saw each other on the weekends. They worked out of the same clinic, the same hospital, but most days they stayed so busy that their paths didn't cross. How sad was that?

"I'm dating someone." Now why had she been so vague with her answer?

"Is it serious?" Maybe he'd picked up on her hesitancy.

"He's asked me to pick out an engagement ring." Several times, but not lately, she realized, trying to recall just how long it had been since Brian had last hinted that they make it official, and unable to pinpoint when it had been. Was it wrong that she hadn't noticed that he hadn't mentioned getting married in months?

"Serious enough." Linc was quiet a moment. "Is he good to you?"

Good to her? What did he even mean by that? Brian was a thoughtful person, a hard worker and a loyal friend. They understood each other's long work hours and dedication to their patients. Her parents had adored him.

"Yes. He's good to me. He's covering my patients while I'm here. He was very gracious to tell me to not worry, that he'd make sure everyone was taken care of at the clinic."

He's a real find, Lottie. He's going to make you such a great husband.

"He's a cardiologist, too, then?"

Blinking to clear her mother's voice, she nodded. "We have a lot in common."

"That's nice." Linc didn't really sound impressed, more as if he was just acknowledging her comment.

"We met at school, were in a study group together for a class, and became fast friends and study partners. With as much time as we spent together, I suppose it was natural that we became a couple."

They never fought, never disagreed or argued other than about Gram and on that they had agreed to disagree. Their relationship was easy, rather than one of hot emotion. She glanced toward Linc, her gaze connecting with his, and more guilt hit. *That's not just guilt hitting you*, a voice deep within corrected. *That's the hot emotion that has always flooded you when you're near Linc.*

Because he was my first love.

Your first love imprinted itself on you like no other.

"I know it's been a few years, but I'm sorry about your parents."

Lottie's heart squeezed. "Me, too. I can't believe I lost them both in the same instant, but they loved each other so much that I don't think one would have wanted to survive without the other."

"That's a deep love."

"They definitely loved each other." Her mother had been the yin to her father's yang. "I always wanted a love like theirs. It's what they wanted for me, too. Mom loved Brian so much and wanted to plan our wedding someday. I hate that she'll never be able to."

"I'm sure they did." Linc's voice sounded a little hoarse and he cleared it prior to adding, "Your mother certainly never felt that way about me."

Lottie's breath caught. Heat burned her cheeks. Adrenaline drove her heartbeat faster and faster. Why had she said what she had? What was wrong with her? "Mom only met you that weekend she and Dad came to visit, Linc. She didn't know you. If she had, she'd have liked you, too."

He shrugged as if it didn't matter. "It's water under the bridge."

But there was such an odd look on his face.

Lottie remembered introducing him to her parents, and and they hadn't hidden their looks of disapproval. Her heart ached. She'd known their dismissal of him as not being important had bothered Linc, and she had done her best to reassure him. In the end, it hadn't mattered, but other than when it came to her mother's relationship with Gram, it was the only time she hadn't understood her parents' behavior.

"Linc, I'm sorry about how they treated you that weekend. They were just being overprotective parents, but I know they bordered on rude." Her mother had even acknowledged that once, apologizing, but reminding Lottie how much better off she was with wonderful Brian. Feeling her mother had needed reassurance, Lottie had nodded. With as much as Linc's rejection had hurt, maybe Lottie had even believed it.

"Like I said, water under the bridge." Linc glanced toward his watch. "My next patient arrives soon. Got to get back to the therapy room. Shoot me a text when you hear something about Jackie."

Had he really needed to leave? Or did he just not want to discuss her mother and the past? Who could blame him when he was right; it was water under the bridge.

"Okay." But even as she said it nausea hit. Had he forgotten that after her tearful, almost desperate call, he'd made sure she couldn't reach out again? "I don't have your current number."

When she hadn't heard from him after leaving her miserable voice mail, she'd tried calling again. The number had been disconnected. She'd double-checked that she hadn't dialed the wrong number a few times before admitting the truth to herself.

Linc's left eye twitched ever so slightly, clueing her in

that he wasn't as calm as he sounded when he gestured to her phone and asked, "May I?"

She handed the device to him.

He punched in a number, hit dial, then disconnected the call. "Now you have my number and I have yours."

"Just like old times," she said without thought.

"Not even close."

Realizing what he meant, Lottie winced and tried to clarify. "I meant, not like old times as in you and me old times, but…" Shaking her head, she swallowed and started over. "You know what I meant. Go. Your patient will be waiting on you. I'll let you know when I hear something about Gram. Maybe you'll answer this time." Oh, that had been an ugly dig and beneath her. He'd said his goodbye, that it was better for them to end, and he'd stuck to that. Just because she hadn't believed him, had thought he'd come after her to Boston and they'd find a way to make their relationship work, he hadn't done anything wrong.

Linc's face blanched, but he remained silent, just staring down at her as if trying to read beyond her words.

Uncomfortable beneath his stare, she rushed on. "Hopefully I'll hear something soon because I'm worried that Gram's surgery is taking so long. But other than that, you won't hear from me." She tilted her chin upward in a show of bravado she didn't really feel. "Nothing. Not even a peep."

Rather than leave, he stood there, studying her, then raked his fingers through his hair, leaving a fresh rumbled wake. After a moment, his tension eased and he half smiled.

"Not even a peep, eh?" Storms clouded the blue of his eyes, then he stunned her by kissing the top of her head. "Ah, that's more like old times, wouldn't you say?"

Watching as he left the waiting room, Lottie reached up to touch where his lips had lightly grazed her hair.

Her heart pounding as she tried to decipher what had just happened, she whispered, "Not even close."

CHAPTER THREE

"RAISE YOUR LEG a little higher, Jerry. I know you can do it." Linc observed the seventy-year-old huff out a long breath and instead of raising his leg higher, drop it flat against the mat table he lay upon.

"Tell me again how raising my leg is going to make my knee get better."

"It's to strengthen the muscles around your knee so that it stabilizes the joint. Now, get back to work." He'd explained previously, but Jerry, although good-natured, tended to ask the same questions over and over. Linc understood. He'd been doing the same thing, asking himself over and over what he'd been thinking with his foolish kiss to Lottie's head. What had he been thinking? That was it. He hadn't been thinking. So much vulnerability and emotion had shown in her eyes when she'd referred to that unanswered call, that unlike twelve years prior, he'd acted on instinct. "Stupid. Stupid. Stupid."

"Fine. I'm working, but you don't have to call me names," Jerry grumbled, lifting his leg. "I seem to recall you mentioning something about stabilizing the joint."

Linc needed to stabilize his brain. Was there an exercise he could do for that?

"Sorry, Jerry. I was thinking about something I did earlier that I shouldn't have done." Which was all he was going to say out loud on the matter. "Now give me twenty with your toes pointed and twenty with your toes pulled in toward you."

Rather than continue with his leg raises, Jerry's gaze went to something behind Linc. Or more like, someone.

"Ah, now I understand." His patient grinned. "She's pretty."

Even before Linc turned, he knew who Jerry looked at. Only one person had ever made his pulse jump that way. Steeling himself for whatever Lottie had come to say about his idiotic kiss, he faced her. Rather than lambaste him, she tucked her hands into the pockets of her flowy red pants and, a thousand questions in her big green eyes, said, "Sorry. I didn't mean to interrupt. I thought you must be finished with your patient when the receptionist told me to come on in."

"Interrupt. Please interrupt," Jerry pleaded, earning a glare from Linc. "Fine. Ten pointy toes and ten pulled in toes. Got it."

"It's twenty, not ten," Linc corrected Jerry to give himself a moment. "Besides, rumor has it you missed me when you had your therapy on my day off work."

"You're old enough to know better than to believe rumors," Jerry said, but the man's grin took the edge off his words.

"You'd think I was," Linc agreed. You'd also think him old enough to know better than to have kissed a woman who'd shredded his heart more than a decade ago. Sure, he'd been the one to not call back, but he'd done so for both their sakes. He hadn't needed her mother's interference to know that he'd never be good enough for her precious daughter. He hadn't even blamed Lottie's mother for begging him to stay away and let her daughter have a better life than he'd ever be able to give. Weren't Vivien's words part of what had driven him past every failure and humbled him at each success over the past twelve years?

First making sure Jerry's form was correct, Linc then glanced toward the woman who had turned his insides out the past few days by simply being on Fripp. "Jackie's out of surgery?"

What had Lottie thought about his kiss? It was only a peck to the top of her head, he berated himself. A peck that had him off-kilter. Had it done the same to her? Was that why she'd come in person?

Eyeing him, she nodded. "Again, sorry if I shouldn't be here. I was tired of sitting so after Dr. Collins let me know about Gram, I thought I'd stretch my legs by walking down here to tell you."

Was she wrong to come here? Her eyes seemed to ask. She shifted her weight, first making him wonder if her foot was bothering her, but as she hadn't taken the weight off her right foot, he didn't think so. Instead, he thought she was nervous. Because of him. What did that mean?

"You could have just peeped."

Pink stained her cheeks and he realized that's why she was there. Stubborn, proud, beautiful girl hadn't wanted to call or text. Not even a peep, she'd said.

Oh, Lottie.

He probably needed to stay away from her completely. That would be best. And yet, he knew he wouldn't.

"You think?" she asked, her weight shifting again.

"Stretching your legs is good, too." His imagination immediately jumped to stretching her legs and that was somewhere he definitely needed to keep his mind, and hands, from. To get his brain back on track, he nudged his patient. "See, Jerry, some people intentionally stretch. You should take note."

Jerry rolled his eyes but kept raising his leg. Not as high as Linc would like, so he placed his hand beneath Jerry's ankle and lifted it an inch higher. "Like this."

"Yeah, yeah," Jerry mumbled, but didn't show any signs of discomfort at the increased range of motion. "Just so long as you keep your hands off her, she'll be fine."

Lottie's cheeks went hot pink. Jerry's comment was innocent, but Lottie looked as if she might bolt.

Linc cleared his throat. "You do realize, Jerry, that I'm going to up the ante another inch because you're embarrassing my friend?"

The older man laughed, then gave Lottie a repentant glance. "Sorry. This guy's torture session is affecting my mind. Despite how I'm convinced he enjoys making me hurt, he's a great person. The best. You're lucky to be his girl."

Lottie's mouth opened as she obviously sought a way to tell Jerry that she wasn't his girl. But she had been. For one glorious summer, Lottie had been all his. And he'd willingly let her go.

Even knowing how he hadn't been able to forget her, he'd do the same thing again. Doing the right thing wasn't always easy or pain free.

"I, uh—" she began, but paused.

Knowing he needed to rescue her and the situation, Linc sighed with great exaggeration. "Now you've really embarrassed her, and me, too, Jerry. She's just a friend."

Just a friend. Linc supposed they were friends. She'd wanted the long-distance relationship when she left for school, but with distance, life circumstances and her mother against them, time would have changed her mind. He'd stayed behind, working and living in a different world from her upper middle class one.

But she was back and thanks to some wise real estate investments, there was no longer an economic disparity between them. Not that Lottie had ever seemed to mind their different backgrounds. Vivien Fairwell had, though. His stomach knotted at the memory of Lottie's mother and her distain that Lottie cared so much for him and how she worried he was going to ruin her baby girl's future.

"Just friends? You should do something about that." Jerry raised up onto his elbows to waggle his brows. "She's much too pretty to be just a friend."

She was pretty. Beautiful. But it had always been more about the sparkle in her eyes and the pull she had on his heart than anything reflected in Lottie's mirror. She had an elusive something that held a power over him that no woman had ever been able to replicate.

"She's only visiting South Carolina because of her grandmother, who happens to be my neighbor, and is in surgery this morning. Lottie came to let me know how Jackie is. Plus she's in a long-term relationship back in Boston."

Had he pointed out the latter as a reminder to himself or for Jerry's sake?

Scratching his balding head, Jerry glanced at Lottie's bare left hand. "I may be missing something but looks as if you've still got a chance. Don't waste it."

Lottie had said the man wanted her to pick out an engagement ring, but she wasn't wearing one. Did that mean she'd declined and that if he wanted to risk it, he had a second chance with her? Loving Lottie had messed with his head and heart for years. Did he want to risk repeating that devastation when she left to go back to Boston?

Because she would go back. It would be foolish to think otherwise.

Whether Lottie was wearing a ring or not didn't matter.

Only, he knew that wasn't true. Everything about Lottie mattered. Always had.

Wishing he could see beyond her lovely face to know what was going on in her mind, Linc met her gaze. "Just as soon as you walk away, I'm unleashing an Intense Pain 101 therapy session. Ignore his screams for mercy and my heinous laughter as I grant him none."

As he'd hoped, Lottie smiled. "Ah, Linc, you should go easy on him. Really, there's no need for the Intense Pain 101 lesson." Her tone was light. "For the record, Linc and I have known each other since we were teenagers, I know what a great guy he is."

Little more than kids? Was that how she saw the people they'd been that summer? Kids who hadn't known better than to love so freely? What would happen if they were just now meeting for the first time, if he didn't know she'd be going back to Boston and her life there? If they didn't have a past that overshadowed the present?

"Just as I know what a great woman she is."

Lottie's breath caught at Linc's compliment. Her gaze connected to his, and his smile dug deep dimples into the corners of his mouth. Even confused as she was, Lottie smiled back. Smiling around Linc came easily. It always had. It was the not being around him that came later that held such heartache and tears.

She never should have come to the therapy room. She'd just been so excited that Gram had come through surgery and done great that she'd needed to tell someone who understood and cared about her grandmother, too. She'd needed to tell Linc.

As it had done often since her arrival, Jerry's gaze bounced between them.

Deciding to make light, she waved her thumb toward Linc. "Jerry, if this guy keeps giving you a hard time, we'll have to rustle up an Intense Pain 101 session for him, instead."

Raising his leg, toe out, Jerry laughed. "You think so?"

Linc's eyes glittered like sunshine bouncing off the sea on the clearest blue day. "You want to make me hurt, Lottie?"

"Maybe," she said with a bright tone and waggle of her brows at Jerry, causing the clueless man to chuckle again. But she faked the lightness, because Linc's question was a valid one. His not wanting to continue their relationship and subsequent ignoring her call had hurt so badly. She'd often thought of someday making him eat his heart out at what he'd rejected. Was that the same thing as wanting him to hurt?

Linc knew. Knew what she was thinking. His smile was still in place, but his gaze had grown intense.

"Everything okay, Linc? Do you need me to finish with Jerry?" A pretty brunette joined them, giving Lottie a look that left no doubt that her interest in Linc went way beyond being his coworker.

Linc hesitated, as if he were considering accepting her offer, which had the woman's smile faltering. She'd obviously expected him to use her interruption as a way of telling Lottie that she needed to leave. Jerry was doing his leg lifts, but Lottie did need to get out of the way.

"Hi, I'm Lottie, an old friend of Linc's." She stuck out her hand toward the woman. "I'm in South Carolina for a week or so while my grandmother recovers from a fall. She lives near Linc. It's nice to meet one of his coworkers."

Was the woman more? The look she was giving said she was trying to decipher the same thing about Lottie. A myriad of emotions hit, jealousy taking up a huge chunk of the pie. Jealousy Lottie had no right to feel.

"Oh, um, that's… Hi." First giving Linc a questioning look, the brunette shook Lottie's hand. "Shannon Simpson, I'm a physical therapist."

"Awesome." Lottie put on her brightest smile, then met Linc's gaze, wishing she could read what was going on behind those guarded blue eyes. Confusion, she guessed. The same as confusion was overwhelming her. "I've got to get to my grandmother's room. Hopefully, she'll be out of recovery and back to herself soon." With that, she smiled at Jerry, then the pretty therapist. "Nice to meet you, Jerry and Shannon. Y'all keep Linc in line."

Y'all? Since when did she say y'all? Since being back in the South, apparently.

Shifting her focus back to the man whose gaze hadn't left her, she waved. "Goodbye, Linc."

The words seemed to echo around the room, bouncing back to smack her with the past and ringing with a finality that went beyond a casual visit. If only she meant it.

"I'll stop by to check on Jackie before I leave this evening," he told her. The way he looked at her suggested he'd like to say something more, but, with their audience, wouldn't.

"Gram will like that." And so would Lottie because he confused her. How nice he was to her, how he'd kissed the top of her head, how there was something deeper when he looked at her that she wished she could fully understand.

"She's one of my favorite people in the world."

"Mine, too. Thanks." Lottie turned to leave, but almost immediately paused at the panicked voice of the woman Shannon had been working with prior to asking Linc if he needed help.

"Shannon? Come quick. Something's wrong."

Shannon, Linc, Jerry and Lottie all looked toward where she had stopped pedaling on the stationary bicycle and was holding her chest. The woman was in her late sixties or perhaps early seventies. Her face was pale. Sweat glistened on her skin surface and dampened the hair along her scalp. Genuine fear showed on her face.

"Mrs. Stephenson?" Shannon crossed the fifteen feet to where her patient tightly gripped the therapy bike's handlebars. "Are you okay?"

Linc and Lottie joined Shannon.

"I… No, my chest is hurting." Grimacing, the woman rubbed her sternum. "It's getting worse."

"Let's get you off the bike," Linc suggested, putting his arm around Shannon's patient to steady her.

Not that Linc needed her help, but Lottie automatically got on the opposite side to assist. He'd obviously meant to guide her to an empty mat table, but Mrs. Stephenson motioned that she wanted to sit immediately so he lowered her to the floor and knelt beside her. "Are you having indigestion? Heartburn?"

Taking a deep breath, then wincing, Mrs. Stephenson shook her head.

Kneeling on the opposite side from Linc, Lottie introduced herself. "Hi, Mrs. Stephenson. I'm Dr. Charlotte Fairwell. I don't work at this hospital, but I'm a cardiologist in town visiting my grandmother. Is it okay if I check you?" The woman's gaze shifted to her, and she nodded. Lottie placed her finger on the woman's radial pulse and wasn't pleased with the thready, irregular beat beneath the woman's clammy skin. "Do you have a heart condition, Mrs. Stephenson? An arrhythmia or history of angina, maybe?"

Still rubbing her sternum, the woman shook her head. "I don't think so since I don't know what those things are."

Lottie glanced at Linc. "Do you have aspirin or nitro-glycerin?"

He shook his head. "Unfortunately, no."

Lottie was afraid of that.

"Mrs. Stephenson, we need to get you to the emergency room," Lottie continued, keeping her voice gentle, but firm.

"I don't want to go." Mrs. Stephenson's voice trembled. "I'll be fine in a minute. This happened earlier and passed. I already feel better just being off the bike. After my knee replacement, I don't need another medical bill."

"I understand that, but you do need an EKG and cardiac enzyme laboratory tests." Lottie leaned forward to place her ear against the woman's chest, listening to the unsteady thumping. "There isn't really a choice." Straightening, she met Linc's gaze. "We need to get her to the emergency room. Do whatever needs to happen to get her there. STAT."

Something Lottie didn't have time to explore shone in his eyes as he nodded. "There's a wheelchair by the reception desk."

"You stay. I'll get the wheelchair," Shannon offered, already back on her feet. "I can take her to the emergency room to have her checked and will give her orthopedic surgeon a call to let him know what's up."

Keeping a finger on Mrs. Stephenson's pulse, Lottie nodded as Shannon left.

"Mrs. Stephenson, at the minimum your heart is out of rhythm." Lottie motioned for Linc to elevate the woman's legs, nodding her approval when he did so. "Linc and I are going to put you into a wheelchair, then we'll get you to the emergency room."

"No." Sweat beaded on Mrs. Stephenson's forehead. "I'm

not—okay." She winced, gasping a little. "I'll go. We should probably hurry."

Glad Mrs. Stephenson wasn't going to waste more energy, and perhaps time, protesting, Lottie kept her gaze locked on the woman, who'd closed her eyes. "Mrs. Stephenson?"

"Hmm?" The woman's eyelids fluttered a little but didn't open, not even when Shannon returned with the wheelchair and said her name.

"Are you hurting worse?" Lottie gently shook the woman's shoulder.

Her eyes opened. "I'm dizzy."

"Okay. We're going to help you into the wheelchair." Linc, Lottie and Shannon got the woman into the wheelchair and wrapped a strap around her to secure her in. The last thing they needed was her falling out as they rushed her to the emergency department.

"Let's go," Lottie said the moment they had the strap tightened. She had meant Shannon, but Linc grabbed the wheelchair's handles.

"Finish up another round of sets, Jerry," he called over his shoulder. "You know what to do. I'll be back."

"Will do."

They'd barely made it into the hallway when Mrs. Stephenson said, "I may pass out."

Her head bobbed, pressing her chin into her chest.

Linc stopped pushing the wheelchair. "Mrs. Stephenson?"

Lottie bent, putting her ear to the woman's heart. The beat was there, but weak and irregular. She shook her shoulder, harder than before. "Mrs. Stephenson? Can you hear me, Mrs. Stephenson?"

Nothing. Lottie flattened her palm against the woman's chest, then swore under her breath. The erratic beats had stopped. To Linc, she said, "Help me get her out of the chair and onto the floor. She needs CPR now."

To Shannon, she said, "Call a code and get us help now. We're out of time."

While Shannon made the call, Linc and Lottie lowered Mrs. Stephenson to the floor. Lottie immediately started compressions. Linc got into two-person CPR position and delivered two breaths.

Arms pressing deep into Mrs. Stephenson's chest, Lottie counted out loud, going to thirty, then pausing for Linc to rapidly deliver another two breaths. Lottie started over, delivering the compressions, counting them out loud to help maintain her rhythm and to let Linc know when to give more lifesaving breaths.

"Just tell me if you need me to take over compressions," Linc offered in between breaths.

Lottie nodded. If the code team took much longer, she'd have to take him up on that. Her arms were gelatin from the exhausting movements. Who would have ever guessed that someday she and Linc would be working together to try to save a woman's life? That he'd let her take charge and would do as she asked without question? That he'd look to her with such confidence that she'd know what to do and let her? Brian would have taken over. Not a fair thought. Brian was also a cardiologist. Linc was a physical therapist. Of course he'd let her run the show during a myocardial infarction.

"Oh, God. Please don't let her die," Shannon said from where she fretted near them. Lottie glanced her way long enough to make sure the therapist wasn't going to lose her composure. Linc must have wondered, too, as he motioned for Shannon to sit beside them.

"If anyone can save her, it's Lottie." The pride in his voice was so pure, so strong, that Lottie's gaze shot to his as she continued to compress and count. Pride and something more shone there. Something raw and intense that made her own heart do a funny flip-flop.

It seemed to take forever for help to arrive, but Lottie knew from experience that it really hadn't been more than a few minutes at most.

When the nurse arrived with the crash cart, Lottie continued compressions until the defibrillator was charged and ready to give a two-hundred-joules shock to Mrs. Stephenson's heart.

"All clear," the nurse ordered.

Lottie moved back as the paddles were placed on the woman's chest and delivered the voltage, causing Mrs. Stephenson's body to jerk.

The second the paddles were removed Lottie began compressions again. "One. Two. Three. Four," she said in rapid succession, continuing her count.

"We have a pulse!" the nurse who'd rushed to them with the crash cart announced. "It's weak, but we have a pulse!"

Lottie kept compressing Mrs. Stephenson's chest, afraid to stop too soon, but relief spread through her when the woman sucked in a breath on her own. *Yes!*

Another hospital employee arrived with a gurney. Lottie stopped compressing, remaining on the floor as Linc and the man lifted Mrs. Stephenson onto the gurney and another of the code team took over rhythmically compressing the woman's chest. Within seconds, she was being rushed down the hallway toward the emergency department.

Lottie's shoulders slumped, and she rubbed her palms over her trembling biceps. She always thought she was in decent physical shape until she had to perform CPR. That never failed to be an eye-opener.

"You okay?" Linc stretched out his hand to help Lottie up.

"Fine, but I'll probably be sore tomorrow." She automatically took his hand so he could assist her back to her feet. The second his hand closed around hers, her insides jerked to life as surely as if he'd hit her with the defibrillator paddles. He must have felt it, too, because as soon as she was standing, he let go and rubbed his palm against his thigh.

"That was unexpected," Shannon said from beside them, no doubt referring to Mrs. Stephenson's heart attack, but as Lottie stared at Linc, she thought he was what was so unexpected. He'd been so wonderful while they'd done CPR, so supportive and perfectly in sync with her compressions.

"Yes, it was." Lottie stuck her hand into her pocket to keep from also rubbing her stinging palm against her thigh. Still staring at him, she swallowed. Why? Why did he have to be in Fripp? She was content with her life in Boston. It was what she'd worked toward, and yet, looking into Linc's blue eyes, everything back home just seemed drab.

"Lottie—" he said, his voice a bit breathy. Was it from what had happened with Mrs. Stephenson or what was sparking between them?

"I've got to go." She couldn't deal with the emotions bubbling inside her, not in front of Linc and his coworker. Maye not ever. "I've got to get to Gram's room." Anywhere to have a few moments to decompress and sort through all the questions that coming face-to-face with Linc again was raising. "She should be there by now. I hope Mrs. Stephenson will be okay." She glanced toward Linc, found him studying her with concerned eyes, and she quickly averted her gaze because her emotions were stretched in a tug-of-war between reason and something akin to hope. But hope for what? She'd reached out to him all those years ago and he'd rejected her. She'd moved on, was in a stale, but safe relationship with a good man. So why did looking at Linc fill her with what-ifs?

"Are you okay?"

Lottie glanced up from where she sat next to her sleeping grandmother's hospital bed. She'd been going through messages, several from Brian wondering when she was coming home, and thinking about the fact that she was responding to other texts but not his.

Linc's dark scrubs intensifying the blue of his eyes, he stood inside the room and watched her in a way that made her wonder how long he'd been standing there.

"Of course. All in a day's work."

"Not in my day's work. It was a stressful situation." One corner of his mouth lifted in a half grin. "I'm glad you were there."

Her heart did a funny pitter-patter thing that she was positive it shouldn't be doing. Funny how a teenage love could still have such an affect. Or maybe it was that Linc was a gorgeous man, and that grin would have had her heart fluttering even if she'd never met him all those years ago. Maybe both was closer to the truth. She clutched her phone tighter.

"You made quite the impression on my patient." Glancing toward where Gram lay in her hospital bed, eyes closed, breathing evenly, Linc came into the room to stand close to where Lottie sat. He kept his voice low. "You're Jerry's hero."

His tone was a mix of admiration and teasing. Lottie's stomach took a cue from her heart and got all jittery. Her phone vibrated in her palm. Although her roommate Camilla's name popped up on the screen, the reminder of the unanswered messages from Brian caused guilt to flicker through her. She should have answered his messages. Why hadn't she?

Brian's the perfect man for you, Charlotte. You're going to have such a great life with him. You make me so proud.

Heart squeezing, Lottie took a deep breath.

Oh, Mama, I miss you so much.

"Mrs. Stephenson was only in the ER a few minutes before they had her in the cath lab. Fortunately, she made it through her stent placement and her doctor thinks she's going to be okay."

That the woman had survived was a true relief.

"I'm glad the nurse arrived with the defibrillator when she did, that Mrs. Stephenson's heart responded and that she was able to get to the emergency room so quickly."

"Thanks to you," Linc said, smiling as he moved closer to where she sat. "I'm with Jerry. You're my hero. I'm proud of you, Lottie, of the woman you've become. I always knew you were destined for great things, but watching you today, well, you hammered home just how amazing that young girl I once knew grew up to be."

Embarrassment replaced her relief. Embarrassment and deep pleasure that Linc was proud of her. Wasn't that what she'd dreamed of for so long? For him to see her and recognize that she'd been worth his giving their long-distance love affair a chance to work? Why had he been so adamant that they cut all ties and then done just that?

"I didn't do anything you wouldn't have done if I hadn't been there." Because despite his having let her do what she needed to do, he'd been calm and she knew he would have gotten Mrs. Stephenson the care she needed. "I was just at the right place at the right time to make me look good."

"Thank God you were." He quietly moved a chair next to hers and sat down. "Emergency medicine isn't my thing."

"Nor mine," she admitted, staring at her sleeping grandmother to keep from looking toward him. He was so close she'd swear she could smell the crisp scent of his soap. Crazy, as it would have been hours ago when he showered. If she looked at him, would he see her inner turmoil? Would he know that seeing him again had everything she'd thought she'd known about her life, her future, up in the air? "My patients are usually fairly stable when I get to them as I do more interventional cardiology than emergent."

He shrugged. "Either way, you impressed me and Jerry. He couldn't stop talking about you."

"Was he offering more dating advice?" Now why had she brought that up? She didn't want to discuss Jerry's misguided thoughts. Or to talk dating with Linc. She didn't have to look his way to know he studied her.

"Just to Shannon." His soft answer had Lottie's gaze cutting toward him. The blue of his eyes burned into her and had her fighting a gulp. "He told her that she'd better up her game since there was competition in town."

Lottie gave in to the gulp.

"That not only were you beautiful, but you're smart and a doctor to boot. I reminded him that although everything he said was true, you were involved with someone so there wasn't competition. He just laughed. Crazy old man." Linc paused. "Like I said, he was quite impressed with how you saved Mrs. Stephenson."

"We saved her," she reminded him, because he'd been right there with her doing the CPR, and to give herself a moment to process that he was involved with the pretty therapist beyond a working relationship. The realization stung. How much she was bothered by the realization stung even more. "Interesting advice. I thought you weren't dating anyone."

His gaze didn't waver from hers. "What you asked me was if there was anyone special in my life."

"To which you said no," she stated, doing her best to keep her gaze locked with his despite struggling with the fact that she had no right to question him, to feel such angst over the idea of him with the woman.

"I told you the truth." Linc's voice was steady, just as his gaze was. His gaze was also curious, no doubt wondering why she pressed him about things that shouldn't matter to her. She agreed. His dating life shouldn't matter. The nausea in her stomach suggested it did.

"You're dating Shannon, but it's not serious?" At least, not on his part. The way the other woman had looked at him suggested she would welcome a serious relationship.

"I'm not dating Shannon. We went to dinner a few times after I first moved here, but nothing serious and nothing recently."

"Sorry," she said and meant it. "I had no right to pry." Nor should she have felt such a green surge at the thought of him with the woman or the wave of relief that he no longer was. "You'll have to forgive me." She'd obviously lost her mind. "After the excitement in the therapy room, I've sat in silence all afternoon while Gram has slept except for a few waking moments here and there."

His gaze narrowing, he seemed to consider saying something more, but instead glanced toward Gram. "Has Dr. Collins been around? What's he saying about how her surgery went?"

Relieved that he wasn't pressing for why Lottie had pried, an answer she wouldn't have been able to give, she sighed. "That she did great, and he doesn't foresee any complications. If she does well tonight, he's transferring her to a rehabilitation facility tomorrow."

"I'm not going to a nursing home," her grandmother informed them in a firm voice that hinted that she hadn't just awakened.

Lottie's gaze went to the petite woman lying on the hospital bed. Happiness hit at the spunk in Gram's voice. When she'd awakened earlier her voice had been weak, and she'd still been disoriented.

"Ah, so you've been faking it this whole time, leaving me twiddling my thumbs," Lottie accused, wincing a little as she recalled her and Linc's conversation. How much had her grandmother overheard?

"Amazing the things you learn while sleeping." Paler than her bravado would suggest, Gram reached for her bed's controller, pressed the button to raise the bed. "When did you ask Linc if there was someone special in his life?"

Lottie winced. Gram had heard too much.

"Today while I was in the surgery waiting room. He stopped by to check on you." Not answering would just have Gram digging deeper. Better to answer as if the question was no big deal. It wasn't, right? Just as whether or not he was involved in a serous relationship wasn't a big deal? Why couldn't she convince herself of that? Lottie glanced toward Linc. Although unreadable, his features appeared relaxed. "We were catching up while waiting to hear news about your surgery. Asking if there's someone special in one's life is a natural question that friends who haven't seen each other in a long time ask each other."

There. Hopefully that would satisfy her grandmother and, also, let Linc know why she'd asked.

Gram snorted. "Natural if you're still interested in each other."

Lottie shot another apologetic look toward Linc to see how he'd taken Gram's comment. He'd been the one to reject her even after she'd poured out her heart. She hadn't forgotten or forgiven him for that. Not really. Had the way he'd looked at her, teased her, kissed the top of her head, been because he was still interested? And if so, then what? Would she throw away her relationship with Brian, no doubt causing her mother to roll over in her grave, just to risk having her heart shattered again?

"Excuse her." Lottie rolled her finger in a crazy motion. "The anesthesia has affected her. She doesn't know what she's saying."

"I know exactly what I'm saying. Just because I'm trapped in this bed, it does not mean you can get away with saying things such as I'm not in my normal state of mind," Gram overprotested, causing both Lottie and Linc to smile. His smile sent sunshine through Lottie.

"You're right. Sorry, Gram. You're the epitome of brilliance."

"The Einstein of modern days," Linc added, his eyes sparkling.

"Tesla would have been wowed by your supreme intelligence." Lottie loved how Gram's color had brightened from the pasty white of when she'd first awakened.

"I know I'm wowed," Linc continued. "By that and your card playing skills."

Gram harrumphed and Linc chuckled. Lottie had been going to ask how he knew about Gram's card shark ways, but then he winked. Conspiratorially rather than anything overtly romantic, but still, her rib cage contracted around her lungs, taking her breath and momentarily she couldn't do anything other than stare at him in wonder.

Who would have ever thought she'd be in a hospital room teasing her grandmother with Lincoln Thomas? That being near him would put the same excitement in her belly that it had when she'd been eighteen and hadn't had her heart broken by him yet? But she wasn't a teenager anymore and had a life that was so far removed from this room and the girl who had cried herself to sleep for months at his rejection. But with the giddiness filling her at his simplest gestures, maybe she wasn't so far removed from the young girl she'd once been.

"No doubt the Fripp Card Club will be holding new elections while you're incapacitated and will vote you off the island—I mean, club." Linc's lips twitched.

"They wouldn't dare." Stiffening, Gram narrowed her gaze, then, glancing back and forth between them, she relaxed against her pillow. "Look at you two picking on me when I've had a rough couple of days. Not that I'm surprised that y'all fell right into sync just the way you always did."

They had, hadn't they? Not that they'd picked on Gram back in the day. Jackie would have tanned their hides, perhaps rightly so. Still, Gram was right. Even as adults, she and Linc shared a connection that Lottie had never experienced with anyone else.

"That anesthesia really has you not thinking clearly." Maybe there really was some lingering in the air because Lottie didn't feel as if she were thinking clearly, either. If she was, her mother's voice telling her how perfect Brian was for her and to hang on to him no matter what would be playing loudly in her head. Instead, Lottie refused to listen to the voice that she usually welcomed in no matter what words were being said. How could she not when she missed her mother so? But she didn't want to think about Brian or how disappointed her mother would be if she knew what Lottie was feeling while looking at the one and only boyfriend her mother had ever disliked. Had Vivien known Linc had been destined to hurt her?

"My thinking is just fine," Gram countered. "Who's Jerry?"

"The patient I was torturing when Lottie saved a woman's life." Linc tone was full of pride, causing Lottie's gaze to reconnect with his. If she didn't know better, she'd think he felt he had a personal stake in her success. If anything, he'd almost wrecked her to the point she'd wanted nothing more than to curl into a ball and cry her days away.

But she hadn't. She'd done what needed to be done and she'd moved on with her life. Without him. Because that's what he'd chosen. Linc had claimed to love her and yet he'd willingly shattered her.

Gram's brow lifted. "So, you saved a woman, rescued Linc's patient and caught up on his dating life? You've been busy this morning."

"Your granddaughter is a special woman," Linc said to Gram. His eyes remained focused on Lottie, though, almost as if he sensed her inner turmoil. No wonder she liked this adult version of him; he was kind, funny, considerate and physically…well, physically, Linc had always done it for her. Part of her wanted to throw caution to the wind and explore the way being near him made her feel. Yet, another wanted to scream and demand to know why he hadn't loved her as much as he'd claimed.

Not pulling her gaze away, Lottie willed for him to know how much he'd hurt her, that no matter how attracted she was to the man he'd grown into, she was older, wiser and would never again allow anyone the power she'd once given over her heart, Especially not him.

CHAPTER FOUR

"HOW'S OUR GIRL TODAY?"

Glancing up from where she had been skimming through a continuing medical education article on her phone while sitting next to her grandmother who was watching an *I Love Lucy* rerun, Lottie's heart rate picked up at the sight of Linc entering her grandmother's hospital room. Had navy scrubs ever looked better? *Wowzers.*

"She's not too good." And neither was Lottie. She didn't want to feel anything when she looked at Linc. Not attraction, not whatever else that was thumping around inside her chest. She wanted it gone as it should have been years ago. Didn't he know this would be easier if he'd just stay away? Why wasn't he?

Gram scowled. "I can answer for myself. It's my foot that's broken, not my vocal cords."

Turning off her phone, Lottie sat up straighter in the semicomfortable chair.

"Aren't you just a ray of sunshine," Linc teased, coming over to stand by Gram's hospital bed and taking her hand. "What's wrong?"

Gram had a momentary look of repentance. "Rough day."

"Tell me about it."

Gram did just that, explaining how her going home plans had yet again been waylaid by a faulty blood pressure cuff and how Dr. Collins didn't plan to discharge her unless she agreed to go to a rehabilitation facility.

Whether she wanted Linc there or not, Lottie soaked up his gentle tone as he explained how Gram would heal faster with the proper care. The boy she'd loved had grown into a gorgeous, compassionate man.

Almost as if he sensed her thoughts, Linc's gaze met hers. What was he thinking? She wished... No, she didn't wish that. Wishing things where Linc was concerned was off-limits. He was off-limits. Once Gram was out of the hospital, their paths wouldn't even have to cross again.

"Is there something I can do to help you feel better, Jackie?"

"You can convince my granddaughter to stay in South Carolina so Dr. Collins will agree to let me go home, and then you can agree to do my therapy there so they will let me out of this place," she immediately responded, shooting Lottie a pointed look.

No. Tell her no, Lottie mentally demanded.

Linc was saved from answering by a knock at Gram's door. Gram's nurse came in, saw Linc and gave him a big smile prior to addressing her patient. Seriously, was every female employee infatuated with him? Or was it just that Lottie found him so irresistible that she automatically thought every woman must, too? Ugh. Why couldn't he have grown up into some inconsiderate jerk who repulsed her so she'd have tucked memories of their summer together away as a fortunate near miss?

"Oh, hi, Linc. I didn't know you were in here." The pretty brunette's cheeks pinkened, then she smiled at Gram. "Dr. Collins put in orders to get you up in a wheelchair for a while to see how you do with sitting."

Gram's brows vee'd. "Has he forgotten that I've been sitting up in this bed?"

"Not quite the same thing." The nurse turned toward Linc. "Would you mind helping me get her into a chair? You probably already know since you're here, but Dr. Collins also ordered a physical therapy consult for you to do an assessment and start treatment."

"It's never a problem to help with a patient, Amy."

Beaufort hospital wasn't so huge that employees wouldn't know each other, especially those whose paths crossed routinely, yet that Linc and the nurse knew each other's first names triggered another dreaded green surge.

What was wrong with her?

She'd never been the jealous type. Not that summer with Linc and certainly never with Brian.

While Lottie's stomach gnawed at itself, Linc and the nurse got Gram into position sitting on the side of the bed, chatting with Gram and each other as they did so.

"I'm going to let you sit upright for a minute or two, just to acclimate you to being upright. Then, we'll get you into the wheelchair."

Gram huffed out a deep breath, then shook her head. "I don't need a wheelchair."

Lottie disagreed. Even as distracted as she was with watching Linc and Amy, she wasn't so blind to have not noticed how breathy Gram had gotten with the position change.

"Doctor's orders," Amy reminded Gram, doing another quick vital check on her.

Beep. Beep. Beep. Amy's pager sounded. The nurse glanced at it and grimaced.

Lottie stepped closer to her grandmother. "I'll help Linc if you need to take that page."

The nurse looked torn, as if she didn't want to go, but

knew she needed to. After the brief hesitation, she nodded. "Thank you. That would be wonderful as I do need to get this one sooner rather than later." She glanced toward Gram. "How are you feeling? Any light-headedness?"

Too proud to say otherwise, Gram insisted, "I'm fine."

"Great. No worries as you're in good hands with Linc. He's the best therapist in the hospital." She sent Linc a glowing smile to go with her praise. "If you need anything, hit your call button. I'll be back as quickly as I can."

"She's cute, Linc," Gram pointed out after the nurse had left the room. "You should invite her out to the island and cook her one of those yummy shrimp dishes you make."

Lottie fought the urge to place her hand on her forehead. One minute Gram was pushing her and Linc together and the next she was encouraging him to ask a nurse to dinner?

"Is she?" He seemed oblivious as he made sure the locks were on, then positioned the chair to where they could most easily get Gram into it. "I'll keep it in mind, but I doubt she would be nearly as appreciative of my grilled Cajun shrimp as you are."

Lottie blinked. Linc had cooked for her grandmother?

"Then her taste buds are dead. My mouth waters just thinking about them. Sneak me in some. That'll make me feel better."

Moving to the opposite side of where Linc inspected the chair, Lottie filled the spot the nurse had vacated. "I'll let dietary know you'd like shrimp," she offered, "but I bet it's not on their menu due to someone possibly being allergic."

"Poor souls," Gram said, her palms against the bed with her fingers curled around the mattress edge as if she wasn't quite as confident in her strength as she verbalized.

Linc gestured toward the wheelchair. "You ready to transfer?"

Gram nodded and so did Lottie. It had been a while since

she'd help transfer a patient, but she'd done so many a time over the years, especially during the early stages of residency.

"I was born ready," Gram assured him, gaining smiles from both Lottie and Linc.

"Great." Linc looked directly into Gram's eyes. "We're going to do this without you putting any weight on your casted foot, okay?"

"Sounds simple."

"It won't be," he stated. "But the main thing is to make sure you don't fall. I want you to put your arm around my neck so I can help support you."

He lowered to where she could more readily reach her arm over his shoulder.

"That's a good line. I bet you say it to all the girls." Gram put her arm around his neck.

"Only the ones I like." He grinned. "How are you feeling? Light-headed?" Linc asked as they helped Gram reposition.

"Like the world is one big merry-go-round."

"I thought that might be the case."

Linc's gentle tone, the way he maneuvered Gram into the chair with ease, and immediately knelt to elevate her casted foot on the footrest had Lottie feeling a little as if she'd joined her grandmother on that merry-go-round. Was his bedside manner this wonderful with all his patients? Having witnessed the teasing rapport with Jerry, she suspected so.

Quit being so wonderful.

"Better?" Linc asked.

Gram nodded, but still looked pale. Linc must have had the same impression, because he stayed in the kneeling position, talking with her for a few minutes prior to straightening.

"I'll log in to see what orders Dr. Collins has written."

He glanced at his watch. "I have a therapy session starting in a few minutes, but I'll be back afterward."

When Linc had left, Gram sniffled. "I just want to go home, Lottie. I miss Ole Bessie and Maritime. Please do whatever it takes to get me home."

"It's true, then? You're staying in South Carolina?"

"Yes." Word had sure traveled fast at Boston Memorial. Gripping her phone tighter, Lottie winced at the unhappiness in Brian's tone.

A nurse aide had come by to change Gram's bedding while she was in her chair, and to give Gram a sponge bath. After the woman had left, Lottie decided to watch a nature program on TV with her grandmother. When her cell phone rang and she'd seen Brian's name, she stepped outside the room to take the call.

"I'm staying until Gram gets steady enough on her feet that I feel comfortable leaving her. Hopefully just a few weeks, but maybe a month or two."

"A month or two?" Brian sounded incredulous. "Can't you hire someone to stay with her? There has to be someone better suited to grandma-sit than someone with your credentials. You have an important job and commitments, Charlotte. You can't just be gone from your life for that long."

"I also have obligations to Gram. I'm all she has." And vice versa. "I want to do this for her. Besides, it was Human Resources that suggested I take a family medical leave." Other than quick trips to see Gram and the occasional vacation, Lottie never took time off work. She had quite a bit of built-up paid time off she'd thought to put to good use staying with Gram, but the HR manager had advised her to pursue short-term leave for a couple of months, stating Lottie could return sooner but that would cover her just in case. "Greg Abbott even called not long afterward. He understands that I need to be here right now."

Which was saying more than Brian. Seriously? Could she hire someone to sit with Gram? This wasn't about money. It was about family and taking care of one's family.

"It would seem I'm the last to know."

"That wasn't my intention, Brian. You were with patients this morning, so I texted and asked you to give me a call when you had a free moment. I didn't want to interrupt something important," she replied, frustrated that she was having to defend the desire to take care of Gram. No, he and Gram didn't jibe, but Gram was her only living relative. He knew that. Shouldn't he be showing some concern? Some empathy and understanding of why she'd want to be there?

"You could have texted more details."

"I thought it was something I should tell you in person."

There was a pause, and then he sighed. "Do you know how embarrassing it is that the receptionist whom I corrected when she said how sorry she was that you were having to take an extended leave to take care of your ill grandmother was actually correct and knew more than I did?"

Was that the real problem? Not that Lottie hadn't told him, nor that she wasn't coming home, but that he'd been embarrassed?

"I knew my patients would need to be rescheduled and wanted to give HR as much of a heads-up as possible."

She and Brian had been together for over five years. She understood his point. She should have given him more details in her text, possibly, but she hadn't counted on the grapevine getting to him first. He was frustrated, and wouldn't she have been if the situation had been reversed?

No, because you'd have been with him. You'd have set

everything aside and gone to South Carolina to help in any way you could, even if it was just emotional support.

Which wasn't a fair thought since he was helping by taking the overflow of her patient load.

"I'm sorry that you're upset, Brian, but I promised Gram I'd stay as long as she needed me and that's what I intend to do." Seeing her grandmother so broken earlier had done Lottie in. She'd have promised her the moon if it had meant drying the unshed tears in Gram's eyes.

"And it doesn't matter if I need you here?"

His question surprised Lottie. These days they rarely interacted during work hours, not even making time to grab lunch together. When had they stopped doing that? Why hadn't she noticed? She enjoyed when they were together, but was that because they were mostly with their friends or with Lottie's roommate, Camilla? How long had it even been since they'd done more than a quick peck to the lips? Not that she'd ever felt great passion at his touch, but shouldn't her feelings be something more than lukewarm?

"Do you need me there, Brian?"

Was his long hesitation due to his frustration at having heard that she was taking family medical leave from someone else or that he really had to think that hard to know the answer?

Why did knowing his answer seem so imperative? Did Brian need her there? Did he need her at all? Did she need him? Or were they just together out of habit and an affection for one another than kept them from not wanting to cause the other pain? Why did her stomach squeeze so tightly as she contemplated questions that she suspected had been there a long time, but that she hadn't wanted to deal with the ramifications of asking? Brian was who her mother thought was the perfect husband for her. Her father had liked him. Why was Lottie even questioning his role in her life?

"We'll talk later. I've got patients waiting," he finally said, which really didn't give Lottie resolution to the questions swirling through her mind.

"I—okay." Maybe he'd had a rough morning. Maybe she'd had a rough morning, because her own annoyance and discontent with their current status quo wasn't abating.

Likely, it was being here, in South Carolina, having seen Linc again that made everything back in Boston seem less sparkly. She liked her job, the apartment she shared with Camilla, her usually undemanding relationship with a man she respected and admired—usually.

"He never asked how Gram was." Mumbling, she turned to go back into the hospital room. As she did so, her gaze lit on the man standing a few feet away. "Linc!"

"Sorry, I didn't mean to eavesdrop, but you were deep in conversation and looked upset, so I didn't want to interrupt." His gaze searched hers, for what she wasn't sure, nor was she sure she wanted him to find it. "Dr. Collins did get Jackie's PT ordered so I'm back to do her assessment and get started."

Realizing she had been leaning against the closed door of her grandmother's room, she grimaced. "Sorry I had the door barricaded."

"Making sure Jackie doesn't escape?"

Appreciative that he hadn't questioned her about her phone conversation, she half smiled. "I'm not sure both of us blocking her door could do that at whatever point she decides she's had enough. I should probably get in there before she climbs out the window."

Although lingering concern swirled in his eyes, he chuckled. "You're right, but short of Jackie busting it, you're safe on a window escape since they don't open. How did she do with sitting in the wheelchair after I left? Any light-headedness?"

Was he intentionally repeating his question to ask how Gram was? Had he heard Lottie's grumbled complaint that Brian hadn't asked? Or was that her mind connecting dots where dots didn't exist? And why would she connect dots where Linc was concerned? She didn't want to like him. Lord, her insides were a jumbled mess.

"She seems tired. The nurse aide came by to change her bedding and bathe her. I imagine that's worn Gram out even more. But other than in protest of being kept here, she's determined to not utter a word of complaint about actual symptoms for fear that Dr. Collins will decide that she can't leave tomorrow."

"You think he's going to discharge her with her wanting to go home instead of to a rehab facility? That's why you've decided to stay longer?"

So, he had heard at least that much.

"I hope not since I'll be the one having to handle her at home. I don't want Gram miserable, but I also want her taken care of to where she can heal properly without falling or reinjuring herself because I didn't do something right."

"You being here is right enough, Lottie." Oh, how his words spread balm over her raw nerves. "If she hasn't told you, then I'll say it for her. She's ecstatic you're here." He gave her an empathetic look. "As far as once you do get her home, I'm just down the street if you need help."

Knowing his offer was genuinely given, Lottie wondered just how long she was going to be able to hold on to her inner anger. Seriously, why did this adult Linc have to be so great? "Thank you."

"No problem. I'm at your service, have duct tape and

make a credible alibi." He waggled his brows. "What more could you need?"

The tension in her shoulders eased. "I'll keep that in mind if she gets too out of line."

Memories of his helping Gram with dozens of things around her home that long ago summer popped into Lottie's head. Based on what she could tell, they'd picked back up on that with his moving to Fripp. He and Gram had always gotten along. Too bad her parents hadn't thought much of her summer infatuation with a construction worker. They'd loved Brian, though. Her mother had often commented on what beautiful grandbabies she and Brian's upper-middle-class parents would someday have. Lottie had always smiled, nodded, assumed that someday she and Brian would marry and have those grandchildren her mother mentioned. But for the life of her she couldn't picture those brown-eyed children her mother had described. Closing her eyes, she tried, but instead saw blue-eyed, sun-kissed imps with dimpled grins smiling up at her and wrapping her around their adorable fingers.

Startled at the vision, Lottie forced the image from her head, sucked in a deep breath and met the bluest eyes she'd ever looked in to. Heart pounding, she glanced away, scared he'd see what had been in her mind. It didn't take a genius to know who those imaginary kids had looked like. What was wrong with her? Obviously, she was having a stress reaction to having her life upheaved by Gram's fall and coming face-to-face with Linc after all this time.

"I'm serious, Lottie. If you need something, I'll be there."

She'd once needed him, and he hadn't been there. But he'd meant for Gram. Despite his kindness and the way his gaze lingered at times, Linc didn't have feelings for her anymore. Nor did she want him to. Not in any way more than the way that was normal for you to want your exes to see you and wonder why they ever let you go.

"When Dr. Collins lets her go home, I would appreciate help in getting her into the house." And so many other things if her grandmother wasn't able to hobble around on crutches. Avoiding Linc would make Lottie's life easier, but Gram came first. "Can you imagine me trying to get her up those steps and into the house?"

He grimaced. "Don't attempt it, Lottie. It's not worth the risk of her falling and injuring herself further. I'll get her inside."

He was right. It wasn't worth the risk of attempting to do things without his help. At whatever point Dr. Collins discharged Gram, she'd enlist him to get Gram into the house. Once there, hopefully, Lottie could manage the rest.

Leaning back against the wall, Lottie sighed. "Stubborn woman. Things would be so much simpler if she'd go to rehabilitation. But other than the circumstances, spending a few weeks with her on the island isn't such a tough pill to swallow."

His eyes softened, then averting his gaze, he glanced at his watch. "I better get started."

Lottie stepped aside, meaning to go into Gram's room with him, but her phone buzzed. Thinking it was likely Brian to say he was sorry for his earlier attitude, she glanced at the screen. Camilla. Good. She hadn't wanted to talk to Brian again anyway. Not unless he really had been calling to apologize.

Men. Maybe she was finished with the whole lot of them.

Lottie had sat with her grandmother until Jackie dozed off. After getting back to "Ole Bessie," she'd thought she'd sleep herself as she was at a deficit for the past few nights. That was saying something because she never got much rest. Yet now that she'd picked up Maritime from Mrs. Baker's house and could sleep until the next morning, restless energy stole her slumber. Rather than uselessly lying in her bed, she sat in the covered porch's swing and stared toward the canal. Reflections from the homes on the other side of the water twinkled, and an occasional shadow passed by a lit window.

It wasn't that late, barely nine, but still, she should be exhausted. She was exhausted. And yet her mind raced. She knew why, so didn't bother trying to delve into the reasons she couldn't sleep. Her mother had thought Brian the perfect man for her, but Lottie wasn't so sure. Maybe she never had been. He had called and apologized, but Lottie had cut the conversation short rather than say the things wanting to burst free from her. Things like, *Let's just be friends.*

No, you can't do that.

Sighing at her mother's voice, wishing she could hear it for real, rather than just echoes from the past, Lottie grabbed her shoes. Maybe a walk to the beach and back would help.

"Woof!"

Lottie winced. Taking the dog with her would significantly decrease odds of having a peaceful walk, and yet with the dog's expectant look and knowing she'd likely been cooped up inside Mrs. Baker's for most of the day, Lottie couldn't bring herself to not take her.

"Fine. I'll bring you." She hooked Maritime's leash to her collar, and for once the dog cooperated. "Good job."

The moment they stepped outside, the dog bounded down the stairs and waited impatiently while Lottie undid the gate's lock. As she lifted the latch, she gave Maritime a stern look. "We'll walk to the beach and back, but you have to be quiet. No barking."

The dog let loose a few loud barks in response. Lottie

rolled her eyes and gave the leash a firm tug. "Shush. It's not too late for me to change my mind, you know? I don't know what Gram sees in you."

The dog gave another loud bark. Lottie suspected if she could interpret the sound it would translate to something along the lines of Maritime didn't know what Gram saw in Lottie, either, other than that they were blood related and Gram couldn't really help that. But rather than more barked protests, Maritime fell into step beside Lottie as they took off down the paved road that ran in front of Gram's and led to the beach.

The ocean cut through the silence of the night.

When she walked past the McMahon place, Maritime tugged on her leash.

"Stop that," Lottie ordered, but the dog continued to pull, hard, and began to bark. Scanning the dimly lit house's yard, Lottie didn't see anything warranting Maritime's ruckus. "It's probably just a deer, you silly girl. Stop barking."

She tugged on the leash, trying to prompt the dog to continue their walk, but Maritime wasn't giving in.

Lottie stepped a few feet into the driveway, loosened the length of the leash to give the dog more room to wander and hoped that would satisfy Maritime's curiosity. At least, she'd stopped barking. While the dog sniffed the ground beneath a palmetto tree, Lottie glanced toward the house again. What was Linc up to?

None of your business, she told herself. *Go, walk to the beach, sit in the sand and watch the moonlight shimmer on the water.*

She'd had no idea what Linc had been up to for twelve years. She didn't need to know now, either.

"Hurry up," she told the dog, but Maritime didn't even turn her way, just took off toward the freshly painted gate that led to the stairway and on to the elevated porch entrance to Linc's house. As the leash length ended, the dog came to a halt, then began his barking again.

"Shush, Maritime," Lottie ordered, pulling on the leash. She didn't want the noise alerting Linc that she was there.

Still barking, Maritime gave another tug on the leash and managed to pull free from Lottie's hold.

"Get back here," she called as Maritime eluded her attempts to recapture the leash. Instead, the dog jumped up, used her nose to undo the gate's latch and bounded up the steps. "No!"

Lottie took off after the dog. "Get back here now. See if I ever take you on another walk."

Pawing at the front door, Maritime took to barking, again.

"Got you!" Lottie announced, grabbing hold of the leash. "Don't expect to sleep in my room tonight. If not for Gram, you'd be toast." Not looking as if she believed Lottie, Maritime gave a yelp of protest as Lottie practically dragged all sixty uncooperative pounds of her back down the porch steps. "Stop. We're going home. And you have no one but yourself to blame when I go on future walks without you."

She'd just reached the gate, when the front door opened and Maritime launched a renewed and noisy effort to make her way back up the steps.

"Lottie?"

Bark. Bark. Bark.

"Maritime, please be quiet." Amazingly, the dog listened. She not only stopped barking but plopped down on her behind as she stared up toward the porch. Giving the dog a look that she hoped conveyed that she was on to her, Lottie then glanced up. Linc had come out onto the porch and stood at the railing. Wearing only shorts, he stood there silhouetted by the house's lights. Broad shoulders and chiseled pecs narrowed down to his slim waist and hips. Good grief, he was beautiful. Lottie swallowed. Would Maritime rein her in if she took off up the stairs in a heated pant?

Having spent his days doing hard, manual labor on a construction site day after day, Linc had had a fit body at nineteen. But nothing that compared to how he'd filled out; he was simply perfect now. Lottie's hand gripping the leash grew clammy. Ha! Despite the ocean breeze whipping around her, her whole body had grown clammy.

"Is everything okay?"

No. Everything was not okay. Far, far from it. The past few days had completely unraveled the anger that had gotten her through the past twelve years, and all that was left was confusion. How could she look at him and want him so badly when she knew he'd never loved her the way she'd once loved him?

"What are you doing here, Lottie?"

Great question. Knowing she was fighting a losing battle, she shrugged. "Would you believe the dog dragged me?"

"I might." Amusement laced his words. "Do you want to see the house?"

Maritime answered for her, jerking the leash free of Lottie's sweaty hand and taking off up the stairs.

As her inner jitteriness grew with each step, she prayed, *Lord, please don't let this be a mistake.*

CHAPTER FIVE

WAS HE COMPLETELY CRAZY? Linc wondered as he knelt to scratch Maritime behind the ears. Inviting Lottie inside his house was nothing short of certifiable.

He'd never had a heartbreak like the one he'd had at her hands. Not that she'd intentionally hurt him. She hadn't. All she'd done was change the course of his destiny one summer long ago. She'd changed him that summer.

For the better. Not that he'd known it at the time. He'd just known that he'd let someone special slip through his fingers because deep down he'd known her mother was right. He hadn't been good enough for Lottie, not then. As the years past, he'd convinced himself that he'd built up Lottie in his mind to pure goddess status and that was why she still haunted his dreams, why he'd catch himself comparing women to her memory.

Maybe that's what had driven him to want to settle on Fripp, to buy the house she'd once loved. Whatever, inside this house had been the first time he'd had a sense of peace, a sense of belonging somewhere, a sense of finally being good enough. For what, he hadn't been sure since he hadn't seen Lottie in years, but he had felt better than he had since…since Lottie had left Fripp to achieve her lofty life goals. And she had. He'd achieved some lofty life goals, too.

What would her mother say if she were meeting him

now for the first time? He'd made a small fortune flipping properties and getting lucky on a few property investments. He no longer had to work, but loved helping others. Would Vivien look at him and still see someone unworthy of her daughter? Or would she embrace him the way she had the cardiologist?

"Hi." Lottie sounded a little breathy, or maybe it had just been the way the wind caught her words making them seem so. Just as the wind, making its way onto the porch, was toying with her hair, making it dance about her head.

"Hi yourself," he said back, moving aside to let her into his house and suddenly feeling self-conscious of his home. "Just remember it's still a work in process. For the most part, I've focused on a few rooms, finishing them, but feel as if I've barely begun with the changes I plan to make to others."

"Oh, I love the kitchen." She moved past him and headed straight to the granite countertop, running her palm across it. "This is gorgeous."

Pride filled him. He'd picked the granite slab himself and had it cut and transported to the island. "Thanks."

She turned. "I take it you started with the kitchen?"

He shrugged. "A man has to eat."

At his comment, her gaze lowered, running over his bare upper body. A blush rose in her cheeks and she hurriedly glanced away, commenting something else about the countertop, he thought, but wasn't sure as his brain had lagged on how Lottie had looked at him.

With interest. Female interest. Which was highly interesting since she was the one in a serious relationship. That phone call hadn't sounded as if it were going well, though. Maybe Lottie wasn't as happy as she'd wanted him to think.

She doesn't have a ring on her finger. The guy was an idiot not to have scooped Lottie up years ago.

Which meant what? That Linc thought he was also an idiot? That maybe they'd been given this second chance for a reason? To see where their relationship would have taken them had they been older and at a different phase of life? He struggled with that. To his knowledge, he'd never intentionally made a move on another man's woman even if that woman felt as if she belonged with him instead.

Aside from the guy in Boston, she had a job, an important job that she loved, in the city. She'd be leaving in a few weeks, and they'd be back to where they'd been all those years ago.

Not quite. Vivien was no longer there reminding him that he had to do the right thing.

The thought made his head spin, just as the fact that Lottie was here, inside his house, had his knees weak.

Needing a moment, he knelt to show Maritime more love. "Hey, girl." He scratched her favorite spot behind her ears. "Who's a good girl?"

"Not her," Lottie said, shaking her head. "We were supposed to be walking to the beach, not making a detour. She wasn't having it and refused to move past your place."

Hands still rubbing Maritime, he glanced up, met Lottie's green gaze and revealed way more than he should. "Like I said, good girl."

Eyes widening she studied him a moment, not with disgust or disapproval, but more with the same confusion he felt. When she finally did speak, she'd steered the conversation away from anything personal, which was perhaps for the best. "So, you started the remodel in the kitchen. What was next?"

"My bedroom." And there he went taking it right back to personal. And that particular personal was too much for him to deal with. He wasn't taking Lottie into his bedroom.

Doing so would have him forgetting everything except begging to discover the lovely woman before him, letting her replace old memories. Yeah, they needed to stay out of the bedroom. "I was working in the main bathroom when I heard Maritime at the door. Some buddies and I hung drywall in a few rooms a few days ago, and I've been taking it room by room to putty, sand and paint. I'd planned to get at least the first coat on that bathroom tonight."

"You're working tonight after working twelve hours today?"

He shrugged. "It's a labor of love. Besides, who are you to talk, little Miss Take-a-Walk-at-Night?" Which he really didn't like. The island entrance had a guard shack, but there were a lot of people coming and going with short-term rentals. "Next time you feel the need to go for a walk after dark, call and I'll go with you."

"I was fine," she assured him. "With Maritime to protect me, what could go wrong?"

The dog glanced toward her, then nuzzled her head against Linc's hand. "I'd still feel better if you weren't out walking by yourself after dark."

An amused light shone in her eyes as she arched a brow. "You didn't mind when I used to sneak out after dark to meet you."

Linc swallowed the lump that formed in his throat at just why Lottie snuck out, where they'd go, what they'd do, and yet as powerful as those memories were, it was the woman before him that he saw, that had his breath catching. "I was a kid who didn't know any better and had ulterior motives to wanting you to sneak out back then." He wanted the brilliant woman she'd become just as much, more even, but never at risk of her safety. "Come on. Let me show you the rest of the house."

Perhaps not sure how to take his comment, probably because his frustration with himself was coming out, she said, "I, uh, okay. Thank you, then I'll let you get back to work."

"And finish your walk?"

"I guess that depends on Maritime. She seems to think she's in charge, so getting her to go down to the beach area might be difficult if that's not where she wants to go."

"She's looking pretty content right here."

"That's because you've been loving all over her since we got here. Who can blame her for not wanting to leave?"

Lottie's lower lip stuck out in a pout, drawing Linc's gaze to her mouth. He wanted to kiss her, to suck that lip into his mouth and gently nip it between his teeth, to taste her sweetness.

Trying to clear the images from his mind, he asked, "Jealous?"

Yes, but Lottie wasn't telling Linc that. Especially not after his comment about being a kid and not knowing any better. Had he meant that as his not knowing better than to mess around with her or that he hadn't known any better on the safety of her sneaking out? She'd never felt unsafe on Fripp. Not then and she hadn't tonight.

At least, not due to anything except how her own body betrayed her.

How else could she describe how being inside the McMahon place—Linc's home—messed with her senses? Ha. It wasn't the house messing with her senses.

Maybe she should tell Linc to put on a shirt. Or two or three. A parka, even.

He should cover up those feet, too. Not that she usually found feet sexy, but there was something about his bare toes that got to her. Maybe memories of playing in the sand and surf with him.

Or memories of rubbing against those feet with her own when—

"I'd love to see the rest of the house," she said in a rush, not letting her thoughts play out. With her comment she took off, startling Maritime who gave a loud, annoyed bark.

"Sure thing." Straightening, Linc followed her. "Had you been in the house before? Back when the McMahons lived here?"

"I peeped in the windows once, but had never been inside," she admitted. "I just wanted to know what the inside of the house looked like but couldn't really tell much beyond the living area on the bottom level. I remember they had it decorated with old movie posters."

"The family moved all those things out. I have workout equipment down there now."

That explained a lot. Those arms. The shoulders. She swallowed. Those abs. Maybe even the calloused hands.

"You're welcome to use it while on the island."

His body?

Hoping he couldn't read her thoughts, she took a deep breath. "Gram will be workout enough once she's home. She ran me crazy the last time I visited. I can only imagine how it's going to be during her recovery."

"When was that?"

"I flew out for a long weekend at Christmas. I tried to convince her to come to Boston so we'd have more time together, but she refused."

"Leave a sunny South Carolina island to go to blustery cold Boston?" He clicked his tongue. "How did she ever manage to say no?"

Lottie's lips twitched. "You have a point, but at least she'd have had a white Christmas."

He didn't look impressed. "Sand's white."

She laughed. "You don't see many holiday ads promoting that as what is meant as a 'white Christmas.' At least, not outside the travel industry. But I admit that coming here for a few days during the cold was a nice break." She smiled wryly. "I hate the circumstances but being here is nice. I miss her."

"She misses you, too." His empathetic look dug deep within her. "She talks about you."

Lottie's brow rose. "To you? What does she say?"

His face color heightened, as if he realized what he'd said and wished he could take the admission back. "Mainly, she mentions how busy you are and that she worries that you work too much. I think it's after you've talked."

"We text some during the week, but I always call her on Sunday mornings. It's our time. Sometimes things come up at the hospital that delay what time we talk, but we always talk."

Those brief Sunday morning calls with her grandmother were each week's highlight.

"Jackie stops by here a few minutes every Sunday to check on the house's progress and for a cup of coffee when she walks Maritime."

Hearing her name, the dog cocked her head toward him, wagged her tail, then moved closer for another round of attention. Linc didn't hold back but lavished the dog with a good rub.

No wonder the dog knew to go to his place and was so familiar with him. Not once had her grandmother mentioned Linc in the months since he had moved to the island, but she was obviously repeatedly mentioning Lottie to him. Why hadn't Gram told her he was back? Had Gram purposely been holding back that knowledge? Of course, she had. Question was, why? Had Gram worried Lottie would find excuses not to return to Fripp if she knew Linc was there?

Realizing he was eyeing her oddly, probably because she'd yet to respond to his comment, Lottie smiled. "I'm glad there's so many people on the island who she knows. She has so many friends here who are practically family. Most of my life, I thought Mrs. Baker was blood related, as she had me call her Aunt Mary from the moment I first met her."

"The all-the-timers are definitely a family."

"You're one of them now," she mused. Who would have thought the young teen boy who'd come to Fripp to work would someday live there?

"Yep. I've no plans to go anywhere. Fripp is home and its residents are family. I see myself staying here for the rest of my days. Come on. Let me show you the rest of my house."

Although much of it was in a state of remodel disarray, Lottie loved the insides of the McMahon place. Entering each room, she'd envisioned how it must look with the sunlight coming through the windows, with the view of the ocean waves, and how gorgeous it would be when Linc finished.

When they came to the bathroom he'd been working in, she eyed the painter's tape. "So, this is what I have been keeping you from?"

"It is." Leaning against the doorjamb, he nodded. "Pretty sure you should stay and help make up for it."

His tone was teasing, but Lottie nodded. "I can do that."

"I was joking, Lottie."

"I know, but I'm serious. I've never painted but I'm willing to learn if you're willing to teach." Why was she trying to convince him to say yes? It was better for them both if she just left. "I usually catch on to new things quickly."

"I remember that about you."

Her breath catching, Lottie's gaze locked with his. "What else do you remember about me, Linc?"

"That you get cranky when you're hungry."

Lottie couldn't argue with that.

"That you love to run to where the waves lap at your feet, turn your face up to the sun and hold your arms out as if you're offering yourself to Poseidon." He painted a memory so vivid that Lottie could almost feel the warmth upon her face and the cold sea at her feet.

"I haven't done that in years," she admitted, wondering at the urge to run out to the water's edge and do so that very moment, embracing the moonlight rather than the sunshine.

"Part of me longs for the girl I was that summer." That was normal, wasn't it? To wish for days that had been stress free? For when she and Linc had been so enthralled with each other that little else had mattered? She shrugged. "Life seemed so perfect back then."

"Maybe it was." His tone was low, but she heard him, heard that bit of yearning for days gone past that she also felt. She also heard the acceptance that that time had long ago passed.

"Look at me now, spending my beach nights offering to help a friend paint." Knowing she needed to get her brain back on track, she picked up a brush and waggled her brows. "Show me what to do."

Thirty minutes later and wearing one of Linc's old T-shirts and drawstring shorts pulled tight so she wouldn't get paint on her clothes, Lottie stroked the brush back and forth, taking pleasure in seeing the dull primer brighten with the paint.

Glancing over at where Linc cut the section around the

ceiling, she bit into her lower lip. He'd put on a shirt when he'd given her the clothes to change into, but with his arms stretched above his head, the hem rode up, revealing slivers of toned flesh that somehow had her mouth going bone-dry and watering at the same time.

"Hey, Lottie?"

She dragged her gaze away from that tempting bit of abs. "Um?"

"Painting works better when your brush actually touches the wall."

"What? Oh." She glanced at the brush she held. He was right. She'd been wagging it back and forth in air strokes. How embarrassing. She shook her head.

Looking amused, he knelt next to her. "Here. Let me show you again." He took her hand into his and guided the brush back and forth along the wall, white covering gray.

Skin tingling at where he held her hand, Lottie made light of her own faux pas. "Oh, so that's how this works. Brush against the wall. Got it."

Still gripping her hand, his thumb stroked across her skin. Breath catching, Lottie watched the gentle movement that was awakening a hurricane of emotion. Slowly, surely, the caress continued until she couldn't resist looking at him.

As she turned his way, he was close. So very close. She could feel his breath against her lips, could see the storm clouds brewing in his eyes as their gazes met. His thumb stilled and his hand trembled. Or maybe it was her hand that trembled. Her gaze dropped to his lips.

She wanted him. This wonderful, thoughtful man, but even as she felt herself lean into him, a voice reminded her that she shouldn't, couldn't kiss him.

Perhaps he thought the same thing because in that same

moment his grip on her hand tightened, bringing the brush up and across the tip of her nose.

"Linc!" she sputtered, automatically reaching up to touch the wet paint.

"What?" he asked, grinning.

"Don't you know that painting works best when the brush actually touches the wall?"

"You don't say? Guess we better get back to it, then."

Nodding, Lottie focused on the wall where she'd been working, but the moment he was back in position, stretched to finish up the far corner of where the wall met the ceiling, that sliver of flesh caught her eye. Without letting herself overthink her actions, she pretended to be turning to get more paint, but instead wielded the brush as a weapon and swiped it across the exposed flesh.

Surprise lighting his eyes, he glanced at his stained flesh and T-shirt, then at her. "Forget where the wall was again?"

"Maybe."

He moved closer. "Perhaps you need me to show you again?"

"Perhaps." Lottie's heart beat faster. "Are you going to? Show me, that is?"

"More like I'm going to give you a lesson on what not to do." With that he dabbed his brush at her.

"No," she squealed, scooting away from him. "Uncle. Uncle. I'll behave."

"Sure, you will." He dabbed the paint again, but Lottie was ready and dabbed back, leaving a wide white streak across his face. "That's it. This means war."

A dabbing paint scuffle ensued that had Lottie laughing so hard her sides hurt as she twisted and turned to protect her face and make a play for his at the same time.

Maritime barked excitedly outside the bathroom door, pawing to get in.

"We should stop. She's going to scratch your door," Lottie warned when Linc had captured both her wrists and held them above her head, having her at his mercy.

Eyes twinkling, he stared at her a moment, seeming torn on whether he wanted to cover her in paint, kiss her, or save his door from Maritime.

"Linc?" she prompted in a voice that was breathy, whether from their scuffle or from how he was looking at her she wasn't sure.

First taking her brush, he lowered her wrists. "You're right. We should stop. Maritime, calm down. I'll be out in a minute to take you outside."

Taking off his T-shirt, he used it to wipe off the bigger paint globs from her face, then his own. "I'll get you a towel."

"Be careful not to track paint through your house," she warned as he went to open the bathroom door.

He paused, grinned. "Now, you're worried about getting paint everywhere?"

Feeling lighter than she had in longer than she could remember, she shrugged. "Better late than never."

Which had her stopping to wonder to just what she was referring to.

"Do we pull off the tape now?"

"Not yet." Glancing at where, paintbrush in hand, Lottie sat on the floor, Linc tapped the lid back onto a paint can.

Linc would have knocked out painting the bathroom much quicker had he not had his helper, but laughing and playing with Lottie had felt right. After putting on a clean T-shirt and taking Maritime outdoors for a bathroom break, he'd turned on the music that he'd silenced when he'd heard the doorbell, fiddling with his phone until a station with songs from the previous decade played over the house's Bluetooth connected speaker system. They'd sang along with the tunes, laughing at each other repeatedly going off-key while they'd finished coating the walls.

"We'll let the paint dry, then we'll run a putty knife along the edges before pulling up the tape."

Disappointment showed on Lottie's paint-splattered face. "We have to wait for the paint to dry? I'd hoped to see the finished product."

"You can swing by the next time you're out walking Maritime."

"Speaking of Maritime, she and I should head back to Gram's."

What she said was true, but he didn't want her to go. Spending time with her tonight had been…nice. "Want me to give you a ride back?"

She shook her head. "It's not that far. I'll walk."

When Lottie got up from where she'd been working, she stretched, the motion revealing a slim line of pale skin as the hem of his tied T-shirt rose. Desire to place his lips there punched Linc so hard that he had to force himself to look away. What was it about Lottie that kept him on sexual edge anytime she was near?

He took her brush, dropping it, along with the brush he'd used prior to rolling the walls, into a plastic bag, then sealed it. He'd clean them later.

"Come on, girl," he told the dog, going into the kitchen and, with unsteady hands, grabbed her leash off the island. Time had gotten away from them. It was late. He was tired. Lottie was a beautiful woman. He needed to keep his brain on track rather than where it had gone because thoughts of kissing Lottie all over needed to be tamped down. "Ready to go outside, Mari?"

When he straightened from attaching the snap hook to Maritime's collar, Lottie joined him in the kitchen, her face freshly scrubbed. He didn't look her way, couldn't look her way. Letting himself would be inviting trouble. She must have felt the same because he could feel her hesitancy.

"I shouldn't have stayed so late on a weeknight. Sorry." A mixture of apology and uncertainty laced her words. "Thank you for showing me your home and being kind when I offered to stay when you knew I would be more hindrance than help. I'll head home."

He followed her to the door. "You know I'm not letting you walk home alone at this hour, right?"

"Which means that you'd be the one walking home alone." She arched a brow and mimicked, "You think I'd let you walk home alone at this hour?"

Despite his inner turmoil, Linc's lips twitched. "There is that. Let me grab my shoes."

When he returned to the living room, she stood on the front porch, Maritime's leash in hand, staring up at the sky as if it were the most fascinating thing she'd ever seen.

"Thanks for waiting."

She didn't avert her gaze from up above. "You thought I wouldn't?"

"I wondered," he admitted. "You've never been afraid to take off on your own."

He hadn't meant his comment as a reference to when she'd left for Boston, or even when she'd first come to Fripp against her parents' wishes, but as soon as the words left his mouth and her eyes cut to him, he realized that's how she'd taken them.

"It would seem that way." Sighing, she gave in to Maritime's tugging against the leash to hurry down the stairway. When they reached the bottom, she stopped just inside the gate, then turned to where he'd followed. "You really don't have to walk me home, Linc."

They'd had a good time. Obviously, his comment had triggered walls to slide into place. Reaching past her, he lifted the gate latch and pushed the gate open. "I don't have to, but it's the right thing to do."

But rather than take off out the gate, she stood there, eyeing him. "Do you always do the right thing, Linc?"

"Not always and never easily." Take when they'd almost kissed. Only at the last moment had he dabbed her with the paintbrush instead of kissing her until they'd both been breathless. Lottie wasn't free, but it was more than just making moves on another man's woman. It was Lottie giving him the right to be interested in her, in her admitting that she wanted his interest, that she wanted a second chance with him.

"You know…" She looked his way and smiled. "We could just keep walking each other back and forth so the other doesn't have to walk alone."

"We could, but something else I recall about you is that you get pretty grumpy if you don't get your sleep. Since you're picking up Jackie in the morning, I think we'd better get you home and then I'll see myself back to my place and be done with it."

"Ha, that's something else that's changed. Medical school, especially residency, got me over my lack of sleep grumpiness. These days it's a great night if I get six hours."

Linc inhaled a deep breath. The night air carried the salty tang of ocean. "You give the impression that Jackie is right in thinking you work too much, Lottie."

They covered several yards prior to her answering.

"I do work a lot," she admitted. "There's so much to be done and never enough time. We're talking people's lives, so it's not easy to just walk away at the end of the day."

Sensing that she was lost in her thoughts, Linc walked silently beside her, not surprised when after a few moments she continued.

"Plus it only makes sense that I would choose to work a lot. I went to school a long time. It would be a shame not to make the most of all those years of studying and that lack of sleep we were just discussing. Giving up all that snooze time has to be justified, right?"

Her tone was light, but her words held depth, as if she were trying to convince herself of their validity.

"Makes sense, but also makes for an off-balance life."

"I have a great life in Boston," she assured him, her expression, barely visible in the moonlight, challenging him to say otherwise.

Her claim was still playing through Linc's head as they headed up Jackie's driveway. She liked her life. So, what if she and Boston Brian weren't as cozy as he'd initially thought. That didn't change the fact that she'd only be in South Carolina for a short time.

"I feel as if I should ask you up, offer you a drink. Something to be hospitable after you took the time to walk me home." She lingered at Ole Bessie's gate. "Thank you, Linc. I've never been skittish on Fripp. But it was nice not being alone."

"It was the least I could do after you helped me paint."

Her laughter was genuine. "Ha! We both know I got more paint on you than on the wall. Fortunately, white looks good on you."

"On me, you, the floor, a little on the walls," he teased,

wondering if the moonlight had ever sparkled so brightly in a woman's eyes.

"Hey, I thought it looked great when we finished."

"We'll know once I pull the tape." He'd never thought a bathroom would be his favorite room in the house, but after tonight, it might.

"Thanks for teaching me the basics. I doubt I'll ever personally tackle painting a room at my apartment, but if I do, now I know how. My roommate, Camilla, would be so impressed."

Which was a harsh reminder that she planned to return to Boston, and he shouldn't forget it. Studying her, he wished he could know what she was thinking, what she was feeling as she fidgeted. His every gut instinct said she wanted him to kiss her. Doing so would be so easy. What came afterward would be anything but. He needed to go home.

"Glad to be able to further your education." As much as he should just turn and go, instead, he leaned forward and pressed a kiss to the top of her head, breathing in the scent of her shampoo and feeling a tiny clump of dried paint scrap the corner of his lips. Pulling back, he gently picked the tiny paint chip from her hair. "Night, Lottie. Sweet dreams."

"I…" Her lower lip disappeared, then she nodded. "Night, Linc."

He took a few steps down the drive.

"Linc?" she called, sending his pulse racing.

"Hmm?" He turned. She stood exactly where she'd been, Maritime nosing into a nearby palmetto that her leash just allowed her to reach.

"Are you sure you don't want me to walk you back?" She shook her head as if rattling her senses into place. "I mean, drive you back? It wouldn't be any problem to run you there."

Was her invitation innocent or an offer of so much more? His heart squeezed; he suspected it was a confused mix of both. "Go inside, Lottie. You need to rest up for whatever Jackie throws at you tomorrow." And he needed the walk home to help clear his head, then he'd clean up the paint mess they'd made in his bathroom. "Go. I'll wait until you're inside."

She hesitated, then nodded. Maritime in tow, she climbed the stairway leading to Jackie's porch. When the house light came on, he saw her silhouette linger, then close the door to disappear inside the house.

Taking a deep breath, Linc crammed his hands into his shorts pocket and took off toward his place in an emotionally tangled mess. With him living on the island and her grandmother being here, running into Lottie had been inevitable. He'd known that. What he hadn't counted on was just how much he'd still want her, how much he'd like the quick wit beneath the Boston exterior of the woman she'd become.

If anything, Lottie attracted him more than she had the summer they'd met.

That was saying a lot.

CHAPTER SIX

THE FOLLOWING DAY, Linc had barely arrived at Jackie's when Mrs. Baker walked over with Maritime's leash secured to the handle of a wagon she pulled over the sandy lawn.

"I spoke with Jackie just a little while ago. They were on Huntington Island so they should be here soon." She gestured toward the wagon. "I baked a few things to welcome her home. There's plenty of those cookies you love in there, too, so be sure to help yourself. While I'm thinking of it, thanks again for unclogging my drain last week."

"No problem on the drain." Linc's mouth watered at the thought of Mrs. Baker's chocolate no-bake cookies. "You trying to fatten me up, Mary?"

The older woman laughed but was saved from answering by Lottie turning the car into the driveway and clicking open the door to the basement garage. From the back seat, Jackie waved as they passed. Maritime went crazy barking and bouncing around to where she freed her leash from the wagon handle. Barking, she charged toward the car that had just parked and excitedly jumped up to peer in at Jackie. *Bark. Bark. Bark.*

Linc and Mrs. Baker took off after the dog, attempting to keep her from scratching the car's paint. Jackie was now talking to the dog, so Maritime wasn't having being pulled away from her favorite person whom she hadn't seen in days.

Bark. Bark. Bark.

"Maritime, shush! Would it have been easier if I hadn't pulled the car into the garage?" Lottie spoke loudly to be heard over the dog. Perhaps giving up, she opened the car's back door. The dog jumped in, licking Gram's face in an excited welcome home. Laughing, Gram loved on the dog. "Don't let her bump your foot," Lottie reminded her, then glanced back at Linc. "I wasn't really thinking about which set of stairs would be easiest to get Gram up. Is this even going to work? I should have hired someone to help you get her inside."

Linc eyed her, wondering at her nervousness and finally attributing it to Gram's coming home. "She barely weights a hundred pounds soaking wet. I don't foresee getting her inside the house as being a problem, do you?"

Lottie's gaze dropped to his arms. Her throat worked. "Uh…no, I guess not so long as I can keep Maritime out from under your feet."

"Hello, I am right here, you two," Jackie said from the car's back seat. "It's my foot that's broken, not my hearing."

Lottie shot her grandmother a look. "Getting you into the house would be a lot easier if it was your hearing."

Linc laughed. "Lottie has a point, Jackie. You sure went to a lot of effort to get me to carry you across your threshold."

Her arms around Maritime's neck as she hugged the dog to her, scratching behind her ears and managing to keep Maritime from licking her face, Jackie snorted. "If I'd wanted you to carry me across my threshold, you'd have done so long ago."

Linc chuckled again. "I imagine I would. You Dunlap ladies are hard to resist."

"I wouldn't go as far as to say that," Lottie mumbled. Linc wasn't sure if Jackie heard over Maritime's excited whimpers and barks, but he had. Did Lottie think his walking away the night before had been easy? Far from it. Under the circumstances, the best thing he could do was resist anything other than her friendship.

"Wrap your arms around my neck, Jackie." He squatted beside the car. "Once you've gotten hold, I'll slide you toward me, then put my arm beneath your legs to support you as I lift you from the car."

"Maybe it's you who has been wanting an excuse to have my arms around you," Jackie accused, doing as he told her and doing a decent job of hiding any pain. Other than having to convince Maritime to move out of his way, he had zero problems scooping up Jackie.

"Get back, Maritime," Lottie ordered, pulling on the dog's leash in an attempt to hold her back. "You're going to trip Linc and hurt Gram."

"She's fine," he assured her, being careful not to let the dog's jumping knock him off-balance or hit Jackie's injured foot.

Lottie followed behind him, fretting as if she worried that he was going to hurt himself. He didn't make a habit of carrying patients, but Jackie didn't weigh much. His biggest concern was making sure the transfer into the house caused her the least amount of pain possible and that Maritime truly didn't trip him up.

"My little girl has missed me, hasn't she?" Jackie crooned, baby-talking to the dog from Linc's arms. "Just a little, haven't you, sweetie? And no wonder, you look as if you've lost weight. Hasn't Lottie been feeding you?"

"Nope," Lottie answered from where she and Mrs. Baker had followed them into the house. Lottie carried a folded lightweight wheelchair, and Mrs. Baker held a bag of Jackie's things. "Only good dogs get fed and that's not what she is."

Linc snorted. He suspected she'd overfed the dog, if anything.

"My Mari is always a good girl, aren't you?" Gram reached down to scratch the excited dog's head. "Linc, have you let Lottie starve my poor baby?"

"I tried to sneak her food, but you know what a stickler Lottie is for rules." Taking care to be gentle with her foot, Linc lowered Jackie onto the living room sofa.

Looking up from where she positioned Jackie's foot on a pillow, Lottie wrinkled her nose. "Your bad dog hasn't missed a meal."

"Maritime is not a bad dog."

"She's not good. Maritime," Lottie said in a strict voice. "Sit."

Four sets of human eyes looked toward the dog. As if to prove how wrong Lottie was, Maritime sat, stared up at Jackie with adoring eyes, and, tongue flopped out of her mouth, panted patiently while waiting for further instruction.

Linc tried not to laugh as Lottie rolled her eyes.

"Of course, she listens when you three are here, but normally, she ignores everything I say. I've even tried treats to get her to listen, and they haven't worked."

"Has she been mean to you?" Jackie asked the dog, motioning for Maritime to come closer. Maritime sniffed at Jackie's bandaged foot. "She knows."

"I imagine she does. She's a smart girl." Linc watched as the dog gently rubbed her nose against the injured foot. "Maybe it'll make her careful not to bump you. We can't have you falling again. Let's practice transferring from the sofa to your wheelchair."

"Maybe later, when I've rested from the drive home."

Linc shook his head. "I'm not leaving until you show me that you can transfer from the sofa to your wheelchair."

"While they do that, how about you and I carry up the goodies I made? They're out in the wagon," Mrs. Baker suggested, placing her hand on Lottie's arm. With one last warning glance toward her grandmother, Lottie followed Mrs. Baker back outdoors.

Turning back to Jackie, he eyed her. "You wanted to come home, which means you're going to have to transfer yourself. Lottie can't do it for you."

"You can just stay. There's another bedroom."

"Not happening." For so many reasons. "My staying wouldn't help you to get stronger."

"I'm plenty strong. My problem is that I can't bear weight."

"Which doesn't mean you can't transfer yourself so Lottie doesn't hurt herself trying to move you."

"You ever heard of hopping one-footed? I got this."

Linc stayed close to catch her if she wasn't as strong as she thought. "Fine. Prove it."

Just as he suspected, Jackie struggled to get into the wheelchair. "You tricked me, asking me to do that when I've had a long day and Maritime wants nothing more than to snuggle. Go help Lottie and Mary carry up the goodies. I'll have more strength after I've eaten."

Recognizing that he had gotten as far with the woman who'd leaned back against the sofa as he was going to get for the moment, Linc headed outside.

He was surprised that Lottie and Mary hadn't been back inside long ago. When he stepped outside on the porch, he grinned at the posse of neighbors who now stood in the driveway, each one carrying a dish. No wonder they hadn't made it back. Lottie must have used brute force to have kept them at bay this long, probably insisting that they couldn't interrupt Jackie's transfer.

"Oh, here's Linc now," Mary said, spotting him. "The ladies are here. Can we see her?"

"Sure thing."

Mary and the other ladies headed up the stairs to visit with Jackie, leaving Linc and Lottie on the lawn.

"Thank you for bringing Gram into the house and working with her when I know she doesn't make things easy."

"Not a problem. She's one of my favorite people in the world."

She gave him an odd look. "You mean that, don't you?"

"Why wouldn't I? She's feisty, but that's one of the things I most love about her." He gestured toward the house. "They'll be here a while so if there's anything you need to do, now would be a good time."

Worry clouded Lottie's eyes. "Tell me what to do so I can help her, Linc. I feel inadequate at being alone with her like this."

"You'll be fine." Linc gave her an empathetic look. He considered staying, but suspected Jackie would have him lifting her each time rather than putting in the effort to transfer herself. Sometimes need was the best facilitator. "She'll tell you what she wants you to do without hesitation, and you've made her extremely happy by doing what was necessary so she can recover at home. She missed her house and Maritime. I'll call to check on her later. If you need me, call. I'm only a few minutes away."

He took off down the drive. When he reached the road, he turned, caught her still watching and waved.

Smiling, she waved back and Linc was tempted to toss his plans so that he could spend the day with Lottie, helping her with Jackie and reassuring her that she had this. She did but he understood her doubts. Seeing a loved one not up to par was never easy, but especially not when it was someone as vivacious as Jackie.

He called that evening to see if she needed help putting Jackie to bed.

"It wasn't easy, but Gram and I got her into her wheel-chair, to the bathroom and back to the sofa a few times. The last time she preferred to go to bed, and she was out within seconds."

Disappointment hit that he wouldn't be seeing her again. Maybe he should have stayed earlier, but… "This is the most active she's been in several days. Hopefully, she'll sleep through the night."

"Hopefully." Lottie yawned. "I straightened things up a bit and plan to call it an early night, too."

As if to emphasize her plans, she yawned again. Had taking care of Jackie worn her out or had she not slept well the night before? That he could relate to. He'd lain in bed for what seemed like hours, thinking over their painting fun and how much he'd wanted to kiss her, marveling at how the grown-up Lottie had looked at him.

"Get some rest, Lottie." If he didn't get his thoughts in check, he wouldn't be getting any sleep tonight, either. As restless as he felt, he'd probably work late into the night. "I'll be by in the morning for Jackie's therapy."

"Thanks. We'll be here."

Linc hung up the phone, then stared at it as a crazy thought occurred.

He had called…but twelve years too late.

* * *

Early the following morning, Jackie frowned at the equipment Linc carried into her living room as she reclined on the sofa. A neon-green-and-aqua pillow propped up her injured foot, and Lottie had styled her sandy-blond-gray hair into a long braid and dressed her in a loose T-shirt and pair of baggy shorts that would have easily gone over her cast.

"What's that?"

"Part of your therapy. Lottie gave me permission to rearrange things however I needed to for your sessions." Placing the folded rowing machine onto the tiled floor, he repositioned a chair.

"Did she now?" Jackie eyed him "I thought I had to be non-weight-bearing."

"Sitting is non-weight-bearing," he assured her, opening the rowing machine. It wasn't the fanciest model but would work great for what Jackie needed.

"You need to maintain good blood flow and to keep your muscles from atrophying. Rowing is a good option as you get cardio, prevent muscle wasting, plus strengthen your core to help with balance and posture. We'll start with just doing upper body and will progress to adding your good leg, then on to using both legs when cleared to do so by Dr. Collins."

Jackie's forehead wrinkled. "You're supposed to help me walk again, not train for the Olympics."

Linc grinned. "I don't think they have a category for sassy old lady, or you'd be a shoo-in for gold."

"Lifetime of training," Jackie agreed, practically giggling even though she still eyed the machine with doubt.

"Are there one-pound weights around here?" Linc glanced

toward where Lottie stood at the edge of the living room, the hand over her mouth no doubt trying to smother a snicker.

"None that I know of." Lottie looked at her grandmother for verification.

Jackie snorted. "Do I look like the kind of person who prances around her house in leotards, leg warmers, and weights in her hands?"

Linc chuckled.

"I can ask Mrs. Baker to sit with Gram so I can run into Beaufort to purchase some," Lottie offered.

Linc shook his head. "No need. We can improvise. Get me a couple vegetable cans."

Lottie went to the kitchen to grab the requested items.

He turned to Jackie. "You're going to stretch, then do weights. After that, we'll move on to the rowing machine."

Jackie crinkled her nose. "When all that work takes me nowhere, that's just useless."

"It's not only not useless, but necessary if you want to get well without setbacks."

"I suppose." Jackie's gaze went beyond him to the window-lined back wall. There was a screened porch to the other side, but the view of the canal was still excellent. "Being cooped up indoors is enough of a life setback."

Linc's heart squeezed at the longing on her face. "How about we make a deal? You do all your therapy with good effort, and I'll put you on the swing beneath your oak tree."

Jackie's face brightened. "You have a deal. I'm going to go crazy if I don't get outdoors soon."

As someone who rarely spent her waking hours indoors, he imagined Jackie was going stir-crazy after her hospital stay.

Lottie returned with a can in each hand. "Look what I found. Sixteen ounces each. Woot-woot."

Jackie cocked a brow. "Where's yours?"

Lottie placed the cans on the end table nearest her grandmother. "I'm not the one in therapy."

"Nope, but most things are easier if you have someone doing them with you and cheering you on." Jackie's expression was expectant.

"I'll be cheering you on." Linc was torn. Part of him wanted Lottie there, to experience her smiles and laughter and have them brighten his day, but another registered that if she stayed, he'd have trouble keeping his mind on Jackie.

"You planning to get out your pom-poms?" A smile played at Lottie's lips. "I can see you now. Go, Gram. Go, Gram. Go—"

Jackie chuckled. "That would be a sight. Our Linc shaking pom-poms and doing cartwheels."

"No pom-poms, but I can do a cartwheel." He paused. "Well, I could do a cartwheel. I honestly haven't attempted one in years but imagine I still can."

"That's what we all tell ourselves and then one day, we can't do the things we once could." Jackie turned pleading eyes toward Lottie. "Stay. Having you here makes me feel better."

Linc had no doubt that Jackie could do the exercises he had planned for her, but the look she gave Lottie was a humdinger.

"Then I'll stay. I'll go grab some cans for me, too."

"You're a spoiled woman, Jackie." Linc scrolled through his music playlists, chose a motivational one, then grinned. "Did I say spoiled? I meant soon to be sweaty."

"A little sweat never hurt anyone." Jackie picked up her cans. "Tell me what you want me to do so I can go outside. There's an ocean breeze with my name on it."

"I love your enthusiasm, but you need to stretch and warm

up prior to going to the cans. We'll be doing similar things as we did during your session at the hospital. Put down the cans and hold your arms directly out like this." Jackie did as he instructed, following each stretching motion. "Now, I want you to make circles. Small ones at first, and then slowly work your way out to where you're doing bigger and bigger circles."

Linc ran through the exercises, having her rotate her arms, do an overhead triceps stretch and a cross-body stretch. Softly singing along with some of the catchy up-beat songs, Lottie did each of the exercises, too. Linc caught her gaze and, without thought, winked. Her gaze stayed locked with his for what seemed a long time but couldn't have been more than a few seconds. Seeming unsure what to do, she looked toward Jackie and thrust her arms back and forth into the air.

"Go, Gram. Go, Gram. You got this."

Smiling, Jackie eyed her granddaughter. "You seem happy."

"Hey, you were the one who said you needed me to cheer you on," Lottie reminded her, still waving her hands around and shaking her hips. "This is me cheering you on. Whoop. Whoop."

"Now, with the cans, do biceps curls. We'll do five sets of five with palm facing upward." There. Linc sounded professional. Rather than like the silly schoolboy he felt with Lottie bouncing around the living room. "When we're finished, then you'll rotate your wrists to where your palms face inward and repeat the five sets of five. After that, we're going to do the same with Arnold presses. That's where you bring your arms in at ninety-degree angles, then up and out. Five sets of five there, too."

Without a word of protest, a testament to how much she

wanted him to carry her outdoors, Jackie pumped her arms in a quick, jerky manner.

"Slow. Steady. With purposeful movements," he said, demonstrating what he meant. Lottie followed suit, raising and lowering her vegetable cans. "Good job, Lottie."

"Teacher's pet," Jackie accused, looking amused.

Lottie arched her brow. "What does that make you, Gram? The class troublemaker?"

Laughing, Jackie slowed her pace, controlling each motion.

Barely into the third set, Linc noted that her arms were shaking. His goal wasn't to exhaust her muscles. Not today. So, he slowed her, having her take ten to fifteen second breaks between her sets of five. She finished the sets, but her arms were a little wobbly at the end.

"Good job. You, too, Lottie," he teased. No wobbly arms there. "Uh, next, we're going to do leg stretches. All non-weight-bearing, of course."

"Of course," Jackie repeated, mimicking him, her gaze going back and forth between them. Was it obvious how Lottie being there affected him? Was Lottie just as aware? Probably. His voice had crackled during that last set of instructions, and then there had been that wink.

"Can you stretch out your injured leg or does it feel too heavy with the cast?"

Jackie lifted her leg a few inches. "It's not light."

"So, on the next exercises I'll leave it up to you as to whether you do them with just your good leg or with both. I want you to stretch out your legs in front of you and just raise them, then lower them. If you can, do ten together, then ten with each leg. If you have any discomfort on the fractured side, then just work your good side."

Jackie lifted her leg off the sofa, then lowered it back. She kept her movements small but controlled.

"Excellent." Linc glanced toward where Lottie had sat down and was following suit. "You, too, Lottie."

"Thanks. This is a good warm-up for my run later."

Had a more dazzling smile ever existed? Or eyes so green?

He cleared his throat. "Stretching and warming up is always a good idea."

Not missing a beat, Gram suggested, "You should go run with Lottie, Linc. Refamiliarize her with the island. Can't have her getting lost."

"Seriously, Gram? I was here at Christmas."

Jackie pretended to be fully focused on her leg movements. "Lots of changes since then. I mean, Linc didn't even live here at Christmas."

"She has a point," he agreed. "The island has changed a lot." They both knew it wasn't true. Yes, older homes were occasionally replaced with newer structures, but his giving the McMahon place a fresh coat of paint and updated landscaping might be the biggest change since her last visit. "I can go for a run with you. Or I can visit with Jackie while you go. Either way."

"I don't want Gram left alone." At her grandmother's eye roll, she continued, "Not yet, anyway."

"Rather than order those weights, you should see about getting a GramCam."

Lottie's gaze cut to him. "A what?"

"New parents call them baby monitors," he stage-whispered.

"I heard that," Jackie grumbled, shaking her head. "A GramCam—that's all I need. Y'all spying on me."

"I was thinking of starting an online channel with you as

the star," Lottie teased, pulling her phone out. "Gram TV, it could catch on."

Pulling his gaze from where Lottie typed something into her phone, Linc chuckled. "That was your last set of those, Jackie. Now, I want you to make small circles."

"More circles?"

"Yep. Only this time, with your legs. Small circles with your legs going toward your center to begin with. Let's do ten and then do ten with your legs going in an outward motion. Do your good leg first, then the other, stopping if the movement triggers pain."

They went through the rest of the exercises, all but the rowing machine and he'd planned to play that one by ear based on how quickly Jackie tired out, anyway.

"No rowing today," he announced.

Jackie looked relieved that he wasn't pushing her to do so. Although she was an active lady, she had spent several days in bed. It didn't take long for that inactivity to take its toll on one's strength and energy.

Expression turning suspicious, Jackie asked, "I still get to go outdoors?"

"Yep. You earned it." Linc folded the row machine and moved it against a wall so it wouldn't be in the way. "I'll check to make sure the swing is ready and then come back to carry you out."

"Best thing you've said all day."

Enjoying the early stages of the sunrise-streaked sky as she jogged along the street, Lottie pulled her cell phone from her waistband phone pocket and, slowing to a walk much to Maritime's displeasure, clicked it on. Gram, still sleeping peacefully in her bed, appeared on the screen. Lottie smiled. Ordering the GramCam Linc had suggested earlier that week had been a brilliant purchase and provided more freedom without worrying that Gram was awake and waiting for help to transfer from the bed to her wheelchair. Or worse, that Gram was doing so on her own to where she might fall. So far, she'd played by the "rules," but Lottie didn't expect that to last.

"Hey, you!"

Maritime barked and did a happy wiggle and tug toward where Linc leaned against his porch railing. Had Lottie subconsciously on purpose slowed in front of his place?

"Hey, you, back," she called, sliding the phone into her pocket. "Good morning."

He'd been so good with Gram that she couldn't help but appreciate him. That was why she was smiling, right? Because of how patient and kind he was to Gram? How he kept both Gram, and Lottie, smiling during the sessions Gram insisted Lottie do each day, too? Not that Lottie minded. She looked forward to seeing Linc work his magic on her grandmother. From the changes he'd already made inside his house, she knew he'd been good at his construction job, but for him not to have gone to PT school would have been a shame. He was an excellent therapist. Then again, as far as she knew there wasn't much he wasn't good at except long-distance relationships and returning heartbroken phone calls.

Linc hurried down the steps and as he drew nearer, Lottie forced her gaze to remain on his face rather than gawk at his impressive physique. He must have just finished working out as the edges of his hair were damp and, in places, his T-shirt clung to his chest.

He fell into step beside her. "Jackie still sleeping?"

She nodded. "Thanks for the GramCam suggestion and helping me set it up yesterday. It works like a charm. I feel better sneaking out this morning knowing I can see if she's awake."

"How'd she do last night? Has adding the rowing machine made her sore?"

"Not that she's mentioned. She was sleeping well when I just checked on her." There. That let him know why she'd slowed. "I appreciate everything you're doing for her, Linc. I know she's happier being at home and thanks to you, it's going better than I'd imagined."

Although Gram would never admit it, Lottie suspected she looked forward to Linc's arrival almost as much as Lottie did.

"You're the one who made that possible, by staying. If I wasn't here, you'd have hired a home health company or just driven her back and forth to Beaufort." Linc pointed toward a neighbor's yard.

Glancing that way, Lottie grasped Maritime's leash tighter, grateful the dog was more interested in something up ahead of them. She smiled at the buck, three does and fawn grazing there. The deer, smaller than mainland deer, were plentiful around the island, and Lottie and Gram had watched them playing numerous times as they fed and cut through Gram's backyard.

"If I could get her up and down the stairs so she could spend more time outdoors, she and I would both be happier. Maybe I need to convince her to have a lift installed."

"I don't mind helping you get her up and down them as often as you need me to. She'll be running circles before they could have it built, but having a lift isn't a bad idea if Jackie can afford it." He offered to take Maritime's leash and Lottie handed it over. So far, the dog had been fairly well behaved but that could change any moment.

"Gram's artwork is quite successful, but even if it wasn't,

money isn't an issue. My grandfather left her well provided for." A car pulled onto the road, and they moved to the shoulder.

Kneeling to hold Maritime's collar to prevent the dog from possibly taking off after the car, Linc waved at the couple as the car passed. "That's good. One less thing to worry about. You never talked much about your grandfather, just mentioned that he died from a heart attack."

Resuming their walk, Lottie brushed some hair that had come loose from her ponytail back from her face. "He died when I was too young to remember much. He was the glue that kept my mother and Gram civil." Her heart clenched at the thought of her mother, and she was struck with the same deep grief of missing her that always hit. "When Gramps died, Mom didn't come back to the island until the summer I was here, and Gram quit leaving."

She'd never understood the animosity between her mother and Gram, and neither had been able to give her a reasonable explanation. Lottie had always thought they'd someday get along, that maybe she'd be able to facilitate that. With her mother's passing, that had never happened and never would. How her mama could have been such a devoted and loving mother and yet a mostly estranged daughter to Gram had always boggled Lottie.

"I'm sorry. I recall you mentioning that he's why you wanted to be a cardiologist. You said you wanted to be a heart doctor so you could prevent as many other kids as possible from losing their grandfather the way you'd lost yours."

Lottie glanced toward him. He remembered that? "We were lying on the beach, listening to the waves and each other's life ramblings when I told you about Gramps dying. You always listened to my ramblings as if I was spouting something brilliant."

"In my eyes, you were."

Warmth spread through Lottie's chest. "I think the same about you."

"There wasn't much brilliant about the kid I was back then, but I was impressed at how you knew exactly where you were going in life. That you'd applied to Harvard and, not just gotten accepted, but also landed a prestigious scholarship."

Embarrassed at his praise, Lottie shrugged. "I'm still not sure how that happened."

"I am. You deserved it. I never doubted that you'd become an amazing cardiologist."

"For all you know I could be an awful cardiologist," she teased to offset the warmth filling her at his praise.

He shook his head. "Even if I hadn't seen how great you were with Mrs. Stephenson, I know better."

"How is she doing?"

"Great. She's scheduled to resume her knee rehab next week."

They reached the beach area, but rather than turning to head back, Lottie crossed through the opening in the large rocks to head toward the water. "Do you mind? The sunsets are beautiful, but don't compare to the sunrises. I've always loved coming here to watch them, but this is the first morning I've ventured out to experience one."

"This is your run, although not as much of one since I interrupted and likely made you miss a good portion of the sunrise. Sorry about that."

The half-mast sun painted the horizon with orange, red and blue streaks. "Don't be. I'm enjoying your company."

He glanced toward her and grinned. "Ditto."

The word he'd used so often in the past, especially when she'd said I love you, had Lottie's breath catching. To hide her reaction, she bent to take off her shoes to keep out the sand and let the waves lap at her feet. "Who would have ever thought we'd be friends?"

First unhooking Maritime's leash to let the dog take off across the empty beach, Linc bent to take his shoes off, too. "It's not that odd. We were on the best of terms when we said our goodbyes."

"You're right. We were."

They'd been on this very beach, sitting on a blanket and watching the sun go down.

"This summer has been the best of my life," Lottie said, stealing a glance at Linc. "I can't believe it's over, that I'll be leaving tomorrow."

Linc squeezed her hand. "It has been a great summer."

"So great you don't want to continue our relationship, though?" she prompted, still not quite wrapping her brain around the idea that tonight was really the last time she'd ever see him.

He loved her. She knew he did. It was in the way he looked at her, smiled at her, touched her as if she were the most precious thing he'd ever know. According to him, she was.

"We've talked about this, Lottie. We end now." He swallowed, though, as if he wasn't quite as sure as he claimed. "You're going to be busy with school. I'm going to be busy with school and work. We'd try to squeeze each other in, managing a few holiday visits at first, but ultimately we'd become disillusioned, holding each other back until one of us called it quits, and we'd never view this summer the same. Don't you think it would be better to keep our memories of each other perfect?"

"I guess."

What he said made sense on the surface. Having a thou-

sand miles between them wasn't going to be easy. But Lottie didn't buy that they'd be better off completely severing all ties. Nor did she buy that he wouldn't change his mind.

She knew he missed her on the rare occasions they'd gone twenty-four hours without seeing each other. A few weeks apart and he'd see that she was right, that although it wouldn't be easy, their love was stronger than any distance or busy schedule. They'd make it work.

Confident in the knowledge that Linc loved her, Lottie leaned over and kissed him.

They'd have their dreams and each other, too...

Memories of that evening, that night, squeezed Lottie's heart, making breathing hard, so she stepped into the inlet's cold water, hoping it would jar her system. How naive she'd been. He'd meant his goodbyes and she'd been the one missing him like crazy, almost throwing her dreams away to chase after him. Walking out until the water was knee-high, she stared across Skull Inlet toward Pritchard's Island where an abandoned University of South Carolina research lab had once stood. It had now been demolished, erasing yet another piece of her beloved Fripp memories.

"You used to run out into the water, arms wide and your face turned up to the sun," Linc said from behind her. "That girl was my best friend."

"For a single summer," she said low enough she doubted he'd hear over Maritime splashing where the dog had followed her into the water. She and Linc had been inseparable, and she'd been young enough not to let what would happen at summer's end prevent her from loving him with all her heart. She'd never been that trusting, that naive, again.

Sighing, she turned to see Linc standing just behind her.

His gaze met hers. "It was a great summer, Lottie."

The best.

Everything that had happened since didn't change the magic she'd felt with him. And maybe that's exactly what he'd meant that day. Not that she agreed, but time had kept pressing forward and so had she.

He took her hand and, clasping it, brought it to his lips. "The best."

Had he read her mind?

Hand in hand, they walked back to the sandy beach while keeping an eye on where Maritime played. Rather than bend to pick up his shoes, Linc let go of her hand and surprised her by leaning forward in a stretching motion.

Curious, Lottie eyed him. "What are you doing?"

From his bent over position, he grinned. "Prepping myself."

"For?"

"You'll see." He put his hands above his head, swayed back and forth in another stretch. Then with a quick motion, he lowered his hands to the ground, rolled forward, and landed back on his feet. Sort of. "Ta-da."

Shaking her head at his silliness, Lottie laughed. "Don't hurt yourself."

Attempting another that was so poor that Lottie knew he wasn't even trying, he pretended to be offended. "Are you making fun of my cartwheel?"

She pretended surprise. "Is that what that was? I'm not saying it was bad, but it might be in the running for the worst cartwheel in history."

"Oh, really?" Grabbing her by the waist, he picked her up and carried her back out into the water. "Take it back, Charlotte Fairwell."

Maritime chased after them, barking and splashing through the water, leaping around as if she were part of their play.

"Or you're going to drop me?" Laughing and clinging to him so she could take him down with her if he did attempt to toss her, Lottie shook her head. Lord, he felt so good against her.

"There you go proving how smart you are again. Harvard would be proud."

Only Lottie wasn't sure she was smart, at all. A smart woman would let him drop her into the inlet, so his arms weren't wrapped around her body, so she wasn't pressed against a body she'd once known as intimately as her own. Or maybe a smart woman would hold on so tightly that he'd never let her go. If she had that goodbye to do over, that's what she'd do. Hold on with all her might, all her heart, to what they shared. Was it too late?

"Okay, okay," she said, giving in. "Since Maritime obviously isn't coming to my defense, I take it back."

"Why don't I believe you?"

"You told me to take it back." She stretched to try to reach the water so she could splash him, but her fingertips didn't quite make it. "You didn't say I had to mean it."

"Yep. Smartest girlfriend I've ever had." To her surprise, as she'd been prepared to be soaked, he lowered her to her feet to where the water was midthigh, dampening their shorts. Rather than dunk her, he even made sure she was steady on her feet and that Maritime didn't knock her over with her excited leaping.

Picking up a piece of driftwood, Linc tossed it toward the shoreline. Excited, Maritime took off in pursuit.

Walking beside him through the water, Lottie couldn't resist asking, "Have there been many?"

"Girlfriends?" Linc shrugged. "A few."

Which didn't tell her much and curiosity got the better of her.

"Any that stand out?"

"Just one."

Heart pounding, Lottie almost face-planted into the water. She didn't have to ask and he didn't have to confirm for her to know who he meant. He meant her.

"I didn't think I'd ever date someone after you," she admitted. "I didn't think it worth risking the pain of another heartache." Need to understand what had happened, to know if she'd been wrong about him, about them, overwhelmed her. "Why didn't you call me back, Linc?"

Jaw tight, he didn't say anything, just took the stick Maritime had retrieved and gave it another fling, then glanced at his watch. "We should head back. If she's not already, Jackie will be waking soon."

Seriously? He was going to ignore her question? Lottie wanted to tackle him, knock him into the water and splash him until he begged for mercy and told her everything she wanted to know. But he was right. Gram probably was awake. Guilt hit that she hadn't opened the GramCam app since he'd joined her in front of his house. She pulled out her phone, looked to see that Gram was indeed awake and reading the note Lottie had left her. "I need to get back."

To Gram's…and to reality.

CHAPTER SEVEN

"WHO WOULD HAVE thought a broken heel would be so much trouble?" Taking a break from the variety of seashells she glued to a piece of driftwood, Gram stared out at her backyard view of the canal. "I miss being on the water."

"You've barely been home a week," Lottie reminded her, sitting on the opposite side of the card table she and Linc had set next to Gram's swing so she could work. Linc had jogged back to Ole Bessie with her, saying that he would get Gram's therapy session done first thing. Otherwise, they'd barely said a word since her asking the question that had haunted her for twelve years.

Gram had cooperated fully thanks to Linc's promise to take her outdoors after her session. After getting her comfortable, he'd escaped Lottie's questioning, and perhaps accusatory, looks to his house with a request for Gram to call whenever she was ready to go indoors. Lottie suspected that might be never with the way Gram had settled into the swing and longingly eyed the occasional boats passing through the canal.

"That's too long."

Lottie imagined it was to Gram who spent time most days on the water, weather permitting. The large oak provided great shade, and a breeze blowing in from the ocean relieved the sticky warmth that Gram seemed impervious to as she semi-lay on the double swing. Lottie had placed a colorful pillow on the cushioned swing to keep Gram's foot elevated. Maritime dozed a few feet away. Keeping her grandmother busy and motivated was going to be the key to keeping her compliant and staying off her foot until the orthopedist released her to start using crutches.

"You'll be back on your feet in no time," Lottie said. "But having this injury happen does make me question you going out to Pritchard's by yourself so frequently."

Gram's expression turned saccharine. "Guess you'll just have to move home so you can keep an eye on me then."

Lottie's stomach clenched. "You know I can't do that. I have a contract with the hospital in Boston. Maybe you should move up north." Gram's expression grew horrified, and Lottie laughed. "You look as if I just suggested something sacrilegious."

"You did." Gram crossed her arms. "I was born in South Carolina, and I'll die here."

Lottie's throat tightened. "Let's not even talk about that."

"Actually, we should talk."

This time Lottie imagined she was the one with a horrified expression. "It probably feels as if you're dying because you're having to remain immobile, but you're going to be fine."

Gram snorted. "I don't mean dying from this blasted foot. I meant, in general, when I die. Eventually it's going to happen, although Lord willing not any time soon. I need to know that you won't sell this place after I'm gone." She reached out to pet Maritime who'd awakened, stretched, then moved next to the swing. "Nor do I want my Ole Bessie to rot from lack of use and love just because I wanted her to stay in the family."

Having seen the McMahon beach house, which she'd

loved, deteriorate more and more with each visit, Lottie understood exactly what her grandmother meant. No doubt the entire island was cheering that Linc had bought the place.

"I can't move here, Gram." Not even if she wanted to, which she didn't. She loved being a cardiologist and taking care of her patients. She loved her life in Boston. Her coworkers and friends.

That Brian didn't immediately pop into her head as a reason to love her life in Boston wasn't lost on her. If she had wanted to return to Fripp permanently, would he have been enough to keep her in Boston? Would she have been willing to change the course of her life to be with him the way she once had with Linc? She adored him as a friend, but he wasn't enough. She knew it. Perhaps he did, too, and that's why he hadn't mentioned picking out a ring for so long. Yet, letting him go felt a betrayal to her parents, to her mother. Vivien had loved Lottie with all her heart and she'd thought Brian was perfect for her, so he must have been. And maybe, at the time they'd met, Brian had been because he'd never made demands of her, never held her heart strings to where he could yank on them at will. She'd never given him that power. Doing that would have been risking getting hurt again.

Oblivious to where Lottie's thoughts had gone, Gram gave Maritime another pat, then picked up a shell and studied the swirling center. "I plan to set up a trust to ensure you can keep the place spiffy so that you can bring my future great-grandchildren here and, hopefully, someday, they can bring their children."

Her children. Grandchildren. No matter how much she tried Lottie couldn't picture children who looked like her and Brian. Not even to honor her beloved mother's memory did she see that ever happening.

"You can teach them about the island and to have an appreciation for the South." Gram pulled Lottie's attention back. Good. Her previous thoughts would open a Pandora's box she knew better than to mess with, but realized she couldn't in good conscience ignore. Brian deserved better than that. And so did Lottie.

She watched the woman she loved so much twist and turn a wire around an end of the driftwood, then attach more shells. Lottie picked up a shell and began gluing it to her own piece of driftwood. They worked in silence until Gram was satisfied with her work and leaned back in the swing to eye Lottie's piece.

"You're pretty good."

"I just glued pieces where they fit."

Gram grinned. "Exactly."

Her genuine praise pleased Lottie and, taking a deep breath, she said, "Gram?"

"Hmm?" Gram looked up from where she'd been loving on Maritime.

"I'm not going to marry Brian."

"I know your grandmother doesn't like me, but I didn't think she'd convince you to end our relationship."

Lottie paced across the sunroom to stare out the window at where her grandmother still sat in the swing with Maritime by her side. Mrs. Baker and another neighbor visited with her, laughing at something Gram was saying.

"This isn't about Gram. It's about you and me, Brian. I adore you, but I'm not in love with you."

That doesn't matter, Lottie. You can learn to love him, her mother's voice whispered.

No, Mama. I can't. I won't.

"You're not in love with me either, Brian. Not really.

Maybe you were once upon a time, but if you're honest, you're more in love with the idea of us as a couple than you are specifically with me."

"If I've done something to give you the impression that I don't love you, then you're mistaken."

"As a dear friend doesn't count," she pointed out, then sucked in a deep breath. "Not when that's all there is. When you've had time to think about what I'm saying, you're going to know I'm right."

Silence came over the phone for long moments. "It's him, isn't it?"

"Him?"

"The guy you were so torn up about when we first met. You told me that you weren't sure about our dating because you hadn't gotten over someone you'd once known. Your mother told me not to worry because she knew you and I were perfect together, but he's always been between us, hasn't he, Charlotte?"

Lottie squeezed the phone so tightly her fingers hurt. "Mama talked to you about Linc?"

"Just to say that she was happy I'd come into your life and brought a smile back to your face. That she'd known from the first moment she'd met me that I was the one to fill the void that had been in your life."

Guilt hit Lottie so hard she could barely breathe. "Your friendship did fill a void in my life. Yours and Camilla's. I love you both dearly. But I'm not willing to pretend that we're anything more than friends. Not anymore."

"I'm not sure what to say, Charlotte. I'm not even sure what you want me to say."

"That makes two of us," she admitted, trying to calm her shaking hands. "This is scary because you've been a part of my life for the past five years and what I thought my future looked like and now I just don't know."

Another pause, then, "I never wanted to be your safety net."

And yet that's exactly what he'd been. Safe, undemanding, unable to wreak the havoc upon her heart that Linc had, and she'd embraced that. Her mother had mistaken that and friendship for something more and because Lottie had wanted to believe, she'd let her mother convince her of the same.

"You deserve better," she said, and meant it. "I hope you find someone who loves you as you deserve to be loved, Brian."

Hanging up the phone, Lottie sank into the sunroom's oversize hanging chair and gave in to the tears streaming down her face.

Forgive me, Mama. I miss you so much, love and respect your opinions, but this is my life and I have to live it.

That evening, after they'd gotten Gram settled on the sofa, Lottie walked onto the front porch with Linc. As always, he'd been amazing with Gram. Part of her had wanted to immediately tell him that she had ended things with Brian, but after his reaction to her question that morning, she held back. Once she'd had her big boo-hoo fest, she'd cleaned her face and spent the remainder of the afternoon playing cards with Mrs. Baker and Gram.

"Thank you for taking such good care of Gram. She had a really good day today with getting to spend so much time outdoors, but I know this has to be slowing down your work on your house."

He shrugged. "Unless some helper mermaids come ashore and finish the job for me, it'll be waiting on me after Jackie is back on her feet. There's no rush."

"Helper mermaids, eh?" Lottie smiled. "Just because there's no rush doesn't make it right for us to take advantage of you, Linc."

"Neighbors helping neighbors isn't taking advantage." He leaned against the railing, staring out into Gram's yard. "Besides, I owe your grandmother. It's thanks to her that I got the McMahon place."

Lottie stared at him. "What do you mean?"

"She's never said anything, but Mrs. McMahon's son said she called and convinced him to take my offer over the others they received."

Gram had done that? Why would she care who bought the house?

He pushed off the railing. "I work tomorrow, but I'll stop on my way home and take her outside for an hour or so. It's not much, but short of getting her out there at the crack of dawn and her being stuck out there all day, it's better than nothing."

"It's wonderful and much appreciated. Thank you." She bit into her lower lip. "Is there anything we can do for you?"

He shook his head. "I'm good."

Lottie agreed. Linc was good. Better than good.

Why wouldn't you answer my question? Would it be so difficult to just admit that you hadn't loved me the way I thought you did? The way I loved you?

"You're blushing, Lottie." Curiosity laced his voice.

"I got a little too much sun today when I was sitting outside with Gram." Because she didn't want to ruin the evening by telling him what she'd really been thinking. If she told him, he'd just change the subject or leave.

"You think?"

She knew.

* * *

True to his word Linc came by after he got off work the following day. Knowing she wanted to do something to show her gratitude for all he was doing for Gram, Lottie had left Gram playing cards with her friends long enough to make a grocery and shrimp boat run. The least she could do was cook dinner. She might have gone a bit overboard though, with steak, shrimp, pasta, rosemary potatoes and spinach salad with fresh fruit.

"Wow." Linc eyed the spread. "If this tastes half as good as it looks, then I'm going to need to spend some extra time working out in the morning."

Pleased by his reaction, she smiled. "Then let's hope you have to rise extra early."

He glanced around the cleaned kitchen. "What can I do to help?"

"Let's get Gram moved to either a lounger or the swing, whichever she prefers, and we can eat outside, if you're okay with that? She's been itching to go out all day."

"Will do."

Her grandmother had been sitting in the living room, watching a television program about couples getting married at first sight.

"Is this not just the craziest thing you've ever heard?" she asked as they came into the living room. Prior to the break, Lottie suspected her grandmother only had the television for her beloved weather station, but "reality" shows were helping fill her time resting on the sofa with her foot propped up. "People volunteering to marry someone they've never met and that a television producer has picked out?" She tsked. "You know this is just for theatrics and not real. Who would agree to something so ridiculous?"

"Maybe someone who has given up on more conventional means of finding love," Lottie offered, half teasing.

"Actually," Linc said with a straight face, "I've been thinking about auditioning. You think they could find my soulmate?"

"No."

Two sets of curious eyes shifted to Lottie at her rather firm response.

"No?" Linc's brow lifted. "I'm that hopeless?"

Far from it. "I mean, there's better ways to find one's soulmate than some random person a Hollywood producer chose to boost ratings."

His blue eyes twinkled with a mixture of mischief and something more. "What would you suggest?"

Why was he teasing her about this? And in front of Gram!

"Take out a billboard with your photo on it." Gram practically cackled. "Women would line up."

Lottie couldn't argue. Linc was a handsome man, but there was so much more to him than his beautiful exterior. He genuinely cared about others, was intelligent and seemed to know how to do just about anything. His smile made a person feel good inside, an innate warmth and friendliness that just spread happiness. At least, that's how he affected Lottie.

Being around Linc did make her happy. Always had.

Linc chuckled. "I doubt that, but I imagine there would be a few takers when they saw my house. The McMahon place might be a real chick magnet."

"You'd have more than a few takers if you lived in a cardboard box," Gram assured him. "Tell him, Lottie."

"Way to put me on the hot seat there, Gram." Cheeks heating, Lottie glanced toward Linc. "I'm sure lots of women would jump at the chance if they knew you were looking."

Linc eyed her. "Would you? If you were single, I mean?"

Yes. No. She didn't know. Wasn't that what she'd been trying to figure out for the past twenty-four hours that she had been single? She was only there for a short time. Linc was her past, her present, but he likely wouldn't be her future outside of precious memories. Would a smart woman grasp at the chance to retaste the sweetness of the best summer of her life when she knew that warmth would only make the winter all the colder?

"I did," she reminded him, knowing she needed to give an answer. "When I was single."

I'm single now. She'd wanted to tell him the moment he'd walked into the house the night before, and it was on the tip of her tongue even now. But after thinking about little else for the past night and day, she hadn't fully processed just what her new relationship status meant. She hadn't even told Gram that she'd officially ended things with Brian. If she had, Gram would have been the one taking out a billboard—multiple billboards along Linc's drive to and from Beaufort and all advertising Lottie.

"That's right. You did." Linc's eyes darkened, momentarily losing their teasing gleam. "Maybe I'll put off my audition a little longer to give myself more time to work on the house, just in case I need a 'comes with an ocean view' tagline as a backup plan."

"If I was in my prime, you wouldn't need a backup plan." Gram gave Lottie a "you're crazy" look.

Chuckling, Linc scooped Gram up into his arms. "Just say the word, Jackie, and I'm yours."

Crazy! Gram's stare reiterated.

Opening the back door for them, Lottie followed the pair down the porch steps and readied the swing for her grandmother, making sure that the pillow was in the correct spot.

Gram was right. She was crazy. Crazy confused. Crazy guilty that she knew her mother was rolling over in her grave that Lottie had ended things with Brian. Crazy with the way her heart leaped when she was near the man who had yet again turned her life upside down.

As he got her grandmother settled, Lottie asked her, "How about I put a little of everything on your plate?" Lottie smiled at Gram's nod. She turned toward Linc. "Stay, rest and visit with Gram. Once I've taken care of her, I'll bring a plate for you, too."

"If it's all the same, I'll make my own."

"Yeah, yeah, leave me out here by myself," Gram mumbled, but didn't look as if she truly minded in the slightest.

"I think you just offended Maritime." Lottie gestured to where the dog had cocked her head.

"Come here, girl. You know I love you," Gram cooed to the dog as Lottie and Linc went into the house.

While he heaped generous portions of the food onto his plate, Lottie poured two glasses of lemonade and one sweet tea.

"This is amazing." Linc popped a potato chunk into his mouth. "When you texted to say not to eat anything as you were preparing dinner, I was prepared for pizza or burgers or something simple. If I'd known you could cook like this, I'd have suggested dinner long ago."

"What? And miss out on all the casseroles the neighborhood ladies have dropped by?" Lottie put her hands on her hips. "Besides, I can cook."

His eyes twinkled. "You couldn't when I knew you."

"I could. I just didn't," she said. "Mama and I had taken cooking lessons. She thought it was something fun for us to do together." Oh, how her teenage self had hated those weekly classes. Now she'd do anything to have those moments with her mother back.

I'm sorry, Mama.

Whether she apologized for not appreciating that precious time with her mother or that she silenced her voice as it started to beg her to rethink the security of her relationship with Brian, Lottie wasn't sure. "For a long time, cooking felt like a chore. At some point during residency, I realized cooking relaxed me and as a bonus I had really good leftovers to eat for the next week."

Glancing down at his full plate, Linc gave a sheepish grin. "I may have blown that 'leftovers for a week' plan."

Lottie shook her head. "If you're okay with it, I thought I'd cook dinner each evening you work and feed you for helping with Gram."

His smile slipped. "Lottie, you don't need to do that. I told you—"

"Please," she said, stopping him. "It gives me something to do to feel useful and Gram, too. I let her pick out the sides and dessert she wanted me to make. She even helped cut the potatoes."

He popped another potato into his mouth. "Well, if she's the one who picked these out, then I need to thank her. She must have thought I was going to be extra hungry."

"I invited Mrs. Baker to stay for dinner, too. She couldn't make it tonight but plans to come tomorrow."

"Lucky her. If word gets out on what an amazing cook you are, the whole island will be showing up for dinner." He set down his plate. "How about I carry out our drinks while you prepare Jackie's plate? I'll come back to bring mine and hers down while you get yours. That way you can join us sooner."

Handing the glasses over, she smiled. "Thanks. That sounds perfect."

They ate, laughed and enjoyed being outdoors, watching as several herds of deer passed. Maritime kept an eye on them, but otherwise ignored them.

When Linc got Gram back indoors and settled into her wheelchair where she'd asked to sit, he said, "I'll get out of you ladies' hair but I'm already looking forward to whatever you're making tomorrow evening. Tonight's dinner was delicious."

Happiness filled Lottie at his compliment. He had eaten with gusto, as if he truly enjoyed every morsel, and she'd enjoyed watching him and Gram bicker over whether Emily Dickinson had been brilliant or off her rocker.

"Yes, dinner really was," Gram agreed. "Lottie's going to make a great wife someday."

"Don't go signing me up for your wedding reality show," Lottie warned, giving her grandmother a please-don't look. "I've no plans to marry anytime soon."

Although the mood was light, Linc's gaze bore into her. "Still no plans to go pick out an engagement ring, then?"

So much for wanting time to ponder her feelings, to sort her thoughts before sharing her news. This wasn't how she wanted to have this conversation. Not with her grandmother or with Linc. Was there even a reason to have it with Linc? But she didn't really see a way around answering him. Not unless she pulled one of his cues and just changed the subject. Tempting.

Instead, she took a deep breath and watched him closely to see how he'd react to her revelation.

"Brian and I are no longer a couple."

CHAPTER EIGHT

LOTTIE WAS SINGLE. Why hadn't she said anything earlier?

Just because she was single did not mean Linc had anything to do with that decision. Nor did it mean that if she was that he should feel so happy. He shouldn't. The pain in her voice when she'd asked why he hadn't called her back had almost undone him. Answering her would have hurt her worse than keeping his silence, so he'd kept his mouth shut. It's what he should do now. Lottie's time in South Carolina was as temporary as it had been the summer they met. In another few weeks Gram wouldn't need her there, and Lottie would return to Boston. She might even realize that she'd made a mistake in ending her relationship with the cardiologist.

"I'm not sure whether to say I'm sorry or congratulations," he said cautiously, doing his best to keep his voice level.

Jackie had no such reservations. "Definitely congratulations. He wasn't the right man for her. Never was even if my granddaughter was too blind to realize that."

Lottie winced. "This turned awkward fast. Let's not talk about Brian."

Worked for Linc. He never wanted to mention the guy's name again.

"Are you sure you have to leave, Linc?" Jackie asked.

"I need to keep my card game sharp, and Lottie's not a good player."

"Gram!" Lottie protested, causing Maritime to let loose with a yelp.

"What?" Jackie turned her hands up, then reached out to pet her dog. "You're not."

"No one's good at everything," Linc reminded her, eyeing the way Lottie's pulse pounded at her throat as if she'd just run to the beach and back. She might be acting as calm as he was, but she was just as on edge. "For the record, if I got to pick whether you could cook like an angel or cheat at cards like your grandmother, I'd pick the food every time."

Eyes searching his, Lottie sent him an appreciative smile. "Thank you."

"Hey," Jackie protested, as Linc had known she would. "I don't have to cheat at cards to win."

Pulling his gaze from Lottie's, he glanced toward Jackie. "Except for when you play me?"

"Does that mean that Linc beats you at cards?" Lottie sounded incredulous. "As in, when you don't have a partner to cause you to lose, he outplays you?"

Jackie frowned. "I wouldn't say he outplays me. He's just really lucky at getting the right cards."

"I beat her. Fair and square," Linc said, grinning. "Haven't you?"

"Rarely and only when she lets me so I'll agree to keep playing. Even then, I can tell she doesn't like it, but believes it a necessary evil because she loves to play so much."

Jackie blinked innocently, then clasped her hands together. "That settles it, Linc. You have to stay for at least one game so I can beat you both."

Linc's gaze met Lottie's, and he attempted to decipher what she wanted him to say. She lifted her shoulders in a slight shrug, but her eyes said, *stay.* "She'll trounce me if you go. Actually, she'll trounce me if you stay, but it would be worth it to see you take her down a peg."

"One game." There wasn't anything at home that couldn't wait. "But that's it. I'm a working man who has to be up early in the morning to work off my dinner."

Eyes still connected with his, Lottie smiled. "One game."

"One game is all it's going to take," Gram bragged. "I have a secret weapon tonight."

Linc pulled the coffee table over near the sofa while Lottie grabbed the card deck, paper and pen. "You think I'm going to let you win just because you have a cast?"

Jackie gave him a smug look. "Nope. Tonight, Lottie is my good luck charm."

"Rummy!" Lottie whooped, slapping her cards down on the table. "I win!"

"Let me see your cards." Jackie leaned forward, making sure Lottie's cards lined up as they should. Her voice had sounded brisk, but there was a light in her eyes that said Lottie's grandmother knew exactly how her granddaughter kept getting exactly the cards she needed and that she didn't mind nearly as much as her protesting would suggest.

Standing, Lottie moved to Jackie's side of the table and took her grandmother's hands, dancing around while holding them. "I want to hear you say the words."

Gram's lips twitched as she shook her head.

Laughing, Lottie happy danced all the more. "Come on, Gram. Say it. I beat you."

"And here I thought you'd be my good luck charm and instead that big oaf was yours."

Lottie's gaze cut to him, and he shrugged. "I don't know

what she's talking about. Congratulations on your win, though."

Lottie laced her fingers with her grandmother's and swayed them back and forth as if her grandmother joined her in her happy dance. "If Linc's why I won, then he's definitely staying for cards again tomorrow night."

Rolling her eyes, Jackie smiled. "You think you can beat me two nights in a row just because he's here? Doubtful, but I guess we'll see."

Linc moved the coffee table back to where it belonged, then told Jackie goodbye, grinning at her I-know-what-you-did look.

When he readied to leave, Linc wasn't surprised that Lottie walked outside with him.

"Thanks for staying." She followed him out the gate, taking care not to let out Maritime who'd come with them. "Gram and I had a great time tonight, especially me. Did you help me win?"

If she didn't know, he wasn't telling.

Linc latched the lock so Maritime couldn't push open the gate. "Jackie would have called me out if I was feeding your hand, surely?"

Lottie's eyes widened and he laughed.

"Linc! She'll get us both if she even suspects you helped me," Lottie accused, pushing against his arm.

Linc knew better. Jackie had enjoyed Lottie's smiles and laughter as much as Linc had.

"I play to win," he told her. As Jackie had suspected, he'd had difficulty concentrating with Lottie sitting across from him, smiling despite making bad play after bad play. He'd figured out real quick that beating Jackie might not happen but, unbeknownst to her, helping Lottie had been easy enough. Her delight had him feeling as if he had won.

She was still smiling and so was he. Not because of the card game, but because Lottie was single.

She laughed. "So you say, but now you have me wondering. You're a really nice guy, Linc Thomas."

"Uh-oh."

"What's that?"

"Nice guys never get the girl."

"No?" Breath audibly catching, smile faltering, she looked up at him. In the glow of the house's lights, her eyes glittered with uncertainty. "Does the nice guy want to get the girl?"

That one was a no-brainer, but he hesitated. There were so many reasons why he should let her down gently and go home before they made a big mistake.

"He does," he admitted, "but thinks getting the girl would complicate both of their lives, especially when the girl just ended a long-term relationship and might be confused about what it is she wants."

"I suppose you're right." She took a deep breath. "What do you want, Linc?"

You.

"Do you want to kiss me? Because in this moment, that's what I want."

Talk about complicating things. Lottie's question, how she was looking at him, sure did that. Or maybe it was how he answered that most complicated things.

Reaching out, he ran his fingers into her hair, letting the silky strands wrap around his hands as he pulled her close enough to inhale the citrusy scent of her shampoo. "I've wanted to kiss you from the moment I rounded the hallway corner and saw you standing there, soaking wet, and wrapped in a towel."

What he'd wanted was to strip off the towel and kiss her all over. He swallowed the lump forming in his throat and took a deep, steadying breath.

"You didn't say anything." Her response sounded accusatory.

"No," he agreed, lowering his hand. "You were bleeding, but more than that, you weren't single."

Lottie flattened her palms against his chest. "You're right, but Linc?"

"Hmm?"

"I'm single now." She stared up at him with such longing in her eyes that Linc couldn't breathe. If ever he'd heard an invitation to kiss a woman, that had been it. Only he couldn't. No matter how much he wanted to, he simply couldn't.

"So, you are." He drew upon every bit of willpower he'd ever had. Fingers still in her hair, he cradled her head in his palms and stared down into her lovely face. "I'm going home, Lottie, but not because I don't want to kiss you. Know that."

Disappointment shone on her face. That both pleased and tormented him.

"Mrs. Baker is sitting on her porch," he pointed out, in case she hadn't noticed her grandmother's neighbor watching them from the next house over. He wasn't sure there were binoculars involved, but light glinting off something metal had been what clued him in to her presence. Part of him didn't care who saw, but having their first kiss in so long watched in that way bothered him.

"Oh!" Lottie took a guilty step back. "I, uh, yes, best not to kiss me when she'd tell Gram and that would have

Gram thinking all kinds of things that just aren't the case."
A nervous laugh escaped her throat. "She'd have us back
together and be picking out names for our kids. What was
I thinking? I never should have said anything about Brian
and I not being together in front of her."

Her prattling had Linc's head spinning. She pressed her
hands together and gave another of the laughs she made
when nervous. That she was so obviously off-kilter put a
huge dent in his willpower, but he managed to keep his feet
in place and not close the distance she'd put between them.

"Perhaps not, but I am glad you said something in front
of me."

Her eyes took on that wide-eyed uncertain look again.
"You are?"

"You know I am, Lottie. I want to kiss you, to know if
your mouth still tastes as sweet as honey and if the surf
pounds my insides when you kiss me back. But I'm going
to admit something else to you." Something he could barely
believe himself. "I'm glad Mrs. Baker is there because as
much as I want to kiss you, I'm not sure that I should."

Because he knew that all the reasons he shouldn't had
nothing to do with her relationship with Boston Brian and
everything to do with the fact that getting involved roman-
tically with a woman destined to leave him yet again would
be a big mistake on his part.

A big mistake he was destined to make.

Linc had worked the previous days but had stopped by each
evening to take Gram outdoors, eat dinner with them and
to play a single hand of cards, Mrs. Baker included. Each
night, Lottie waited on him to say something, do something, that let her know he'd meant what he'd said, that he
wanted to kiss her. He smiled. He laughed. He teased her.

He made her smile and laugh and she teased him back. A crazy mixture of anxiety and anticipation was demolishing her insides.

After she'd practically thrown herself at him, she'd been prepared for awkwardness, but when he'd arrived the following evening, his warm smile, raves about his dinner and feeding her card hand to help her beat Gram in rummy had prevented that.

"Hey, Lottie, would it be okay to pack that up? Jackie has convinced me to go out on her boat to gather driftwood and whatever other treasure I run across. Mrs. Baker is going to come give her a few practice hands at winning cards." Gram grunted and Linc laughed. "How about it? Do you want to spend a few hours on the water with me? We can picnic on Pritchard's."

Just like old times.

Lottie nodded. "I— Sure. If Gram needs more supplies for her art, then we should definitely go see what we can find."

"Right. She needs the card practice, too. What with that three-night losing streak she has going."

"I'll remind you that your losing streak matches my own."

Lottie smiled. "Yeah, about that—"

"Lottie plans to make it four nights so be prepared for another defeat after we're back this evening," Linc warned. "I'll run home, grab my trunks and be back in say, thirty minutes?"

"Sounds perfect."

An afternoon alone with Linc. Yeah, that mixture of anxiety and anticipation was blowing full force, and as scary as she found not knowing what the future held, Lottie planned to run directly into the wind, face up to the sunshine for however long it lasted.

* * *

From the boat's front passenger seat, Lottie twisted to watch Linc drive. Once they'd exited the canal, rather than zooming straight across the bay to picnic at Pritchard's, Linc had headed into the inlet to drive through Gram's beloved marshes, pointing out birds and other wildlife.

"What a great surprise." Happiness flowed through Lottie. "It feels so good to be out of the house."

"Careful. You're sounding like Jackie," Linc teased, glancing toward Lottie. "You look a lot like her, you know. Or how she must have looked at your age."

Lottie nodded. She did resemble the photos she'd seen of Gram at her age. "I think it's the eyes." Lottie breathed in the sea air, relishing how doing so seemed to wash away every care. "As much as I'd love Gram to move to Boston, I'd never want to take away the joy she gets from coming out here. Not that Gram couldn't go out on the water there, too, but boating on the Charles River isn't the same as doing so in the South Carolina marshes."

Rather than answer, Linc just smiled and pointed toward the spartina grass to Lottie's right. He slowed the boat to a stop, cutting the engine a good distance from the tall green blades poking up from the water. There! A bottlenose dolphin broke the surface, then another, feeding, or maybe just playing at the grass's edge.

"Oh!" Excitement filled Lottie. Having grown up in Atlanta, her first dolphin sighting had been at the aquarium there during a field trip her mother had tried to talk her out of. Lottie's first wild sighting had been on Fripp with Linc when he'd pointed out a young calf swimming next to its mother. More than likely that calf, now grown, still lived in the area.

She looked toward him and was shocked to find him

watching her rather than the dolphins. When their gazes met, he gave a lopsided grin that had her wondering if he was remembering how they'd watched for Bonnie and Baby Clyde, as they'd dubbed the mother and calf.

"They're still here."

Had he read her mind?

"Really?" She gazed at him in wonder. "You're sure? How do you know?"

"I've seen them. Bonnie has a new calf. According to the wildlife management agent I spoke with, she's had three since Baby Clyde."

"Three babies? I love that so much." Lottie turned her attention back to the dolphins, watching them play.

"I'd hoped we'd see them out here today."

"Oh!" she exclaimed when one came up a few feet from the boat. Reaching for her phone, she got her camera ready in case it came close again. After a few moments, two arched in unison, not as close as the one had been but midway between the boat and where they'd first spotted them. Lottie clicked away, hoping she'd gotten a few decent shots. Just as she was about to lower her camera, another surfaced close to the boat, perhaps the same one as before. He seemed to look right at her, smile, then duck back underwater. It surprised her so much that she hadn't clicked her camera a single time. Disappointment filled her that she failed to capture such a cool moment, especially since she'd had her phone in hand.

"Can you believe that?" She glanced toward Linc to see if he'd seen the dolphin. His phone was aimed her way. Realizing he'd been taking photos, hopefully catching the dolphin, she automatically smiled a cheesy smile. "Cheese."

Lowering his phone, he smiled. "I thought I got a great

shot when your friend came up for a visit, but that one was better."

"Right." Lottie snorted. "I guess he just wanted to see what we were up to."

"Not sure if he's just curious about why there's someone else driving Gram's boat or if he's letting us know he knows we're here and eyeing his pod." Linc held one hand out to shade his phone's screen as he scrolled through the photos.

Lottie's attention wavered between him and the dolphins who continued to play as they moved farther along the grass edge.

"You'll like this one." Linc handed over his phone.

Lottie glanced down at the screen. He'd captured the dolphin looking at her and her excited profile as she looked back.

"Oh, Linc, will you send me this? I'd love a copy."

"Will do." He leaned toward her, placed his finger on the screen and scrolled the photo to the next one. "Keep looking."

Lottie's favorites were the ones with the dolphin, but the photos he'd clicked of her smiling at him weren't bad. Happiness shone on her face because she was happy. She dragged her finger across the screen again, excited to see the next shot, and paused. It was of her looking at him right before she'd said her cheesy "cheese." In her eyes she saw what she'd always known deep down. Even so, she wasn't willing to throw that label on what she was feeling. Her peace of mind wouldn't let her.

She lifted her gaze, found him watching her still. Did he see what was so obvious in that photo? "They're really good."

"Hard not to be with you in them."

Feeling way too breathy, Lottie handed his phone back,

well aware of how their fingers brushed as she did so. How could she not be when that slight touch had sent electric tingles through her?

"Thank you. I think it's the fresh air and being away from working every day. I obviously needed a change of scenery more than I realized."

Linc slid his phone back into his shorts side pocket, zipping it to keep the phone secure. "We'll go through the marshes for a while longer, then head to Pritchard's and picnic. Afterward, we'll see if we can come across some cool old boards or driftwood."

"Sounds perfect."

Watching him as he started the boat and guided them through the marshes, Lottie admitted that the entire day felt perfect.

Setting up the beach umbrella to provide shade on a good portion of the blanket, Linc stole a glance toward Lottie. She'd possessed an underlying cautiousness the past couple of days, but seemed completely relaxed that afternoon.

He understood her wariness. He felt the same. Part of him wanted to take her into his arms and kiss her until she was as breathless as just looking at her had him. Another part had told him to take things slow so he didn't muddle up either of their lives.

That he'd managed to keep away from the physical, knowing she was single and wanted him, was a testament to just how complicated things were and how he never wanted to hurt her again. He wouldn't. Even if it meant taking some things to his grave.

"Glad to see you enjoying yourself."

Lottie spread her arms. "What's not to enjoy about this gorgeous day?"

"True. We couldn't have asked for better weather."

"Nope." Lottie dug into the beach bag and pulled out plates, napkins, chips and a bag of cut up vegetables.

"Who knew a sandwich could taste this good?" Linc said, taking another bite.

"Agreed. I didn't realize how hungry I was." Lottie brushed crumbs from her lips with the napkin she kept tucked under her plate to keep the breeze from snatching it. "Thank you, Linc. This beats being at the hospital from dawn to dusk any day."

"Tell me about what you do," he requested, finishing off the last of his second sandwich and putting his utensils into the bag they'd brought with them.

Tentative at first, then with enthusiasm, Lottie told him about her work, the fabulous cardiologists she worked with and the innovative techniques for treating heart disease that they were developing. Hearing her passionate answer left no doubt about how much she loved her job.

They finished eating and sat watching the water, both the calmer inlet and the waves just beyond the barrier. Across the inlet, families had blankets spread, kids played in the water and several groups appeared to be playing Frisbee.

"Whatcha think, Lottie? You up for treasure hunting? We can head over toward where they tore down the old research facility and look for items along the shoreline there. I doubt we'll find many shells—we'd have to come early for that—but there's usually some cool driftwood that way."

"There are cloth bags in the boat where Jackie puts things she finds." She'd taken him with her during her treasure hunts a few times. He'd gone, wanting to learn more about the islands, the water and about living on the island. She'd made him a housewarming gift out of some of their first trip's finds. He cherished the piece he'd hung on his bedroom wall.

After grabbing the bags from the boat, Linc and Lottie took off toward the east side of the barrier island. They covered the sandy shoreline and headed into a sparsely wooded area. Most of the trees along the shore were broken, and swayed from numerous storms that had battered the island over the years.

"Gram really has been busy this week and has turned out several new pieces. Well, you know that." Lottie laughed a bit nervously. "It's not as if she hasn't taken great pride in showing them to you when you've come by."

"She's very talented and so are you."

Cheeks turning pink, Lottie ignored his compliment of the piece she'd made. "Not everyone appreciates Gram's style, but I've always loved how she sees the world."

He stretched out his hand to assist her over a fallen tree. "Except when she's trying to interfere in your life?"

She climbed over the log, taking his hand to remain steady as she planted two feet back on the sandy ground. "You mean by sending us off together?"

"That would be one example," he agreed as they made their way through fallen tree debris.

"The latest example. I'm sorry she does that, Linc."

"It could be worse. She could not like me at all."

"She sure didn't like Brian and wasn't subtle about her feelings."

"She never is." He glanced her way, his gaze catching hers. "Regrets about your breakup?"

She shook her head. "Only that it should have happened long ago. We've really been more good friends than anything for way too long. It's what we started as and what we'll hopefully remain once he realizes we weren't right as a couple."

"What if he never realizes?" Had Linc? It had been twelve years and looking at Lottie, being near her again, seeing her smile, hearing her laugh, breathing in her goodness, had him wondering more and more what would happen if he gave in to how she made him feel. What if he gave in to the urge to taste her lips? Would the expected fireworks display instead be a few fizzled sparks? Or would he be so hooked that this time letting her go would be impossible?

If that were the case, then what? He'd heard how she talked about her life in Boston. Just this year he'd finally realized his dream of buying a house on Fripp. Long-distance relationships were hard. Wasn't that why they'd said their goodbyes at summer's end not expecting to someday have their reunion? He'd sure not expected Lottie to call him, begging him to change his mind and to call her. He'd believed when she got back to her reality, the sparkly shine of what they'd shared would dull and she'd realize circumstance had thrown them together and made everything seem so surreal. Recalling the raw emotion in her voice when she'd asked him why he hadn't called her back, he had to wonder if he'd been wrong.

"Hopefully, he will."

Could Linc? When whatever was going to happen between them prior to her returning to Boston, would he be able to just be her friend?

Linc glanced at where she walked next to him. Looking more beautiful than anyone had a right to, she pointed ahead.

"That's where the research lab used to be, isn't it?" Taking care with each step on the shifting sand, she headed toward where the dilapidated University of South Carolina research facility had once stood. "I still can't believe they tore it down. Every time a storm would come through, I'd ask Gram if it survived." She glanced toward him. "She refused to leave during the last big one. I was so worried. Promise me that, even if she's kicking and screaming in protest, you'll drag her off the island if there's another mandatory hurricane evacuation."

Everything Lottie said confirmed that she planned to leave, that staying wasn't an option.

"Why not ask me to promise something easier to keep like that I'll win the lottery or something? But you have to know that regardless of any promise I've made to you that I'd do my best to convince her to leave if I believed she was in danger."

"If only she saw danger the same as I did." She picked up a piece of driftwood. "I like this one."

He moved closer to inspect it. "Good eye."

"Thanks." She turned, smiled at him, and his heart thudded as their eyes met. The ocean sounds around them quieted. As the world stood still, her smile faded and her green gaze deepened. She sucked in a little breath that had Linc's own breath feeling sketchy. His pulse beat as wildly at his throat as the waves pounding against the barrier that protected the inlet.

"Linc?" She pulled her lower lip between her teeth. His gaze dropped. He wanted to kiss her. To feel her lips against his. If he kissed Lottie, he was asking for heartache. He knew that. When he'd invited her out for the day, he'd known. Known they'd be alone, that this moment would come, this decision would have to be made. Never had he dreamed he'd hesitate and yet he couldn't quite close the gap between their lips. Did he really want to do this when he knew how it was going to end? When ultimately, she'd leave him again?

How her eyes had lit up when she'd been talking about her work had him taking a step back.

Don't do this to her. To yourself.

Lottie mustn't have had the same concerns, though. Or if she did, the sunshine had melted them away. She stretched onto her tiptoes and pressed her lips to his.

Fireworks, he thought. No fizzled-out sparks, but massive, light up his world, July Fourth fireworks.

CHAPTER NINE

"THE BOAT'S STILL THERE," Lottie said from where she walked next to Linc, treasures in hand. Had they not found so many excellent pieces of driftwood and even an old piece of a sign washed up from who knew where, Linc imagined they'd have held hands on their way back to the boat.

"Did you think it wouldn't be?" He chuckled. Then again, would he really have been surprised if Jackie had hired someone to take off in the boat, abandoning them on the island? Not that he couldn't have swum across the inlet to Fripp. He'd done it in the past when the tide was lower, but he wouldn't have allowed Lottie as the currents could be tricky and grab hold before one realized.

Physical attraction could be tricky and grab hold before one realized, too.

Lottie's kiss for example. Sweet and that of a siren all in one fantastic moment. He'd kissed her back. How could he not have when he'd tasted the vulnerability on her lips? Linc might have been the one who'd worried he hadn't measured up all those years ago, but Lottie felt emotionally exposed, as well.

If only it was just physical attraction. If that were the case, he'd have made love to her right there in the surf. The physical had been hot and heavy, but it had always been about more than sex with Lottie.

"Those kids keep venturing farther and farther out."

Linc looked toward where Lottie was gazing. Four teens were a good distance from the shore, but didn't seem to be in any distress, just swimming and then floating.

He watched them for a few seconds, then put the larger pieces of driftwood he carried into the boat, along with the bag full of smaller pieces. When he returned, he took Lottie's bag, along with the cooler. "Finish packing. I'm going to load this, then we can head to the house to check on Jackie."

Soon her grandmother would be back on her feet. He wouldn't be needed and neither would Lottie. Then she'd be gone, and his life would return to how it had been for the previous twelve years without her.

Why didn't he believe that?

Nothing was ever going to be the same. Now that he knew how potent her kiss, how bright her smile, how magic her laughter, how could it?

When he returned to where they'd picnicked, Lottie had packed everything except the umbrella base, which she had been unable to pull out of the ground.

"I think it's stuck."

"Let me," he offered. "I drove the base deep to secure it so the wind wouldn't blow it away."

She moved aside, watching as he pulled the umbrella free. "You made that look easy."

"It's all in how you flex the biceps," he teased.

Lowering her lashes, she sent him a tentative smile. "For the record, I like how you flex your biceps, Linc Thomas."

But not enough that she'd stay. He hated that the thought hit him, but it did, and he couldn't shake it. Knowing he owed her an explanation, he searched for words, but her attention had gone beyond him to the water.

"I think those kids are trying to swim to the island. I don't think they should."

Putting the umbrella over his shoulder, Linc glanced toward where the teens had been playing.

She was right. They shouldn't be trying to cross the inlet. The water that had been fairly calm earlier was now choppy. The teen in the back wasn't a very strong swimmer. The others weren't great, but that one was already struggling to keep up.

Hand going to her hip, Lottie frowned with concern. "Have they even thought about the fact that once they make it to the island, they have to cross again to get back to Fripp and the current will be stronger?"

"They'll realize and turn around." Linc hoped so, but wasn't confident enough that he didn't want to keep an eye on them until they'd made it safely to shore.

While Linc pulled up the anchor, Lottie didn't seem able to take her eyes off where the teens were.

"We shouldn't leave until we see what those kids are going to do."

Linc nodded. He hadn't planned to.

"Linc, tell them to turn back." The pitch in Lottie's voice had heightened. "They make me nervous."

"They're not going to hear me over the water." Nor did he expect them to listen. Kids that age felt invincible. He started the boat. "We'll move closer until they make it across."

Once they had, he'd do his best to convince them to accept a ride back to the other side. Hopefully, they'd be smart enough to say yes.

When they'd made it close enough, Linc killed the engine to use the trolley motor to guide the boat closer to the kids so he could pull them into the boat without the wake creating more issues.

"Hey. The water has gotten choppy. You guys want a lift?" he called, but their response was lost on him as the teen farthest away disappeared beneath the water.

One. Two. Three.

Where was he?

"Linc! He's not come up! The one in the back, he's under!" Lottie exclaimed. The teens closest to the boat turned toward where their friend had been.

"Where's Slade?" one asked, looking around at the two friends near him. "He was just here."

"There. There he is," another said as the boy bobbed up only to disappear beneath the murky water again.

"Slade?" they yelled.

Stomach knotting, Linc reached for a life preserver, mentally gauging the distance the current had pulled the boy when he'd popped up, knowing the water could have him anywhere before he could reach him.

Lord, help me with what I'm about to do.

"Call for help, Lottie," he ordered. "Get the others in the boat and call for help."

Realizing what he intended, fear widened Lottie's eyes and she grabbed his arm. "No. You shouldn't go in."

Although logically he knew Lottie was right, that he risked being caught in the current that had the boy, Linc couldn't not go in.

He was that kid's only chance.

No! Lottie wasn't sure if the scream was just in her head or if it had echoed around the islands. Panic seized her throat so tightly she wasn't even sure she was capable of sound.

Linc had kissed her cheek so quickly she questioned if he really had, then he'd dove into the water.

Her instinct was to go after him, to keep the boat so close that she'd be able to get him back aboard. She didn't allow herself to question how she'd do that, just that that's what she wanted to do. But Linc was right. She had to call for help and get the other kids on board first.

Pulling herself together, Lottie shifted her gaze from where Linc's strong breaststrokes cut through the choppy water to the freaked-out teens now clinging to the side of the boat. She had to get them out of the water before there was possibly more than one crisis. Once she had them safe, she'd use the trolley and stayed as close to where Linc swam as she could. He'd be okay. He'd get to the teen and they'd both be just fine.

"There's a ladder I can lower on the other side," she called down to the teens. "It'll make getting in easier. Can you make it there?"

Staying close to the boat and each other, the trio swam to where Lottie had lowered the ladder into the water and, while making the emergency call, was waiting to help them up.

A male teen climbed into the boat, struggling enough that Lottie was glad she'd gotten them into the boat prior to chasing after Linc. Finally, he was on board.

"You next Jill," he called to the sole female of the group, leaning forward to reach for the girl attempting to climb up the ladder.

She grabbed hold, but her arms wobbled.

"I can't do it, Jeff." Tears mingled with the water droplets running down her face. "I'm scared and can't pull myself out of the water."

"Help her, Trey," the teen told the boy still in the water. "Push her onto the ladder."

Lottie dropped her phone, midcall, onto the boat deck to help reach for the girl.

With Trey's assistance from in the water, Jill scrambled up the ladder enough that Lottie and Jeff were able to grab hold of her and pull her onto the deck by falling back and bringing her with them.

Next, Lottie and Jeff helped get the last teen from the water.

Finally, all three were in the boat.

"Here." Lottie tossed the shivering girl the blanket she and Linc had used for their picnic, then gestured to the boys. "There're towels in that bin."

They said something, but Lottie didn't know what. Heart pounding, lungs screaming, head spinning, she searched the water. "Where's Linc? Where is he?"

There was no sign of him or the missing boy, just the life preserver being carried out toward the sea.

Linc's lungs burned. His muscles ached. At some point during his swim, he'd kicked off his waterlogged shoes, knowing they were slowing him down, but not quite sure how he'd gotten them off as he'd never stopped pushing forward.

He'd caught sight of the kid, not fifteen feet in front of him, and then miraculously, he reached him, only to watch the kid be snatched under and back out of sight.

Feeling the water's greedy fingers tugging at him, Linc gave in, diving as forcefully as he could toward the kid, grabbing hold of his lifeless arm to pull him close, then kicking as hard as he could to free them from the water's hold. That the boy was no longer conscious was a mixed blessing as it was going to take everything Linc had to get them to the surface, if he was even able to. Had the boy been conscious and panicked, attempting to get them free would have been a hundred times worse.

Diving in had been foolish, but he'd known he preferred death over not attempting to rescue the kid. He couldn't do nothing and always wonder what if he'd tried.

But now, as lifesaving air seemed so far away, he wondered if this was the end. With that thought came all the life regrets, all the things he wished he'd said, done. Every thought evolved around Lottie. She filled his mind, his heart.

He loved her, always had, always would. He should have told her. He should have kissed her every chance he'd had and not worried about what the future held. He should have embraced every precious moment during her time in South Carolina. He should have—his mind grew fuzzy. He kicked his legs harder, but they were cold, heavy and didn't seem to be propelling him and the boy forward any longer.

"Linc!" Lottie's cry sliced through the water. "Linc!"

Was he dreaming? Her voice a siren's song playing in his mind, beckoning him to find her. She sounded so close. Keeping his grip on the boy and his focus on where Lottie called him, he broke the surface, gulped air, hacked, coughed, gulped more air as he searched for where her voice came from.

"Linc!" And then, there she was, his beautiful rescuer guiding the boat near and tossing a roped life preserver to him.

Arms like gelatin, fingers numb with cold and gripping the kid so tightly, he struggled to get the life preserver around the boy, but finally managed. Getting him into the boat was going to be a feat, but time was of the essence as the teen still lay lax against him.

Kicking them to the edge of the boat, still gasping to

recatch his breath, Linc was able to lift the kid enough to where his friends pulled him into the boat. Lottie leaned forward and extended her hand, obviously thinking she was going to help him. Linc shook his head.

"Start CPR." Talking hurt. He coughed. "Not breathing." Another cough. "CPR."

She glanced into the boat, presumably at the kid, then back at him. "But—"

"CPR now, Lottie." He knew she wanted him out of the water. He also knew that every second the kid wasn't breathing reduced the odds of her getting him back. Linc would be okay, Lottie might not know that, but Linc did. She needed to save the kid. "The others can get me up."

They'd have to. He didn't think he could climb into the boat unassisted if he had to.

Torn, Lottie knew Linc was right. She had to get CPR started STAT. Trey and Jeff were more capable of pulling Linc into the boat than she was, anyway. But leaving him, taking her eyes off him again when she'd felt such devastation at not being able to find him on the water's surface, felt near impossible.

Pulling the life preserver off the limp kid, Lottie scooted it toward Jeff even as she started checking for Slade's pulse. "Get this to Linc. Use it to pull him onto the boat like we just did for your friend. Now."

Her fingers pressed against Slade's cold skin. No pulse. No surprise. She gave the kid a breath, then another prior to starting compressions. Her arms felt disconnected from the rest of her as her insides trembled. Linc was okay, she assured herself. She had to revive the boy Linc had gone to such great heroic lengths to try to save.

"Come on," she urged, counting the reps in her head between compressions and breaths, as she racked her brain to recall what the exact protocol for resuscitating a drowning victim currently was. She'd never done this! Not on a kid whose lungs had filled with water. "Please. Take a breath."

Lottie focused on her patient rather than on the teens' efforts to get Linc into the boat, but from her periphery she was well aware they still hadn't pulled him into the boat.

Over and over, she compressed the boy's chest, tears streaming down her face, knowing she had to keep going rather than look toward the others to see what was taking so long. Had Linc gone back under? Was that why she hadn't heard the reassuring thud of him landing on the boat's deck?

"Lord, please. Please. Please. Please," she whispered, continuing her deep compressions to the boy's chest.

Sputter. Water spewed from the boy's mouth. Cough.

"He's alive! Slade's alive!" Jill exclaimed, distracting the other teens from their rescue efforts of pulling Linc into the boat. Fortunately, he was finally in enough that he tumbled onto the deck and Lottie heard that reassuring thud of a landing.

Thank you, God.

Lottie fought the urge to abandon her post to rush to Linc, but knew Slade wasn't out of the woods so kept up her efforts on him, pressing deeply on his chest.

He had a pulse. A weak one, but it was there.

"Do not ever do that again."

From where Linc sat in the back of the ambulance, a blanket wrapped around him to fight off his chill despite the summer heat, he eyed where Lottie clenched his hand so tightly that he might have bruises.

"It worked out."

"But it might not have." She squeezed his hand even

tighter, then lifted it to press his fingers against her chest. Her warmth seeped into him, abating some of the chill that he'd begun to think would never subside. "Do you have any idea how scared I was that I'd lost you when I couldn't spot you anywhere?"

"I'm sorry I scared you, Lottie." He'd been scared himself. Terrified. "I'm fine." Part of him still couldn't believe he'd made it out of the water. When he closed his eyes, he could still feel the darkness pulling him under, making his lungs burn for air. He inhaled sharply, appreciating the reassuring air filling his lungs. "I'm just waiting for these guys to tell me I can leave so we can go home."

"Dude, she's right," said the paramedic who had given him a once-over as he came back over to the truck from where he'd been speaking with a sheriff's deputy. "You shouldn't have dived in."

Lottie's look said, *see!*

"But it would be a much different story here today if you hadn't," the emergency worker continued, his voice full of gratitude.

"The kid's going to be okay?"

"He'd regained consciousness by the time my buddies got him loaded into their ambulance. He didn't remember you or how he got out of the water, but he asked about his friends, wanting to know if they were okay."

"That's a good sign." Lottie breathed hard, still clutching Linc's hand as if she might never let go. "Hopefully, he won't have any brain damage from having been without oxygen."

"They didn't think so. He could answer their questions and his neuro check seemed okay."

"Good." Linc let the medic go through another unnecessary neuro check on him. "I'm fine, too, just ready to go home."

"Let me have you sign some papers and then we'll release you." The man slapped Linc on the shoulder. "Thanks for what you did out there, man. You're a hero."

"Gram was all hyped up over what happened this afternoon, but she is finally asleep," Lottie said when she came back into the living room and saw Linc was awake and sitting up on the sofa.

"Unlike me who slept most of the evening." Linc shook his head. "Crazy. I never nap."

Moving the blanket she'd put over him, she sat down next to him, scooting as close as she could without climbing into his lap. "You never almost drown, either."

Linc's arm went around her and she felt his face nuzzling into her hair. "Thank you for staying by my side while the paramedic checked me, Lottie."

She leaned back enough to look at him. "Are you kidding? You thought I was going to leave? Linc, if you ever scare me like that again, I—"

He placed his fingers over her lips. "It's okay. Everything is okay. I'm fine. Slade is being kept overnight for observation but is expected to be released in the morning. Everything, everyone, is fine."

"I'm not fine, Linc. Not in the slightest." Lottie wiggled to where she could palm his cheeks and make him look directly at her. "Please do not ever, ever, scare me that way again."

Smiling, Linc stared into her eyes. "Yes, ma'am. You've made your point."

"Why are you smiling? I'm serious, Linc. This isn't funny. You really, really scared me."

He reached up and took her hand into his, lacing their fingers. "Why wouldn't I be smiling? I'm alive, Lottie, and the most beautiful woman I've ever known is beside me. I'm allowed to smile." When she started to say something, he gave her hand a reassuring squeeze and continued, "What I did was foolish. I know that. But I can't say I'm sorry." His hand trembled where it held hers. "I just can't."

Realizing what he meant, she sighed. "I understand. I was just so scared and…have I told you lately how wonderful you are?"

Lifting her fingers to his lips, he pressed a kiss there, sending butterflies dancing in her stomach. "Tell me."

She stared into his eyes, her own a bit glassy. "You're wonderful."

With that, she pressed her lips to his in a soft kiss. "Wonderful," she repeated, dropping more kisses over his lips, his face. She'd thought she'd lost him and that was unacceptable. No matter what happened between them, no matter what the future held, she needed to know Linc was somewhere in the world, making it a better place.

"You doing that is wonderful."

She kissed him again. This time, longer, more fully as she scooted closer and he kissed her back. They kissed until Lottie was as air hungry as if she'd been the one under water, until her heart pounded so hard she thought it might burst in her chest.

Soon kisses weren't enough. She needed more, to feel the life within him, within her. By the way Linc tugged at her shirt hem, she guessed he needed more, too.

Her shirt disappeared, as did his. Kisses turned to touches turned to more kisses.

"You saved me out there today," he whispered against her skin. "It was your voice I heard calling to me like that of Lorelei, only luring me back to the surface and to you rather than to my doom."

Lottie didn't want to think about the water. Not anymore.

Not ever again. She just wanted to feel all the magic Linc stirred inside her, to embrace that and him.

That's just what she did.

Sunbeams broke through the darkness of Lottie's room, waking her. The events of the day before rushed through her mind. Linc! She opened her eyes, took in that she was in her bed. So was Linc. Safe. Alive. Warm against her bare body.

"You're here," she whispered, not quite believing how they'd spent much of the night.

Linc's eyes opened. Staring sleepily at her, concern flooded his blue gaze. "Do you want me to leave?"

She shook her head. "No." Her mind was full of questions, but that wasn't one of them. She wanted him right where he was. Next to her. "This certainly complicates things, though."

The worst part was, she wasn't sure she cared how complicated their having had sex made things. All she'd cared about was that Linc was alive. As if needing to reassure herself, she placed her palm against him, feeling the strong beat of his heart, watching the rise and fall of his chest.

"This only complicates things as much as we let it." He lifted her hand to his lips and pressed a kiss to her fingertips. "We don't have to rush things, Lottie."

She laughed. "Too late. We did that last night."

He scooted up onto his elbow. "Maybe, but maybe it's okay if we don't overthink this. I know you're going back to Boston in a couple of weeks. That what happened yesterday upset you and maybe that's why last night happened. I have no regrets and I don't want you to, either."

"I don't regret last night." How could she when his making love to her had surpassed her most erotic fantasy? Their first time had been hot and heavy, but when they'd gone to her room, every touch had been as if his sole purpose for living was to give her pleasure. He had. Oh, so much pleasure.

Remembering had her stirring in places that should be too sore to stir.

"Why don't we just enjoy what's left of our summer reunion?" he suggested. "We'll figure things out when our time is up."

"Sounds simple enough." But Lottie knew better. She knew how difficult leaving was going to be. She'd done it before and spent twelve years missing him. How much more difficult would leaving be this time knowing the deep ache that awaited her at his absence? An ache she suspected would far surpass what her teenaged heart had felt.

"I can see the indecision on your face, hear it in your words." He cupped her face, looked straight into her eyes. "Lottie, if you'd rather me leave and us pretend that last night never happened, then I'll leave. But don't ask me to pretend that *we* didn't happen because I won't. We happened. We happened twelve years ago, and we happened again this summer."

"I don't want you to leave, and I don't want to pretend we didn't happen. I couldn't if I tried." She wasn't that skilled an actress.

"And last night?"

"Last night happened." She took a deep breath. "I wanted last night to happen."

Linc's grin might be the most beautiful thing she'd ever seen. "Then it's okay if I kiss you good morning?"

Swallowing, she nodded. "More than okay."

She wanted his good morning kiss. Now and forever. She had now and was going to embrace it with welcoming arms, embrace Linc with open arms.

Forever would have to take care of itself.

CHAPTER TEN

"I DON'T WANT to go into the water."

From where he trod calm water just off Pritchard's, Linc eyed where Lottie sat on the side of the boat and knew exactly how she felt. Going in that first time after their rescue hadn't been easy. He'd done so the very day he'd awakened in Lottie's bed. He'd had to. He'd had to wash away the remnants of fear that hit when he'd gone home, stepped out on to his back deck and felt dread at the gentle waves rolling in rather than the healthy respect he'd always afforded the sea. It hadn't been easy, but he'd made himself go in. Just as claustrophobia and panic were hitting, making him think he was going to get sucked under, he hadn't. He'd swam long enough to erase the hesitation that was similar to what was gripping Lottie now. And he'd purposely swam every day since. On several occasions, Lottie had watched from the shore, refusing to get into the water during their nightly watch the sunset "date."

He splashed water her way, the droplets soaking into the red material of her bikini. "I should have made you go in last week."

She shook her head. "There's nowhere that says I have to go in ever again."

"You love the water."

She shrugged. "Things change."

He imagined that's exactly what would happen when she left Fripp, but for now, she was there and he was determined to replace her fear with respect and her bad memories with good ones. In the process, he'd do the same for himself. He'd certainly been making good memories the past week. With Lottie.

"I won't let anything happen to you. Come in and swim with me."

Eyeing him, she sighed. "You're going to make me do this even though I don't want to, aren't you?"

"It's for your own good."

"Fine, but I don't like you very much right now." Sighing again, she pinched her nose and slid off into the water. Linc was by her side within seconds, but let her surface on her own, wanting her to regain her confidence in the water. She flung her hair back, then blinked the water away from her eyes. "Happy now?"

Wrapping his arms around her waist, he kept them afloat with little kicks of his legs. "I've not quit being happy since this beautiful cardiologist rescued me."

His comment had her expression softening. She curved her arms around his neck and her legs linked at his waist. "Tell me more."

"Once upon a time there was this woman," he began. "She came to the island to visit with her sick grandmother. While there, she ran into—"

"The big, bad wolf?" Lottie's eyes twinkled, and he could feel her body relaxing against his.

Laughing, he shook his head. "Although she's wearing a really hot red bathing suit, her name isn't Red. Now, quit interrupting."

"I think a fish just nibbled at my toes, but okay, I won't interrupt."

"She ran into this really awesome physical therapist who helped her grandmother." Linc paused. "Did a fish really just bite your toes?"

She fluttered her lashes. "Maybe." Her legs squeezed his waist. "I definitely felt something."

"Let me check your toes."

Still clinging to his neck, Lottie straightened from where her legs had been wrapped around him and raised her foot out of the water. "See?"

"Looks okay to me."

"How can you tell from that far away?"

"I'm pretty close," he pointed out, not seeing anything wrong with her toes.

With a sudden swivel of her body, Lottie splashed him. Hard. Then laughing, she took off swimming as hard as she could toward the beach.

"I'm going to get you for that," he warned, chasing after her. He could have caught her within seconds but let her get close enough to the shore that they could stand prior to grabbing her leg and pulling her to him. "Hello, there."

Laughing, she splashed him again. "That took longer than I thought it would."

"You wanted me to catch you?"

Wrapping her arms back around his neck, she smiled at him. "Absolutely. Why wouldn't I?"

"Because of this." He dunked them both under the water that was thankfully fairly clear and kissed her, letting his air be hers and vice versa.

They stayed under until Linc's lungs cried for him to surface, but Lottie held on just a little longer, her tongue slipping into his mouth.

When they surfaced, he grabbed her hand. "Come on. We're going back to the boat."

"What? Why?" But her eyes danced with mischief. She knew exactly why.

"We're going to my place for more water therapy." Still, holding her hand and loving the sound of her laughter, he kicked off the sandy bottom and, taking her with him, swam toward the boat. "This time in my shower."

"Swim faster, Linc. Swim faster."

"I can't believe you're leaving."

Lottie zipped her suitcase closed and eyed where her grandmother sat on her bed, watching her. "You knew I was leaving, Gram. I was only here until you were back on your feet, which you are. Dr. Collins was so impressed at your last appointment."

"Who knew being impressive was a bad thing? I could fake another break if it meant you could stay longer." Gram sighed. "You've said goodbye to Linc?"

In some ways, it felt as if they'd been saying goodbye every moment since Dr. Collins had released Gram to start walking on her boot and Lottie had set a date to return to Boston. With the countdown on, they'd squeezed out every moment, Linc even opting to take a few vacation days to extend their time together.

Lottie bit into her lower lip. "Not yet. We'll say our goodbyes when he drives me to the airport."

"You're a fool to leave him."

"I know." She was. Yet, she couldn't stay. Sighing, she plopped onto the bed next to her grandmother. "I have to go back to Boston, Gram. I have a contract, a life. And I like my life there, but the truth is, I like my life here, too. I wish I could stuff you both into my suitcase and take you with me."

"I'd never be happy away from the island, but I am going

to miss you." Gram let out a long breath. "I understand that you have to do what you have to do. Just be sure you say the things you need to say to the person you need to say them to, too."

When Linc arrived, Lottie hugged her grandmother a thousand times and shed close to that many tears. More. "I love you, Gram. Keep doing your therapy and I'll be back to visit at Christmas, sooner if I can."

Christmas, she thought as Linc crossed the bridge leading onto Sea Island Parkway. Christmas felt an eternity away. Maybe she'd be able to pull a few long weekends prior to then. She glanced over at Linc. Would he want to see her when she came back? The past few weeks had been so amazing, but then, they'd done amazing before.

Her stomach clenched. They'd danced all around.

Linc was mostly silent as they headed toward the airport. How could he appear so calm when she felt anything but?

"This isn't easy," she admitted, swiping at her leaky eyes again.

"Goodbyes are never easy."

Lottie's breath caught. "Is that what this is? Are we saying goodbye again, Linc?"

If not for the way he white-knuckled the steering wheel, Lottie might have thought he hadn't heard her. That he didn't immediately answer spoke volumes. Hurt and anger erupted within her. She was doing what she had to do. Did she matter so little that he'd rather say goodbye than to make a long-distance relationship work?

"Is my question such a difficult one to answer?"

He stared straight ahead. "Is goodbye what you want this to be?"

"You know it isn't."

"What do you suggest? That we see each other when you

can sneak away to South Carolina for us to pick back up as if you'd never left?"

"I know it's not ideal, but would that be so bad?"

He sighed. "I guess we'll find out. I'm not willing to spend the next twelve years wishing we'd tried."

Relief filled her. Linc wasn't saying goodbye forever.

"I'll schedule time off to come back. A long weekend in September, maybe, but definitely longer in October." Christmas was definitely too long. "Do you think you could come to Boston at Thanksgiving? I can introduce you to my friends, especially Camilla. I've told her all about you."

His jaw flexed. "A long weekend in a couple of months, a few days in October, and I'll request time off to come to you in November."

"I'll be on call at Christmas but plan to take off the week after. Maybe we can work it to where we'll see each other most months."

He let out a long breath. "Why do I feel as if we're back to where we were twelve years ago? Saying goodbye on a relationship high, but destined to have time and distance pull us apart?"

Lottie's chest hurt. "That's not going to happen. Not for me." She swallowed the lump in her throat. "Is that what you expect to happen on your end?"

"I don't think I'm going to enjoy you being a literal thousand miles away, if that's what you're asking."

"What I'm asking is if you believe in our relationship? Because if you do and I do, then time and distance shouldn't be able to pull us apart."

He hesitated, then asked, "Do you see yourself ever moving to Fripp?"

Lottie thought about his question. "In theory it sounds

great, but I have a contract with the hospital in Boston. I enjoy my job and being a part of the research team that helps develop new lifesaving technologies."

He took a deep breath that had her feeling defensive.

"What about you? Do you see yourself ever moving to Boston?"

To his credit he didn't immediately answer but seemed to soul search his answer. "No, Lottie, I don't."

"I— Okay." She rubbed the sudden throbbing at her temple. "It's okay. We don't have to figure everything out right now. We will make this work." Somehow.

Lottie was still telling herself that when Linc pulled the car up to the airport departure's curb, put the car gear into park then got out to get her suitcase.

"Call me when you land in Boston."

"As soon as we taxi in. I love you, Linc."

"Lottie, you tell me that now? When you're leaving me?"

"I don't know what to say to make this better, Linc. My heart is breaking to leave you and yet I have to go."

He studied her a moment, then nodded. "I know you do. It's what was always going to happen."

He sounded so resigned to their fate that Lottie couldn't stand not touching him a moment longer so she threw her arms around him, kissing him while she still could.

When he pulled back, he cupped her face, stared into her eyes for a long moment, then kissed her with such intensity that Lottie had to quell the urge to jump back into his car and forget about Boston and everything else.

As much as she told herself that he wasn't kissing her goodbye, old doubts plagued that that's exactly what he was doing. That once she was back in Boston, he'd shut her out yet again, and she was destined for the worst heartbreak of her life.

* * *

"You're not coming to South Carolina?" Hoping he'd mis-heard, Linc clicked up his phone's volume to be sure what-ever Lottie said came across loud and clear above the ocean's roar.

When her call had come through, he'd stepped outdoors and onto his back deck. Moonlight reflected off the water, highlighting the whitecaps crashing onto the shoreline. From the point they'd realized a September trip home wasn't going to happen, they'd been counting down the days until this weekend.

"It's not that I don't want to, but we've been so slammed. The hospital administrator and my coworkers were so good to me during Gram's recovery that I can't just leave them hanging."

"But you're okay with leaving me hanging?" His ques-tion was as much for himself as to her. They talked on the phone most days, but those calls weren't as long or frequent as they'd been when she first left. He'd told himself he un-derstood when she canceled in September, but now she was doing so again. He'd gotten a leave authorized in Novem-ber, but would she end up canceling on him? Citing that she wouldn't be able to get off work anyway?

"It's not like that." Her frustration came over the phone line. "You know it's not. I miss you."

"Just not enough to make coming back a priority?" Grip-ping the phone, he ran his other fingers through his hair. More and more he felt the distance between them. Had she gone back to Boston and realized he'd been nothing more than a summer fling? A reunion with her past?

"Airplanes fly in both directions."

He grimaced. She was right. He'd checked flights doz-ens of times, but something always held him back from booking one. He'd been at the hospital for less than a year, but he had some time accumulated and could shuffle his schedule. For that matter, he could go for a few days most weeks. So why hadn't he? Instead, he'd thrown himself into the remodel, working late into the night. It's what he'd been doing when his phone had rung so she could cancel yet again. He'd been excited to see her, to show her his progress on the house, which he'd finished much sooner than he'd originally planned. Why? As an added lure for her to come back to South Carolina? If he wasn't enough, did he really think finishing the remodel of the house she loved would make a difference?

"Linc? Are you still there?"

"I'm here."

She hesitated, then asked, "Just not answering me?"

"I don't know what to say, Lottie."

"The right thing would be to say that you understand and that if not before, you'll see me when you come here in November."

In her big city glitzy world where he wouldn't fit in and she'd see the stark differences between them. Sure, he'd gotten his degree, but working at the hospital in Beaufort wasn't the same as cavorting with her Harvard friends.

"I really don't like the cold."

She hesitated, then asked, "Are you saying you're not coming in November?"

Was that what he was saying? Linc leaned against the railing, stared out at the whitecaps breaking against the shore, breathed in the salty ocean air. He missed her, but ever since she'd left, every doubt he'd ever had had surfaced. He'd even relived his conversation with her mother during several dreams that had left him waking in a sweat. Was this really how he wanted to live his life?

"I don't know."

More silence, then, anger spiking in her tone, she said, "Are you so upset with me that you want to fight, Linc? Is that what you're doing? I'm sorry I had to cancel last month. I'm sorry I have to cancel this month. I was unexpectedly off work for six weeks this summer—six weeks!—and in your world, so it's a little difficult for me to get away from mine again so soon."

His world. Her world. Her mother had been right to point out that difference all those years ago. Hadn't he acknowledged that he was an escape for Lottie? Was that the real problem? That he worried outside of their fairy-tale beach paradise that she wouldn't want him? That she'd realize he wasn't so great when thrown into the world she thrived in? He was just existing day by day, cherishing each call, but deep down, waiting for the ax to drop.

"I don't want to fight."

"That's it? That's all you have to say?" Her tone was accusatory. "Work with me here, Linc. At least a little."

He closed his eyes, letting the roar of the ocean sound around him. The wind had picked up, stinging his skin and whipping at his clothes, hair and the phone he pressed to his ear. For so long he'd dreamed of this, living on Fripp. Here he was with his bare feet planted on the deck of that dream and rather than experience the joy he'd once felt, he lived phone call to phone call. What kind of life was that?

He'd let her go all those years ago. It had been the right thing to do. He hadn't needed her mother to tell him that. If it hadn't been the right thing, he'd have gone after her, right?

Or maybe not, because deep down he'd wondered if Vivien had been right about her other claim, too.

My daughter may think she's in love with you because of your little island romance, but that kind of love never holds

*up when put to the test in the real world. You're both young
and share an attraction, but that will fade, and when it does,
Lottie will move on to someone more suited for her. Don't
ruin her life in the meantime.*

Linc's stomach twisted into knots and, curling his fingers, he tapped his fist against a deck post. Not a punch, but
hard enough it stung. "I can't do this anymore."

"Do what?" Her pitch had gone up several octaves.

"Be in a long-distance relationship. I just can't. Phone
calls and I-miss-yous just aren't enough. I thought I could do
this, that they'd be enough, but they're just not. I'm sorry."

Lottie unlocked her apartment door and flicked on the light.

"Oh! Sorry," she said, apologizing to the couple who
jumped apart from where they'd been making out on the
sofa. "I wasn't thinking, or I'd have made more noise, jig-
gled my keys or something."

Not that her roommate and ex-boyfriend were likely to
have heard her no matter if she'd stamped her feet and beat
on the door. Who knew that when she'd removed herself
from the picture that Camilla would acknowledge the attraction she'd apparently felt for years, but had kept tamped
down out of love of their friendship? How had Lottie missed
what was so obvious? Once Camilla had been convinced
Lottie truly wasn't getting back together with Brian, she'd
asked permission to go for it. Lottie had given her blessing.
Regardless of anything between her and Linc, she and Brian
weren't right for each other. She loved him, but wasn't in
love with him, nor him with her.

Not once had he ever looked at her the way he did at
the woman straightening her clothes while simultaneously
slapping his hands away. Yeah, Brian had never been like
that with her.

"Sorry," Camilla said, a blush staining her tan cheeks. "We were headed out to eat, but then got distracted and… do you want to go with us? We were thinking of hitting that Irish pub over by the Charles that everyone at the hospital has been raving about."

Lottie shook her head. "I'm going to shower and numb my brain with mindless television while vegging out on the sofa."

Her roommate winced. "You still haven't heard from him?"

Fighting the emotions that clawed their way up her throat anytime she thought of Linc, which was often, Lottie shook her head.

"Have you tried calling him?"

She shook her head again. How many times had she started to press his number, but been unable to complete the call? Enough that just thinking about it had hands tightening around her throat. Because what if she called and he didn't answer?

What if she called and his number had been disconnected as he'd done in the past?

She wasn't calling. Much better to not know than to hear that monotonous message about reaching a number that had been disconnected or was no longer in service. Phone calls and I-miss-yous weren't enough. He was right about that. But not having those phone calls and I-miss-yous was tearing her apart.

Why hadn't he called her? How could he have just thrown them away? Being apart wasn't easy, but at least she'd been trying.

Had she really?

Or had she acquiesced too easily when Greg Abbott had asked her if she could cancel her trip to help cover staffing issues? She could have said no and she hadn't. Why not? She'd accused him of purposely wanting to fight, but had she been the one instigating issues?

Camilla hugged her and Brian did, too. "You're sure you don't want to go? Or if you wanted, we could call for take-out and numb our brains along with you."

"Please don't." She shooed them toward the door. "Go. Have fun."

It took a few minutes to convince them that she truly was fine and that in her case, misery did not love company, but eventually they left. Lottie showered, put on her favorite pajamas and curled up on the sofa with a bowl of cereal and the remote control. She clicked on the television.

A dog food commercial played on the television and a big golden dog loped across the screen. Longing tore at Lottie.

"You know it's bad when I even miss Maritime," she mumbled as tears began rolling down her cheeks. She loved her life in Boston, but since coming back, nothing felt the same. Nothing. Not her love for her job. Not her joy in spending time with her friends. Nothing.

She wasn't the same.

She'd left her heart in South Carolina, so how could she expect to love anywhere else?

Which meant what exactly? She had another eight months on her contract with the hospital. She couldn't just up and leave. She didn't even want to.

She'd been the one to call Linc last time, the one to pour her heart out only to be ignored. She'd poured her heart out again, and he'd essentially said what she could give him wasn't enough. Did he expect her to give up her life without him making any concessions so their relationship could work? She wanted a partnership, not someone who couldn't meet her in the middle.

Which meant what? That she no longer wanted Linc? That wasn't right, either. She wanted Linc. She wanted her phone to ring and it to be him telling her how sorry he was that he hadn't called and that he'd need her to pick him up from Logan airport Thanksgiving week.

But she was angry that Linc wasn't putting as much effort into making things work as she'd been.

The commercial ended and the romantic comedy playing came back on. Lottie clicked it off, but the next channel was even worse with an on-screen couple declaring their everlasting love to each other, then embracing.

She clicked the station again and a Celtics came on. Good. Nothing romantic about a basketball game.

Was that what she wanted? Romance?

"I want what Mom and Dad had," she said to the empty room. "They loved each other beyond everything else. I want a love like that."

But her parents had met in college, fell in love and married the summer after they'd graduated. They'd lived in the right neighborhood, socialized with the right people, enjoyed the same things, and wanted a similar life for her. Only, when her mother was planning Lottie's life, she'd missed the key ingredient to her happiness. Vivien had loved Lottie's dad and he'd loved her. Without that, none of the other things mattered. They were just meaningless fluff.

Bored with the ball game, she clicked the channel again and groaned. Seriously? Then again, maybe there were advantages to marrying at first sight.

She glanced at her phone. "Ring." Nothing. "Just ring, okay? Is that too much to ask?"

She picked up a throw pillow, clutched it to her, then buried her face in it to muffle a scream. "Argh!"

Her doorbell rang, and she about jumped out of her skin.

"Lottie?" a voice that might be a hallucination called. "Are you okay?"

Linc had been standing outside Lottie's apartment for longer than he cared to admit. You'd think he'd have had plenty of time to figure out what he wanted to say over the past few days and even during his flight. Apparently not, because he'd gotten there and gotten cold feet that had nothing to do with the twenty degree temperature drop from when he'd left South Carolina.

Lottie's roommate must have thought he had something great to say because when she'd spotted him on the sidewalk as she'd been coming out of the apartment building, she'd done a double take, recognizing him from Lottie's photos, introduced herself and the guy with her, then buzzed him up to their apartment.

"The rest is up to you," she'd said. "If you can't convince her to open the door, you've no one to blame but yourself."

He hadn't been able to argue that, but he'd meant what he'd said to Lottie. Phone calls and I-miss-yous weren't enough. Not nearly so.

He might not be enough either, but he was here to find out, to try his best to be the man she needed him to be.

But standing outside her door, he wondered if he should have given her a heads-up. What if she turned him away? What if he'd blown it with her again because he'd been too cowardly to trust in her feelings for him? To trust in *them*?

Then she'd screamed.

"Let me in, Lottie." He knocked on the door, again. This time louder, more insistent. "It's Linc."

The door swung open. Eyeing him, she crossed her arms

over her cartoon-character-covered pajama top. Blocking the doorway, she tapped her foot. "You think I didn't recognize your voice? I mean, you haven't called, but it's only been three days since you told me you didn't want to do this anymore."

Yep, she was mad.

"Can I come inside?"

She moved aside, allowing him to come into her apartment. He looked around at the modern white-and-gray style. The only thing that looked familiar was the twisted wire and driftwood lamp next to her sofa. He focused on Jackie's art, drawing strength from the bit of South Carolina in the room.

"We need to talk."

"Really?" She arched her brow. "Is that why you haven't called for the past three days?"

Less than thirty seconds and she'd already thrown that at him twice. Not good, but then, had he expected otherwise? Did he even deserve otherwise?

"If I'd called, I'd have said things I didn't want to say," he began, hoping he could make her understand. Walking over to the lamp, he ran his finger over the driftwood. "Some things need to be said in person."

"What things?" She crossed her arms again, probably to protect her heart from the likes of him. Taking in her colorful cartoon pajamas, clipped-up blond hair, fresh face, and bare feet with their orange and black polish, Linc's heart swelled.

"Things like I miss you and phone calls that aren't enough."

She snorted. "I think you said that loud and clear the other night."

"Then you agree?"

"What do you want me to say, Linc? If I say yes, then it

means I'm acknowledging that we aren't working and I'm not willing to do that. If you are, then why are you here?"

"It's not us that's not working, Lottie," he pointed out. "We'd be working just fine if we were together to be working."

"I can't leave Boston, Linc."

"I'm not asking you to."

Lower lip trembling, she looked at him in disbelief and with a light in her eyes that she might start throwing things his way. "You came all this way to end things with me in person? That's what you couldn't tell me over the phone? Seriously? Just leave now."

"I came all this way because I'm not willing to risk things ending," he said.

She blinked. "I don't understand."

"You told me that the airlines flew both ways. That hit close to home. Closer than I've ever revealed to you. I should have already been here, Lottie, but I was afraid to."

"Afraid to? Now I'm really lost. You're the bravest person I've ever known."

He shook his head. "I'm not brave, Lottie. Not when it comes to you." He took her hands in his, marveling at their warmth. "I should have come after you last time. There were reasons I didn't, but those reasons don't apply anymore. Not really."

"What reasons?"

How much should he tell her? Everything. She needed to know the truth. Yet, he didn't want to blame someone else for his own shortcomings. He'd let Lottie's mom influence how he'd handled things. Because he'd believed her when she'd told him that he'd ruin Lottie's life for nothing more than a summer romance that hadn't fizzled itself out yet, and thinking himself altruistic, he'd cut off all ties. In reality, Vivien's words had played into his own deeply held belief that he wasn't good enough for her and that once she left Fripp, she'd realize that their summer had been nothing more than a fantasy. He'd spent the past twelve years trying to make himself into someone good enough.

When push had come to shove, he'd still not felt good enough.

"Your mother loved you with all her heart, Lottie. She knew how much being a cardiologist meant to you and she recognized that I was a threat to that dream."

Pulling her hands free, Lottie studied him. "You were never a threat to me."

"Had I let you come back to South Carolina, I'd have destroyed your dream and eventually your feelings for me."

Clasping her fingers together, she gasped. "That's not true."

"You'd have thrown away your scholarship. As infatuated as I was, I at least recognized that I couldn't let you do that."

Lottie's color heightened, and she shook her head in denial of what he was saying. "If I opted to come back to South Carolina, that was my decision to make. Not hers."

"Maybe not, but it was mine to make sure that I wasn't the reason you threw everything away. I told myself that if how you felt about me was real, then it would still be real when you finished university."

Her eyes filled with accusation. "You didn't answer my call, Linc. I poured my heart out to you and you changed your phone number. How could you do that? Why would you do that?"

"That's where the true cowardice comes in." And this was where the truth came out. "Had I not changed my number, I'd have given in to calling you back, Lottie. I got rid of my phone and all the numbers in it so that I couldn't do that. I couldn't be the reason you didn't achieve your dreams."

She drew in a ragged breath. "You hurt me so badly."

"I know." Oh, how he knew and how he wished he could take that pain away. "There's more."

"More?"

"Your mom convincing me to let you go was easy, because deep down I never believed I deserved your love. I never believed I was good enough for someone like you to love someone like me."

Lottie looked at him in confusion. "Someone like you? You're the best man I've ever known. How could you not be good enough? Any woman would be lucky to have you."

He shrugged. "I've only ever wanted one, and she was way out of my league."

"Why do you keep saying that? Did I ever give you the impression I thought you were beneath me?"

He shook his head.

"It was Mama, wasn't it? You don't have to answer. I know it was." Lottie took a deep breath. "It took me a long time to understand why she and Gram didn't get along, but it's because of that. Mama's love of high society and living a life others envied. She had this vision of how my life was supposed to be and it blinded her to the truth, even when Gram pointed it out to her, which I'm sure she did and that that was the source of their bickering."

"I don't want to say anything derogatory about your mother, Lottie. She loved you, and I've no doubt there wasn't anything she wouldn't have done for you if she believed it was in your best interest."

"That doesn't excuse her interfering in my life to the extend she did. For so long I stayed with Brian because I knew it's what she wanted… It took me much too long to realize that it was up to me to live my life and to make my own choices." She narrowed her gaze. "Why are you here, Linc?"

He sucked in a deep breath. "To tell you I'm sorry I broke your heart twelve years ago."

"That's it?" Her fingers curled into fists at her sides. "You're sorry you broke my heart?"

"I want to make it up to you, if you'll let me." He knew he'd hurt her. He also knew she was worth putting his heart on the line.

"How can you make up for twelve years of nursing a broken heart, Linc?"

"By making sure that the next twelve fill your heart so full it overflows into the next twelve and the twelve after that and so forth." Linc's heart pounded so hard it made keeping air in his lungs impossible. "I'm going to sell my place on Fripp and move to Boston to be near you, Lottie."

Her eyes rounded. "No. You can't do that. You love that house and Fripp."

"I love you more."

Lottie suspected she'd fallen asleep during the marrying a stranger show, was dreaming, and would awaken to Camilla returning any moment. But until that happened, she was going with this dream. Because Linc saying I love you to her was the ultimate dream. One that had her heart flopping around like a fish on Gram's dock.

"You love me?"

"I have always loved you, Charlotte Fairwell. I always will."

"I'm going to wrap my arms around you and tell you how happy I am that you're here, that I love you, too, and if there's nothing there but air and I wake up, I'm going to cry," she told him, still thinking she had to be dreaming. "Please be real."

"I'm real." He took her hands into his again, holding them as if they were the most precious things he'd ever held. "So very real that I worry you'll find me dull outside our Fripp fairy tale."

"Never," she whispered, pulling her hands free to hug him tightly to her and pressing her face against his chest. "Fripp isn't the fairy tale. You are."

"I hope so because I don't ever want to go back to being without you. If that means living where it's cold, then so be it."

"I'll keep you warm." She hugged him tighter. "Until I've fulfilled my contract and we can go to Fripp, I'll keep you warm."

"We don't have to go there, Lottie."

"I miss Gram and Maritime."

"She misses you, too. Jackie says Maritime sits outside your bedroom door and whines."

Imagining the dog doing that, Lottie laughed. "Now I know I'm dreaming."

"She loves you and so do I. We don't have to make any definite plans tonight, Lottie. We can stay here or go to Fripp or to Timbuktu so long as we're together."

"Sounds perfect."

"Almost. I don't want to rush things, but we've wasted so much time already that I don't want to be apart any longer." He reached into his pocket and pulled out Gram's wedding band. "Oops. Wrong one."

Lottie's breath caught as she watched him dig back into his pocket and pull out the other half of Gram's wedding ring set.

"When I asked for her permission to do what I'm about

to do, she insisted I take these." Linc knelt on one knee. "Marry me, Lottie. Tonight. Tomorrow. Next week or a year from now. Whenever you're sure I'm the one you want to spend your life with, marry me."

Choking back tears, Lottie nodded. "How could I say no to a man with an ocean view on Fripp?"

He laughed. "Guess I can let Jackie know I won't be auditioning for that marrying someone I don't know show, after all."

"Definitely not. You're my real-life fairy-tale happy-ever-after."

"Ditto."

* * * * *

MILLS & BOON

CHAPTER ONE

THAT FLUTTER TRAVELED through Valerie Hughes when Owen Clifton entered the break room. She pushed down the awareness of him she always felt when he came near. This time was no different. She had no intention of getting involved with him even if he were emotionally available, which he wasn't. She shifted in the metal chair as she returned her paper cup to the table in front of her.

"Hey, Valerie." A smile formed on Owen's lips as he made his way toward her with a plastic container in his hand. They shared an addiction to sweets. She had no doubt there would be a treat worth eating inside the semiclear plastic box. More than once they'd caught up in the break room over a candy bar. That's how they had become such good friends.

"I see one of your admirers brought you something." She indicated the container with a nod of her head.

"Uh, what? Oh, yeah. Lisa brought me a thank-you gift for helping her out."

Valerie grinned. He did that type of thing all the time. Always helping someone. He had no idea the effect he had on women. Almost every single female in the department had brought him something special to eat at one time or another. What made it so humorous was he had no idea they were flirting with him. Time and again she'd seen it happen.

She had been working at Atlanta Children's Hospital in the anesthesia department for six years. Owen had already been on staff when she'd joined; he was a recent widower. Being one of those men who grew better looking with age and having an engaging personality, the women in the department flocked to him. For her, more than that he was a compassionate and caring doctor. She admired him. He was nothing like the low-life man she had been involved with who not only broke her heart but had been running around on his wife.

Owen didn't look at her as he shifted the box from hand to hand. Why was he acting nervous? They'd been work friends for a long time, and good friends for almost as long. She'd never seen him like this. And she knew him well enough to know something wasn't right. He looked over his shoulder as if expecting someone. His gaze met hers again.

What was she missing? It wasn't her birthday, so it couldn't be a surprise party. Or was something going on in the hallway he was protecting her from seeing? "Is there something wrong? A problem with a patient?"

He cleared his throat. "Um, do you mind if I close the door?"

Owen sounded so unsure, which was very unlike him. Unease welled up inside her, and she sat straighter in the chair. "Of course not. You're starting to freak me out a little. What's going on?" She looked to the door and back at Owen. "Who sent you in here to talk to me?"

In the six years they had worked together, she'd never known Owen to cross the line between professional and personal. Every conversation was held in public, in front of others in the department. This wasn't done by discussion but more as a silent mutual agreement. They sometimes joined groups of coworkers for meals and parties, but never crossed the line to anything more. That suited her just fine. He seemed like a great guy, but she had been misled before by appearances.

Owen stood and shut the door then sat down, pushing a hand through dark hair that had turned white at the temples. "No one sent me. Nothing's wrong. I just have something I want to ask you, and I don't want us to be the subject of hospital gossip."

Now she was really intrigued. She faced him. "Okay. Talk away." Her words sounded lighter than she felt.

"I need a favor," he stated.

All this drama had been about a favor? The tightness in her chest completely disappeared. Through the years they had traded cases, days off and attendance at meetings. What was so special about this favor that it had to be asked in secret? What really held her attention was he'd never asked her for a personal one. She fiddled with her now-empty paper cup, twisting it, then met his look. "What kind of favor?"

"I need a date for my nephew's wedding. Will you go with me?"

Valerie's heart rate started to race. Owen was asking her out! Did he have any idea of the crush she had on him? No, she'd kept that under wraps. She'd manage her reaction carefully. Why would he be asking her out now? Owen had never even suggested he liked her more than as a colleague. She'd never known him to go out with anyone.

"I, uh, hadn't expected that. Not that I'm not flattered but before I answer, can I have a few more details?"

He had the good grace to turn pink. It was cute. Apparently he was embarrassed. He looked down at his hands. "Elaine's been gone now for five years."

Valerie had no doubt he knew the months, hours and minutes since her death. Valerie had never seen or heard of a man more devoted to his wife, dead or alive. Too often Valerie had wondered what it would be like to have someone that much in love with her. She wanted a man who would be that faithful. One who would put her happiness first. Sadly, so far in her life that hadn't happened. The man she'd put her trust in, believed she would marry, certainly hadn't felt that way. He'd used her and then thrown her away like food gone bad in a refrigerator. Now she couldn't help but be leery of it happening again.

"My kids have decided I'm lonely and it's time for me to start dating."

He sounded as excited about that as he would if he were being served dirt for dinner.

"They've been trying to set me up. I've managed to fend them off, but I have a nephew who is getting married in a few weeks. They said I should have a date for this wedding, and if I don't they'd find me one."

Valerie covered her mouth to conceal a grin.

Owen glared. "It's not funny. I've heard about some of those women online. They'd eat me alive. I haven't been on a date in twenty, no, twenty-eight years." He pulled his brows together. "Do they still call it dating?"

At that, Valerie guffawed. "It's still called dating." Not that she would really know. She hadn't been out seriously with a man in ages. At least not out and about. In her last serious "relationship," her boyfriend, Ray, had always made an excuse for them to stay in. She couldn't imagine any reason somebody wouldn't want to go out with Owen though. He was an all-around nice guy. In fact, she'd admired his attributes for a long time. Yet she hesitated to accept his proposal.

He leaned back in the chair with a disgusted look on his face. "I can't take one more phone call or nudge or surprise meeting with the unmarried parent of one the kids' friends. They've even gotten my sister-in-law and brother involved."

His frustration made Valerie's smile grow while her heart went out to him.

"I just want to shut them down. Enjoy the weekend with my family. I thought if I brought my own significant other then maybe they'd leave me alone for a while."

"So basically, you're going to be using me."

He had the good grace to give her a sheepish look. "I wish I could tell you differently, but I guess that's true. I don't know many people outside of work. I don't go to places where there are a lot of single women. I haven't been to a real party in years. I don't want to take a stranger. I like you. We're friends, so I thought of you. We respect each other and I enjoy your company. The wedding is supposed to be at a very nice resort. I thought you might like a chance to get out of town for a few days." He shrugged. "Maybe enjoy the fall leaves."

Owen was using the hard sell, saying all of the right things but leaving out that he really wanted to spend time with her. But that was too much to expect. Probably because he sensed she'd run for the hills if he did. Their friendship worked partly because they knew the other wasn't interested in anything more than friendship. She didn't dare let what happened before happen again.

"Are you sure it's a good idea to be tricking your children or leading them to believe there's something between us that's not there?"

"It's just for a few days, then I can tell them we broke up. All we have to do is share some meals together, smile and have pleasant conversations with my family. I just need them to stop pushing women at me. I'm not ready to get involved with anyone. I may never be."

There was Valerie's confirmation. At least they were on the same plane. If she didn't start to want or expect anything more, all would be good. She did want to help him out. Still, a niggle of doubt made her say, "Let me think about it."

His shoulders slumped.

"Just give me overnight. I promise to get right back to you. I may be on call." She had to admit she wanted to go. Too much. Maybe if she did, she could get over her silly crush. Those emotions she'd learned the hard way she couldn't trust.

"I already checked. You're not."

Wow, he really wanted her to go. "I need a chance to think about it. I don't want to do anything that would hurt our friendship or our work relationship."

He nodded. "It's not like we're going to be sharing a room. I'll see to it that you have our own space."

"Won't your children think that's odd?"

He twisted his lips. "They might, but I think they'll just be glad I brought someone."

A staff member pushed the door open. Owen jumped up, a guilty look covering his face. Would he wear that look the entire time if she agreed to go with him? She had no desire to have him be ashamed of her. She'd experienced that before from other men. That had been enough.

The young nurse glanced between them. "I've been looking for you, Dr. Clifton. They're ready for you in OR four."

"I'm on my way." He glanced at Valerie.

"I'll let you know."

He gave her a nod then followed the smiling staff member out the door.

Owen shook his head while he made his way to the OR. It had been years since he had asked anyone out. At least a woman that wasn't his wife. He couldn't say he enjoyed it much more now than he had in his youth. The fear of being turned down hovered around every word.

Valerie hadn't said no. She'd just wanted to think about it. That he could understand. She had been as shocked as him judging by the nervous look on her face. When he'd first come up with the plan, he feared he might be losing his mind. How could he do it to Elaine? If he were out with another woman, then it would mean that Elaine was truly gone. It made the truth real. He worked to stop the tremble of his hands. That wasn't the way he wanted it.

Time went by with his kids continuing to nudge him to start going out. Kaitlyn, his daughter, had rallied the troops to gang up on him. All the calling and cajoling had him thinking seriously about asking Valerie. Surely it would be better to invite someone he knew, who didn't expect personal involvement instead of being set up with a stranger.

He had been surprised at how eager his children had been for him to start dating. Apparently, they were worried about him, now that they were all away from home. At least Valerie hadn't turned him down right away. That would have been devastating.

But it wasn't until he'd left her that he'd come to that realization. Before talking to her, he wouldn't have thought it really mattered one way or another what her answer would be. For some reason it had become important Valerie go with him. He was comfortable with her.

He'd worked with Valerie for years and he liked her. Maybe if she did just this one thing then his children would get off his case. He would've made the effort they wanted. Still, it wasn't worth worrying over until he found out what Valerie decided.

As an adult he didn't need to prove anything to his children. Still, he wanted them to know he could take care of himself without their pushing and help. His children needed to focus on their lives.

Owen pulled on his surgical cap and stepped up to the scrubbing station. As he scrubbed up, Valerie's face came to mind. She really was an attractive woman. It wasn't until recently that he had started to notice women again. For so many years he'd kept the blinders on. He loved his wife too much to run around on her. As far as he was concerned, he was still married. Growing up, he'd seen the hurt inflicted by infidelity. His mother spent more than one night staying up late waiting on his father. The fights that followed were nasty. Owen had promised himself as a child he would never treat his wife that way. And he hadn't. He believed in honoring those he loved.

An OR nurse approached him. He held up his hands, letting her pull on his gloves. He shouldered his way through the OR doors. This procedure shouldn't take long. A three-year-old girl getting ear tubes.

"Let's get this young lady asleep and comfortable." He stepped to the head of the table. "She's in good health? No fever or issues?"

"All good, Doctor," one of the OR staff responded.

"Then here we go." Owen placed the small rubber mask over the girl's nose and mouth. When the child was anesthetized, he moved her head to the side, making sure the airway remained clear. He positioned her head so the ears, nose and throat doctor could insert the first tube. Soon Owen was able to swap sides for the surgeon to place the second tube.

"Done," the ENT surgeon announced.

Owen backed off the gas. He placed an oxygen canula under the child's nose, then rechecked the monitors. "I'm ready for her to go to recovery."

"I'll clean up and speak to the parents." The ENT removed his mask, gown and gloves. "Thanks, Owen."

"Anytime."

Owen finished disposing of the used equipment then headed to recovery, where he joined the nurse caring for his patient. "How's she doing?"

"Well." They both glanced at the monitor.

The nurse looked at the IV placement then made a note on her electronic pad. Owen gave her his report then left the recovery room. He was on his way to the nursing station when he heard his name being called. It was Valerie.

"Owen!"

Their eyes met over their masks before her attention returned to her patient. Even dressed in blue scrubs with a scrub coat over them Valerie had an appeal he'd given little thought to before today. It was clear she had lovely curves. The unflattering clothes did little to hide them. Her surgical cap had large pink flowers on it, adding a pop of color in an otherwise monochromic space. He'd never realized how Valerie had a way of lighting up a room. Seeing her always made him smile.

He shook his head. For years he'd known her and never given her this much thought. More than once he'd asked her to help him. Since asking her to the wedding she not been far from his thoughts. She hadn't even agreed to go with him, and he'd become fixated on her. The idea made him a little sick to his stomach while at the same time gave him a buzz of excitement. All of a sudden it mattered if she went along with his plan. But what he needed to do was concentrate on his charting.

"I need help."

"What procedure did your patient have?" Owen demanded.

"Appendectomy." Valerie pressed down on the boy's incision area, her gloved hands covered in blood.

A nurse appeared at her side, tearing open a packet of padding.

"On three," Valerie said. "One, two, three." She lifted her hands, and the nurse quickly applied the absorbent material, pressing down. Valerie's hands went on top of the nurse's.

Owen listened to the boy's heart with his stethoscope. His pulse was faint, weak. "I need a bulb here."

A nurse handed him one. He placed the mask over the boy's mouth and nose and pressed in on the plastic bulb, giving the boy oxygen.

"Call Dr. Powers. Tell him we're bringing his patient

back. Stat." Valerie called over her shoulder, then looked at the monitors. "BP still going down. Get fluids on board."

Another nurse arrived with the drip stand and fluid bag, then set it up.

"Take over here." The nurse applied her hands as soon as Valerie moved hers. Seconds later Valerie pushed the needle into the port.

"Eighty over fifty," Owen called.

Other staff joined them.

"Let's get him moving," Valerie said.

Owen continued to monitor the boy's heart rate as they ran alongside the gurney into the OR.

Dr. Powers rushed in as they transferred the patient onto the table. "Patient status?"

"There's a bleeder somewhere." Valerie continued the compression.

Owen squeezed the handheld ventilator at a constant pace.

"Get two packs of O in here. We need to get this child open and find that bleeder."

"Owen," Valerie said, "will you do the intubating and handle the anesthetic?"

"Sure. Intubating kit. Stat."

"Here you go." The OR nurse handed him the items as the words came out of his mouth.

Less than an hour later the problem had been found and the child stabilized. Valerie had insisted on staying at the boy's side until he was moved to the ICU. He would have one night of observation before going to a room.

Owen looked up from where he sat behind the nurses' station. Valerie stood over the boy watching while his gurney went through the door Her skin had turned pale. She looked beat. He went to her. "Hey, Valerie, are you okay?"

Her hands visibly shook. "Huh?"

He'd never seen her rattled. She was now.

"I'm fine. I'm fine. I need to clean up, then go back check on him."

Owen placed his hand on her arm. "You need to take a moment to regroup before you do that. This isn't like you."

"I'm fine. Really, I am."

"You don't look that way. What's going on?"

Valerie offered him a weak, apologetic smile. She scanned the area as if making sure no one else was around before she eased onto the bench between the row of lockers. "I had something similar to what happened to my patient today happen when I was just starting out on my first job. It didn't end as well as it did today. I'm just a little upset. I'll have it together in a few minutes. I know it's unprofessional. It just got to me a little."

Owen sank down beside her, making sure to leave plenty of room between them. "That's understandable. We're human after all."

She gave him a weak smile. "Thanks for looking out for me."

"Not a problem."

Valerie stood. "I appreciate the pep talk."

"No problem. I've had to have plenty of pep talks in my life. It doesn't hurt to share one." Heaven knew after Elaine's death he'd been sobbing in his office more than once when his brother had come in and consoled him.

Her smile grew. For some reason that made Owen's chest expand like he'd ridden to her rescue.

"I'm going to clean up and go make my evening rounds." She started toward the bathroom at the back of the room.

"I'll leave you to it then." Owen headed toward the door.

"Owen."

"Yes?" He stood up to face her.

"Thank you."

He nodded. "Anytime."

The next morning the surgery department hummed with staff and patients. Valerie didn't have time to do little more than prepare for her first case. She looked for Owen. Not finding him, she released a sigh of relief. She'd come close to falling apart emotionally in front of him, which was highly unprofessional. That hadn't happened in twenty years, then it did just after Owen asked her to spend a weekend with his family. Could the timing be worse?

All night long she'd rolled around in bed thinking about his weekend proposal. She had done all the "what-ifs" to see if it was a good idea to agree to the plan. After more hours than she wanted to admit, she had concluded she would go. She liked Owen and was honored he'd asked her. What could it hurt? Maybe it would help her get over her crush on him. That would be a good thing.

"Hey, Valerie."

She jumped at the deep voice that came from behind her. Owen. Her heart leaped. "Good morning."

He stepped closer. So much so she warmed. "How're you doing? I thought about you last night. I hope you got some rest."

His concern shouldn't affect her in the way it did. He was just being nice. "I'm good."

"I'm glad to hear it."

One of the nurses called his name. "Got to go. Have a good day."

It wasn't until after lunch that she saw him again.

He came to stand near her. "How's it going today? All good?"

"Yes. Thanks for your concern and help yesterday. I'm all right. You don't have to worry about me." But she had to admit she sort of liked it. Too much of her life had involved a man not caring.

"I'm not worried. Just wondering." He picked up the next day's schedule.

"I appreciate you asking. I'm just embarrassed."

His gaze met hers, the sincerity in his eyes reassuring her. "No reason to be."

Valerie studied him. She liked the white at his temples; it gave him a distinguished air. He wasn't wearing his silver wire-rimmed glasses at the moment, but she liked those on him as well. He removed them when he wasn't working. She knew him well enough to register that small detail. Despite her near emotional collapse, he put her at ease.

She glanced around. Seeing no one nearby, she met his gaze with a direct one of her own. "I've been thinking that if I agree to go to the wedding with you, we should practice being around each other outside of the hospital. Your children will never believe us otherwise."

"You're agreeing to go?"

"I thought a lot about it last night. After yesterday I owe you a favor." She hadn't been sure about it until a moment ago though. She wanted to go. Wanted to get to know Owen better.

He smiled with obvious relief. "Thank you."

"Is there a problem with us talking about it here? Do

you not want anybody to know?" She didn't try to keep the note of hurt out of her voice. In her last relationship, Ray had kept her hidden away. Never wanting them to be seen together. It had taken her a while to understand why, but when it had become clear, it had been crystal clear. Even in a fake dating situation she wanted the man to stand beside her.

"No, I just didn't think either one of us would want to be a topic of gossip. Since it's just one weekend I think it'd be all right for this to remain between us." He put the schedule back on the counter.

"If that's the way you want it." She'd been humiliated before. Maybe this wedding weekend was a bad idea after all. She had no intention of going there again. But surely he wasn't ashamed of her, or he wouldn't have asked her to meet his family.

"Thanks."

He shifted on his feet as if he might run, but then settled. "You said something about us getting to know each other better. Like how?"

She shrugged. "We're supposed to know each other well enough to be dating. We should know more than the work aspect about each other. Our favorite colors. Vacation dreams. Stuff like that." As much as they gravitated toward each other at work, they never really shared deep feelings. Things that people dating would know about each other.

He didn't say anything, as if giving the idea thought, then, "Well, that sounds reasonable."

It might but he didn't sound enthusiastic about it. Yet she wasn't surprised. "I suggest if we're really going to do this, then we should spend some time together outside the hospital."

His brows rose as if that idea had never occurred to him. His insecurity showed as he stammered, "Uh, y-yeah. Okay."

Valerie found it rather adorable. The poor guy was struggling. Just how did he expect to get through an entire weekend playacting when he wasn't an actor? She had to help him. "How about we start with a simple meal at a restaurant?"

His head went to an angle as if he'd never heard of such a thing. "Okay. I'm on call tomorrow night so that's out."

"I'm on call the next." She watched him fidget with a pen.

He put the pen down with a thump. "So that leaves Friday night. Now about seven o'clock?"

"Sounds good." Too good. She wouldn't get her hopes up.

"Then I will pick you up then." Owen seemed perplexed by that idea.

Valerie gave him a pat on the arm. "I've got to get back to work."

He offered her a tentative smile as if he suddenly wasn't sure what he'd agreed to. "I'll see you Friday if not before."

"I'll be ready," Valerie said as she passed him on the way to the door.

CHAPTER TWO

FRIDAY EVENING OWEN pulled into Valerie's condo development right on time. He didn't want to appear too eager or make her think he didn't care enough to arrive on time. The problem remained that he wasn't sure which side he fell on. His pulse ran fast at the thought of spending time with a woman who wasn't his wife while reminding himself this dinner out would be necessary to convincing his children he and Valerie were a couple.

He took a parking spot in front of Valerie's building. Her condo was part of a group of two-story structures not far from the hospital. He knew of the complex because he passed it on the way to work, but he'd never been to Valerie's home. The red-brick period building had large windows. He studied the flowerbeds, shrubs and manicured lawn. Everything looked neat, orderly and proper. All of it reminded him of her personality and her work ethic.

The seasonal wreath on her front door wasn't quite what he'd expected, but he liked the touch. She didn't strike him as a froufrou sort of woman. That had been Elaine. His chest tightened. Taking a deep breath, he pushed the thought away.

What he had thought of as being a simple plan had moved past that. This going out and getting to know each other better went beyond them spending a weekend together. Somehow this seemed more personal. Real. As if they were really dating.

In fact, he wasn't sure what he had gotten himself into. When he had formulated his plan, he apparently hadn't thought it all the way through. The last time he had a date was so long ago he wasn't sure he knew what to do. He'd been married so long. He still *felt* married. A thread of guilt tugged at him. Wouldn't it be betraying Elaine if he had a good time?

It had taken him an inordinate amount of time to dress. Elaine would have laughed him. He'd never been a clothes horse, but still he couldn't decide what to wear. Eventually he had pulled on his favorite jeans, added a button-down shirt, tucked it in and added a belt, then a sport jacket. Done, he turned as if to ask Elaine's opinion. His chest tightened.

How long had it been since he'd cared how he looked? He studied himself in the mirror. His hair had strands of silver, but it was still thick. He kept it clipped short, but it needed a trim. He would get one before the wedding.

What was he doing?

He would go out to dinner tonight because he couldn't stand up Valerie, then he'd call off their appearance at the wedding. Afterward he'd straighten his children out. Tell them he'd handle his personal life.

Taking a deep breath, he slowly let it out. He exited the SUV, then made his way up the concrete walk. He didn't make it halfway before a door opened. Valerie stood there with a reassuring smile on her face. Had she been watching him? Or was she making sure she didn't have to invite him in? Maybe she'd just peeked out to see if he was there. He didn't want her to know how long it had taken him to approach her door.

"Hey." The word sounded rougher and more nervous than he intended.

"Hello. I need to get my sweater and purse." Valerie returned inside, leaving the door open.

She wore a simple floral dress. Her brown hair framed her face and fell to just above her shoulders. The majority of the time her hair remained under a surgical cap. The dress was a nice change from hospital scrubs. He couldn't stop watching her. Valerie looked lovely tonight.

Her eyes were green. Like the dark jade of summer leaves. Why hadn't he ever noticed that before? As she reappeared, he appreciated her curves; mature ones that she'd maintained well. Wow, he hadn't had that thought about a woman in a long time, and certainly not about Valerie. What was happening to him? His reaction to her was so out of character.

Still, he couldn't understand why he hadn't noticed all this before. Could it be because he'd been so focused on himself? That idea wasn't a comfortable one. The urge to run consumed him, but he held steady as she turned off the hall light, leaving a lone lamp on.

"I'm ready." She patted her hair.

Was Valerie as nervous as he was? Why would she be? "Uh, yeah. Let's go. I hope you're hungry." When she paused to lock the door, he waited on the walk then led her to his vehicle.

"How are you, Owen?"

"I'm fine."

"Are you sure?" She studied him. "You look a little green."

His throat tightened. Was it that obvious how uptight

he was? "It's the first time I've been out with a woman in years. I'm not sure I know how to do this."

Her face turned curious. "Have dinner with a friend?"

Some of his anxiety ebbed away. "More like a female friend."

"I understand. Let's go get something to eat and enjoy ourselves. What do you say?"

"I can do that."

He saw her into the passenger seat and climbed behind the steering wheel. "I hope you like the restaurant. I've always thought it was good."

"You go there often?"

"Yes, I guess I have." It was Elaine's favorite place. In truth he hadn't been out to eat much since she'd died. Or to a party. A movie or anything that might involve couples. It was just too painful. "On second thought, I think you should pick where we go. Got any ideas?"

Valerie took a seat at the table for two outside the bistro in Decatur. The sky had turned to orange in the west as a light breeze ruffled the leaves of the tree above her head. The sound of traffic was muffled by the two blocks of buildings creating the square.

She hadn't been to this bistro before and had always wanted to try it. She hoped the relaxed atmosphere would lessen Owen's anxiety. He seemed as tight as a wound-up rubber band. The amount of time he had spent sitting in his car before coming to her door had been a clue. He had even admitted to being nervous. She'd give him positive points for that.

When she had asked where they were going to dinner, the odd look on his face and the length of time it took him to answer had been telling. Her best guess had been he'd planned to take her to his and his wife's usual place then thought better of it.

There it was again. He got another point for that. Progress.

She had no idea when she suggested them getting to know each other on a more personal level it would be so difficult for him. A couple of times she thought about letting him off the hook. Yet he'd been the one who had put all this into motion. Owen needed her help. His children were right. He needed to move on.

Their friendship had been based on the superficial things in life. Patients, their shared sweet tooth, the other staff members... They'd always held back on talking about their hopes and dreams, places they'd like to travel to, what they *really* wanted out of life. She'd been afraid to that with him. Had it been the same for him? Now this crazy weekend wedding plan left them no choice but to open up. But she would only go so far. Some things Owen didn't need to know about.

Still, if tonight didn't go well, she'd call off the weekend. There would be no point in them going any further. All the same, she found it endearing that a man so controlled in the OR was so out of sorts around her. That he had such strong ties to his loved ones and cared about his children enough that he was prepared to do this to make them happy. Even if it was for appearances only.

Owen looked up from the drinks menu. He looked around. "This is really nice."

"I've always wanted to try this place. I hope the food is good."

Valerie couldn't suppress the little burst of joy that he acted as if he were relaxing some.

The waitress came to the table to take their drink orders.

"Where did you learn about this place?" Owen put his menu on the table.

"A couple of the nurses told me about it." She placed her menu on top of his.

He leaned back. A horrified look crossed his features. "You told them we were coming here?"

Valerie didn't care for the note of concern in his voice. "No. I was just listening to them talk about places they liked to go. Would it have mattered if I had told them?"

"No. Yes. I don't know." His eyes pleaded. "I'm just not ready to be the talk of the OR. I had enough of the whispered concern when my wife died. I don't want to do that to you."

He was worried about her? Her heart softened. But hadn't she heard that from another source? And it had been him covering up his lies. "I'm a big girl. I can take care of myself."

"I know, but I don't want to be the reason you're the discussion at the coffee machine."

Surely he wasn't ashamed to have her be seen with him. After all, he was the one who asked her to the wedding. Yet that would just be his family. Not the people he worked with every day.

The waitress returned with their drinks and took their orders.

Owen took a long draw on his drink. "I'll say I appreciate the service."

Valerie smiled. They were back to talking about nonpersonal, safe subjects. It was time to shake him up again.

She put her elbows on the table, clasped her hands together and rested her chin on her hands. "So, Dr. Clifton, tell me one of your dirty secrets."

Owen blinked and he swallowed hard.

She fixed him with a look that didn't waver.

He took the bait and met her head-on. "Where do you want me to start?"

"Wherever you want to." Valerie continued to watch him.

Owen took a deep breath, as if he planned to tell her something of super importance. "I smoked behind my grandfather's barn when I was seven."

A laugh burst from her. "That was good. Now, tell me about your family."

He grinned. "You don't waste any time, do you?"

"No. I figure we have a whole lot of personal stuff to learn about each other." At his wince she said, "Why don't I go first." She smiled at the look of relief on his face. "I was born in Chicago. You know I have a brother and two sisters. I've talked about them before. But you might not remember my brother lives out in California. I don't see him much, but I talk to him often. One of my sisters still live in Chicago. The other lives in Louisiana. They have children. Mostly all teenagers now."

"You're a good aunt. I've heard you talking about what to buy as presents for their birthdays." His gaze had turned intent as if he were remembering a scene in his head.

"I spoil them all whenever I can." Valerie grinned. She loved doing it. They were a nice replacement for the children she didn't have.

"They're just a little younger than my children."

"Yes." Was he wondering if she would get on with

his children? Or wondering why she didn't have any of her own.

"I know you went to Texas A&M to medical school then worked at Houston Children's, but you've never said what made you decide to move here."

Valerie didn't much want to talk about that time in her life. She would tell him the surface information and let that be it. "Owen, I do believe you are getting into the spirit of things. You asked a question."

He twisted his lips. "Maybe I am. Answer my question."

"I wanted a change." She raised her hands. "And here I am. I really like Atlanta, and I don't think I'll be leaving."

"A change? Any particular reason why?"

She had his interest now. But not for a reason she was comfortable with. She didn't want to talk about that time. Not even with Owen. "Let's just say it had become awkward at work and it was time to move on."

"I see." His eyes had clouded with concern.

She doubted he did. Did he know what it was to love someone and learn they had been deceiving you? She'd had to get away. From the gossip, the despair, the humiliation, the breaking of her heart and trust. The only way for her to survive had been to move and start over. To work to regain her stability.

"So, tell me about you." Valerie crossed her arms on the table and leaned forward. She didn't want to miss a word he said.

"There's not much to tell that you don't already know."

"There has to be. There's always something to tell." She wouldn't let him get away with dodging her questions. "Why don't you start off by telling me who'll be at the wedding? You said it was your nephew getting married?"

"Yes, it's my brother Will's son."

"Where does your brother live?" Valerie hated having to pull answers out of him, but she would.

"Will lives here in town. He works for an engineering firm."

She watched as Owen sat straighter. His movements were smooth and relaxed, like an animal that knew its environment and was secure in its place in it. He took good care of himself. "Are you guys close?"

"Yes. He and Sarah really helped me out the first few months after Elaine died. I was a mess. I think you'll like Sarah."

Would Sarah like her after she found out Valerie and Owen had only been pretending to be in a relationship? "How will she feel about me being at the wedding with you?"

"She'll be pleased. She thinks it's time I start dating too." He rolled his eyes.

A tightness formed in Valerie's chest as she formed the next question. "You really don't want to do that, do you?"

He shrugged. "I don't know. I don't like to be pushed into it. I'm not sure I'm ready. But I don't like my children worrying about me. And, heck, I'm just plain out of practice."

"You seem to be doing a pretty good job tonight." She gave him her best encouraging smile.

He looked at her for the first time that night with warm eyes. "I know you and like you, so it makes it easy."

Heat flowed through her. Valerie had to watch it or this man would charm her into doing something she shouldn't. "Thank you."

The waitress returned with their dinner orders. They concentrated on their meals for a while.

"I know your children's names and a few things about them from you talking about them at work, but give me a refresher."

Owen took a long draw on his iced tea. He really didn't enjoy talking about himself. He feared Valerie might see behind the "okay" facade he'd built over the last few years. He gulped. Where had that come from? Until tonight he'd thought he'd been doing fine.

He had been wrong. This evening with Valerie proved how backward his life had turned. From his dressing to please his wife, to the feeling of guilt he carried, right up to not wanting anyone they knew to see them together. Valerie having dinner with him had eaten away at the floodgates holding back years of pent-up emotion.

Owen got a momentary reprieve when the waitress returned with a refill of their drinks.

Valerie gave him a sympathetic look. "You know we don't have to do this if you don't want to."

Did she want out of their agreement or was she being nice enough to offer him the chance. "I don't mind."

"Well, you could've fooled me."

He leaned forward, placing his elbows on the table. She returned his gaze without a blink. "I know I'm acting like I'm not having a good time. But I assure you I am not having a bad one." He waved his hand around. "I just haven't done this in a long time."

"You keep saying that. Why haven't you done it?"

His gaze held hers. He wasn't going to tell her he felt disloyal to his dead wife. How crazy did that sound? He was uncomfortable having a good time and disappointed in letting Valerie down There was no winning. "I guess I just haven't wanted to."

She placed a hand on his. Hers was warm, soft and re-assuring. "We're just talking. One friend to another."

Valerie was his friend. They'd been working together for years. All he had to do was think of her as a colleague again. Why was he even letting thoughts of her as a woman enter his mind? As long as he kept her in the right spot in his head, then he'd be okay.

"Hey, I don't expect anything. Nothing more than you can give. Now, will you tell me about your children?"

Owen took a deep breath. He could do that. He was a proud, doting father. "Kaitlyn is the oldest. She's married and lives in Marietta."

"Yes, I remember you talking about her wedding."

"Yeah. I don't see her so often, despite how close she lives. She does something with computers, and her husband works in the city engineering department. They both are busy people. She's the one who rallied the troops to convince me I need to go out. The boys will agree to anything just to get her to hush."

Valerie nodded as she continued to watch him.

"Rich is my middle child. He is tall and thoughtful and the most like his mother, yet he has a powerful personality. He's finishing college and thinking about medical school. I'm trying not to influence his decision. He has a girlfriend. She's a nice girl. I expect they'll marry when she finishes school."

Owen had to admit he needed to talk. Living alone had done him no favors in that regard. Just to have a conversation with someone who listened and showed interest in his life. He'd missed the give and take of talking to someone.

"John's your youngest, isn't he? He's the one who just started college."

"Yep. He made me an empty nester, but he comes home more than the others. So I get to see him pretty often."

The waitress interrupted them to take their dessert order.

As they ate their desserts, Owen's attention settled on Valerie's lips. Why was he only just noticing how soft and plump they looked? He'd seen her with colleagues, patients and their family members and never noticed her lips before. She'd always had something about her that put them at ease. Just as he was around her. Valerie really cared about people, him. Subconsciously he must have been noticing her more than he realized. He liked it when she'd talked about her nieces and nephews. Her face lit up. She liked children. That had been one of the things that had run through his mind when thinking about going out with someone, before quickly discarding the idea. He was a man with three children after all.

After paying for the meal, he escorted her toward the door. When a customer stood up quickly, pushing out his chair in front of Valerie, she stopped. Owen placed a hand at the small of her back to steady her. His hand tingled at the contact. The man apologized, and Valerie moved past him. Owen missed the contact between them, yet his heart still continued to race. This wasn't the reaction he wanted or expected.

Valerie continued to weave between the tables and chairs, Owen following as she made her way to his SUV.

There Valerie faced him. "Owen, thank you for the nice time tonight."

"I enjoyed it."

Her eyes widened, and she tilted her head as if she questioned that statement.

"Don't look so surprised."

"I have to admit I am. During most of it you looked like you might run at any second."

Owen chest tightened. He didn't like the idea of her not believing he'd appreciated her company. "I know I bumbled my way through most of it."

She placed her hand on his forearm. He immediately felt the reassuring heat. "Hey, nobody said there were any rules."

"Thank you. So do you think it'll work out for a weekend away?"

She removed her hand then gave him a firm nod. "I think we can make it work."

The ring of his phone stopped their conversation. He answered. "Yeah, I'm on my way. I'll be there in about ten minutes."

He had hardly ended his call when the ring tone sounded on Valerie's phone "Yes. I'm on my way."

"Apparently this isn't the usual emergency. They need both of us." Valerie climbed into the car.

Owen got behind the wheel, and they headed out of the parking lot.

Valerie sat with her hands clasped in her lap. "The nurse said something about a major automobile accident."

"Sounds like we have a night ahead of us." Owen turned into the hospital parking lot.

Without a word they climbed out of the car and headed for the staff door, up to the second floor to the surgery department then into the locker room. A couple of the staff members' eyes widened when they entered together, obviously dressed for dinner, yet no one made a comment.

As Owen went to his locker Valerie said, "I'll see you in there."

Less than five minutes later they met again in the surgical scrub area. Both were dressed in mint green scrubs, and Owen stood beside her as they sanitized their hands. Valerie already wore a mask. He marveled at her emerald eyes, which reminded him of fresh grass in the spring.

She wore one of her kid print surgical caps to cover her hair, but he much preferred the look of it down and flowing around her shoulders. Whoa, that was a wayward thought. They'd had a simple dinner, and his thoughts made him feel like a man smitten by a woman. That had to stop. They had a friendship between them and that was it. He couldn't handle anything more.

Valerie met his look. "Is there a problem?"

"No." Panic rippled through him. He'd been caught staring. "Thank you for coming to dinner."

Her smile reached eyes that glowed. "You are welcome."

He had the good grace to look ashamed. "I can't say it was the easiest thing I've done. But I also have to admit that it was nice to have somebody to talk to outside the hospital."

Her mouth took quirked. "Thank you, I think."

He stepped closer. "Really, despite all appearances, I had a good time."

A nurse came in through the side door. "Ready for gloves doctors?"

"Yep." Valerie held up her hands letting the scrub nurse help her. When she was finished with Valerie, the nurse turned to Owen.

"Which OR?" Owen asked.

"Number five," the nurse stated. "By the way, it's going to be a tough one. Dr. Horton is on his way along with Dr. Wilson. The gastro guy has been called in as well. The rest of the staff should be here in just a few minutes."

"What happened?" Valerie asked over her shoulder as she headed toward the OR door.

"The kid took a hit from an SUV with his motorcycle. The SUV won. He's got internal injuries. And a number of broken bones." The nurse followed them.

"Sounds like a long night ahead," Valerie said with resignation and determination.

Their assistants were already at the operating table. Owen stood beside Valerie as they listened to the report on the patient from the ER doctor. They had just finished when Dr. Horton entered the room.

"Someone tell me what we've got here."

One of the ER staff spoke up. "Boy's motorcycle collided with an automobile. He's got a broken femur, a broken arm and there's internal bleeding."

"Let's go in and get the bleeding under control before Ortho and Plastic show up to see what they can do tonight." He lifted a large pressure bandage from the boy's abdomen. "Suction."

Owen and Valerie moved quickly into position near the patient's head.

"I'll see to blood," Valerie announced, not waiting on him to answer before she went to work.

Owen stepped to the end of the table. There he double-checked the anesthesia setup, making sure the mask was secure to the patient's face. "If you get tired, we can swap if we need to."

Valerie nodded then took a seat on the rolling stool. She asked the nurse, "Has the request for blood been called in?"

"It's on the way," Mark, one of the newer interns, said. She glanced his way. "I hadn't expected you to be called in too."

"I was still here when the boy came in. I thought I'd hang around in case you guys needed help."

"That's good of you." Her attention turned to the patient.

Owen was surprised to see Mark as well. The intern offered his help, and Owen would take it. His focus went to the machine beside him as he reviewed the numbers. He spoke to Dr. Horton in particular and the group in general. "The patient is sedated. We're ready when you are."

As the hours ticked by, Owen kept vigil on the patient's heart rate and rhythm, breathing, BP, and checked his body temp and fluid balance while the surgeon worked. Every so often Owen would rub the back of the patient's head and beneath his shoulder blades to keep circulation moving to help prevent pressure sores.

Once during the long hours Mark offered Valerie a break, and she took it. She returned and did the same for Owen.

The OR door opened. Dr. Wilson, the orthopedic surgeon, entered. He did what he could until the swelling went down. The boy also needed some time to recover from the internal surgery. The young man would have many more surgeries to come.

An alarm went off.

"Give me the numbers," Dr. Horton demanded.

Valerie called out vitals. Her voice held a tight note, but remained even and sure. Owen turned off the high, loud squeal as he reviewed the lines on the monitor.

"Let's get this boy stabilized and out of here. The rest will have to wait," Dr. Horton said to the orthopedic surgeon.

It was nearly 5:00 a.m. when Owen and Valerie escorted the patient to recovery and another hour before they handed the boy off to the ICU doctors and nurses. Afterward, they walked up the long quiet hall toward the surgery suite.

As they went by the OR they'd just been in, Mark exited. He looked surprised to see them but soon recovered. "Night, y'all. I mean, mornin'." He grinned and kept moving down the hall.

"I would've thought he'd have been long gone." Valerie glanced back at Mark.

"He must have gotten caught up in helping straighten the OR. Nice guy. Eager to learn." Owen pulled his head covering off. "That's a night I don't hope to repeat."

"Hey, we still have reports to give." Valerie yawned.

She pushed the door to the dictation room open. Taking a seat, she went to work. Owen did the same. Valerie finished before him, giving him a wave as she left the room.

Five minutes later he found her in the locker room. She'd changed out of her scrubs back into the clothes she'd worn to dinner.

"I'll be ready to go in a few minutes to take you—"

A couple of doctors entered the room, coming to work for the morning surgeries. By the look of interest on their faces, they had heard what he had said. Horror washed through him. The one thing Owen didn't want to have happen was the rumor to get out he and Valerie were involved.

She must have seen his reaction. The joy left her eyes. She glanced at the doctors as they moved into another part of the locker room. Her mouth formed a thin line. "I'll wait for you near the staff door."

He blinked. He'd mess up. "Valerie—"

"I'm tired, Owen. I'm ready to go home to a hot shower and bed." She opened the door to the hall.

Owen grabbed his wallet and keys, leaving his dinner clothes in his locker for later and hurried after Valerie. When he joined her, she pushed through the door and walked to his SUV without saying a word.

Moments later Owen pulled out of the parking lot. "Valerie, I'm sorry I acted like we'd just gotten caught in a compromising situation. I'm just sensitive to gossip. Too often after Elaine died, I was the topic of conversation."

"It's okay. I get it. Maybe someone else is better suited to go to the wedding with you. There're any number of the women in surgery who would go with you. Maybe you should ask one of them."

Owen glanced at her. "I'm sorry. I didn't mean to act that way."

"Let's just not talk about it anymore. I'm tired and want to go home."

He had to fix this. They had been friends before he suggested she help him. He wanted to keep that.

CHAPTER THREE

TWO DAYS LATER the morning light was just reaching around the buildings when Valerie entered the hospital. She'd spent most of the day before in bed after her long night in the OR. The rest of the day she did her chores and read.

Far too often Owen slipped into her thoughts. She'd already had a man in her life who acted ashamed of her. Worse than that, he'd lied and humiliated her. To discover he had been cheating on his wife with her had been the ultimate betrayal. He had been a visiting doctor, and she'd been swept off her feet. Nothing good had come out of it. She had no desire to experience that again, not even with someone she'd had a crush on for years. Owen obviously didn't want people to know they had been out together. And that hurt. Too much.

All too in her life she'd loved someone who didn't love her back. First it was her father leaving her family when she was five. When her mother remarried her stepfather, he barely tolerated her. Valerie's brother and sisters were already out of the house, leaving her to take most of the stepfather's verbal abuse. Valerie had no intentions of being drawn in by feelings she couldn't trust. She intended to tell Owen he needed to find someone else to help him keep his children at bay.

Making her way to the floor where her patients waited for surgery, she prepared for a quick visit to reassure them since she hadn't been there to do it the night before. She loved this hospital and her patients. She was happy here. When she'd moved to this metropolitan hospital, she feared she might be overwhelmed but instead she'd found her home.

She spoke to a number of the staff as she made her way to the nurses' station. Being a part of helping children filled her need to give. Here she was appreciated and useful. As an anesthesiologist she had little ongoing interaction with patients, yet she took great pride in knowing she had helped patients handle the pain of surgery.

Wearing only her dark blue scrubs, with her stethoscope around her neck, she checked in at the nurses' station and picked up her list of patients and their room numbers. She pulled her glasses from where they hung in the V of her shirt. Slipping them on, she studied the list.

She had purposely left her white lab coat behind. Many adolescent patients had white coat phobia. Especially the chronically ill ones. What the patient and family faced was traumatic enough without adding more uncertainly.

Owen joined her at the desk. "Mornin', Valerie."

"Hey, Owen."

"You recovered from the all-nighter, I hope."

She glanced at him. After the way they had left things the other night, he sure acted friendly. "Yep. I got plenty of rest yesterday."

"I'm glad to hear it. What kind of schedule do you have today?"

"It's pretty full. Especially since I didn't get to visit my patients last night. I've got to get to it this morning." Valerie studied the paperwork in front of her.

"That's right, you like to visit them in the evenings, don't you?"

She blinked. Owen had paid that much attention to her schedule, her routine. They were friends. He'd noticed her habits. Maybe she was being too hard on him. Maybe her expectations were too high, even unrealistic. He didn't know her background because she hadn't wanted to share it. Therefore, she couldn't blame him for something he didn't know anything about. "Yes, I like to visit in the evening. It always seemed harsh to me just to pop in in the morning and say, hey, I'm going to put you to sleep and then leave. Then they don't see you again until they wake in recovery and that's for only a couple of seconds."

"You're right. I hadn't thought of it that way. I may change my method."

"Part of our job is reassuring the patient. I don't think that necessarily happens in just three minutes of conversation."

His gaze met hers. "That's one of the things I admire about you. You really are so patient aware."

It was nice to have Owen confirm her belief, especially one so important to her.

"Do you think—" he looked around "—we could talk for a few minutes? I want to apologize for how things were left the other night."

"No apology necessary." She didn't want to go into it. They had a great friendship, and she wanted to keep it at that.

"I think there is. I value our friendship, but I'm selfish enough to beg for your help on the wedding weekend. I couldn't do it with anyone else. What can I do to convince you to help me?"

He sounded so pitiful and earnest her hackles lowered. "Look, I can't talk about it right now. I've got patients to see. Maybe when we're both done this afternoon."

Owen put up a hand. "Okay, okay. You're right. We both have people waiting on us. I'll check in with you later."

Valerie watched him stroll down the hall. She shook her head. Why did she have to have a soft spot for Owen of all people? She feared getting into a tangled web she might not be able to get out of. At least not with her heart intact. She hadn't noticed another man after meeting Owen, and the issue only became worse when she found out he was available. If she seriously considered his crazy idea for the weekend, she had to control her feelings for him. Those same feelings that had gotten her in trouble last time. Maybe spending more personal time outside of the hospital would help her squash those emotions from her mind and heart.

Valerie huffed. At forty-two, she was too old for all this nonsense, but she was going to play along for him. Picking up the tech pad, she headed toward her first patient's room.

Later that afternoon she went in search of Owen. She found him in the small room that was his office. She tapped on the door. At the sound of his voice, she entered. She closed the door behind her and took the only empty chair in the tiny space. "All right, tell me what's expected of me on this wedding weekend."

A look of surprise came over Owen's face as if he'd been taken off guard by her arrival. He recovered well, leaning causally back in his desk chair. Crossing his arms across his chest, he said, "We'll drive up to Blue Ridge. I mentioned that the wedding is at a resort. My brother and sister-in-law have rented a lodge and cabins there."

"Is everyone staying together?"

"Yes and no. It's a large resort. The cabins are on the property. All the events, I guess, take place at the lodge, but we would be staying in a cabin."

"Your children will be staying in the cabin with us?"

He shook his head. Thank goodness that wasn't going to happen. "No, my children are in the wedding and will be staying in the lodge with the wedding party."

Relief washed over her. Maybe it would be easier to get though a weekend with Owen if his children weren't watching over them all the time.

"We'll have separate sleeping arrangements," he quickly added. "I want you to feel as comfortable as possible."

"While we mislead your family." Valerie hated lying. She'd lived a lie and nothing but hurt had come out of it.

Owen winced. "It sounds dishonest when put like that." His look met hers. "I just want them to be happy. To live their own lives. Stop worrying about me."

"Have you considered talking to them?"

"I have. Sort of, but my daughter is determined. She and her brothers in the cause. They aren't listening."

"Then I guess we need to prove to them that you're a happy, well-adjusted man who's out on the prowl again."

He scowled. "I wouldn't exactly put it that way."

She smiled at his discomfort. "Okay, maybe that was overdescribing it some. I still think we need to get to know more about each other. I don't know that much about you outside of the hospital. I'm afraid they'll ask questions I can't answer. I also think I should be able to recognize them. Wouldn't they think it strange that I haven't seen a picture of them?"

"I have some pictures on my phone." Owen dug into his pocket. He scrolled through trying to find ones that might show his kids. "All of these are so old. I can't believe I don't have more recent ones. What you need to do is come to the house. I have some that were taken the last time we were all together."

"I'd like to see them. Also, where you live. If we were in a real relationship, I think I'd have been to your house."

"Then let's make it happen."

At the ring of the doorbell, Owen hurried to the front door with relief. The catering service had delivered the meal on time. The young man handed him a large box, and Owen gave him a tip before sending him on his way. He expected Valerie to arrive any moment. If anything, she was punctual.

He had gone out on a limb, an emotionally shaky one, when he had invited her to his house. Looking around his kitchen, he felt a prick of dishonesty slither through him. This had been Elaine's domain. Everything about the space captured Elaine's personality: from the pale green walls to the butcher block island that she'd insisted they needed, to the white table and bank of windows along the back of the space. Even the knickknacks she'd placed on the top shelf of the cabinets watched over the room with the black-and-white-tile floors. He hadn't added a new utensil since her death. It was all there waiting for her to return, despite him knowing she never would.

And he had invited another woman into Elaine's world. What had he been thinking? Valerie was a friend, a trusted one. He liked her. She wanted to know about him and his family. What better way than for her to see where he lived, and his children grew up. He could get through this.

He pulled containers out of the box, placing them in the oven to warm. He just managed to throw the delivery box out in the carport when the front doorbell rang. Quickly wiping his hands on a towel, he hurried through the house. He opened the door. Valerie stood on the stoop studying his house.

Her hair hung loose around her shoulders. He enjoyed the sight as much tonight as he had the other time. He resisted touching it. Was it as soft as it appeared? She wore a simple shirt that flowed around her. Slim jeans covered her shapely legs, and black flat shoes were on her feet. She looked casual, comfortable, completely at ease with her world.

Owen hesitated a moment, staring. Had he bitten off more than he could chew by inviting her to his home? He wanted her to know more about him so they would be able to carry off their weekend together, but this could be going too far.

"Are you going to invite me in?" she asked sweetly, her tone revealing a note of humor.

"Oh, yeah, yeah, yeah." He opened the door wider and stepped back.

"You have a nice home, Owen. Just what I thought you'd live in." She smiled and came into the hall leading to the back of the house.

Owen wasn't sure if her statement was intended as praise or not.

"Sorry I'm late. They had a drug count just as I was

headed out the door. Something about the counts lately have been off."

The stealing of drugs was deplorable. He had no use for people who did that. "Great. That means we'll be under scrutiny for a while. We'll have to count and recount."

"I never have understood going into medicine with all those years of study to throw it away on taking or stealing drugs."

"I agree. Come this way. We are going to eat in the kitchen if that's okay?" He started down the hallway again. "I hope they find who it is quick."

He watched Valerie as she looked around, studying everything. He was in no doubt she didn't miss a detail. He wasn't sure he liked being so closely scrutinized. What could she be learning about him that he didn't want her to know? Owen shook his head. Did it really matter? Was there anything? After all, they were friends.

"Wow, what a nice kitchen." Valerie walked round the space, her fingers drifting along the butcher block. "I love all the windows. The afternoon light makes it look so warm and homey. My condo doesn't allow for such natural light."

Owen didn't miss the note of wistfulness in her voice. He had never thought about it. It had been what Elaine wanted, and he'd seen to it she got it.

"I'm glad we're eating here instead of some stuffy room." She looked at him, eyes wide with distress. "I'm sorry. I shouldn't have said that. I'm sure none of the rooms in this house are stuffy."

He chuckled. Something he found he did more around her than he did others. "I'm glad to hear it. Our formal dining room is rather stuffy. If it weren't for the cleaning lady, the dust would never be removed in there. It's rarely used. The only time it's put to use is on holidays or when the kids come home. I spend most of my time in here and in my den."

"I see why."

"Actually, this house is too big for just me, but I like having a place for the children to come home to."

"Wouldn't they do that wherever you are?" she asked casually, but the words held weight.

Why did she keep asking hard questions? Why did he feel the need to justify himself? "Yeah, but this is familiar. Where they grew up. Why don't you have a seat?" He directed her toward the table he'd already set for two. "The food is already warming in the oven."

She turned toward the stove. "Is there something I can do to help?"

"Nope. I've got everything under control. All I have to do is pull it out and set it on the table." Soon, he had everything arranged. "I'm not much of a cook, so I thought I'd just have it catered."

"I love to cook. Especially baking. I'd really make use of this kitchen."

"That's right. You bring all that delicious bread to the hospital. I had no idea you baked it yourself." He already learned something new about her. It was sad he'd never ask before if she baked it.

"I do."

"You're welcome to use it anytime." Owen heart fluttered. What had he been thinking? It wasn't like he was known for blurting things. The words just seemed to pop out. Valerie baking bread in his kitchen, Elaine's kitchen, was too personal.

Her brows rose in anticipation. "Do you mean it?"

He swallowed hard. "Sure. On your next day off you're welcome to it. Remind me and I'll give you the key."

Valerie shook her head. "I'd never come when you weren't here."

He'd rather she did. This idea of getting together for a weekend had become more complicated. "For tonight let's just enjoy what I've got here." Owen pulled the aluminum cover from the chicken casserole, green beans and corn. He set a plate with rolls on the table.

"This looks great." Valerie acted more relaxed in his home than he felt at the moment.

"I did manage to put something together on my own for dessert."

She leaned in to smell the food. "I'm intrigued."

Owen paused with a spoon in the air above the casserole container. "You must finish all of your supper before you can have dessert."

She laughed. "Then serve it up, please."

The sound of her humor rippled through him, filling his chest with a warmth he never expected to feel again.

"Remember my sweet tooth." She held her plate out for him to serve.

He chuckled. It felt good. "How can I forget?"

They had been eating for a few minutes when Valerie asked, "What's your favorite color?"

Owen swallowed and put down his fork. "That question came out of the blue."

She shrugged. "That's something people who are seeing each other know."

"Really? I never thought about it."

"So, what's your favorite color?" Valerie pinned him with a look as if demanding an answer.

He thought a moment. "Blue."

"I like yellow."

Owen wasn't surprised. "That figures. You're a sunny type of person."

She smiled. "Thanks. That's a nice compliment. Now you ask me something."

He looked at her. Really looked. Her face was flush from the heat of the kitchen. Her eyes had a twinkle in them along with curiosity. The lines at the corners of her eyes came from more laughter than age. Were her lips as soft as they looked? Owen shook his head clearing that thought. He'd envisioned a business meeting between friends, and this had turned into something else. Did he really want to know all this personal stuff? He had to direct the subject to more even ground. "I need to think. I want to ask the right one."

She gave him an odd look but returned to her meal.

"Mark Lewis is really doing a good job. He's the most devoted young doctor we've had in a long time."

She picked up a roll and set it on her plate. "It seems that way. He has certainly stepped in when I have needed him."

"For me as well. He should make a great doctor if he keeps this up." Owen focused on his meal.

"He should." She gave him a direct look. "You do know your children won't quiz us about Mark."

How like her to call him on the carpet. "I know, but I find it more comfortable than talking about me."

She placed her hand over his for a moment. "You don't have to go through with this wild idea of yours. My feelings aren't so fragile that I can't accept you changing your mind. Just tell them how you feel. That they need to live their lives and you'll live yours."

"I've tried and there isn't any stopping Kaitlyn. She's got my stubborn streak. I promise I'll get with the program."

"So where were we with the questions? What's your spirit animal?"

His brows rose. "What? Is that some modern age guru question?"

She laughed. "It did get you out of that sad look. After all, if you know my favorite color then I should know your spirit animal."

"Okay. That's fair. Mine would be a tiger."

"That figures." She sounded disappointed.

"What's yours?" He became determined to know.

She proudly stretched her neck. "A giraffe."

He threw his head back and laughed. Something he hadn't done in too long. "Really? I wouldn't have guessed that. Why?"

"I love the majesty of their long necks, sweet humor and the fact they look so graceful running. What's your favorite pet?"

"I'm a dog guy." This was fun.

Valerie looked around. "I haven't seen one."

"I don't have one right now. In fact, I've been thinking about getting one, but I'm not sure I want to go through all that house training, and I work long hours." That was true, but there was more to it than that. Mostly the busier he was the less time he had to think about the loss of his Elaine. Being in their house alone had no appeal.

"You do know you can adopt an older dog and work fewer hours. I know you work far more overtime than necessary."

Owen did. His problem was he didn't want to become attached. To love a dog and lose it. To have his heart torn out again. That was a chance he refused to take. "Why don't we go to the living room for coffee and dessert? My children's pictures are in there."

"Let me help you with the dishes and putting away the food." Valerie scooted her chair back.

"You're a guest but I'm going to agree. Domestic stuff, I have found, isn't my thing. I'll do the food if you'll handle the dishes." He swallowed. The dishes he and Elaine had received as wedding presents.

Over the next few minutes, they worked together to put everything away. He marveled at how smoothly they accomplished the tasks. They worked well in and out of the OR. Owen served brownies and brewed the coffee.

Valerie found herself watching Owen. He was a handsome man. Tall, slim except for a little extra weight around the middle, which did nothing to detract from his appeal. The gray in his hair only made him look more distinguished. When he finally loosened up over dinner, he had been charming. Instead of liking him less, she found she really enjoyed his company. It was a shame he was still so hung up on his wife.

He led her to the living room, placing the plate on the coffee table. She handed him one of the two mugs she carried.

Valerie studied the formal area with the light blue floral sofa. The two matching armchairs and oak tables only added to the unlived in feel. Family pictures lined the mantel. She placed her mug down and picked up a vase on the table next to the chair. After admiring it she returned it to the same spot.

Owen adjusted it an inch. Valerie watched him. Their

looks met. She attention fell to the vase once more. "I'm guessing you haven't changed much since your wife died."

He looked away from her and mumbled, "Not really."

"She had excellent taste."

That seemed to ease his trepidation. "I can't take any credit for it. My wife was the decorator. It's all I've ever known."

Valerie walked to the other side of the room. "So, tell me all about these handsome people." She pointed to the three portraits in a line along one of the living room walls.

"The girl is Kaitlyn. The oldest and ringleader in the need to set me up. The next is Richard, but we call him Rich. He's my namesake. Owen Richard Jr. The last is John."

Valerie studied the portraits then turned to him. "Kaitlyn's been married…a little over a year. If I remember right."

"Yep. You have a good memory."

He had been anxious and out of sorts in the days leading up to it. Valerie had worried about him going through such a happy time without his wife. "Must've been difficult for you to handle a wedding without Elaine."

Valerie didn't miss the pain that washed over his face. "I'm not sure how I got through it. It was hard but a good day. It was not only hard on me, but it was hard on the children as well."

Valerie placed her hand on his arm. Her heart went out to him. "That's understandable. You said Rich was thinking about med school." She needed to get them back to a positive note. "What will his degree be in?"

"In chemistry. Like me."

She grinned. "Apparently the apple doesn't fall far from the tree."

"Yeah, we have more in common than our name. It often made us butt heads. Still does. Then there is John who wants to please everyone. He isn't sure what he wants to do. He thinks he wants to go into the business world." Owen shrugged. "Who knows?"

"They sound like wonderful and interesting people."

"Thank you. I'm proud of them. I just wish they didn't worry about me as much as they do. They have enough to focus on without worrying about their dad."

"Yeah, but I consider that a major sign of their love and your closeness with them." Owen somehow brought that out in her as well.

"We do have that. Thanks for pointing it out."

She took the seat at the end of the couch. He chose the overstuffed chair across from her. "My turn. It's time for me to learn something more about you."

"What would you like to know?" Valerie wasn't sure she wanted to share everything with Owen. But he deserved answers to his questions just as she did to hers. She leaned back on the couch and placed her hands in her lap.

"I don't know. How about why aren't you married?"

Easy one. Maybe he wouldn't dig any deeper. "Let's just say it's never worked out."

A winkle formed across his forehead. "No children either?"

"No." The faster she said it the easier it was to answer. Her chances had narrowed significantly.

Owen shook his head. "I don't understand why not. You're an attractive person, self-confident and have much to offer in a relationship."

That was nice to hear coming from Owen. "I could say the same about you."

"I've been married." He looked away.

She said the words quietly. "Yeah, but you haven't even been out on a date in the last five years."

Owen shifted and looked directly at her as if to put her on the defensive. "How do you know?"

Valerie shrugged. "You told me. Remember? It's been twenty-eight years since you've been on a date. Besides, the hospital grapevine is very efficient, especially where single doctors are concerned."

His face tightened. From his reaction the other day, he didn't like being talked about. "If I'd said anything."

She gave him a half smile. "Things like that get out."

"I guess you're right. But now I can say that I have been out on a date. This is the second time we've had dinner."

"I thought this was a friendly meal. Not a date." She grinned.

He had the good grace to redden. "I guess I have gotten set in my ways."

"Will you tell me about your wife?" Valerie asked softly.

He said nothing for a while. She wasn't sure he would answer her.

"Elaine was the perfect wife. We met in college. She worked to support me through school. Before I finished, we were expecting Kaitlyn. It was a struggle, but we managed. Elaine took everything as a challenge. Sometimes I wasn't sure we'd get the bills paid but somehow, she made it all work."

"She must have been a wonderful woman."

Owen continued as if she had said nothing. "She was from a small town in South Georgia and I from one in North Georgia. We met in the middle—Atlanta—at college. We planned to build this house about ten years into our marriage. It was the dream home where we were supposed to retire." He shook his head as if trying to remove the sad memories. "Then she got sick. Soon after, she was gone."

"Elaine sounds like somebody I would've liked and admired." She placed her hand over his.

He looked at her hand a moment. "Thanks, Valerie. I think she would've liked you too. Your enthusiasm over the kitchen alone would have been your common ground."

Valerie moved to the front of the chair. "I'd love to see more of your family pictures."

A phone rang in the distance.

"I need to get that. It might be the hospital or one of the kids."

Or a perfect way to get away for a moment to gather his thoughts and calm his nerves. She watched him leave the room. Had her presence and questions been too much for him?

CHAPTER FOUR

VALERIE WAITED TEN MINUTES, then went in search of Owen. She picked up the low rumble of his voice coming down a short hallway off the main one. Following that sound, she wandered in its direction. He'd said he had a den. She bet he'd gone there to talk on the phone. The more she was around Owen, the more curious she'd became about him.

She located him in a dark paneled room. A large wooden desk sat in the center of the space with a row of windows at the back. Owen stood looking out of them. To his left was a wall of shelves filled with books and pictures, including what looked like small family memorabilia. In the center was a large TV. On the other wall sat a leather sofa and a table along with a straight wooden chair that didn't encourage anyone to visit very long. This space was obviously where Owen felt most at home.

Owen turned when she stopped in the doorway. He pulled a face, giving her an apologetic look. *It's okay*, she mouthed as he returned to reassuring whoever was on the other end of the phone.

She went to the shelves, picking up a framed picture. Owen's family stood in the traditional stance for a young family. He held the smallest of the children. His wife stood beside him with her hands on the shoulders of the two other children. They each wore smiles that didn't reach their eyes. Valerie smiled.

"That was Easter over twenty years ago," Owen said from beside her so close she could make out the citrus scent of his aftershave. "Sorry about that call. My sister-in-law was filling me in on all the wedding weekend activities. She's so wound up about them I didn't have the heart to cut her off before I did."

"You're a nice guy, Owen."

He chuckled. "No, it's more like I live in fear of her. She runs her show."

"Sounds like an interesting person."

"She can be a force to be reckoned with." He took the picture from her and placed it back on the shelf.

Valerie had been afraid she done something wrong by touching his picture until he picked up another frame and handed it to her. "Here we were on vacation. It's a much happier group. This is one of my favorite pictures."

"You all look so…perfect family."

He chuckled.

It rolled through Valerie like a warm drink on a cold day, making her shiver. Owen sounded happy.

"Not exactly perfect but a family. Elaine had a way of holding us together."

Valerie studied the tall, willowy woman with blond hair. The direct opposite of her. "I can tell she enjoyed life."

He took the frame again, looking at it. "That she did."

"You still miss her." That was an understatement, but Valerie felt she needed to say something. What would it be like to have someone love her like that? Stand by her, love her so much he would not hesitate for others to know.

To be the center of his world? Sadly, she was jealous of a dead woman.

Owen's look went off into the distance. "Every minute of every day."

He sounded so sad she wrapped her arms around his neck and hugged him. After a moment's hesitation, he returned the hug. How long had it been since someone other than his family had given him a hug?

Owen pulled away but didn't let go. His gaze met hers, held. A flicker of uncertainty went through his eyes before his head lowered. His lips were gentle on hers, as if testing their texture. Her heart held a beat waiting to see if he would continue or back away.

His mouth pressed closer as his hands tightened at her waist. He tasted of coffee and the sweetness of their dessert, which was almost as pleasurable as the kiss. Her hand clutched his waist and she leaned into him wanting more. Owen was a good kisser; the experience was living up to her dreams.

The sound of footsteps registered seconds before Owen pushed her to arm's length as if she were suddenly a bad disease he was afraid to get. His hands came to her shoulders, steadying her before they dropped away.

"Hey, Dad. I'm home." A young man's voice carried into the room.

She looked at Owen. He appeared flustered as he stumbled back.

"I shouldn't have done that," he said so softly she almost missed it, but she hadn't.

The hurt of years built up, flooded Valerie. Her lips tightened. She'd dared, for a moment, believe someone wanted her. That a man would be proud she belonged to him. Owen's words were a slap in the face. The indignity and disappointment of years ago washed over her.

"Whose car is in the drive?" Moments later a tall, youthfully thin male pulled up short just inside the door of Owen's den. His eyes went wide as he looked between her and Owen.

A coolness Valerie could attribute to Owen moving farther away from her grew between them. Those old hurts began to bubble. Now many times had her ex pushed her aside? Refused to admit she existed except when he needed her?

"John. I wasn't expecting you."

Owen's son continued to watch them, curiosity making his face almost comical.

Owen gestured toward her. "John, this is Dr. Valerie Hughes. We work together at the hospital."

"Hello, Dr. Hughes." Owen's son continued to watch her with curiosity.

Valerie forced a smile. "Hi, John. It's nice to meet you."

An awkward silent settled around the room.

"I should be going." Valerie stepped toward the door. She needed to leave before her distress showed. The last thing she wanted to learn was that Owen would treat her just as her ex had.

"I'll walk you out." Owen made a stiff movement toward the door.

As she passed John she said, "Good night, John. It was nice to meet you."

Valerie didn't slow down on her way to the front door except to pick up her purse. She said nothing and neither did Owen as he followed her.

As she circled the back of her car he said, "He didn't tell me he was coming home. I'm sorry if you were uncomfortable."

"I think you were far more uncomfortable. You had nothing to be ashamed of. We were just two adults looking at pictures in your den." She wanted to stand by Owen, but he needed to let go of the past and look to the future. Even if they were a pretend couple, she wanted him to respect her and be proud of her. Was that so much to ask?

"Yeah, but he's never seen any other woman in my den but his mother."

She offered him a wry smile. "He seemed to be handling it well. Maybe you're the one who needs to get used to the idea."

Owen got into the hospital early Monday morning. He wanted to speak with Valerie before their day got started.

Could Friday night have gone worse? She hadn't been happy when she left. He couldn't blame her. He had kissed her then acted like he was embarrassed and ashamed of her when John showed up.

John had almost caught them. Owen had acted like he was a teenager doing something wrong. Except he was an adult in his own home. There was no reason for him to have acted the way he had or for him to make Valerie believe he regretted kissing her. On the contrary, he enjoyed kissing her. Too much.

Afterward he hadn't been able to look her in the eyes. Shame filled him. And what he said to her. He hung his head. Could a grown man be more insensitive? When their gazes had met, it had been clearly visible she'd been hurt.

She was due an apology. He had asked her to do him a huge favor then insulted her.

What had he been thinking? That's the problem: he hadn't. Instead, he'd been feeling. It felt too good to have a woman in his arms again. To kiss her. To have her kiss him in return. He wasn't sure he would have stopped if John hadn't interrupted them.

He just hoped she would listen to his apology. After the fiasco of Friday night, he anticipated she'd change her mind about attending the wedding. Maybe reconsidered their friendship. That kiss certainly had shifted the relationship. Suddenly it had become more important than ever that she go with him. He wanted Valerie beside him at the wedding. Still, he wouldn't blame her if she refused.

Her reaction to him backing away had been just as over the top. What had the other men in her life done to her? He would find out. If nothing else, he wanted her to feel safe with him. He wasn't sure why it mattered so much but it did.

He pushed through the swinging door of the OR suite, walking down the hall in the direction of their offices. He planned to straighten this out now. He slowed at the department desk and spoke to the clerk. "Good morning, Melissa."

"Dr. Clifton." She handed him the device that held the information on his patients for the day.

"Have you seen Dr. Hughes?"

"She's already in OR three preparing her first patient."

"Thanks." He logged into the device. Giving the list of his patients a quick review, he then hurried down the hall.

He didn't plan to interrupt a procedure, but if Valerie hadn't started yet he would have a word with her. After scrubbing and gowning up, he stepped into the operating room. Valerie was there, but the patient had not arrived. She stood with her back to the door, organizing the tubing.

"Valerie, could I speak to you for a moment outside?"

She looked over her shoulder. "Can it wait? I'm expecting the patient any moment."

"I'd really like to talk to you now." Owen hadn't noticed Mark Lewis across the room until he spoke up. "Dr. Hughes, I'll be glad to get things going."

Valerie hesitated a moment, and Owen feared she would turn him down. Then she looked at Mark. "You don't mind?"

"Not at all." The man's voice was cheerful behind his mask.

"Thanks. I appreciate that." She went out the door.

Thankfully there was no one in the scrubbing area. They could talk in private.

"Owen, this really isn't a good time."

He agreed, but he had to get this off his chest. "I'm sorry about what happened Friday night. I should've handled it better. You were hurt and I didn't want that. I'm sorry."

"You said that Friday night. I recognize rejection. I've seen it before, and I promised myself I wouldn't put myself in that position again."

Owen stepped back. Whoa, he hadn't expected that. "What brought that on?"

Her look turned contrite, as if she'd said more than she had intended. "It's nothing."

"That didn't sound like nothing to me. Where did you get that idea? I haven't rejected you. I still want you to go with me to the wedding."

"Are you going to treat me like I have the plague there

as well? You kissed me for a reason. I'd like to think it's because you like me. But I don't think you've moved past your wife far enough to be having dinner with a woman much less planning to spend a weekend with her. We wouldn't fool anyone into believing we're seeing each other. You just need to talk to your children and leave me out of your madness."

"I would call it off, but John called Kaitlyn and Rich. They know about you now. I'm sure my brother and sister-in-law do as well. I'm too deep in to call it off."

"And you still want me to spend a whole weekend surrounded by your family as a couple and you can't bring yourself to touch me without feeling guilty?" She shook her head, disbelief in each movement.

"I can do better. I will do better. I promise not to hurt you again. I've put you in a bad position. I get that. Please give me another chance."

Her look bore into him. "What happened Friday night won't happen again?"

"The kiss or the denial?"

"Denial."

"I promise." He held up his hand. Would she turn down his kisses?

Her sigh came out heavy. "Then we'll give it another try. You have to loosen up though."

"I'll try. You have my word."

She made an impolite noise in her throat. "Think again. If we're going to make them believe us, then you'll have to learn to touch me. Hold my hand. Even kiss me."

Something he feared he might enjoy too much.

A staff member entered the scrub area, giving them both a curious look.

"I have a patient waiting. We'll talk about it later." Valerie left him with a determined glint in her eyes before returning to the OR.

Relief washed through Owen as he watched her go. At first, he believed he want to convince her to keep their plans for the wedding weekend to save him from his children. Now he realized he wanted the chance to spend more time with her. The chance to kiss her again. To see if he felt as alive the second time as he had the first. He smiled at the staff member as he went out the door.

Valerie had had to remind herself to focus over the last few days. Her thoughts kept returning to Owen's kiss. It was as sweet and perfect as she had imagined. Until his son had come home. For those few minutes, Owen was Owen. Not a father, a widower, a doctor, but a man who was enjoying kissing her. The moment had been perfect. So much so that it had cut like a scalpel when he had acted as if she weren't important.

She had experienced enough rejection to last a lifetime. She had hoped Owen would be different. Quickly she learned not to expect more from him. She shouldn't have let his reactions affect her so, but she hadn't expected him to rebuff her so bluntly. That part of his personality he covered well. If she was to be his plus one at the wedding, he would have to do better than he had the other night. She hadn't realized Owen's grief went so deep. She had agreed to spend the weekend with him only because she felt sorry for the position his children had put him in.

Thankfully she hadn't seen him in the last couple of days. She'd needed the break to regroup. They'd had full caseloads and were coming and going into operating rooms at different times. She only knew when he was in the department because his name appeared on the OR schedule board near the department desk. For some reason she couldn't resist looking when she came into work.

She looked down the hallway. Owen stood beside the department desk talking to two of the young staff nurses. Their smiles were those of hero worship, just a tad too bright. Then there were the giggles as they left him, his attention immediately returning to the iPad in his hands. Valerie shook her head. He had no idea how he charmed woman. He had that personality that attracted women without him even trying. She had been pulled into that net and gotten caught too.

On Wednesday, the anesthesiology department head, Dr. Dale Rhinehart, stopped her in the hall between cases. "Valerie, you're going to be needed in surgery tomorrow to help Owen. We have an abdominal aortic aneurism. I've cleared your schedule so you can help. You and Owen work well together. Get with him. The boy has been his patient since infancy. Owen can bring you up to date."

"Okay." Had Owen asked for her to assist? It was a rare thing for two anesthesiologists to be needed for a case. Interestingly, the first case had occurred so close to this one. One thing about medicine was she never knew what would happen from one day to the next.

Dr. Rhinehart continued, "You both will have earned that long weekend you have coming up."

Had Owen told him that they were going away together? No, he wouldn't have done that. He didn't want people at work to know they were seeing each other, even if it was pretend. Just as her ex had been pretending. Except Owen didn't want the gossip whereas her ex didn't want his wife to find out he was cheating. The idea still made her sick.

"Speaking of which, there's Owen. I'll leave you two to discuss the case." Dale turned toward his office.

Generally Owen offered those around him a ready smile, but today a serious look covered his face. The lift of a corner of his mouth didn't reach his eyes. A heaviness of concern filled them instead. This Owen tugged at her heart. "I understand we're going to be in the OR again together."

"Yes, difficult case ahead." He slowed so she could match his steps.

"You're familiar with this patient?"

"Very. I've put him to sleep a number of times in his life. He grew up in this hospital. I'm just on my way to talk to him and his parents. Would you like to come along?"

"Sure. Give me a minute to do some dictation, and I'll be ready."

"Okay, I'll be in my office."

Fifteen minutes later Valerie entered Owen's office to find him studying the tech pad. She settled into the chair in the corner of the small room made tinier by Owen's presence.

He turned off the device and locked it away in his desk.

She studied him a moment. The lines around his mouth were deeper, and his eyes didn't have their usual spark. "Are you okay?"

"Yeah. Just tired. I was reviewing Rob's case."

"Rob?"

"Yes, the boy that we're going to take care of tomorrow." He pushed back from the desk.

This was the Owen she really liked. The one with the

caring heart. "You must know him really well to call him by his first name."

"I do. He's a good kid and has a great family. He's been coming here since he was a baby."

"Tell me about him." She had the sense Owen needed to talk.

"His name is Rob Martin, and he's fourteen years old. He was born with hyperplastic left heart syndrome."

Her mouth pursed. "That's a tough one."

"Yeah. He's done great, but it's taken time and fortitude. It also took three surgeries and a transplant before he was two to get there."

Valerie didn't say anything, waiting on him to get it all out.

"For years I put him to sleep every six months for his heart biopsies." He smiled. "Even once to fix a broken arm. I've gotten to know all the family well. Five months ago, Rob started having difficulty, but we couldn't figure out want the problem was. The blood work didn't even show the problem. It turns out it was endocarditis, and it's manifested itself at the point of his original surgery. The infection settled in his, aorta which as you know is the weakest part of his body. He's a tough one. And now he has this aneurysm on his aorta."

The pain in Owen's voice made Valerie want to go to him but instead she gripped the arms of the chair.

"He's been in the hospital for the last three weeks with a PICC line and antibiotics going in him. The endocarditis made his aorta blow up like a balloon. It's a wonder it hasn't burst."

"He's been on bed rest this entire time?"

"Yes." Emotion vibrated around the single word. "All

patients matter, but this one is special." Owen ran a hand through his hair making the waves more pronounced. "I know we aren't supposed to get personally involved with a patient, but there are just certain ones who come along that get to you. You can't help yourself."

She never experienced that, but she could understand. In an odd way she felt like that was what he'd done with her. Owen had gotten under her skin. "Between us and Dr. Dillard, Rob will be in good hands. We'll see to it. He's the right surgeon for the case."

"I believe so too but it'll be tough. Long hours."

"Still, I'm confident we'll take good care of him." He needed the encouragement.

"That's the plan. I'm glad you were assigned to the case. We've proven we work well together."

Valerie stood. "Why don't you introduce me to Rob?"

Owen squared his shoulders then stood. "Okay."

She followed him out of the office. Walking beside him, they made their way to the elevators. Neither said anything as they entered one.

Owen glanced at her. "I haven't seen much of you lately. How have you been?"

"Fine. Just busy here. I've also been looking for dresses to wear to the wedding."

"I didn't even think about you doing that. Please let me pay for it. After all, you're doing me a favor."

She glared at him. "I will not."

Owen rolled his shoulders and took a deep breath. They had been in the OR for five hours already, and there were many more to come. Rob had been holding his own as the surgeon worked. Replacing an infected aorta took patience and a steady hand, both of which Dr. Dillard had. The operation had been as brutal as Owen had feared.

He looked at Valerie. She had been in her position as long as he had. He massaged the back of Rob's head, moving down to his shoulders and slowly under his back to his shoulder blades, going as low as he could along the boy's back.

When Valerie looked at him, he asked, "How's it going over there?"

She nodded. "Steady."

Mark, along with a few others, had come in to observe. "If you need a break, I'll be glad to fill in."

Dr. Dillard said, as he placed the tubing for the bypass machine, "If you guys want a break, this would be a good time. After we are on bypass, things will get intense." He turned his attention back to placing the tubing.

Owen looked at Valerie. Their eyes met above their masks. "You go first. Let Mark sit in for you."

Mark moved toward Valerie.

She checked the monitors then stood and stretched her back. As Mark sat on the stool Valerie had vacated, she said, "Thanks."

The operation ground on as Dr. Dillard worked in the open chest of the boy.

Owen continued to massage Rob's neck and shoulders, keeping constant watch on the monitors making sure Rob remained stable. This was a difficult surgery at best, but when the patient had been sick for months it became more difficult.

When he'd discussed the case with Dr. Dillard, he'd believed Rob had a good chance for survival. Owen hoped it would be the case. Dr. Dillard was a good surgeon, but the odds could so easily tip in the other direction.

Valerie had been very kind to Rob and his family earlier. And she'd been just as kind to him. It had been nice to have someone he could trust to talk to. Rarely did he let his feelings about his work show. Valerie had been there for him to unload on. His nerves had been on edge until she settled him.

The hours ground on. He and Valerie changed positions every couple of hours.

She remained alert, but he could tell by the slump of her shoulders that the long, tedious hours were wearing on her. Next weekend he would gift her with some time at a spa. She would have earned it.

Finally Dr. Dillard announced with satisfaction, "Well done everyone. Let's close him up and keep a close eye on him."

There was a sense of rejuvenation going through the room at the idea that they had saved a life.

Valerie stood then twisted one way then the other.

Owen glanced over. Even in the nondescript OR scrubs he could make out her feminine curves. Valerie sure had what it took to attract a man. He blinked. Where had that thought come from? Up until a couple of weeks ago he'd only thought of her as a friend, never a woman he wanted to kiss. Now he was too aware she was a woman. It had been a long time since an unrelated female had been his concern, but Valerie had moved into that position.

He spoke to her. "You go on home. I'll see Rob settled in the CICU."

"No, I'll walk with you."

Owen wasn't surprised she'd turned his offer down. In fact, he found it admirable she wanted to see the case through.

A CICU nurse was there to receive Rob. She immediately went to work overseeing the bank of pumps sending medicines into the youth's body.

Satisfied with Rob's care and pain level, Owen turned to Valerie. "I'm going to speak to his parents."

She moved toward the door. "Do you mind if I go with you?"

He appreciated the support. "Thanks. That would be nice."

They walked quietly through the dim nighttime hallways to the surgical waiting room where Rob's parents were waiting to visit their son.

Both adults stood as he and Valerie entered through the glass doors. They looked as exhausted as he felt. It had been a long tense day.

"Dr. Clifton, is there a problem?" Rob's mother asked as she hurried toward them.

He held up a hand. "Rob is fine. Dr. Hughes and I just left him. His nurse is getting him settled, and you'll get to see him very soon."

"Thank goodness." The mother visibly relaxed.

Owen placed a hand briefly on her shoulder. "Dr. Dillard did a great job. I'm sure he's already been by to see you."

"He has," Rob's father said.

"Rob did as well as expected. I know you remember from the past that the first twenty-four hours are important, then getting out of ICU." He looked from mother to father.

The mother nodded. "We know only too well."

Owen gave her an encouraging smile.

Valerie stepped up beside Owen. "Rob did great. There's no reason to think he won't continue to do so."

"Dr. Hughes is right. During the night, don't hesitate to

call me if you're worried." Owen looked from one parent to the other. "I mean that."

"Thank you, Dr. Clifton. Dr. Hughes." Rob's mother hugged him. She hesitated a moment, then wrapped her arms around Valerie. Valerie returned the hug.

"I'll see you tomorrow. Get some rest." Owen started toward the door with Valerie at his side.

As they returned to the OR Valerie said, "You were great with them."

"That's not hard. They're a great family. You were good with them too. Rob's mother needed your care."

"You're right. They aren't hard to care about." Valerie yawned.

"You're worn out."

Their gazes met. "No more than you must be."

"What I really am is hungry. I'd love breakfast. How about joining me at an all-night diner."

"I know something better. Why don't you come to my place, and I'll fix us some breakfast?"

He lowered his chin and studied her in amazement. "You want to cook after the day and night we've had?"

"It's just breakfast. I'll make it short and simple so we both can get to bed." Her face went beet red. "I didn't mean—"

He chuckled dryly. "I know what you meant. I'm too hungry and the diner too far away for me to turn down the offer."

"Good. I'll see you in a few minutes at my place."

Valerie wasn't sure what had made her suggest she fix a meal. It just seemed like the natural thing to do. She was too exhausted to go out to a diner. She needed to eat, and

Owen did too. It was easier and faster for her just to prepare them breakfast at her place.

Valerie gathered the eggs and bacon from the refrigerator and got the bacon started. When she let Owen in
the door he asked where the bathroom was; he wanted to
wash up before eating. She pointed him in the direction of
the hall. "Make yourself at home. The towels are fresh."

She smiled to herself. His hair was in disarray, and she
could tell he'd just chucked his clothes on. He wasn't his
usual put-together self. He'd been in a hurry to get to her
place. Had he been afraid she'd change her mind about the
meal if he didn't get there right away?

For some reason he seemed to fit in her home. They
needed to know each other better, but for her they were
slipping over the edge into an emotional relationship. Could
he possibly feel the same? She shook her head. No. Owen
was still involved with his dead wife. How could she ever
compete with her? What Valerie did know was that at this
rate she would get hurt. She didn't intend to spend her life
being second to somebody she couldn't even compete with.

Owen returned to the kitchen with his hair combed and
shirt tucked in. He looked as attractive as ever. The only
thing that could attest to their long night was the deepen-
ing of the lines around his eyes.

"What a day." He sighed. "What can I do to help, despite my less than skillful kitchen abilities."

"Want to fix the coffee? Everything is over there by
the machine."

"Now, that I have experience with." He stepped around
her.

The galley kitchen felt tiny with them both in it. She
pulled a bowl out from under the cabinet, then pulled the

flour canister toward her, being careful not to poke him in the ribs with her elbow.

He glanced over her shoulder. "What're you doing?"

"I'm making biscuits."

"I haven't had scratch biscuits since my grandmother was alive." He smacked his lips. "I can hardly wait."

She giggled. And she didn't giggle. What was happening to her having Owen in her personal life? He stood close enough to look over her shoulder. She could feel his heat.

"The only biscuits I know how to make are bap biscuits."

"Bap biscuits?" She looked at him, her mouth only inches from his.

She watched his lips move as he said, "You know, the kind that you hit against the counter and they pop open."

She laughed.

He stepped back. "That's a nice sound this early in the morning. Or anytime for that matter."

"Thank you. That was a nice thing to say." Her heart made an extra thump. She turned back to cutting butter into the flour before adding milk. Using her hands, she worked the ingredients into a dough.

Owen continued to watch her with interest. Intently enough that he made her nervous. "This is fascinating. I didn't know anybody still made biscuits like this."

"I hope they turn out good." She floured the cutting board.

"I know at this point I could probably eat a rock."

"I hope that's the last thing these taste like. I'm going to roll this dough out. Why don't you cut them out and put them on the cookie sheet while I get the eggs started and tend to the bacon."

Owen stepped back. "Hey, I told you I wasn't any good in the kitchen."

"I think if you can put someone to sleep for surgery you can handle cutting dough and placing it on a pan. It'll be your chance to learn something new."

He released a resigned sigh. "When you put it like that, I guess I'll have to."

"I knew you were a team player." She gave him a light slap on the back. "The biscuit cutter is that round metal thing with a handle. I'll get the cookie sheet and line it with parchment paper."

Valerie's look drifted to Owen as she found another bowl and added eggs and milk to it. Owen was being precise as he cut and placed the biscuits on the baking sheet, much as he was with his patients. Was he the same when making love? If so, she bet he was a wonderful lover.

She placed the eggs into the hot skillet too quickly, making them sizzle. Jerking back so she didn't get burned, she pulled the pan off the burner and turned it down. She needed to get her attention back to what she was doing. Those types of thoughts weren't what she should be having. "I hope scrambled is all right with you."

"Sounds wonderful. The biscuits are ready to go in the oven."

Valerie slid the pan in. The loud ramble of Owen's stomach drew her attention.

He gave her a sheepish look. "Sorry about that. I'm starving."

"Give me five more minutes and I'll have you fed. How about handing me a couple of plates? They're in the cabinet above your head. The silverware is in the drawer next to you."

He did as she asked. She finished cooking the eggs and bacon and put two plates of them on the table in front of two bar stools. A basket with the biscuits went in front of them. Owen took a seat and she the other. Without discussion they both ate.

Valerie looked at Owen. It was nice to share a meal with someone in her home. Especially one who obviously enjoyed the food as much as Owen did. He was already on his third biscuit.

Between bites Owen lifted his biscuit. "These are really good."

"Thank you. I pride myself on making tasty ones." It felt particularly good to have him enjoy them.

He took another bite. "You can make these for me anytime."

"You just let me know when you'd like to have some, and I'll make it happen. They're not that difficult."

He made a sound of pleasure. "My only problem is that if I eat them all the time, I'd be as large as this room."

"I doubt that. You look trim enough to me." She looked him up and down.

"Life is too short not to enjoy things. I know that too well." Owen's voice turned sad.

Once again his wife had worked herself into a happy moment.

"I'll take care of the cleaning up since you did most of the cooking." He stood and picked up his plate.

Valerie needed to walk away before she said something she might regret. "Thanks. I'm going to take you up on that. It's past time for a shower."

With her shower completed and feeling like every step she took required effort, Valerie tightened her housecoat securely at her waist as she went to the living room to see if Owen had left.

She smiled. He lay on the sofa with his head on a cushion. One of his legs stretched across the length of the sofa while the other remained on the floor. As if half of him wanted to leave while the other wanted to stay. Despite that, he looked like he belonged there. Pulling the throw off the back of the sofa, she covered him with it. He'd earned his rest.

In her bedroom, she crawled between her sheets and drifted off to sleep to the sound of Owen's soft snores.

CHAPTER FIVE

THE VIVID BLUE of the sky and the beauty of the fall day made Valerie feel glad to be alive as they drove toward the mountains. The sunshine warmed her face through the passenger window as they traveled north.

"How much farther?" She shifted in the seat.

"A couple of hours," Owen said from behind the wheel. "Take a nap if you want."

She looked out at the trees that had turned golden, red and orange. It was beautiful. "I don't want to miss this amazing view."

"You'll get plenty of it before the weekend is over."

"I don't know if that's possible." She needed this getaway.

Owen glanced at her. "Have you ever been to Blue Ridge before?"

"Once, just after I moved to Georgia. But it was the middle of the summer. It was beautiful then, but it's amazing now."

"This is one of my favorite places in the world."

"I can understand why. Have you traveled much?" Valerie wanted to know all she could about him.

"We traveled as a family a lot before Elaine... We've done very little but get through the days since."

Valerie studied his profile. His strong jaw had tightened as he spoke. Sometimes he'd run a hand through his hair making it stick up. She itched to smooth it back into place. "Do you always judge your life by 'before Elaine' and 'after Elaine'?"

"I've never thought about it before, but yeah, I guess I do."

Valerie wanted to move away from the direction the conversation had turned. "Now that the kids are gone, do you want to travel more?"

"By myself?" The note of surprised impossibility filled his voice. He sounded appalled by the idea.

"You can travel on your own, you know!"

He shook his head. "I don't think that's for me."

"So your plan is to remain alone, by yourself, for the rest of your life and do nothing but work?" She asked the question in a teasing tone, but she meant every word. Someone needed to tell Owen it was time to move on, to live again. As a friend, it had fallen to her.

His mouth twisted as if she made him uncomfortable with her questions. "To be truthful, I hadn't thought about it."

"Maybe you should."

Owen stayed quiet. Had she said too much? It might have been the truth, but she didn't want their weekend to start off on the wrong foot. Especially since it was shaky to begin with.

At a gray stone entrance, Owen made a left turn. They drove along a tree-lined paved road that wound up a mountain, crossing over a brook twice. Dark green laurel grew low to the ground while the evergreens mingled with the bright colors of the trees that had changed color, creating a canopy over the road. The wind sent lost leaves dancing in front of them.

She gasped as the lodge came into sight. It was amazing. The two-story A-frame was built of natural wood, and the afternoon sun reflected off the smooth surfaces of glass panels. A separate wing stretched out from both sides of the main structure. In front was a manicured lawn with flower gardens bordered with stone. The look was rustic elegance in the woods. "Mercy, this place is beautiful. I could come stay here forever."

Owen chuckled. "I'd see how the weekend goes before you say something like that. You haven't felt the full force of my family yet."

"I'm sure it's going to be fine." He'd loosened a little. Right now he was doing a good job, but as they drove closer to the lodge she noticed him growing more anxious.

"I wouldn't be surprised if all three of my children are waiting for us at the door."

She watched him. "Oh, that's right! John let them know about meeting me the other night."

Owen's gaze met hers. "I'm sure they're all excited."

Valerie clasped her hands in her lap as her stomach churned. Her self-confidence had started to wane.

Owen took her hand, squeezing it. "Hey, there's no reason to be nervous. I'll run interference. Promise."

He pulled around the circular drive and stopped under the stacked stone portico. Large wooden double doors stood between them and the lies they would be telling.

"Owen, are you sure you want to do this? We'll be misleading all the people who love you the most. There's a real chance it won't end well."

"It'll be fine." Owen gave her an encouraging smile and

opened the driver's door. He came round the vehicle and helped her out as a valet unloaded their bags.

Her eyes widened when he offered her his hand. She slipped hers inside his larger one. This was the first time Owen had made an overt move toward her since their kiss. He was trying to keep his word to stand by her. Maybe they could pull this off after all.

As they approached the doors to the lodge, they opened. Stepping inside, Valerie realized that as glorious as the lodge appeared from the outside, it was more so from the inside. The ceiling soared to a peak with a walkway across the middle and a wide stairway leading to it. At each side of the room were large stone fireplaces high enough for her to stand in. Each had a softly flickering fire. Surrounding them were overstuffed, generously sized leather sofas and chairs that begged her to curl up in them and read. Animal skin rugs adorned the floors. Two large, heavy-looking tables sat in the middle of the room, end to end, separating the two areas.

Off to the side was a bench desk with a young man and woman waiting behind it. Owen led her in that direction. He spoke to the man. "I'm Owen Clifton. I believe you have a cabin for us."

The man smiled. "Let me have look." He checked his computer screen. "Yes. The Lakeside. You're with the wedding party." He nodded to another young man standing nearby. "Please show Mr. and Mrs. Clifton to the Lakeside cabin."

Valerie felt Owen flinch beside her. She started to correct the title, but decided it was a waste of time.

Soon they were following the man out a side door to where a golf cart waited. Their luggage had already been loaded in the back. Owen helped her into the passenger seat and climbed in beside her. In the tight space his thigh pressed against hers. She couldn't help but be hyperaware of his nearness. When the driver took off, she grabbed the rail on the front seat and Owen's thigh.

Owen's arm came around her shoulders holding her against him. "I'd hate to lose you before the weekend really gets started."

She appreciated the support as well as his touch.

As the golf cart driver motored around sharp turns, she leaned into him. To her astonishment Owen acted pleased to have her pressed against him. Soon they rode over a small bridge with a swiftly flowing brook beneath it. They made another turn that went up a short trail to a rustic-looking cabin with a porch along the front.

Valerie loved it immediately.

The young man pulled the golf cart to a rocking halt. Owen's hold tightened briefly as he said, "Mr. Toad's Wild Ride."

Valerie giggled.

Owen stepped off the cart then helped her down. They started toward the stairs leading to the cabin's porch while the young man unloaded their smaller bags.

On the porch she went to stand beside the railing. The view took her breath away. She inhaled deeply. It was like being in a treehouse with the world spread out below her. The foliage surrounded them and a glade beyond had another brook flowing through it. She couldn't imagine anything more beautiful.

Owen came to stand beside her.

"I love it. I may never leave."

He chuckled. "Let's go inside and see what we have."

In front of the door the man said, "I'll show you inside then finish getting your luggage." He turned the doorknob and opened the door wide.

Owen let her enter first. She walked to the middle of the room. A stone fireplace dominated one side, with a plush looking sofa in front of it. Two armchairs sat at each side. On the shiny wooden floor lay a bright braided rug. The area screamed cozy and romantic. She wasn't sure she had prepared for either of those things. Directly opposite the living area on the other side of the room stood a large bed. Off the bedroom area she noticed a door she assumed went to a bath. In the back corner of the space was a kitchenette, which included a tiny refrigerator.

Just one bed. She would just deal with that.

The walls were decorated with pictures of animals. She guessed they had been painted by local artists. They added to the warm feeling of the space. "This is just perfect."

"I'm glad you like it."

Owen sounded distracted, but she didn't have a chance to ask him more before the young man returned with their second load of luggage.

The man put the luggage near the bed. "When you're ready to come to the lodge just give the desk a call. Someone will come get you. Of course, you're free to walk."

"Thank you." Owen handed the driver a few bills.

When the young man was beyond hearing distance, Owen said, "After that ride I think walking would be safer if he's driving."

Valerie laughed. "It was a rather interesting one." Especially the way she felt pressed against Owen. Her body still tingled at the memory.

He started toward the kitchenette. "I'll let you get settled in. We were supposed to have two bedrooms. I'll call the front desk and see if they have something we can use. Or if you don't mind I'll just take the sofa. Then I don't have to worry about explaining to the kids."

She studied his stature then looked at the sofa and back again before turning her attention to the large bed. "I don't think you'd be very comfortable on it. You're longer than the sofa by at least a foot. I think we can manage in this large bed."

Owen's eyes narrowed. "I don't know."

"Just think about it. I'll stay on my side, and you can stay on yours. It shouldn't be that hard."

"I'll think about it." His tone implied he'd already made up his mind.

Valerie went to unpack, leaving Owen to figure out what he wanted.

A knock on the door brought them both to attention. Before either one of them could answer, a woman's voice called, "Daddy, it's Kaitlyn."

Seconds later a pretty, willowy woman entered, rushing to Owen and giving him a hug. The love was obvious between them. What would it be like to be wrapped in that emotion? Outside of her family Valerie wasn't sure she'd ever known it. She sure hadn't from her ex despite his constant words of love. What he had felt had everything to do with selfishness.

"Is she here?" Kaitlyn stage-whispered.

Valerie stepped from beside the dresser into view. "Are you referring to me?"

Kaitlyn had the good grace to turn red. "John said you were pretty."

Valerie nodded. "Thank you. You must be Kaitlyn. Your father has told me a lot about you."

The younger woman looked from Owen to Valerie and back again. "Dad surprised me when he said you were his date for the weekend."

"Kaitlyn." Owen used a warning tone. His eyes narrowed at his daughter.

"I'm sorry if I've been rude. What I meant was, up until a few weeks ago we didn't know he was dating you, Dr. Hughes."

"Please call me Valerie." She walked into the kitchenette. "Can I interest you in a cup of tea, Kaitlyn?"

Before she could answer another knock on the door drew their attention. Owen laughed. "That must be the reinforcements." Going to the door, he opened it. "Come in Rich and John. Kaitlyn is already here. This has certainly been a grand welcome."

Valerie smiled. She could appreciate his sarcasm.

"I'm glad you're here. I can make the introduction once." Owen pushed the door wide before coming to stand beside her.

His sons entered.

This would be the true test of how well her and Owen's "relationship" story held up. Valerie feared little made it past the scrutiny of Owen's daughter. They studied each other. She undoubtedly was the image of her mother, who had been a very beautiful woman. And by all standards a saint now.

Owen cleared his throat and put his hand lightly at Valerie's waist, which did nothing to calm her nerves. To the group of three, Owen said, "I've got someone I'd like you to meet." His fingers tightened briefly on her back.

That earned him a point with her. He intended to stand up for her.

John jumped out and said, "I've already met Valerie. She's really nice."

Valerie couldn't imagine how many nice things he would've learned about her from just a short meeting, but it reassured her to hear him. She could appreciate his support.

"Valerie, you've already met my daughter, Kaitlyn. You know John and this is Rich." Owen indicated him with a hand.

"Hi, Rich. It's nice to meet you all. Your father speaks highly of all of you." She made brief eye contact with each of them. Her smile brightened for John.

Rich smiled.

Kaitlyn continued to study Valerie. "We look forward to getting to know you."

"I'm sure with you all being in the wedding party it won't leave you that much time to hang out with us." Owen's hand pressed against Valerie back.

Kaitlyn watched Valerie closely. Owen's daughter might say she wanted him to date but clearly Kaitlyn wanted to pick that person out. Valerie smiled brighter. "Owen, you have a handsome family."

He pressed her against him. "Thank you. I wish I could say their manners were better."

She gave him a light slap on the chest. "Maybe if you talked about me a little more then they wouldn't be so curious." She looked at the children. "Being part of the wedding party sounds like fun."

"Yeah, it should be a good weekend," Kaitlyn said offhandedly. "I brought you a copy of the schedule." She handed it to Owen. "I fixed it so we could all sit at the same table tonight at dinner."

Valerie felt Owen tense as she did. This was definitely becoming overwhelming. She stayed glued to Owen's side. Not a single one of his children missed her action.

Owen spoke up. "That sounds good but for right now I think Valerie and I need to unpack and take a few moments to acclimate ourselves to the place and look over the schedule. We can see each other later this evening."

Kaitlyn hesitated a moment. Rich took his sister's arm and gave her a tug toward the door. "They're waiting on us at the lodge. Aunt Sarah has some kind of get to know each other wedding party mixer planned."

Kaitlyn shook off his hand. "I can take a hint." She glanced back at Valerie and Owen. "I guess we'll see y'all later."

Rich gave Valerie a genuine smile as he followed Kaitlyn out the door with John behind him.

Valerie released a breath she hadn't realized she'd been holding. "I'm glad you were here when they stopped by."

Owen's smile had turned resigned. "I'm glad I was too. I'm afraid I may owe you big time for helping me when this weekend is over."

She smiled. "What're friends for?"

"I'll let you finish your unpacking in peace." Owen sank into a chair. He hadn't expected to feel so defensive on Valerie's behalf. The need to protect her from his lies to his children made him tense.

He thought he and Valerie would have time to settle in and get used to being in such close quarters before they were invaded by his children. He should have known Kaitlyn would be watching for their arrival.

"I had no idea it would be like this," he said loud enough for Valerie to hear him from the bathroom. "I apologize for the surprise attack. I knew Kaitlyn could be protective, but I didn't expect her to be quite so much so."

"Hey, it's nothing to worry about. I'm good. She just loves her daddy and there's nothing wrong with that."

"I had no idea they'd barge in on us so soon." Apparently, he'd underestimated the situation.

"You had no way of knowing. Why don't I fix us some coffee or tea and we go outside on the porch. We can read the schedule and see what we need to plan for."

"I'll get the drinks. You go on out. Catch your breath for a minute."

A few minutes later Owen carried two mugs of steaming liquid outside. He handed one to Valerie, who sat in a chair.

He took the end of the settee closest to her. "It seems there's a dinner tonight for everyone in my family. It's a barbecue so it's casual dress. Then tomorrow there's golfing for the guys and looks like a spa day for the women. I want you to do that if you wish. You deserve a day of pampering after I got you into this mess."

"Quit worrying about me. Let's concentrate on enjoying the weekend. This is too beautiful of a place to spend our time doing anything but enjoying it." Valerie looked toward the glade.

She really was an attractive woman. The breeze ruffled her hair, and she pushed it back into place. "We do need to take a few minutes to get our stories straight. I promise Kaitlyn will compare hers to what we tell Sarah or Will."

"Let's just tell them the truth. We started seeing each other about three weeks ago. That we've had dinner a few times. That we've known each other for years."

Owen's eyes narrowed in doubt. "Do you think that's going to satisfy Kaitlyn?"

"It'll have to because it's the truth."

He shook his head. "I'm not sure anything is going to satisfy Kaitlyn. She wanted me to find someone, but she sure doesn't seem pleased I found someone."

Valerie made a noise in her throat. "She wants her father happy but doesn't want him to forget her mother. It's only natural."

"Don't let her constantly badger you." The last thing Valerie deserved was that.

"I won't."

Valerie sounded more confident about that happening than he felt. "I'll have a talk with her just to make sure."

Valerie placed her hand on his arm. "Please don't. She just loves you and wants you to be happy."

"I get that, but it doesn't give her the right to interrogate you. Or to make my life miserable either."

She cupped his cheek. "You're sweet. Don't worry about me. I can take care of myself. We haven't really talked about your brother and his wife. Why don't you tell me about them."

"They are the best. I don't know what I would have done without them after Elaine died."

His breath caught. That's the first time he said those words. *Elaine died.* She had passed. She was gone. She left us. But never the reality. The hard fact.

He swallowed the lump in his throat and continued, "Sarah held the house together while Will, my brother, held me together. I think you'll like them. But keep in mind Sarah will be acting crazy this weekend with the wedding and all."

* * *

Two hours later, after they'd changed into sweaters and jeans, Owen took Valerie's hand as they walked across the back lawn of the lodge toward an awning containing the wedding party. Music hung in the air while people laughed.

Hoping to calm his and Valerie's nerves, he leaned down to her. "You look lovely tonight."

"Thank you. You don't look half bad yourself."

She'd dressed while he stayed out on the porch. There was something too intimate, too real, too special about sharing a small bathroom with Valerie. He hadn't done anything so personal with a woman in a long time.

When he did go inside, she didn't act the least bit concerned about him being there. Maybe it was because they'd known each other so long. His problem stemmed from him noticing her as more than a friend. Now all he could think about was sliding an arm around her waist, pulling her close and repeating their kiss. Only making it last longer.

She had awakened his body, and his mind hadn't caught up. His heart remained even further behind. Not that he would let that get involved again. Elaine had taken it with her.

"Are you ready for this?" He looked over at the tent.

Valerie's chin rose. "I am. I look forward to meeting all your family."

"You're brave, I'll give you that." He pulled her hand through his arm.

She gave him a tight smile. "I appreciate your support."

For some reason it bothered him that she was only drawing close to look the part of his woman friend for the others. He would have liked it if being near him mattered to her.

As they stepped under the canopy, a tall, dark-haired man who looked like Owen stopped talking to a group and hurried toward them with a smile on his face. "Owen. It's great to see you." They hugged each other, with back slaps.

Owen pulled away to draw Valerie close. "Valerie, I'd like you to meet my brother, Will."

Will smiled warmly at Valerie. "I'm so glad you could join us. Really glad."

Owen's heart hurt for the worry he had caused his brother.

Sarah rushed over to join them. She treated Valerie just as warmly. It pricked Owen's conscious for a moment that he wasn't being truthful with them. He'd come clean when given a chance.

Sarah pulled on Will's arm. "We have to go. It's almost time for our welcome." She looked at Owen and Valerie and waved toward the long buffet table. "Go help yourself. We'll see you later."

They were halfway down the table when Owen heard Rich's voice behind him. "Hey, Dad, we're at that table at the back." He pointed. "We saved y'all seats."

"Okay." With Rich gone Owen brushed Valerie ear with his lips. "Are you ready for this?"

She smiled. "As I'll ever be."

Owen couldn't help but be proud of Valerie's attitude.

A few minutes later with their plates full, he and Valerie joined his children. He wasn't surprised to learn that Kaitlyn had arranged the seating so she would be next to Valerie.

Valerie had thought it through while dressing. The best defense was an offense. Now was the time to see how it worked. She smiled at everyone at the table as she slid into the seat next to Kaitlyn. Giving the younger woman her attention Valerie looked past her to the thin young man sitting on her right. "Your daddy tells me you're married. This must be your husband."

Kaitlyn's eyes widened. "Yes, this is Robert."

"It's nice to meet you, Robert." Valerie offered him a smile.

He returned a shy one. "It's nice to meet you as well."

Valerie settled her napkin in her lap and looked at her plate. "Wow, this looks great."

Before she took the first bite she said to Kaitlyn, "Y'all are staying in the lodge. How're the rooms?"

Kaitlyn took the bait and started describing in detail their room. Valerie listened patiently and continue to ask more questions when Kaitlyn paused.

Owen pressed his thigh against hers, making heat run along her leg. She glanced at him. He grinned. Valerie looked at Rich. "I understand you're thinking about being doctor like your dad. He's a really fine one."

Rich told her about his struggle to decide what direction he wanted his life to take.

Owen shifted and lay his arm across the back of Valerie's chair. The tips of his fingers caressed her shoulder. Once again, the action did not go unnoticed by his children. He played his part well. "I think it's time y'all give Valerie a break and let her finish her meal."

A woman Valerie didn't recognize stood behind the microphone in front of the group. "I need all of the wedding party up here."

Owen's children shuffled out of their chairs.

Valerie commented to no one in particular left at the table. "I could use some dessert."

Kaitlyn's husband volunteer to go after it.

As he left Owen chuckled. "I had no idea you were such a great actress."

It was nice to know she could surprise Owen and had his gratitude. She twisted her mouth into a funny little grin. "Maybe I wasn't acting." Now she was flirting.

Owen's gaze met hers and held it.

Will approached them, interrupting the moment. "Owen, I have you down to play golf in my foursome tomorrow morning, but one of the guys has dropped out. We need to find someone to fill his spot. Do you think one of your boys would be willing?"

"I never could get Rich or John interested." Owen shook his head. "I'm not much help."

Will's lips formed a tight line. "If I don't find someone to fill the spot, we'll have to forfeit. I hate to do that. I have a little money on the game with the father-in-law to be."

"Could I help?" Valerie offered.

"Have you played any golf?" Owen asked.

"Some."

Will thumped the back of her chair. "Then you're in. A warm body is better than no body. I'll see you both at the club house in the morning. We have an eight thirty tee off." He hurried away with a smile on his face.

"I didn't know you played golf." Owen looked at her with curiosity. "You've never said anything."

"I've never had a reason to do so. The subject has never come up."

Robert returned with her dessert. She took a bite. A perfect apple pie.

Owen watched her eat. She had a way of moving her lips across a fork that made his middle quiver. "Are you sure you want to spend the day on the golf course instead of at the spa?"

"I think some spa time would be great after a round of golf. Maybe you could join me."

"What?" He shook his head as he sat back in the chair.

She grinned at the squeak in Owen's voice. "You don't like spas?"

"I wouldn't know."

Her look dared him. "You should try it. There's nothing like a good massage."

"Maybe I will." What had gotten into him? He'd never thought of going to a spa before in his life. "Why don't we call it a night? I think we've both had about all we want for one day, and apparently, we'll have a full one tomorrow. That restful weekend I promised you is slowly turning into a lie."

She could not argue with that. He stood and pulled her chair out. Owen was a gentleman and she liked that.

"Do you want to take the golf cart back or walk?" He led her out from under the tent.

Valerie looked at the star-studded sky. "I think I'd enjoy a walk. It's a beautiful night."

He took her hand as they started across the lawn. It reassured her to have her hand in his. She had started to like too many things about Owen. Even when they moved along the lit path to the cabin, he continued to hold her hand. They walked in silence. A little breeze ruffled the dried leaves at their feet and caused others to fall around them. Somehow the quietness wasn't uncomfortable, instead peaceful.

It wasn't until they reacted the cabin that Valerie remembered they would be spending the night in small space—together. Had it crossed Owen's mind as well? They were both adults so they could handle the situation. She had no doubt Owen would be considerate and would never apply pressure to do anything she didn't want to. The puzzling bit was that she now wanted more than she should.

Owen followed her up to the porch. She waited as he unlocked the door then allowed her to go in first. They stood in the living area for a moment as if unsure about what to do next.

He cleared his throat. "It's a little cool in here. I think I'll turn on the fire."

"I'm going to have a cup of tea. Would you like one? Or coffee?" She needed to do something to keep busy.

"Tea is fine."

Soon the gas logs were glowing.

Valerie's hands shook slightly as she made the tea. She could have been on her first date as nervous as she acted around him. What was happening between them? Despite having a crush on him for years, she'd never felt the sexual attraction she did this evening. It stimulated her and scared her at the same time. The right thing to do would be not to act on it.

She carried the steaming mugs over to where Owen sat in one of the two chairs. He had pulled them closer to the fire. His shoes were set on the floor while his bare feet were on the hearth and crossed at the ankles. She'd never seen him more relaxed. A direct contradiction to her rattled nerves.

Valerie handed him a mug and then eased down into the

other chair while holding hers. She took a sip of the hot liquid, letting it heat her from the inside out.

"Mmm…" rolled from Owen's lips. "I'm not normally a tea drinker, but this is really good. It hits the spot tonight." He set his mug down on the table nearby before he laid his head against the back of the chair and close his eyes.

Valerie watched him. Owen had aged well and probably would continue to do so. No wonder all the nurses, young and old, had a crush on him. She couldn't help but be a member of his fan club too.

"Valerie, tell me why you're not married or don't have someone special in your life. The truth if you don't mind. It won't go any further than me. Promise."

Her heart jerked. Could she share that ugly story? She looked at him, but his eyes were still closed. "How do you know I don't?"

"Because you're here with me. You would never be disloyal, and if you belonged to me, I'd never let you go off and do something like this with another man. Even if you were just friends."

If he only knew.

"The more I'm around you the more amazing I find you. You were a real champ tonight. I just don't understand why you don't have anybody special."

Glad his eyes remained closed she said, "It's not because I haven't had the chance."

Owen rolled his head to the side and opened one eye. "What happened?"

"He decided he wanted his wife more." She didn't try to hide the bitterness.

His eyes opened wide, and he sat up. "What?"

"Yes, I had an affair with a married man. Only I didn't

know he was married." She would get it all out and be done with it. Owen could send her home if he wished. "You asked me why I moved to Atlanta. He was why. He was a visiting doctor and swept me off my feet. Only thing is, he never wanted to be seen with me. Sometimes he would disappear for the weekend and not say where he'd been. One day I heard some of the nurses talking about seeing him, his wife and their kids at the zoo. I couldn't get to the bathroom fast enough to throw up. When I said I would no longer have anything to do with him, he retaliated by making sure everyone knew I had been sleeping with him. I had to start looking for a job elsewhere. Now you know my dirty big secret."

Owen shook his head. His hands fisted on the arms of the chair. "He was a… I can't think of a word strong enough to describe him."

"I can't disagree." Her attention went to the fire.

"Now I understand why you reacted the way you did when I was a jerk. It reminded you too much of him. I'm sorry."

She closed her eyes and open them again. "You didn't know. I haven't exactly had a great track record with men. I tend to be left behind. Even my father left when I was five."

"That must've been very difficult."

"My mom and siblings, we worked through it. After I got through school, I just focused on my job. It was one place where I felt security. The men in my life haven't exactly proved worthy of my admiration. Present company excluded."

"Thanks. I sure hope I'm not lumped into your usual group of men. I will endeavor to be better than that."

She stood. "I'm sure you are already." If anything, he

was loyal. He proved that by how he clung to his dead wife. "I'm going to get ready for bed unless you want the bathroom first."

"No, you can have it."

A few minutes later, when she exited the bath, she found Owen stretched out on the sofa with a pillow under his head and a blanket pulled over him. She quietly slipped into bed and turned off the light.

"Good night, Valerie. I'm glad you came with me."

Warmth like a furry blanket on a freezing day went through her. "You're welcome."

CHAPTER SIX

OWEN WOKE TO the smell of coffee. It had been a long time since that had been the case. He stretched. Looking over the end of the couch, he saw Valerie moving around the kitchenette.

How could any man have treated Valerie with such callous disregard? She was a wonderful woman who didn't deserve the kind of treatment she received in her life. Any man in his right mind would want her. To make matters worse, he'd acted as if he were ashamed of her more than once. No wondered she looked at him as if he had kicked her. If he were available, he would make her feel as appreciated as she deserved.

Dressed for the day in a pullover sweater and tan slacks, Valerie had tucked her hair under a ballcap. She looked both very appealing and ready for the golf course. "Good morning." His voice came out as a gravelly whisper. He cleared his throat. "Mornin'."

Valerie turned. "Hey, sleepyhead. How about a cup of coffee?"

"Sounds wonderful."

She brought a mug to him.

"Coffee in bed. I could get use to this." There was a number of things about Valerie he could get used to. A tint of color came to her cheeks. It was refreshing to see someone her age could still blush. It made him feel rather manly to have her respond that way. "I see you're ready for the day."

"I am. You better get moving. I've let you sleep as long as I could. We won't make our tee time if you don't hurry." She returned to the kitchenette.

He raised the mug. "Let me get this coffee down and I'll be ready to go in just a few minutes."

"I found some muffins in the cabinet with a note that they are for us." She pulled a couple of plates from a shelf.

"Great. I'm starving." He pushed the covers back as he placed his feet on the floor.

Valerie's stare made him wonder what was wrong. He'd forgotten he only wore his boxers. He watched her studying him. She flattered him with her interest.

After a few moments she said, "I'll get out of your way and finish up in the bathroom."

Owen grinned. She was so bold in some ways then timid in others. He found the combination intriguing.

He finished his coffee and had a muffin before he strolled into the bedroom area. Valerie brushed passed him on her way into the living room. Yes, this was fine morning entertainment. He missed moments like this. Sharing a space with someone.

Forty-five minutes later they were outside the clubhouse ready to start their game. Owen had rented Valerie a set of clubs and golf shoes. He had been surprised at the time and attention she had given to picking both out.

Will introduced him and Valerie to the father of the bride, who was heading up the foursome they were playing against. The other man in their foursome was Sarah's brother.

Promptly at eight thirty the men teed off. Owen was pleased with his drive.

"Do you want to drive the cart or shall I?" he asked Valerie when it was time to move up to the women's tee.

"You're welcome to do it." Did she suspected he was one of those guys who'd rather drive than be driven?

Owen stopped beside the women's tee. Valerie found her driver club and took her stance, ready to swing. He had enjoyed too much the movement of her hips as she warmed up. He had to get his mind back where it belonged. Nothing in their agreement said anything about him ogling Valerie.

With a beautiful swing, she contacted with the ball and sent it flying. It landed not far from his in the fairway. He whispered in admiration, "Nice shot."

The other men agreed.

After she returned to the cart, Owen gave her a narrow-eyed look. "You've been sandbagging me. Last night you implied you haven't played much, but I don't think that's true."

Her look turned sheepish, and she wouldn't meet his gaze. "I haven't played much lately. At least not in the last few years."

"But you have played a lot at one time."

"I had a golfing scholarship for college. We won nationals two years in a row." She squinched up her face. "I had the best handicap."

He chuckled. "I should have known. I shouldn't be surprised, but I am. You've never said anything about enjoying golf. Obviously there're some mysteries about you."

She winked. "If you hang around more, you just might learn what they are."

Owen laughed. He might like that. "We'll start with planning to play a round or two of golf on our next day off."

"Sounds like a plan. Now let's finish this one."

They continued to play the hole. On the second shot, Valerie and he both made the edge of the green. With chip shots they were in a good position to the hole. He made the cup in two putts and her in one.

"You were amazing. Excellent playing."

"I'm glad you like it. I'm a little rusty." She went pink with pride and pleasure at his approval.

"I'd hate to play against you if you weren't rusty."

Her eyes twinkled. "I'd hate it for you too."

Hours later their foursome returned to the clubhouse as the victors.

"You were wonderful." Owen gave Valerie a hug. She returned it. It continued longer than necessary, but she liked being surrounded by Owen.

Will joined them, making them break apart. "We had a ringer, and we didn't even know it. I was glad to have you. I needed this win. Gives me bragging rights."

Valerie smiled as she finished cleaning her clubs. "I'm glad I could help."

Owen took her bag from her. "Now it's time you do something for yourself. I'm sending you to the spa for the afternoon."

"Right now, I'd rather have some food." She looked toward the lodge.

Owen nodded. "Food first, then the spa."

They returned her clubs and shoes and stored his equipment to be picked up later before they strolled to the lodge.

"I had a good time this morning." Valerie lifted her face to the sun.

Owen took her hand. "I did too."

As they sat at a table near a window, Valerie picked up one half of her club sandwich.

"What's on the schedule for this afternoon?"

"As far as I know, for us nothing. Free time." Owen bit into his hamburger. "While you're at the spa I'll just go back to the cabin."

"You could come to the spa with me." She looked at him with half-lidded eyes.

He shook his head. "I think I'll just go watch some TV. Maybe check in with the kids. I'm not much of a spa person."

"You can't knock it until you've tried it. I think you might be surprised how much you like it. Think steam room, hot tub, massage, facial, pedicure, manicure—"

Owen held up a hand. "No facial, pedicure, or manicure for me. But I have to admit a good steam room sounds nice."

She laughed. "But I want you to get a massage as well. I promise you'll like it. As far as I'm concerned, you haven't lived until you've had one. So what do you say?"

He said nothing for a few moments. "Okay, I'll go along. This time."

Two hours later, Valerie lay on her stomach with her face pillowed through a hole in the masseuse's table. Wrapped in nothing but a towel, Owen lay next to her in the same position.

She grinned every time she heard a moan or a groan from him.

Soft music played in the room. She had been shocked when he had suggested a couple's massage. Apparently he hadn't realized they would be undressed in a room together. For him to do something so private surprised her. He'd spent the last few weeks keeping her at arm's length. Yet she had to admit he had loosened up. She questioned his judgment, but he insisted it was the way he wanted it. He had even accused her of being insecure.

"Oh, that feels good. That's the spot," Owen softly muttered.

Did he make that type of noise when making love? Her body stiffened and heated.

"Are you okay ma'am?"

"I'm fine." As long as she didn't think about Owen lying naked only a feet away.

"You're done sir," Owen's masseuse said. "Just lie here and take it easy for as long as you wish. Be careful when standing and be sure to drink a lot of water."

Owen released a slow sigh.

A few minutes later her masseuse said the same to her as Owen's had and slipped out the door. She and Owen were left wearing nothing but a towel. The lights remained dim with soft music playing.

Valerie's nerves prickled. She hadn't counted on this situation. And she'd thought staying in the cabin was close quarters. Hearing nothing from Owen for a few minutes, she wondered if he was sleeping or just pretending.

Finally, the soft sound of his voice surrounded her. "I'm glad you made me do this."

"I didn't know I made you."

"I wasn't a willing partner." He shifted on the table.

"That I'll agree with." She turned her head to look at him.

His gaze met hers. "But I have to say I'd be willing to do it again. I now understand why people want to go to the spa."

"I'm glad you enjoyed yourself." His look heated her body.

"I've really been having a good time with you. I'm glad I asked you to come along. This weekend would've been much harder without you."

Her feminine parts had begun to tingle. "I've had a good time as well. I guess if we're going to make it to the rehearsal dinner tonight we'd better get moving. Even though I hate the thought of getting up."

"Me too."

She wanted him out of the room for when she crawled off the table. The chance of losing her towel was too great. "Why don't you go first, then I'll meet you outside the dressing room." She didn't shy away from watching him roll from the table. The view was too tempting.

Thinking he had left, she tried shifting off the table, but her muscles didn't want to cooperate. She groaned.

"Hey, are you okay? Do I need to help you?"

Valerie jerked to a stop. Owen stood beside her. Securing the towel around her, she rolled over hoping the towel didn't flap open. She wiggled from the table, but her muscles were so weak her knees buckled.

Owen moved quickly, steadying her. "Let me help you."

Valerie looked at him. His eyes were on her lips. Her skin burned where his hands touched. Her breathing was ragged. He was going to kiss her. She wanted this. Craved it. She gripped his forearms. His lips had just found hers when there was a knock at the door.

She jerked back, her towel catching on the table corner

and tugging it loose from where it had been tucked in at her breasts. "Oh." Valerie grab for the material but it went to the floor.

The knock came again.

"We'll be right out," Owen answered, eyes never leaving her body. He reached for her towel and handed it to her. "You'll want to cover up, I'm sure. Do you need help?"

With a heated face, she snatched the towel from him and quickly wrapped it around herself. She walked out the door with her head held high. Moments later with robes on, they walked toward the locker room.

As they were entering the room, Kaitlyn and Robert stepped out dressed in robes. The entire group stopped short, in shock.

"Hey, Daddy."

"Hi, honey. I hope you've been having a good day." Owen acted as if it were no big deal for them all to stand there in almost no clothing.

"We have. What have you two been up too?" Kaitlyn looked from one to the other of them.

Valerie feared she might be hot enough to combust.

Owen took Valerie's hand. "We played golf this morning and just got out of the most amazing couple's massage." He squeezed her hand. Was he teasing his daughter?

Kaitlyn's look focused on their clasped hands. "I didn't know you got massages."

"There's a lot of things you probably don't know about me, honey."

Kaitlyn gave Valerie a perplexed look. "I'm glad to know you're having a good time."

Owen pulled Valerie close to his side. "We're having a

great time. We're off to get ready for the rehearsal dinner. See you there."

Kaitlyn didn't look overjoyed with idea. "Okay."

With the door to the locker room between them, Valerie looked at Owen with a grin. He returned it and they broke into laugher.

Owen kissed her temple. "She wanted me to have someone to do things with. Now she's gotten her wish, but I'm not so sure she's happy about it."

An hour and a half later Owen dressed in his navy blue suit in the living area, listening to Valerie getting ready for the evening. He kept his eyes squarely on the football game playing on TV. Yet he had no idea what the name of the teams were nor the score.

He couldn't believe it. He'd almost kissed her. Again. Then when her towel had dropped away, his breath had left him. He hadn't wanted a woman since Elaine died. Before that he'd been in college. Despite their friendship, all he could think about was touching and holding Valerie. There was nothing friendly about his feelings. He'd planned a simple weekend that had spiraled completely out of control emotionally. The need to have her had become almost a living thing. Too old for this kind of nonsense, he had to control his actions. And reactions.

"I'm ready if you are," Valerie said in a cheery voice.

He turned to find her standing there wearing a deep royal blue dress that wrapped her waist and tied at one hip. It complemented her coloring perfectly. Small diamonds twinkled in her ears. A necklace that matched the diamonds hung around her long neck. A gleam of confidence filled her eyes.

Wow. "What's the plan? To outdo the bride?"

That made her eyes sparkle brighter. A smile appeared on her pink-covered lips. "You sure know how to make a woman feel good. Thank you."

"Hey, I'm the one feeling good. All the other men are going to be envious you are with me." So many times he had seen her in scrubs with a surgical cap on her head. He'd glimpsed her curves, but tonight Valerie was all woman. She would be his woman, on his arm. He would be proud to say she was with him.

Until the end of the weekend. Would he be ready for them to go back to just friendship? He couldn't say that he would.

Her smile grew. "I had no idea you were such a silver tongued devil."

"I, too, have some surprises left in me." He offered his arm.

She wrapped hers through it. "I look forward to finding out what they are."

Was Valerie flirting with him? He liked the idea. "I called for a golf cart. I didn't think you'd want to walk down there in your high heels."

"That's thoughtful of you."

He stayed close as she made her way down the steps. He didn't want her to fall. The protection of Valerie was a new emotion for him. He'd never been that way with Elaine.

The golf cart arrived just as they made it down the stairs. Soon they were pulling up to the lodge.

The night's festivities had been planned in a large, elegant room off the lobby. The space consisted of an open area with a high ceiling and walls of windows. Round tables laid with crisp, snow-white tablecloths and sparkling silverware filled the room.

As they entered, Will buzzed by them long enough to say that Owen and Valerie would be sitting at his and Sarah's table that evening. Will pointed in the direction of the front left. Soon they found Sarah holding court at the table. Searching the place markers, they found their seats.

His children were seated at the next table. Valerie stood beside him as he greeted each one of them.

"Hey, Dad. Tell us about having a massage. I didn't know you went in for those sorts of things." Rich's voice held a large dose of teasing. The grin on his face confirmed it. Kaitlyn had no doubt been on the phone with her brothers before he and Valerie left the spa.

"As a doctor I highly recommend one." Especially the kiss afterward. But he wouldn't say that.

He glanced at Valerie. She had a shy grin on her lips. She acted as if she enjoyed him being put on the spot.

"I've never known you to go for a massage." John looked perplexed by who his father had become.

"I haven't. But I have to admit the experience was quite invigorating." He winked at Valerie whose cheeks pinkened. "I look forward to doing it again."

"I didn't take you as the kind of person who would go for a couple's massage." Kaitlyn watched him and Valerie closely.

Owen shrugged. "You know, you never should get too old to try new things."

Kaitlyn's jaw dropped.

He looked at each one of his children. "Isn't that what you guys told me just a few weeks ago?"

"Yeah, but—"

A woman behind the microphone cut off the rest of Kaitlyn's sentence.

"I can tell you all about it later." Owen heard Valerie's soft giggle. He smiled at her as he helped her into her chair.

"You're being mean to them," she whispered.

"They deserve it. They have been messing in my business."

She hissed, "They're going to think I'm some floozie who's corrupting their father."

He found her hand, lifted it to his lips, then kissed the back of it. "Aren't you?"

She leaned closer. He picked up a hint of something floral on her skin. He wanted to tug her nearer but dare not. "I think you're starting to enjoy this tall tale we've created. Especially the shock value for your children."

"I can't say that I'm not." All of it. Especially touching her. "That's a cherry on top of my weekend."

Valerie's eyes looked worried. Her lips thinned. "I just hope it doesn't backfire on both of us."

Over the next hour and a half, they enjoyed the conversation with those at their table. Valerie fit in perfectly. He couldn't have made a better choice about who to ask to the wedding. If it hadn't been Valerie, he didn't know who he would have asked. It didn't matter because she had come, and she was great. Almost too great. One day he would have to own up to his family what he had done.

When it became time for the speeches, he couldn't resist reaching for Valerie's hand. She accepted it. He held it, not caring if anyone saw them. At one point he leaned in close to her ear. "I'm sorry to put you through this."

"I don't mind. I'm enjoying the chance to get to know your family."

"I'm not sure it's the way I want you to know them."

The speeches dragged on. The event wouldn't be over

soon enough for him. He looked forward to spending some time alone with Valerie. He planned to finish that kiss he started.

By the time they were leaving, thunder rumbled off in the distance. They made a mad dash for the closest empty golf cart. It had started sprinkling by the time they got to their cabin. They hurried up the steps, just making the porch before the downpour begun.

Valerie moved toward the settee. "I love to listen to the rain. I think I'll sit out here for a few minutes."

"Do you mind if I join you?"

"No at all. That would be nice." She patted the cushion next to her.

"Would you like a cup of tea to go with the rain?"

"That would be wonderful. I'll go fix it." She moved to get up.

He waved her down. "I'll get it."

Owen hurried to the kitchenette and started the water for tea. While it heated, he turned on the fire so the room would be warm when they came in. Pulling a throw off the back of the couch, he stepped out long enough to hand it to Valerie.

"Thank you."

He soon returned with two steaming mugs in hand and joined her on the settee. He liked that he could feel her heat all the way up one side of his body.

She wrapped her hands around the mug. "This is great. I'm glad you thought about it."

"Warm enough?"

"Yes. You have taken good care of me. The blanket is keeping me warm and the tea hits the spot."

They were quiet for a few minutes, just enjoying the peace of the rain.

"You have a very nice family. I hope they won't be too mad when you tell them we are just pretending." She took a sip of tea.

"They'll get over it. My family loves me. They won't kick me out."

"That's nice to know. Not everyone has that type of security. Your nephew seems to be marrying into a very nice family." She took another sip of tea.

"He is." Owen put his mug down on the floor of the porch.

They returned to listening to the rain as it drummed against the tin of the roof. After a few minutes Owen turned to Valerie, taking her mug and setting it beside his.

She gave him a quizzical look.

"I'd like to finish what I started in the massage room. Let me know if you have a problem with that." With no objection on Valerie's part his lips found hers.

There was nothing tentative about the meeting of their mouths. This time Valerie wrapped her arms around his neck. She leaned into him. He accepted her assent while requesting she opened her mouth. He entered and found heaven.

His hands tightened on her, bringing her securely to him as he deepened the kiss. Pure moments of bliss followed. Owen wanted more. This and so much more he'd been missing in his life.

Placing a hand on his chest, Valerie pulled back. "Are you sure this is what you want? Just a couple of weeks ago you ran away. Headed for the hills anytime somebody even saw us together. I can't take being pushed and pulled. I'd rather not to begin with."

He couldn't help but hang his head in shame. "I know I've been slow to get used to it. Elaine and I had been together for a lot of years. It's hard for me to think about kissing, touching or have anything to do with another woman."

"Yet here you're kissing me."

"Yeah, I couldn't be more surprised." He looked at the crack in the wood floor.

"I'm not sure whether to be flattered or upset about that statement."

He tugged at his collar. "I can assure you it's to be flattered. You're the first woman I've wanted to touch in years."

Valerie smiled. "That I can be flattered about. But I don't want us to take things too fast. Make a step that you're not going to be uncomfortable with or will regret. Especially since we're cooped up together this weekend. It could just be that I'm convenient. I think we need to take it slow and easy."

"I don't know how easy that's going to be. I sure do enjoy your kisses."

Valerie chuckled. "I didn't say it would be easy." She stood. "Come on. Let's go in. I'm getting damp out here."

The rain had become a downpour. He hadn't noticed until that moment. They left the porch and entered the cabin. "Want to sit by the fire for a while?"

"That sounds nice. Let me get out of these clothes, especially the heels. That's one of the best things about being in the OR. I can wear my clogs." She headed for the bedroom area.

Owen shrugged out of his suit jacket then pulled off

his shoes. He sat on the sofa, propping his feet up to the warmth of the fire. Valerie returned in PJs. The message was clear. The sign obviously read closed for the night, and he would honor her wishes. She was right; they needed to take it slow. The one thing he didn't want was to ruin their friendship or make it impossible to work together.

Valerie sat down beside him. To his pleasure she scooted close and took his hand. "This is nice." She laid her head against his shoulder.

"I agree."

For a long time, they said nothing as they watched the fire. These were the kind of moments he had missed, wanted again. Just something as simple as the companionship of having another person in the room. Valerie had a way about her that soothed his soul.

Soon her head became heavier against his shoulder and her hand relaxed. She slept.

Slowly scooting away from her, he gently shook her awake. "Valerie, it's time we get you to bed. You fell asleep." She made the sweetest moan, but he remained focused on the issue at hand. "Come on, honey, let me help you to bed." He urged her to stand then led her to the bed. Flipping the covers back, he said, "Let me get this housecoat off you." Beneath he found she wore classic pants pajamas, which did nothing to detract from her sexiness.

She lay on the bed and he pulled the sheet and blanket over her. "A man couldn't ask for a better fake girlfriend than you. I appreciate your friendship. I couldn't ask for a better one." He kissed her on the forehead. He turned off the light and headed back to the sofa.

Her sleepy voice came from behind him. "You're too big for that sofa. Sleep in the bed tonight."

His back and legs would appreciate a wider and longer space. But could he manage to spend the night without touching her? He would give it a try. Removing his clothes, Owen climbed into the bed. A gulf lay between him and Valerie that he intended to maintain until she was ready to build a bridge. It might be difficult, but he would do it.

Rolling on his side away from Valerie, he pretended she wasn't there all warm, sweet smelling and kind. He hoped he could get some rest, yet he'd set himself up for failure.

Valerie woke huddled against warm skin. Her back pressed against something hard. An arm hung over her waist. Her eyes whipped open. She lay snuggled against Owen. On his side of the bed. Apparently during the night she'd gotten cold and been drawn to his heat.

His breathing ruffled her hair at the shell of her ear. She couldn't deny it felt good being pressed against him. She had been the one to set the boundary, then she'd gone and crossed it. She needed to move or decide on what she wanted their relationship to be. She wasn't prepared to do so yet.

But she wanted to stay. She needed to go. But she was so warm. She had to get up.

She wanted him to recognize she wasn't a substitute for his dead wife or not there just to be a fun time. She really cared for him. More than a friend, but she had to protect her heart, too. She'd been left behind enough, betrayed, and she didn't care for Owen being another man on her list who had left her. She would rather they remain friends.

She shifted.

Owen's arm tightened. "Where are you going? You're nice and warm."

"It's time to get up."

"We have a few more minutes, don't we?" His voice rumbled near her ear. "This is the way to wake up every morning. I've missed you."

Every muscle in Valerie's body tensed. Owen thought she was Elaine!

Valerie wasted no time moving out from under his arm and across the bed. She got up, not bothering to look at him as she grabbed her clothes. "I'm sorry. I didn't mean to get over on your side."

He rolled to his back. "No problem at all."

She glanced at him, but her look stuck on his bare chest showing above the sheet that had dropped to his waist. "We better get moving."

"What's the hurry? The wedding isn't until this afternoon. We have the day to ourselves."

She headed toward the bath. "You didn't read the schedule. We have a family brunch this morning. They'll want you in the family pictures they're taking afterward."

Owen groaned. "I'd rather stay here cuddled up in bed with you."

"Not an option." She threw the words over her shoulder. That wasn't going to happen. He didn't even recognize the difference between her and his dead wife. That might be the supreme rejection.

He stretched his arms over his head and flexed. "You go on without me and tell me about it later."

Valerie glared at him. "That's not going to happen. I'm getting dressed. Why don't you start the coffee?"

His brows narrowed. "Are you running away from me?"

"No."

"Seems to me that you're trying to put some space between us."

She turned, walking to the end of the bed to glare down at him. "Just who did you think was in bed with you just a minute ago?"

"Well, you, of course."

"So why did you make it sound like you thought I was Elaine? You said you missed me." He had the good grace to look ashamed. "I'm sorry. I must not have been awake yet. I would never intentionally hurt you."

"I'm not a replacement for your dead wife. Please keep that in mind."

He didn't blink. "I know that."

She continued to glare. "When you're kissing me, are you thinking of her?"

He jerked to a sitting position. "I can assure you I'm thinking of you. Come here. I can prove it."

"I don't know if I can believe you." She marched to the bathroom.

She had her coffee in hand when Owen entered the kitchen area wearing a T-shirt and jeans. His bare feet padded across the wooden floor.

His bigger body boxed her in. "Hey, I didn't mean to hurt your feelings. I can assure you I know exactly who you are. You're sweet, caring Valerie who I've seen talk to a scared child and have them laughing a few minutes later. You're the doctor who worries over her patient even when they've been discharged. The friend who helps out a friend when he has a crazy idea." He took a step closer. "You're the woman who can beat the socks off most men on a golf course, including me. You're the person who went along with the idea of getting a couple's massage when I suggested it." He walked closer. "You're the woman who has bested Kaitlyn, which I wouldn't have thought possible."

Valerie chuckled.

He cupped her cheek. "You're the woman who has me thinking about nothing but kissing her again." His lips found hers. The kiss was gentle and sincere. She melted against him.

He pulled away. "Am I forgiven? It won't happen again. Promise."

She smiled and nodded.

"Good. We only have one more day in this beautiful place, and I'd like to make the most of it."

"Sounds like a plan. I guess we start by having brunch with your children."

Owen made a face. "I had other ideas but if we must."

Valerie couldn't help but forgive Owen for his faux pas after the sweet speech he gave. Few people saw through her as well as he did. They just had today and tomorrow before they were back to the real world, and she didn't want to spend the time angry. Yet it better not happen again.

The sun shone bright, so they agreed to walk to the lodge for brunch.

She looked at the sky. "It's going to be a beautiful day for a wedding."

"Yeah. I'm not much into weddings. I'm only here for Will and the kids. Otherwise, I could pass on the wedding."

"I had no idea you were such a cynic." She didn't really mind. Lots of people didn't care about weddings.

"And I had no idea you were such a romantic."

She swung their hands between them. "There's nothing wrong with being a romantic."

He grinned. "Or being a cynic."

Owen's children were already in the dining room when they arrived. Valerie was determined to win over Kaitlyn. Smiling warmly, Valerie greeted each of them. "Kaitlyn, do you mind if I sit beside you?"

The look of surprise on the woman's face spoke volumes. She hadn't expected that from Valerie. She smiled to herself. Valerie had already gained the upper hand.

"Sure." Kaitlyn moved so Valerie could more easily take her chair.

"Great. We really haven't had a good chance to get to know each other."

"Uh, no, we haven't."

Valerie reached for her napkin. "I'd like to change that."

"Really?" The word was but a squeak.

Owen's soft chuckle beside Valerie spurred her on. He started a conversation with his son-in-law.

Valerie turned to Kaitlyn. "I understand you and Robert live in Marietta. How're you enjoying that?"

"We're happy there. We're starting to look for a house."

"That sounds like fun. I've lived in apartments or condos most of my life. Every once in a while, I think about buying a house."

"Why haven't you done it?" She had Valerie's full attention now.

"I guess I think of a house as being a place for two people. It's just me..."

"You've never been married?"

"No." Valerie just hoped she didn't ask why.

"So, no house?"

"So, no house."

Kaitlyn face turned serious and thoughtful. "Dad lives in the big old house we grew up in."

"It's a lovely home." Valerie looked at her with understanding.

Kaitlyn had a moment of thought. "That's right, you were there the other night when John came home."

"I was. Your dad showed off all your pictures. Including your mom. She was a lovely lady. You look a lot like her."

The pleasure on Kaitlyn's face let Valerie know she'd said the correct thing. Valerie placed her hand over Kaitlyn's. "I know you miss her every day."

"Yeah, I do." Her eyes glistened.

"Your dad does too. I'm glad he has you guys." Valerie looked at her brothers. "It's good to have someone around you who loves you."

"I've been worried about Dad. He's been pretty resistant to going out. We were all surprised to learn about you."

"You were?" Valerie offered Kaitlyn her best innocent expression, pushing the guilt down about misleading Owen's children.

"Yeah, he didn't say anything to us about dating you. You were a complete surprise when he announced he'd be bringing someone to the wedding."

Valerie glanced at Owen. "Your dad and I have been friends for a long time. We've worked together for a number of years."

"I can remember hearing him mention your name a few times but never as a girlfriend. I'm just surprised because he was so firmly against me trying to fix him up with somebody."

Valerie lowered her voice, keeping it even. "What are

you most aggravated about? Is it that your dad's found somebody or that he did it without your help?"

Kaitlyn leaned back with a shocked look as if that had never occurred to her.

"Yeah," John said from the other side of the table, then chuckled. "She's not the one in charge."

Kaitlyn glared at her brother. "I just want Daddy to be happy."

"I think spending time with me makes your father happy. We enjoy each other's company. Isn't that what you want for him?"

Kaitlyn was slow to answer. "I did. I do. I have to admit he doesn't seem like the same person he was even a few weeks ago."

"That's because you're seeing him in a different light now. He's a person as well as being your father. He has a life outside of what you're used to."

Rich spoke up. "She's got you there, Kaitlyn."

After that Valerie turned her attention to Rich. It turned out they both liked old movies. They got into a debate about which was the best. Soon the topic of conversation for the entire table went to football and what teams were playing that day. It became a family discussion that fascinated Valerie.

At one point Owen reached under the table and squeezed her thigh. She looked at him. His gaze met hers. He mouthed *Thank you.*

With brunch at an end, Valerie and Owen walked the long way back to the cabin while his children went to go get ready for the wedding.

Owen took her hand, holding it securely. "You were

great with Kaitlyn. I think you have gotten her off my
back about dating."

"Kaitlyn and I came to an understanding. I still hated
to mislead them about our relationship."

"It's a risk I'm willing to take if it'll give me peace."

Later that afternoon Owen was once again dressed in a
suit waiting on Valerie. He tugged at his black-and-gray-
striped tie that looked best with his black suit. The afternoon had turned cool. He waited by the fireplace, warming
his hands.

When Valerie came out to meet him, she was dressed
in a light pink beaded dress with long sleeves. Her high-
heeled shoes matched the color of the dress. She'd pulled
her hair, now in waves, back on both sides. The diamond
studs and necklace she'd worn the night before were in her
ears and around her neck. Valerie looked lovely.

"Is there any chance we can forget the wedding and stay
here. I hate to share you. The bride will be angry when
everyone is looking at you."

She laughed. "I had no idea you could be such a flat-
terer."

"It's no lie. You look amazing."

She smoothed the dress down. "After I've spent this
much time getting ready and a fortune on this dress, we're
going."

He went to her, slipped his hand around her waist and
gave her a soft kiss next to her mouth. "You'll be the most
beautiful woman there."

"You know that you don't have to say things like that
when no one's around."

"I do if they're true. Everything I say isn't just for show."

He didn't like that she had the idea he only said admiring words because of the charade they were playing.

"That's nice to know." She smiled.

"You deserve to be told daily. You should have somebody in your life saying those things all the time."

It wouldn't be him. He wouldn't or couldn't make that commitment. Still, he wished he could.

Owen called for a golf cart. It arrived by the time they made it down the stairs. The drive took them to a chapel built in the woods, not far from the lodge. The building had been constructed completely out of glass, letting the beauty of the outside in. The pews were already filling up, and they were told their seats were at the front on the left-hand side.

Valerie slipped her arm through John's so he could escort her down the aisle. Owen walked behind her proud she was his date. Valerie continued to surprise him. He could hardly keep his eyes off her. He slid into the pew next to her along with his extended family. Taking her hand, he held it during the ceremony. Soon they were strolling to the reception, which was being held in a tent on the lawn.

"I love twinkling lights," Valerie murmured. "They're so beautiful."

"Reminds me of Christmas trees," Owen grumbled beside her.

"There you go being a cynic again." She gave him a swat on the arm.

"I'm just not that into weddings. I had my one and never again."

Valerie missed a step and he steadied her.

They looked for their assigned table but soon learned there was no seating arrangement other than find your own. The wedding party had place markers, but the rest of the guests were to mix. They took two empty seats at a table with a group they didn't know and soon made new friends. While a small ensemble played in one front corner of the tent during the dinner, they laughed and enjoyed themselves.

Owen made a point not to say anything more about weddings. He'd learned to read Valerie's body language well enough that when she tensed, he realized that his comment about not marrying again had disturbed her, causing her to misstep. Why, he wasn't sure.

After dinner other band members joined the ensemble. People started to move to the dance floor. Owen stood and offered his hand to Valerie. "Would you care to dance?"

A small smile parted her lips as she took his hand. "I don't do much dancing."

"I don't either. We'll do the best we can." He led her to the dance floor.

Owen took her into his arms and whispered against her ear, "I'm really more interested in holding you than I am dancing." They swayed among the other dancers.

"I've told you, you don't have to say things like that when others aren't listening."

"Or maybe I just want you to hear them regardless." He pulled her closer.

Kaitlyn and her husband danced nearby. Owen smiled at her. Kaitlyn's attention stayed more on them than Robert.

At the song change, John cut in and danced Valerie away. She grinned at Owen as she left him on the dance floor alone. Owen couldn't help but feel disappointed not to have Valerie in his arms as he stepped off to the side. He watched as John led her through the dance. The next dance was a faster one. Rich claimed Valerie. Owen heard her laugher as Rich showed off his best moves. She'd won over his sons.

The boys had had their fun. Owen couldn't help but grin. He appreciated that at least the boys liked Valerie and were enjoying their fun at his expense. Just as he moved to re-claim Valerie, Kaitlyn dragged him onto the dance floor. His gaze followed Valerie back to her seat at the table.

Valerie made her way between the tables. She'd enjoyed the look on Owen's face when his boys had whisked her away to dance with them. Earlier her expectations had dimin-ished about her and Owen having anything truly meaning-ful when he intentionally or unintentionally made it clear theirs wouldn't be a permanent arrangement. She'd begun to hope for more with some of the things he'd said to her, and the way he'd acted. Yet they had only been part of the pre-tend. She would have to enjoy what she could of Owen this weekend because they would soon be back to the real world.

As she made the last turn to her seat, she noticed a girl of about twelve sitting at a table nearby. Something about her coloring wasn't right. Along with that she was tripod-ing, sitting with her hands between her legs and leaning forward.

Valerie hurried to her. Pulling a chair close, she sank into it. "Are you okay?"

The girl didn't answer.

The girl's breathing was short and shallow. "Do you have asthma?"

This time the girl looked at Valerie, giving her a slight nod.

"Everything is going to be just fine. I'm a doctor. I'm

going to see that you get help. Does your mother have your inhaler?"

The girl looked at her again as she struggled to breath.

"Is she the woman who was sitting beside you?" Valerie had seen the girl earlier with a woman.

"What's going on Val?" Owen's voice came from beside her.

"This child is having an asthma attack."

She looked up. Kaitlyn stood beside him. "Kaitlyn," Valerie said, "I need for you to find this girl's mother. She about five-five, wearing a black dress and has blond hair. Tell her we need her daughter's inhaler right away. We'll be outside the tent."

To Kaitlyn's credit she didn't ask questions but instead turned and headed toward the dancing crowd.

"Owen, we need to get her outside where there is cool damp, air. Bring a couple of chairs." To the girl Valerie said, "Your mother will be here in a minute, but we need to take you outside. It'll help you breathe better. Just walk slowly and take slow, easy breaths. This'll all be over soon." Valerie helped her up and they moved outside the tent.

Owen hurried to set up the chairs. He saw them settled before he announced, "I'm going after my bag. I'll be right back."

Before Valerie could respond, he was gone. Her focus remained on the child. "Just take it easy. Concentrate on slowly breathing in. And slowly breathing out. That's it. Slowly in. Slowly out."

Valerie picked up the girl's hand and looked at her nail-beds. Despite the dim light, she could see that they were getting darker. She glanced inside the tent trying to locate Kaitlyn. *Hurry.*

As if on cue, Kaitlyn came rushing between the tables and then outside with a woman right behind her.

"Oh, God." The woman dropped to her knees in front of the girl, handing her the inhaler.

Valerie placed her hand on the girl's back and slowly rubbed it. "Now take a squirt and breathe deep."

The girl did as instructed. Still, her breathing hadn't improved.

"Once more," Valerie said, encouraging her.

The girl squeezed her inhaler.

Seconds later Owen pulled up next to them in a golf cart. He quickly had his stethoscope in place and listening to the girl's chest. He also checked her pulse and heart rate. He looked at Valerie. "We need to call 911."

"Agreed."

He stood and pulled out his cell phone.

To the hovering mother Valerie said, "We're doctors. I'm Dr. Hughes and this is Dr. Clifton. Your child will be fine, but she still needs to be seen at the hospital."

The child's breathing had improved marginally, but she needed the care only found at a hospital.

The mother said, "Should I take her?"

"No. This is gone on too long. I can't in good conscience let you drive her."

Owen looked at the girl. "We're going to take a little ride to the front of the lodge and meet the ambulance. Dr. Hughes and I will be right beside you. And your mom can go too."

He handed Kaitlyn his phone. "You come along. The hospital is still on the line."

Valerie had to admire her; once again she didn't question. She was her father's child.

They loaded themselves on the golf cart with the girl sitting between her mother and Valerie in the back. Valerie could still hear the child's gasps for air.

At a slow but steady pace, Owen drove them to the lodge.

The mother held the girl while Valerie continued to check her respirations, Owen having handed her his stethoscope when he'd got behind the wheel. They pulled round the corner of the lodge as the ambulance drove up the road using only its running lights.

Quickly they transferred the child to the care of the EMTs. She and Owen gave them a report and the ambulance left.

Valerie heard Kaitlyn say behind her, "Valerie's pretty impressive, isn't she?"

Owen's voice held admiration. "Yes, she is."

CHAPTER SEVEN

OWEN, VALERIE AND KAITLYN rode back to the wedding reception in reflective silence.

At the tent Owen had to explain to the golf cart driver why his cart had been commandeered.

Kaitlyn started toward the tent. "I better let Robert know where I've been. I'm sure he's has been looking for me."

"Kaitlyn, thanks for your help," Valerie called.

"Not a problem. You were both great. I see now why Dad likes you."

Valerie smiled. "I appreciate that."

Kaitlyn waved and hurried off.

Owen leaned into Valerie so he could be heard over the music. "I'm ready to get out of here. How about you?"

"Before the bride and groom leave?"

He winked. "They'll never miss us."

They slid out of the tent without saying any goodbyes, even to his children. When she asked him about it, he said, "Oh, they'll figure it out. I've got one more night with you, and I'd like some time alone."

"How about taking us the long way around," Owen said to the golf cart driver as he settled in.

The driver nodded and started off.

* * *

Owen put his arm around Valerie's shoulders. "You know I was actually envious of my boys tonight."

She gave him a questioning look.

"I was afraid I was going to have to stake claim to my date."

Valerie laid her head on his shoulder. "That's a nice compliment." A few seconds later she said, "I heard what Kaitlyn said to you."

"She's right. You are amazing. In fact, you've been amazing this whole weekend." More than he ever imagined. "You won her over. The boys as well. Me too."

She studied him a moment. "I didn't know I needed to win you over."

"You didn't, but I have to admit I've seen you in a different light." One that he wasn't sure he was completely comfortable with.

"As I have you. We've known each other all these years and how little did we actually know about each other. I think we've grown closer, don't you?"

"I do." He brushed the top of her shoulder with the tip of his fingers. He couldn't stop touching her. Which was an entirely foreign idea for him. Even with his late wife, he had never been overly affectionate in public. Valerie did something to him that he couldn't explain. Yet he found it exciting. He felt more like himself. He was slowly coming back.

Too soon the driver stopped in front of the cabin. Owen cupped her elbow and helped Valerie up the stairs to the porch. "Would you like to sit out here for a while or go inside?"

"I'd like to sit out here, but I'm going to get out of this dress and these heels first."

"I could do without this monkey suit as well. I'll tell you what. I'll fix us a cup of tea while you change."

"You really are a nice man."

He raised his brows. "Was there ever a doubt?"

Owen had just finished brewing the tea when Valerie returned wearing her silk pajamas.

She picked up the mugs. "I'll meet you outside."

He quickly removed and hung up his suit before pulling on a sweater and jeans. Then he went to find Valerie outside with her legs tucked beneath her on the settee. He took the spot next to her. "I'm going to miss this."

"I will too. It's nice and peaceful here."

"Maybe we can come back again sometime." What had him saying things like that? They had made no plans to continue the pretend relationship beyond this weekend.

Valerie placed the mug on the floor beside her. "I'd like that."

Their relationship had moved beyond his control. Oddly, he liked it.

They continued to sit quietly as he finished his tea. Valerie shivered against him. "You're getting cold. Come on, I'm taking you inside and turning on the fire." He picked up both mugs with one hand and with the other helped Valerie to her feet. With a hand at her waist, he nudged her toward the door. She didn't resist. "You go finish getting ready for bed and I'll clean up in the kitchen."

"Are you sure you have those kitchen skills?" she teased.

He quirked a corner of his mouth. "That much I can do." He waited in the living room until she finished in the bathroom. He couldn't help but watch as she dropped her robe and slid under the covers.

What did he do now? He wanted to go to her. Kiss her. Take her to bed. He was out of practice and couldn't afford to mess this up. He'd always been steady, confident, but this was Valerie.

He would act as normal as possible. As if getting into bed with Valerie happened all the time. Returning from the bath in his boxers, he found the lights had been turned off. The only light came from the glow of the fire in the distance.

Valerie lay on her side facing his side of the bed with her head in her palm. "I was wondering if you were ever going to get out of there."

"Were you timing me?" He climbed under the covers.

"No, but you do have to admit this is unusual for us. The sharing the bed part."

"Which I appreciate you doing. Sharing the bed. Along with other things."

"Not a problem."

He took the same position facing her.

"You know, I've had a crush on you for years." She didn't look at him, her fingers playing with a wrinkle in the sheet.

"I had no idea. I'm flattered." He was. All this time she'd been right there. So near. He couldn't see. He'd been wandering in a fog of half existence until Valerie woke him. Until recently he'd gotten up every day and put one foot in front of the other to make it through the day, with the hope of sleeping a few hours at night. He'd lost his way when Elaine died.

In the last few weeks with Valerie and especially this

weekend, he had started to find his way back home. It felt good.

He pushed back a lock of hair that had fallen across Valerie's forehead and cheek. She didn't try to stop him. Instead, she watched him. Her eyelids closed as if she were savoring the movement when his fingers brushed her skin.

"Valerie, I'd like to kiss you. I want to do more but that's not what we agreed on for this weekend. I don't want to mislead you. I like being with you. I want us to enjoy one another, but I can't promise you more. My heart is closed. I just can't care like I once did. I'm not capable of giving you more than the here and now. We're good friends. I believe we would be great as lovers, but I can't offer you beyond that. Will that be enough for you?" He held his breath waiting for her answer.

"You would never mislead me. I trust you. I want this too." Valerie leaned toward him.

Owen didn't pass on the invitation. His mouth found hers. She rewarded him with a sigh. It only encouraged him. He wanted more. All of her. Valerie lay back, sweet and trusting as he rolled to half cover her. Her arms circled his neck and clung to him as their kiss deepened.

She opened her mouth for him. Their tongues did a dance of desire. His need spiraled to a dizzying height. He couldn't be more entangled if she'd cast a net around him. His thoughts, his cravings centered on Valerie.

Owen's hands traveled along her rib cage to her waist. He wanted to touch her everywhere. To experience all of her. To return the pleasure.

He released her lips to have his skim over her cheek

to nuzzle at her ear then leave kisses at her temple. "You smell wonderful. Taste even better."

"Mmm, that's always nice to hear." Valerie kissed his shoulder.

His blood ran hot. Had he ever wanted a woman more?

His hand cupped her breast. Valerie pressed into his palm. He fingered a button of her pajama top. "May I?"

"I wish you would."

His fingers worked the button open then moved to the next one. The low firelight flickered off the skin he revealed. As he pushed her top away with the intension of revealing a breast, Valerie's hand stopped him.

"I'm not one of those girls at the hospital who flirt with you. I'm not as young and nimble as I used to be. I don't want you to be disappointed."

"You disappoint me? That never occurred to me. I don't think that's possible. I've only made love to one woman in the last thirty years. I'm the one terrified here."

She cupped his face as she offered him a reassuring smile. "Don't be. I hear it's like riding a bike—it comes back to you."

"I sure hope so because I want you so much I'm willing to make a fool of myself."

Valerie took his hand and placed it over her breast. "Touch me, Owen."

"Your wish is my command." He pushed the slick material back, exposing a luscious globe that made his manhood thicken. He lifted her breast, weighed it before his lips found her nipple.

Valerie's hands went to his hair, her fingers holding him steady as she arched into his mouth. Her moan of pure female passion rippled through him. His length throbbed.

He had to have Valerie naked. To see all of her. To have her open to his worship. He released the last of the buttons of her top, pushing it away. He leaned back and admired the feast before him. It had been so long, too long since he'd allowed himself to enjoy a woman's body. His hand trembled as he traced the outline of her nipple. His blood heated at her shiver. Wasting no time, his mouth found her nipple, savoring it, twirling his tongue around the nub until it stood firm.

Valerie moaned low in her throat as she ran her hands across his back and up once more.

He moved from one breast to the other, giving each the same attention. Her breasts were luscious and full. More importantly they were his to explore. He pulled back. "This shirt needs to go."

Valerie lifted off the bed enough for him to remove the concealing clothing. He threw the top to the floor as she pulled him down to her. Her heated flesh meeting his chest had his manhood screaming with need.

As she gave him an open mouth kiss, Valerie's hands ran along his sides and down to his butt. Her fingers slipped under the elastic band of his boxers. They retreated to tease him again as if she couldn't get enough of him. His ego soared. If he doubted his ability to want a woman again, it left with Valerie's gratifying attention.

"These need to go." She pushed at his boxers.

"Say no more."

He climbed out of bed. With a jerk of the covers, he sent them to the end of the bed, leaving Valerie exposed. She pulled a pillow over her.

"Please don't. You are magnificent. All ripe and ready

in all the right places. So perfect. Please don't ever hide from me. You're a gift in so many ways."

Valerie's eyes glistened. She removed the pillow. "Now it's your turn."

She didn't have to ask him twice. He shoved his boxers to his ankles and stepped out of them.

Valerie's eyes widened as his manhood came into view. She boldly studied him. He shouldn't have been surprised. With a look of satisfaction, she reached out a hand.

He rejoined her on the bed. His lips found hers again. Could he ever get enough of her nectar? Heavens, he became a sappy romantic poet around Valerie. His hand kneaded a breast as he kissed behind her ear.

Enjoying the silkiness of her skin, his hand brushed over it on the way to the pajama pants waistband. He teased her just as she had done him. Flicking his fingers farther and farther beneath her clothing. She squirmed beneath him.

"Now who has on too many clothes?"

Without a word she lifted her hips off the mattress. Owen tugged until her pants were down. She kicked them away. He sat back taking in the full length of Valerie by firelight. "You are breathtaking."

Valerie watched him with dreamy eyes, but seemed unsure of his estimation.

"I mean it. Scrubs cover up a treasure trove of pleasure."

Her smile turned soft.

He touched her lips with the tip of a finger. Then trailed it along her neck and down her chest to follow the slope of her breast out to the tip. From there he went along her breast to run down her chest. Her muscles rippled as he moved over her stomach. He circled her belly button, causing her to quiver. He kissed her belly button before continuing downward until he reached the nest of curls at the juncture of her legs.

"Owen." His name was little more than a whisper.

His gaze met hers. "May I touch you? I've dreamed of doing so."

She closed her eyes and relaxed her legs.

He lay beside her. His lips found hers as his finger slipped between her folds to find her wet, ready entrance. As his tongue plunged into her mouth, she flexed toward his finger taking all he had to give. She grabbed at his shoulders, her fingers digging into his muscles as she rode his digit. He pulled out and entered again. With a flicker of his fingertip, she tensed. He released her mouth in time to watch her face fill with pleasure. It was the most remarkable moment of his life to have witnessed her come apart in his hands. She finally, eventually lowered to the bed with a long moan that made his heart swell.

He leaned away from her but continued to stroke a finger along the line of her hip.

Her eyes opened. She smiled. "You have talents you've been keeping to yourself, Doc."

Owen chuckled. "Thank you. It's always nice to know when your skills are appreciated."

She propped herself up on her elbow, pushing him down. "And they should be reciprocated. It's my turn to explore."

Her lips found his in a soft kiss that left him wanting more as her mouth moved to his ear. She nipped and tugged at the lobe before kissing his neck. One of her hands bushed his chest hair, moving lower and lower then up again. He needed her to touch his manhood, wanted it.

His breath caught as her hand ran lightly over the length of him.

"You like?"

"Hell, yeah."

He felt her smile against his skin. Taking her hand, he placed it over his manhood. He didn't have to ask for more. Valerie's fingers wrapped him and pumped. Could life get any better than this?

Valerie gave him a deep seductive kiss that had him on the road to losing control. He rolled away and jerked the bedside table drawer open. Pulling out a package, he quickly covered himself. In the next seconds he was above Valerie.

"Are you sure about this?" If she said no, he might die.

She placed her hands on his hips and pulled him to her. "So sure."

Owen plunged into her. Unable to stop himself he plunged and returned. It had been too long and Valerie was too desirable. He couldn't go slow and easy. The need for release was wild and hot. With one more thrust he threw his head back and groaned. He shook, savoring the completion of a powerful moment.

He fell half on Valerie and half on the bed. His face rested in her neck. Her arms came around him. In a soothing motion her fingers moved across his back.

Heaven help him, he'd stepped over into territory he'd never intended to enter. Even now he wanted her again.

Valerie pulled the covers over them. He'd rolled onto his back and now snored, yet his hand still touched her. She'd moved away, but he'd murmured before finding her again. Her heart clung to that, holding tight.

She was in love with Owen. For years she suspected as much, but after this weekend she had no doubt. The bigger question was what could she do about it? Would Owen, or could Owen let himself feel the same?

The ghost of his wife still ran his life. Valerie didn't want him to forget Elaine because their life together had made up so much of who Owen was. But room must be made for him to live again. Here in this bed, they had been living. She wanted that forever.

His fingertips tickled her side. "Hey."

"Hey yourself."

"Sorry I went to sleep on you. Literally and figuratively." His finger traced the line of her jaw.

"Not a problem."

"I'll do better next time." He kissed her shoulder.

"I thought we did pretty good this time."

He chuckled. "For an old man who's out of practice."

"We can work on the practice part. And you aren't old."

"Thanks for the compliment, but I'd like to show you I'm not always so quick on the draw."

She grinned. "Hey, I'm not complaining but you feel free to show off anytime you want."

"Give me a little time to recover and I'll see what I can do."

Valerie kissed his hand when it passed her lips. "Promise?"

"Count it. Come here." He tugged her to him. "I want to hold you. Let's get some sleep."

Valerie tucked into his side in spoon fashion. She wanted this forever. To be wanted. Needed and desired by Owen.

The sun had yet to lighten the sky when Owen woke her. His hand cupped her breast as he nuzzled her ear. "Valerie, I want you."

His need pressed long and hard against her butt. Valerie wiggled against him.

At that invitation, he shifted so she lay beneath him. "This time I promise you'll be treated the way you should be."

She'd had no problem with before, but she would cherish whatever Owen was willing to give for as long as he would. Their time was running short, and she planned to absorb all of him she could.

He kissed her mouth slowly and gently, her toes curling, before his mouth touched her eyes, the tip of her nose. "You're so wonderful. In bed and out. Thank you for sharing yourself with me."

She gripped his biceps as his mouth found her breasts again. He kissed one then the other. "Perfect."

His hand drifted to her stomach. It fluttered in anticipation of his touch.

"Are you ready for me, sweet Valerie?" His finger found her center. He nuzzled her neck. "You are. What a nice reward." He moved away.

"Owen?" She hated sounding so needy. It had been a while for her too. Now that Owen had opened her desire, she was ravenous.

He chuckled. "Just a moment. I'm not leaving you." He opened the drawer again.

"Do you always come prepared?"

"Are you asking if I expected this? No. Rich slipped these in my hand last night." He covered himself.

"I'll have to tell him thank you."

"No, you will not. I'll not have my children involved in my sex life. Now, where were we?" He kissed her. "I believe I found the right place." Sliding over her, Owen said, "Open for me Valerie. I want you sweetheart."

She did as he asked. He slipped inside her as if he belonged. As far as she was concerned, he did. He rose on his hands. Her hips flexed to meet him. His strokes were long and deep. He'd pull away until she feared he was gone before he'd slowly return letting her appreciate every nuance of what he made her feel. He seemed in no hurry.

"Valerie, look at me. I want to see your pleasure." He dipped again.

"Oh."

He did it again. Pressure built in her becoming an untamed, unruly need. She pushed toward him, desire growling at her. Owen kept the steady pace as her hands gripped the sheet. She flexed and begged, head moving back and forth in her demand to have more of him.

His breathing was heavier, but his gaze remained locked with hers. "We're going to do this together."

With quick deep thrusts, he sent her over the edge. She floated into darkness where only Owen's touch existed. Pure bliss like she never experienced before washed through her. He continued moving in her, holding her in paradise. Then slowly she drifted back to the world of Owen howling his own release.

Valerie wrapped her hands around his waist and pulled him to her. She never wanted to let him go.

"Valerie, sweetheart, nothing has ever been as good as you."

CHAPTER EIGHT

VALERIE WOKE TO an empty bed. She ran her hand over where Owen should have been. The sheets were cool. He'd been gone for a while. There was none of the warm cuddling of the morning before. Their heated lovemaking had been even more than that. She pulled the covers up over her naked body.

She looked around the room. The sun shone brightly. It must have been late in the morning. She spied Owen's head on the other side of the sofa in front of a cold fireplace. He must have turned the gas off when he got out of bed. Their lovemaking by firelight had been all she could have dreamed of.

Untangling herself from the covers, she found her PJ jacket, put it on and padded to Owen. She took the seat next to him. He sat with his elbows on his knees and a mug of coffee in his hands that no longer steamed.

Her heart tightened when he continued to look at the mug, not acknowledging her. This was what she feared the most. She felt her heart cracking. Owen had gone back into his widower shell. She sat there for a moment, fearing what he might say.

Finally, he straightened. He looked at her briefly. "I'm sorry, Valerie."

"What do you have to be sorry for?" If she made light

of his attitude, pretend not to know what he meant maybe it would go away. "I had a lovely evening and night."

He shook his head. "I'm sorry, but it can't happen again."

"Why can't it happen again?" Her stomach clenched.

"I just can't." He sounded so miserable. Conflicted.

"Talk to me. Tell me how you're feeling." They had always been able to talk to each other.

He huffed. "All right, if you insist on knowing. I feel like I've been disloyal to Elaine. I never ran around on her. I might've been tempted, but I never crossed that line."

"You're an honorable man. There's nothing wrong with you wanting another woman now that she's gone. We're two consenting adults. We're certainly old enough to know what we're doing. Are you going to live your whole life looking over your shoulder and letting Elaine dictate what you do even though she's nowhere around? I thought the whole point of this weekend was to distract your children. But it turns out it's not them you're really worried about it. It's your dead wife."

Owen's face darkened. He slammed the mug on the table, splashing the liquid over the side. "You don't know what it's like to lose someone."

She'd obviously stepped into an area he wasn't prepared to exam. "No, I've never lost someone to death, but I do know about being left. The hurt, the shame, the humiliation, the disappointment, the loneliness. You aren't the only one who has ever lost someone."

"You think I don't know that? That I don't live with it every day?"

"I know you do. Do you think Elaine would want you to be living alone, feeling guilty every time you enjoyed yourself?"

"Of course not! She'd want me to be happy. But I don't think she would appreciate me going to bed with women."

Valerie liked to think she wasn't just any woman. "You're not going to bed with 'women.' You made love to me. You, we, did nothing wrong." She reached out to touch him. He flinched and she pulled back. "In fact, we did everything right as far as I'm concerned."

Owen sat straighter. "I didn't mean to imply you did something wrong."

She glared at him. "The part I'm not enjoying is the morning after discussion."

He hung his head. "What I don't enjoy is the guilt I feel."

Her heart softened. Owen looked miserable, but he had to face what he wanted now despite what was in the past. "I know the conflicting feelings you're having must be difficult to deal with. I get that, but you're going to have to figure out what you want. How badly you want it. I'm sorry about Elaine. About your pain. I wish I could make things better for you because your happiness does matter to me. Yet I can't let you hurt me. I promised myself I'd never let that happen again. If you want to feel guilty for something, you should feel guilty about this conversation. I'm going to get dressed. I'll be ready to go in a few minutes."

"I'm sorry, Valerie. Truly I am. I never meant to hurt you. That was never my intent."

"I'm sure it wasn't, but that doesn't mean that it hasn't happened." She moved into the bedroom area.

"I should never have come up with this crazy scheme of bringing you up here or anybody else for that matter."

"That's true. It's my fault I agreed to go along with you." She was tired of trying to get him to care for her. She had been hurt by her ex, and now Owen had done virtually the same thing for the same reason. His heart belonged to his wife, be she dead or alive. She'd let Owen slip under her defenses.

"What I'm most sorry about is how you feel about the weekend, particularly last night because my memories are wonderful." With that she went into the bathroom and closed the door. She managed to make it that far before tears ran down her cheeks.

Once more she'd had been rejected. She'd let her heart become involved again. Then, bam, it had gotten stomped. She shouldn't have expected any better. That was her destiny being thrown to the side by some man. Why did she think anything would be different with Owen? Love had gotten her nowhere. With her heart crushed and alone once more, was she destined to be the "goodbye girl" forever?

She turned on the shower and stepped under the heated spray.

Owen's loving had been more passionate than she'd ever expected to experience. What made it so painful was the one man she wanted the most was still hung up on his wife, his dead wife. Nothing Valerie could say or do would ever change that. She refused to live with a ghost. Too many times she'd been pushed away for someone else to take her place. It was time she stood up for herself and demanded she be the center of someone's universe.

Somehow, someway she would try to move their relationship back to the friendship zone. Yet she was confident nothing would be the same. Too much had passed between them in the last few days. There would be no going back. The problem with the rejection this time was it hurt deeper, cut more acutely than it ever had before. Worse than that, she feared it would be a chronic condition for her to always love Owen. He was everything she'd ever wanted in a man: kind, loving to her and his children, funny, charming, considerate, loyal and proud.

Her tears fell with the water. Her hope to find a spot in his life gone like the water down the drain.

Thirty minutes later she stood in the living area with her luggage at her feet. "I'm ready to go when you are."

He'd dressed while she had been in the bathroom. Apparently he was as eager to leave as she, his bags already by the door. She glanced back to bed where she'd spent some amazing hours.

Reaching for her bags, Owen said, "I'll get that for you."

"I can handle it."

He looked like a balloon that had lost its air. "Valerie, it doesn't have to be like this. I'm sorry I hurt you."

She must stand her ground, or she would break down. "I think it does have to be like this. You and I both know from watching surgery, it's better to cut it away with a sharp knife. The dull ones only cause infection and a painful death."

Valerie didn't miss his wince. She'd hit a nerve. She didn't care. Her feelings were hurt as well. Deeply. "Owen, can we go now. I don't want to talk about this any further. We're just going around in circles."

She handed her luggage to the golf cart driver waiting at the bottom of the stairs. The young man placed it on the cart then took Owen's. She sat in the seat closest to the front. Owen moved in beside her but didn't touch her. For that she was thankful. If she could just make it home without falling apart. They came to a halt in front of the lodge. Owen went to see about the car. Now if she could manage not to see his children before they left.

The mother and daughter from the wedding the night before came out of the lodge. Valerie smiled at the young girl. She looked much better than she had at the reception. Valerie took a careful look at her coloring. "How're you feeling this morning?"

"I'm fine." The girl gave her a tentative smile, which was more than she done earlier.

The mother and child walked over to where Valerie stood. "I didn't have time or the mindfulness last night to introduce myself. I am Michelle Warren." She put a hand on the girl's shoulder. "This is my daughter Ashley. I want to thank you for helping her last night. For being so aware of what was going on. You and the other doctor saved her life. We're both very grateful."

Valerie looked at the girl. "You're very welcome. I'm glad I was there when you needed me. Be sure to keep that inhaler with you at all times. It's important."

"I will."

Owen joined them.

"This is Ms. Warren and Ashley from last night."

His demeanor changed slightly to the one she'd seen him use with patients. "Of course! I'm glad to see you up and about. You certainly look better than you did last night."

The girl smiled, as did her mother. Owen had charmed two more women. "Thank you very much for your help. I don't know what we would've done without it."

Owen looked at her. "I'm glad we were both there." The valet pulled up in Owen's car. "We have to say goodbye now. Take care of yourself."

As the mother and daughter walked away, Owen and the valet loaded the luggage. Valerie opened the front passenger door to climb in.

"Dad. Valerie."

With a sinking heart, Valerie turned to see Kaitlyn hurrying toward them with her arm up. They had almost gotten away.

"I went by your cabin, but you'd already left. I wanted to say goodbye."

Owen joined them beside the car.

Kaitlyn spoke to Valerie. "I just wanted to say thank you for making my dad smile again."

Before Valerie knew what was happening, Kaitlyn had her arms around Valerie pulling her close. Valerie couldn't help but be touched.

Just as quickly Kaitlyn let go then hugged her father. "I'll see you guys back in Atlanta."

Without a word Valerie got in the car. On top of feeling like the dregs in a teacup over the trashed relationship with Owen, now it was made worse by deceiving Kaitlyn and her brothers. This weekend had gone worse than she had anticipated it might.

They had been traveling for an hour when Owen said, "I'd like for us to at least try to be friends."

The pain in his voice pulled at her heart. "I don't know if I can go back."

"Maybe with more time I'll be able to have a real relationship."

She refused to let his sad voice take hold of her good sense. "Owen, I'm in my forties. I'm not waiting on any man anymore. What if you're never ready?" Or she didn't want him anymore when he came around. That wouldn't happen, but she wasn't going to tell him that.

"I just need more time." His tone had turned pleading.

"Take all you want." She laid her head back against the seat. At least if she slept her heart wouldn't hurt.

Owen rubbed his chest. The tightness in it wouldn't ease. He'd figuratively kicked Valerie in the teeth. Now he didn't know what to do about it. He'd been honest with Valerie about how he felt. Even so, she had the right to feel horrible.

He couldn't get away from the memory of their perfect night, of Valerie being warm and snug in his arms. He wanted more of those moments. Thank goodness he hadn't said so out loud. To have led Valerie on more than he already had would be wrong. What had he been doing making love to Valerie when he was still bound to Elaine? All the guilt had washed over him when he woke.

Owen hadn't given up that part of his life completely. He wasn't ready for that. Didn't feel emotionally stable enough yet. Until the last few weeks, his passion had been locked behind a door. Valerie had opened it, releasing a Pandora's box of desires.

He needed to sort through them, but he had to be honest with Valerie as well. She deserved that. Still, that honesty had hurt her. He glanced her. She remained asleep. They had been up most of the night after all. Vivid, sweet moments assaulted him. She looked just as lovely at this moment as when she had dressed for the wedding or when the firelight had reflected off her skin in bed.

Even though he wanted to caress her cheek he wouldn't let himself. She'd shared her pain with him. About how careful she had been with men. Then he'd gone and treated her exactly the same way. She had the right to feel devastated. To have no use for him.

He'd set her at arm's length. No, he'd pushed her across the room, out of the house and down the road. He wouldn't blame her if she never spoke to him again. He'd stepped over the line and lost his friend.

Now his guilt was twofold: Valerie *and* his wife. How could he get past this to regain Valerie's friendship? If he didn't find a way, he'd have lost both of them. The idea of that happening crushed him.

Once they arrived at her condo he offered to carry in her luggage.

"That's not necessary. I've got it." She started up the walk.

"Valerie, is there any way I can make this better?"

She faced him. "Owen, please don't say anything you don't mean. Just leave it alone. We've both said what we feel. We'll adjust and move on."

Feeling gut punched, he said, "If that's the way you want it."

"It is." She started up the walk again then stopped. "Owen."

"Yes?"

"Be kind to yourself." With that she squared her shoulders and walked to her condo. Without looking back, she closed the door behind her.

Why had that simple action seemed as loud as a ten-foot-thick metal door slamming. Too final. He wanted to run after her, bang on that door and beg her forgiveness. Yet that wouldn't be fair to her.

Valerie had opened up to him. Had shared all of herself and he'd thrown it back at her. It had been a long time since he had been in bed with a woman, but he recognized when someone cared for him. The problem stemmed from the fact that he cared about her as well.

He'd work his way through this. When Elaine had died, he'd had to do the same thing. Stay busy. See the kids more. Visit friends. Play more golf.

Maybe with time, he and Valerie could become friends again. If she agreed. But after the way he treated her this morning he didn't see her ever trusting him again. With the weight of sadness hanging over him, he drove home to his large empty house that offered him no peace.

Valerie breathed deeply before she entered the OR the next day. Monday mornings tended to be overwhelming on the best of days and today it was worse. She would have to face Owen. Even the hours they had been apart hadn't ease her pain. The hardest time had been when she tried to sleep without him. In just a short while her body had begun to crave his warmth.

"Hey, Dr. Hughes," Melissa, the woman behind the department desk said. "How was your weekend?"

Valerie swallowed hard. "It was nice to be off. How was yours?"

The sounds of footsteps drew her attention. She glanced back to see Owen approaching. Had he heard her response? Unable to remember what Melissa said Valerie responded, hoping it was appropriate. She took the OR schedule. "Thanks."

Her hands shook as Owen came to stand beside her. She would get through this. The first time would be the hardest. She didn't meet his eyes. "Good mornin', Owen."

"Mornin', Valerie."

She waved her schedule. "Have a good day." On shaky

legs, she somehow managed to walk away without running into anything. Owen's look remained on her as surely as if he'd been touching her on the back.

Inside the scrub room she took a deep breath. Meeting him would get better. Each time easier. It had to. She couldn't live like this until she retired. Should she consider a transfer to an outpatient clinic? But that would be running again. She done that before and didn't want to do it again.

She hated that her life had been turned upside down. It hinged on him, and she didn't like it. She'd known better but let her emotions rule her head. When she had visited his home, she had seen all the signs that he wasn't ready to move on with his life. It wasn't that she didn't know better; she just didn't want to give up his attention. Having it had made her feel whole. She started to believe their story of being involved, had enjoyed it too much. Now she'd let a wonderful night of pretend end her carefully crafted life.

Really, when she thought about it, she should have felt ashamed of how she'd treated him. Maybe she should have been more understanding. He had loved his wife so much he felt disloyal to her. Yet he had treated Valerie with little respect. Still their weekend together had been a nice one up until yesterday morning. More amazing than she ever dreamed possible. That was the problem with dreams. Sometimes they come true then turned into nightmares. She couldn't trust them. Daring to dream was foolish.

The days dragged. Valerie was grateful for the ones she had off because she didn't have to face Owen. Yet she hated not going in because she didn't get to see him. The pain was double-edged. Her emotions remained in a state of constant flux. Just when she thought she had started to recover, she backslid to where she had started. That happened on the days when she saw Owen the most often.

She had managed to keep him at a distance as much as possible. If he came in the locker room, she left. When he happened to come in the snack room, she made an excuse to leave. The share-a-candy-bar days were over.

Owen gave her as much space as possible as well. He wasn't pursuing her or asking her questions. There hadn't been a call from him. He was respecting her wishes. In an odd way, she wished he wouldn't. She missed him more than she wanted to admit. Her life went along as a long, drawn out, dreary movie in black-and-white. More than once she wondered if Owen was having as difficult a time as she. She liked to think so.

Two weeks passed before they were forced into close proximity. Any anesthesiologist, including fellows, not in the OR were invited, strongly encouraged, to observe a difficult case of a three-year-old who had an extremely larger goiter. These cases made intubation difficult, but this was a very difficult case. Dr. Dale Rhinehart, the head of the department, was the attending on the case. Despite his authority, all were invited to offer suggestions about the procedure. It was a rare case; few of them would see this type of operation but once in their career.

Preparing to do the intubation, Dale offered one of the doctors an opportunity to assist. Valerie smiled to herself when Mark jumped at the chance. She wasn't surprised. The rest of the group gathered in closer. In an effort to make sure she didn't find herself pressed against Owen she moved off to one side. His gaze found hers from where he stood on the other side of the room. Her heart fluttered. She made herself look away. That's when she saw it happen. From her vantage point, she had a clear view of Mark from the side. He palmed a vial of fentanyl and slipped it into his pocket.

Valerie's pulse skittered. Had she seen what she thought she had? In her shock she looked at Owen. Their gazes met and his brows furrowed in question. Her attention returned to Mark.

Surely she had been seeing things. Mark couldn't be the person stealing drugs. He was a good guy, willing to help anytime. He had the makings of a great doctor. Would he do it again? He had to show a count at the end of the surgery. How would he account for the missing drug? Her mind raced with questions.

"Be careful not to obstruct the airway at this point," Dale said.

With everyone except Valerie's attention focused on the deliberate, slow movement of Dale's hands, Mark reached into a different pocket and removed a vial. That was how he was doing it! The count would be good for the number of vials while the amount of anesthetic would only be half.

"Another cc fentanyl."

"Here." Mark removed the clear liquid from the vial with a syringe before inserting it into the port of the IV.

Valerie's teeth clenched. Mark made it look like he had anticipated Dale's need instead of what he was really doing—covering up his theft. Suspicion would fall on the whole team; that wasn't fair. Far worse than that, he might be high while caring for a patient.

Valerie seethed. How dare this upstart of a doctor mislead the entire department into believing he was something he wasn't? The whole situation made her angry. She planned to do something about it. Now.

She hung back, talking about the operation with a few of the other doctors, waiting for the room to clear. She was keeping her eye on Mark, who had volunteered to set the anesthesia area in order. Valerie pretended to look over the supply cabinet.

When only she, Mark and a nurse remained, Valerie said to the nurse, "Sally, would you mind getting a few more intubating kits out of main supply for this room?"

With Sally gone, Valerie stepped over to Mark. "I saw what you did."

"What do you mean?" A flicker of panic filled his eyes before they filled with belligerence.

"I saw you put the vial in your pocket."

"I don't know what you're talking about." He went back to replacing a tubing.

"I believe you do. You have a problem. You need help. I want to help you."

He turned his back to her. "I still have no idea what you're talking about."

She moved up beside Mark, forcing him to look at her. "I think you do. You're too smart. Too good a doctor to waste your life stealing drugs."

"You're wrong." He continued to clear away the equipment.

"I saw you take a full vial and replace it with a half used one. I know what I saw. I'm going to have to tell Dale. He'll get you help."

Mark leaned toward her. "You're crazy."

"Look, the board is getting ready to start a criminal investigation. When the police get involved, it'll be harder to stay out of big trouble. You need to get ahead of this by turning yourself in."

A snarl curled Mark's lips. All pretense of being innocent washed away. He leaned in closer. "It's your word against mine. All I have to do is put the blame on you. All of the medicine was accounted for."

"Except you put a half-used vial back when you took a full one," she spat. The anger she'd been banking had bubbled up.

"You can tell them that, but I'll say you did it." His voice had taken on a superior note. "It'll be your word against mine."

He was right. She didn't have any way to prove what she saw. Yet she couldn't let it just go by as if she'd seen nothing. That would make her an accomplice. "I'm going to give you a day or two to come clean. Then I'm going to have to say something. I don't want to ruin your career. You can get help for this problem."

Mark's face twisted into a mask of anger, eyes flashing. "You hear me, Dr. Hughes. You say one word about this to anyone, and you'll be sorry. I know people who aren't very nice. If they find out I can't supply them, they will not be happy. You keep your mouth shut. What happens won't make you feel good."

Sally came through the door. She and Mark quickly separated.

Valerie's entire body shook as anger ran hot through her. She helped Sally put away the supplies then left. She never would've dreamed she'd be involved in this type of situation. To be threatened made it terrifying.

She stalked down the hall. It wasn't until Owen spoke that she noticed him. He took her arm, stopping her. A shot of electric awareness rippled through her.

"Hey, are you okay? Did something happen in the OR? I saw the look in your eyes."

"I can't talk about it here."

She and Owen may be having their own problems, but she needed someone she could trust. Owen. She knew it as surely as she knew her name. He cared about his patients, this hospital, his family and her. Right now, she needed him.

"Come in here." He pulled her into an empty OR that hadn't been sterilized for the next operation. "What's going on? You look like you're scared to death."

"I can't believe it. Mark is the person who's been stealing the drugs. He says he's selling them to someone, but I suspect that he's an addict." She wrung her hands as she told Owen the entire story of what happened in the OR. "To top it off he threatened me!" She paced the room and back again.

Owen's face had darkened. "He did what? I'm going to find him right now. I'll see him arrested."

Valerie appreciated his solidarity.

He started for the door but she caught his hand. "Wait. You can't do that. We have to catch him in the act. He's right, it's his word against mine."

"They say it tends to be the person who is extra helpful and eager who is able to steal because those are their opportunities to do so." Owen's jaw muscle jumped.

"Yeah, but I would never have thought Mark could be that person. He would be the last person I would've imagined. Sometimes I'm not as good a judge of character as I would like to be."

Owen wasn't sure if that remark had been meant for him, but he felt the punch just the same. "We need to formulate a plan. If it's going to come down to his word against yours, then we'll need to do something to catch him in the act."

Valerie shook her head. "This isn't your problem. I saw him. I confronted him. I'll see about it. You shouldn't get involved."

"If you're involved then I am too."

"Why should you be?"

"Because you're my friend. You need help." He wanted to say more, but he wasn't sure what he should say. "I'm going to talk to Dale. Let him know we need to meet him off-campus to talk about this. I don't want Mark to get the idea you told anybody."

"I don't need your help. I can talk to Dale. I can take care of myself."

Owen's pressed his lips together as he looked at her. "That may be so, but in this case I think you can use all the help you can get. I'm not going to let anything happen to you."

"I still don't understand why."

She just didn't get it. He cared but he couldn't say that. "Let's just say that I don't like to know that my friends are being threatened."

She threw up her hands. "All right."

"Now that's settled, I want you to go to the locker room and get your purse. Don't bother to change clothes. Head straight home. I'll speak to Dale. You don't want Mark to even have a hint that you might tell anyone."

"Don't you think you're overreacting a bit?"

He gave her a stern look. "No. Drug addicts can get desperate. Unpredictable. At home keep your doors locked, pull all the curtains closed and don't open the door to anyone."

A stricken look covered her face. "Okay."

He studied her a moment in disbelief. "You're going to do what I asked without an argument?"

"Yes. You think I should be cautious so I will be."

The relief that went through him wasn't measurable it was so great. "Thanks, Valerie. I'm glad you're taking this seriously."

"I have to admit he scared me."

Owen didn't like the sound of the quaver in Valerie's voice. He fisted his hands so tight his knuckles turned white. The idea of Valerie being threatened by anybody, but in particular Mark, who they both had admired and trusted, made him livid. He had a hard time believing it, but he couldn't ignore what Valerie said she saw. It wasn't something she would lie about.

Regardless of the gulf between them for the last two weeks, he couldn't ignore his need to protect her. If he could, he'd put a indestructible bubble around her. Whether she liked it or not. Something in him he'd never experienced before came to the surface when she'd been telling him about being threatened. He'd always been a peaceable man, but right now he'd like to beat Mark to the floor.

Two hours later, Owen opened the restaurant door, allowing Valerie to enter ahead of him. Dale was meeting them there. He'd been curious about the request, but Owen had said he would explain over dinner. His boss had no idea that Valerie would attend as well. Owen didn't want Dale to accidentally say something that he shouldn't.

Owen's idea had been for it to look as if their group had

gotten together for an impromptu meal between longtime coworkers in case anyone saw them together. He wouldn't be surprised if Mark was watching Valerie. At this point he wouldn't put anything passed him. Owen feared that she had said enough that Mark might be provoked into doing something horrible.

Owen found Dale sitting at a table in the back corner and led Valerie there. They took their seats and placed orders. Dale then looked between them before he said, "Exactly what's this about? Are you going to tell me you're dating?"

"No!" Owen and Valerie said at the same time.

Dale sat back. "Apologies. I must have misread that. That's what I get for listening to department gossip."

Owen was surprised that he didn't actually mind the idea of being the object of department gossip. In an odd way, he wished he and Valerie were. At least they would be friends again. He glanced at Valerie who fiddled with her napkin. He cleared his throat. "Valerie needs to tell you what she saw today. Then you'll understand."

She wasted no time in sharing in detail what had occurred between her and Mark.

Dale shook his head when she finished. "He's right. It's his word against yours. He could just as easily accuse you. Confronting him isn't the answer. We have to outsmart him."

"I've given that some thought. I wondered what you think about this." Owen looked at Dale as he laid out his plan. "What if we changed the label on a paralyzing drug. While Mark is preparing for a patient, he's left alone. That would be his opportunity to grab the drug. Instead of him shooting up with fentanyl, he paralyzes himself. He wouldn't get hurt, but we could catch him red-handed when he couldn't move. He couldn't deny what he'd done. Plus we'll take pictures and document what we did."

Valerie smiled. The first Owen had received in a long time. "That's quite ingenious. You have a sinister mind."

"Thank you. I'm glad I could impress." And he was. It had been too long since he received a compliment from her, or her even act as if he was worthy of praise.

Dale leaned back in his chair. "That just might work. The question is how do we know when to set him up?"

Owen grinned. "You make the assignments. In a couple of days assign him to me. I'll make sure he goes after the vials."

"Hey, you can't leave me out or he'll know I've said something. It has to happen naturally."

Owen touched her arm. "I don't want to take any chance of you getting hurt."

"I'm not going to get hurt. Mark is more likely to do it in my OR because he knows he has the upper hand around me."

Owen's jaw tightened. "You can't take that chance."

"If you can I can."

"Uh, hum." Dale brought their attention back to him. "Let me handle the placement of Mark. You two just be prepared for him when the time comes. Keep a low profile for the next few days. Be as normal as possible. Valerie, let him believe he has you under control. If we rush this, we might lose our only opportunity."

"That's a good idea," Owen said.

Valerie nodded.

Dale continued, "I'm going to notify the board about what's going on. I don't want anything negative coming back on the department." He gave them a pointed look.

"There can be no heroics. I don't want anybody getting hurt. Neither of you and certainly not the patients."

"Agreed." Owen looked at Valerie, who nodded. She was being too quiet. She was either scared or planning something of her own. Which she better not be.

"There's one more thing." Dale looked directly at Valerie. "I'm concerned about his threats. I don't think you should be alone any more than necessary. I'm going to see about one of the security guys staying with you at night."

Valerie jerked forward. "I don't need—"

Owen stopped himself short of taking her hand and holding it. "I've got that covered."

Valerie's mouth opened and closed like a fish.

"I'll be staying with her."

CHAPTER NINE

VALERIE AND OWEN said their goodbyes to Dale before she turned on Owen outside the restaurant. "What made you say that in front of Dale? You're not going to stay with me."

"Then you can stay with me," Owen shot back. "Either way I'm not leaving you alone until this is over. Mark threatened you. That's enough for me."

She didn't want to admit to herself or him that she would feel safer if somebody was with her. Looking over her shoulder all the time wasn't fun. She huffed. "All right, you can come to my place."

In his car a few minutes later Valerie said, "Now that I think about this more it's ridiculous. Mark is not going to come after me. Not in that kind of way. I don't need a babysitter."

"Too late. You've already issued the invitation. You can't take it back."

She couldn't help but smile. Something that had been difficult to do in the last few weeks, and with this situation with Mark it didn't look like life would get better.

"Like I've said, you never know what he might do. Until Mark is caught, then you're with me or you're at work. I went by my house before I picked you up to get some clothes and toiletries."

She groaned but didn't bother to complain further. Ev-

erything about Owen's demeanor and tone said he would
have his way.

At her condo she flipped on the lights and dropped her
purse in the chair. "You know where the bath is. The extra
bedroom is across the hall from it."

"I promise to be a good houseguest." He hoped to cajole
her into accepting his presence.

"I wish you weren't here."

Owen placed his hand over his heart. "How inhospi-
table of you."

"I'm sorry. That did sound awful, and very ungrateful.
I'm glad to have someone here with me."

"Just not me."

She studied him a second before she turned to leave the
room. He was right and she hated to admit it.

A few minutes later she walked into the living room
headed for the kitchen to find Owen wandering around
looking at her pictures and examining a wooden box that
had been her father's. Having him touch her things seemed
so personal, as if he had done the same to her. "I'm going
to have a cup of tea. Do you want one?"

He said without turning around, "That'd be nice. You
have a great music collection. Do you mind if I put something on."

"I guess not."

His face tightened and brows narrowed. "I'm not here to
make you miserable. If you don't want me to play music,
just say so. If it would make you more comfortable, I'll
go to my room."

"You're right. I'm sorry. No, don't go to your room."

Owen picked out a jazz record and put it on. He sat on

the couch. How fast life changed. Valerie could barely tolerate having him around, and it hurt deeply.

A few minutes later she sank into a chair near him. "I still can't believe this. How wrong I was about Mark."

"I like to think I'm a fair judge of character."

She looked into her teacup. "Do we ever really know others? Isn't that why we get hurt?"

Owen shifted his feet. "Are we talking about Mark now?"

Her gaze met his. "Maybe not."

"I know I hurt you. I hate that I have to be here making you uncomfortable. I wouldn't be if it wasn't necessary." His eyes were sympathetic.

Her lips thinned into a line.

Owen went over to sat in the chair next to hers. He leaned forward, giving her a pleading look. "Hey, I didn't mean that like it sounded. In fact, I've missed you."

"Owen—"

"The fact is if Mark is capable of stealing drugs, then he's capable of doing other things to protect himself."

"You can't stay forever." He'd disrupted her life far too much already.

"I don't know that forever will be necessary. What I do know is I'll be here until Mark is caught. I realize there are problems between us, but let's put those aside until we handle this one. Regardless of what has happened or hasn't happened between us, I still care about your welfare."

He just didn't want her heart.

Owen looked down to the end of the hall at the bedroom door firmly shut against him. It was closed as resolutely against him as her attitude had been for the last few weeks.

He couldn't blame Valerie. Yet he hated himself for the way their relationship had deteriorated.

That was fine. He was here for a colleague who needed help. He would do what he was doing for anyone. Hell. Now he had started fooling himself. He was here because of Valerie being in danger. She wasn't just any colleague. Valerie meant more to him than that.

He didn't care to examine how much more important. If something happened to her, he would be devastated.

Owen hadn't hesitated to insert himself into Valerie's life, and condo. He had a mission. No one would hurt her if he could prevent it. He didn't think being a man on a white charger was part of his personality, but apparently it was.

When he'd entered her home, he'd dropped his bag and wondered around looking at her belongings. Everything was neat and tidy. The kitchen had a long counter, which included barstools. The space looked adequate but was nothing in size compared to his kitchen. Valerie deserved more than what she allowed herself. She had a wonderful stereo system and great taste in music.

Now he had to try to sleep with her just steps down the hall when all he wanted was to knock on the door and ask if she would like to dance. He lay down with his hand behind his head, listening to the sounds of Valerie moving around in her room.

What would it be like to experience this each night? One of the aspects he liked about being married was having another person around him, being a part of someone else's life. He had been lonely for so long. Maybe that's why he had latched on to Valerie so easily.

He hadn't found real sleep since the night he and Valerie had made love. His arms craved her now. How many times had he relived those moments? Wished he had them back. Still his guilt held him prisoner.

A noise at his door made him look up. Valerie headed toward the living room.

She jumped when he came up behind her. "It's just me."

"I guess I'm more spooked than I thought. I can't seem to go to sleep." She turned on a lamp beside the sofa. "I didn't mean to wake you up. I was going to get something to drink."

"I wasn't asleep so you're not bothering me. How about watching some TV until we get sleepy? Work a puzzle? Play a game of cards?" Anything to spend time with her.

"An old movie might do it." She turned on the TV and flipped the channels, finding a black-and-white movie. "Do you want popcorn and something to drink?"

"Sure."

She soon had a bowl filled to the top with popcorn, and brought Owen a cold drink. When she started to sit in a chair, he said, "I can't reach the popcorn from over here."

Instead, she headed to one end of the couch and set the bowl between them.

Valerie made sure the boundaries remained defined. Wasn't he the one to blame? He shouldn't complain. It wasn't fair to give her mixed signals, pushing then pulling her back again. Yet he couldn't stay away from her.

He tried to focus on the movie as much as possible. Once he reached for popcorn at the same time as she did. The hot sizzle of awareness rippled through him at their touch, leaving him with a desire he couldn't act on. How little it took to make him want her.

She jerked her hand away.

He made himself focus on the movie. Glancing at Valerie, he found her head lolling to the side. She'd fallen asleep. He placed one of the decorative pillows from the sofa on his thigh then gently guided her head to rest on it. She pulled herself into the fetal position with a sigh. Tugging the throw off the back of the sofa, he spread it over her.

Owen continued to watch the movie, much happier than he had been when she wasn't within touching distance. He let the TV roll into another movie but turned the volume down. Soon he drifted off to sleep.

Too many nights he hadn't slept. Tonight, he would. Because Valerie lay next to him.

Valerie woke unsure where she was. Something heavy lay across her shoulders. She recognized that noise. It was Owen snoring. How had her head ended up on a pillow?

She and Owen had slept on the sofa. Where was her pride? First chance she got she snuggled up to him. As if they couldn't be separated. She looked up to find Owen with his head back on the sofa and his eyes closed. He'd have a crick in his neck when he woke.

She didn't need to add more to her agenda where Owen was concerned. When this business with Mark was over, they would go back to the way things were. Polite, but distance friends. Not that she was excited about that. She'd been more miserable then than when they weren't talking to each other.

He needed to understand she wouldn't be falling into bed with him just because of his proximity. Not that he had asked her to. He had abided by her wishes and kept his distance, been a gentleman. She'd like to think he had been as unhappy as she, but she couldn't tell that by his actions.

Slowly easing out from under his arm, she sat up, stiffly.

"Hey," a rough-edged voice said.

She hadn't been stealthy enough not to wake him. "You should've woken me and told me to go to bed."

"I was just glad you were sleeping."

"You'll certainly need to get some good rest tonight after sleeping on this sofa."

There was still some time before they should be at the hospital. She went to the kitchen, started the coffee maker then pulled out flour and eggs and milk. Her way of dealing with anxiety was to bake. Owen was the definition of anxiety for her.

Fresh bread was in order. There was something about kneading dough that soothed her nerves. She had made a lot of it in the last two weeks. To the point she had a freezer full, and the neighbors had begged her to stop bringing them any because they were getting fat. She hadn't taken all of it to the hospital because she didn't want it to get around how much bread she was actually making. People would wonder why.

Now her frustration lay on her couch. Yep, she needed to make some bread.

She filled a bowl with ingredients. It felt good to have her hands active when she wanted to put them all over Owen. Just more thoughts she shouldn't be having.

In a few hours she would have Mark to deal with. She might believe Owen was overreacting by staying with her, but it did make her feel securer knowing he was there. Dealing with Mark or that type of crime wasn't something she was familiar with.

Her back remained to the living room as she punched a roll of dough down before putting it into a greased bowl.

Strong arms circled her waist bringing a yelp from her. Warm lips touched the skin behind her ear. That was her soft underbelly. The spot that made her melt every time.

Her eyes drifted closed as she leaned back against the hard wall of Owen's chest. After a moment she gathered her wits and pulled away. "Please don't do that."

His arms dropped away. "I'd like to say I'm sorry, but I couldn't resist. You look so adorable standing in a cloud of flour."

She settled her voice, finding a nicer tone. "Just don't do it again."

"I can't promise that either." As if he hadn't heard what she said he looked around her. "What're you doing?"

"I'm making bread."

"At this hour?" He looked toward the window. "It's not even daylight."

"It's my stress reliever."

"Hang in there, it's all going to be okay in a few days, I think."

Yeah, but not where he was concerned. After this stay it might even be worse.

"Well, at least it's useful. Unlike other things you could do. Do I get any?" He looked hopeful.

"Maybe if you behave. Now move out of the way so I can get cleaned up. Coffee is ready."

He gave the bowl a hopeful glance. "Aren't you going to bake it?"

"It has to rise. I'll get ready for work and put it in the machine. It'll be ready when I get home this evening." She gave the dough an overly zealous punch.

"Don't you mean when we get home?"

"Yeah, you too." The idea made her nervous.

He took her hand. "Can't we be friends again?"

She studied him a moment. "Nothing has really changed, has it?"

Owen took a moment before he said, "I guess not."

Valerie shook her head sadly. "There's coffee. Have all you want. Make yourself at home."

Thirty minutes later, Valerie joined Owen in the living room.

He said, "I'll drive this morning."

"No, I'll drive. We'll tell anyone who asked that you had car trouble and I picked you up." She needed some control over her life.

"Okay. If that's the way you want it."

As they entered the hospital he whispered, "Remember, don't antagonize or let yourself be by alone with Mark. Take no chances."

She nodded.

His fingers tangled with hers. "I know you don't believe this, but I do care about you. I don't want to see you hurt for anything in the world."

Valerie's heart swelled as ripples of warmth flood her. "I appreciate that."

To her surprise, the day went smoothly.

Mark acted as if nothing had happened between them. His smile was as bold and bright as ever. He asked to help, but she never saw a false move out of him. Maybe their talk had made some headway. That was until she passed him in the hall when no one else was around. His eyes narrowed in a glare, making it clear he remembered their conversation.

Valerie shuddered and continued walking.

On the way home she told Owen about what happened.

"At this point I'm not surprised by anything."

"I'm fine."

"I know you are. I just wish it was me instead of you. I hate for you to be his focus. Still, let's try not to think about him tonight. How about dinner and a movie?"

"It's been a long day. I'd prefer to cook. Takes my mind off of having all this nervous energy."

"A home-cooked meal would be a real treat for me."

A couple of hours later they sat at the counter finishing their meal. Owen had never felt more at peace. There was something right about having a good meal, with a woman he liked in a cozy home. He missed the intimacy.

"This bread is truly amazing." He held up the last of his third slice. "Why haven't I had more of it? I guess the rest of the staff gets to it before me."

"Maybe you're just not paying attention."

"Do I miss so much around me or just things about you? I'm sorry. I should have been a better friend."

She touched his arm briefly. "Don't worry about it. You've been in a bad place for a long time. You're being a great friend now."

The next evening, Owen sat in his car waiting on Valerie to exit the restaurant. He had begged her to make an excuse not to attend the baby shower, but she insisted on going. The nurse who was expecting was one of her favorites. Valerie assured him she would stay with the crowd and not leave until he had texted her he was outside so he could follow her home.

He would have driven her to the event, but she didn't want anybody asking questions about them. This time he was the one bothered by her trying to hide him. He didn't have to imagine how she must've felt when he'd treated her that way. He didn't appreciate it a bit. Truly resented it.

She'd left him standing in the kitchen the night before, sure the last few minutes had been another crossroads in his life, and he'd chosen the wrong road. Again. He wasn't sure he liked that Owen.

She then said goodnight without inviting him to her bedroom. It saddened him that she was seeing to it they remained distant. He had hoped they'd made some progress back to their friendship. She had made it clear she wouldn't be having any more physical contact than necessary. He'd crushed her heart and was paying for it.

While Valerie remained safely inside the restaurant, he'd driven to his house to pick up more clothes and to check on things. His footsteps echoed inside the house. He'd never noticed that before. The warm comforting place it had once been had turned cold. The smell of cooking, the hum of life, or soft music playing weren't there. They were at Valerie's. Here it was nothing but a huge empty house. It wasn't a haven of peace anymore.

Since Elaine died, he'd let the house remain as a monument to her. He hadn't moved a picture or a trinket in five years. If someone moved something, he moved it back to where she'd left it.

He walked into his den. The area that had always been his. It, like the rest of the house, hadn't changed since Elaine had died. Owen shook his head. She owned the room more than he did. All this time he'd been fooling himself.

It was as if his world had stopped. Then he asked Valerie to be his pretend girlfriend, and the world started to spin once more. He'd started to breathe again. His heart started to beat. He'd started to dream, hope, and wish for more than work and to exist. He had an interest in his life. All of that because of Valerie.

He trudged upstairs to his room, his and Elaine's room. He stopped in the middle and turned around. He looked at her portrait. "Elaine, it's time I moved on. I'll always have the memories of our years together. Our children are a precious gift you have given me. I know you would want me to be happy. Please wish me the best."

Owen gathered the clothing he needed. With lighter steps than he'd had in years, he headed down the stairs and out the door. It felt odd but wonderful to look forward to life. For too long he had been going through the motions. His insides rippled with nervous excitement.

Leaving through the kitchen with a new attitude, he stopped to looked around. Valerie needed something like this instead of the small kitchen in her condo. She would bring it to life.

Before he climbed into his car, he looked at the house that was no longer his home. He didn't need its support anymore. His children came but never stayed a long time. They had moved on with their lives. It was time he did the same. This weekend he would call a Realtor and see about putting the house up for sale.

Arriving back at the restaurant, he'd parked where he could see the door and the parking lot. Texting Valerie, he let her know he was outside.

She returned:

I'll be out in a few minutes.

* * *

As good as her word, she exited the restaurant along with a couple of other ladies, chatting as they walked over to their cars. Once Valerie pulled away, he drove up behind her and followed her home. As they entered the condo, he said, "I've decided to sell my house."

She turned. Surprise ringing clear in her voice. "Why?"

"I don't need it anymore. It's too big. Lonely."

"Why now?"

He shrugged. "It just seemed like too much when I went home. Like it was time to make a change."

Valerie pursed her lips and nodded. "I'm glad for you, Owen." She continued down the hall to her bedroom and closed the door.

He stared at her door. That wasn't the reaction he'd expected. Why had he thought she would care either way? Why did it matter?

CHAPTER TEN

BETWEEN OWEN LIVING with her and waiting on Mark to make a move, Valerie's nerves grew taut with apprehension. She'd spent the last two nights hanging out in her room so she wouldn't get used to Owen being so close. Keeping him at a distance was the only way to protect her heart from further hurt.

When he'd announced he planned to sell his house, she'd been shocked. Should she read something more into it? What had him making such a huge change? Had he started to see that he'd been existing instead of living? Or had something else brought it on? Whatever it was, selling the house would be a big step for him. She wished him the best, but to keep her sanity she couldn't be more involved than that. Even if she wished she could.

After all, that really wasn't her business, but somehow, he made her feel that his decision might've been related to her. Yet when she'd given him the opportunity to say something he hadn't. She intended to stand up for herself and what she wanted. Never again would she give without getting. Too often she'd been let down.

She didn't want to think of Owen as one of those people, but he'd already done it once. What made her think he wouldn't do it again? Yet he had shown such concern for her. Enough he had interrupted his life to stay with her.

She didn't trust her judgment enough to know his true motives. After all, she believed Mark was a good person. She certainly had been misled by her ex, and just a few weeks ago Owen had disappointed her. What she needed from Owen was a grand gesture. Proof that she mattered.

The problem remained that her heart was involved. Owen carried it around with him. He just didn't know it. Or maybe he did, and he didn't care.

She entered her kitchen to see Owen with his butt against the counter, ankles crossed and coffee cup in hand. He looked at home in her small condo. Too much so for her comfort.

"Mornin'…" The soft rumble of his voice made her tingle. Moments like this were what she dreamed of the most. Had wanted all her life. The feeling of belonging and being wanted. She couldn't help but wish for this every day.

"Good morning." She gave him a bright smile. It was nice to get up with another person. Especially Owen. She'd known the first time she'd snuggled against his warm body her life would never be the same. But she couldn't trust this feeling. He would be gone when Mark was caught.

"You know I've had about enough of this."

Owen's eyes lost their glimmer and narrowed. "Are you referring to me or what's going on at the hospital?"

"At the hospital." She wasn't rude enough to say it included him.

His body relaxed and his eyes brightened. "Hey, it'll be over soon. Mark won't last long before he'll need to get a fix. Just hang in there."

"I hope so. If that doesn't happen soon, I'm going to need to be on anxiety meds."

Owen placed a reassuring hand on her shoulder, giving it a gentle rub. "You've got this."

It was a nice reminder he was in her corner regardless of her efforts to shut him out. With the exception of her family, she'd never experienced that before. For Owen's support she would always be grateful.

Before they entered the hospital, he once again reminded her of the need to remain calm and to take no chances. "I've got your back."

She pulled the door open. "Who's got your back?"

"He might take it if he's in my OR, but I doubt it. Unfortunately, I expect he's going to do so in yours. Especially because he thinks he can control you since no one else has questioned him. As grueling as the last few days have been, we've given him a false sense of security. He believes his intimidation worked. He's feeling safe."

She hadn't thought of it that way. With that security he'd be more likely to act.

"Go have a good day."

"After that little speech, how's that supposed to happen?" She started down the hall toward the surgery department. Owen followed.

With a wry smile, he said, "Okay, the best day you can."

"I'm already looking forward to tomorrow. I need the day off." She could use a day away from the hospital.

"I'm off too. Do you want to do something together? Maybe a round of golf?"

"Owen, I don't think that's a good idea. Nothing has really changed between us." She couldn't keep acting like he wasn't hurting her with their togetherness.

"I'm sorry. You're right. It won't happen again." He didn't look happy with the decision.

It was midafternoon, and Valerie's last case when Mark entered the OR. Even with a mask on she could tell he had a smile on his face. The humor in his eyes changed when he met her look. They became serious with an edge of desperation. This was it. Today he would be stealing again. She would bet money on it. The medicine sat on the table beside her, waiting for him. She just had to keep her cool and not give anything away.

He spoke to those in the OR then came up beside her. "I've been assigned to this case with you."

Valerie swallowed. She stilled her shaking hands. This would be his opportunity, and she would give it to him. Lifting the IV line, she checked it. "I'll do the injection if you want to handle monitoring the gas."

He lowered his head, giving her a direct look. In a low voice he said, "I'd rather do the injections."

She received the message loud and clear. He wanted his drugs. She nodded.

"I like working with you." He made sure to say it loud enough that the others heard it.

Valerie wished she could say the same. Now it was her job to see that her patient came to no harm while trying to catch Mark. She watched him closely but never saw a wrong move. Occasionally they made eye contact. Each of them performed the duties necessary to keep the patient asleep and pain free.

The surgeon had almost completed his job when Mark said, "I need more fentanyl."

This was her chance. Valerie's heart rate picked as she handed the bottle she'd prepared for this moment to Mark.

She had watched close enough to know the patient had plenty of pain medicine in his system.

Not actually seeing Mark put the vial in his pocket, she had no doubt he had done so. He filled a needle from a vial that was half-full. She had handed him one that was full. He filled a cc of the liquid and put it into the IV line. The extra cc wouldn't hurt the patient or Valerie would have stopped him.

With a satisfied look in his eyes, he placed the vial on the table beside her. He had gotten what he wanted. Valerie all but held her breath until the procedure was complete, fearing something would go wrong. She'd tried her best not to watch Mark too closely.

With the surgeon finished, Mark volunteered to see the patient to recovery. Valerie was good with that. With her blood racing, she searched for Owen and Dale.

Dale wasn't in his office. Panic welled. She had to find help. On her way to the department desk, she saw Owen approaching. She nodded, her look not leaving his.

When he reached her, she grabbed his arm. "He took the bait."

"He did! Let's just hope he uses it here." Excitement flashed in Owen's eyes.

She looked down the hall. "We have to find him. He'll disappear to shoot up. Where's Dale? We'll need security."

They walked to the department desk. "Have you seen Dale?"

"I think he's finishing up a case in OR three."

They started that way when Dale exited the room. The look on their faces must have given them away.

"Where is he? I'll get security." Dale took long strides toward his office.

She and Owen quickly followed him. "We don't know. He went to recovery and hasn't returned."

"Then we need to find him. I wondered how much longer it would be before he went after it again. I'll call security. You two stay out of this." Dale continued down the hall.

"Come on, Valerie." Owen took her arm. "We'll wait at the department desk. I don't want you to be by yourself if Mark happens to realize you gave him the wrong drug and comes looking for you. If only half our plan works, he could still be dangerous."

"Shouldn't we look too?" She started down the hall away from the department desk.

Owen's grip tightened. "No." His word stopped her. "We're going to do what Dale said. Security will handle it from here."

"Okay. But I'm not hiding." She lifted her head before turning toward the other end of the hall. Valerie had never had somebody protect her as vigorously as Owen. She liked the feeling of being a priority to him. Something she'd never been to any man in her life.

Minutes later she watched from the desk as Dale met two large security guards when they entered the department. If they were going to catch Mark, they had to find him soon. The medicine would be starting to take effect by now. They didn't dare have him recover before he was located. She needed peace of mind. Today this had to end.

The guards methodically went from room to room. Soon they entered the break room. She could only wait for their return. Owen moved closer. She appreciated the reassurance. They waited. Waited.

"Shouldn't we go see what is happening?" She took a step forward.

Owen took her elbow. "Let them do their job. You've more than done yours."

"He's right." Dale continued to watch the door through which the security guards had disappeared. The time clicked by on the large industrial clock on the wall above the desk. A crowd of curious staff gathered around them. The guards usually steered clear of surgery.

"What's going on?" people asked from behind them.

Valerie held her breath. The guards were taking a long time. They must have found him. She clutched her hands in front of her. Soon this would be over. Then her life would return to what it was. No Owen there every day. Sadly.

One of the security guards stuck his head out of the break room door. "We found him slumped over on the floor by the bathroom."

The group started toward the break room. Valerie's heart jumped. She raised her chin. "I'm not missing a minute of this. I've earned it."

They entered the break room to find Mark lying on the floor. His eyes were open, and he could hear everything happening but couldn't move. One of the guards came out of the restroom with a plastic bag in hand. Inside was the vial Mark had taken from her in the OR along with a syringe.

The air whooshed out of her and strong arms wrapped around her waist. Owen lifted her into the air.

Without a thought Owen grabbed Valerie and pulled her to him. His mouth found hers. "We did it."

At her startled look, he glanced behind them to see the staff watching them with a mixture of surprise and smiles.

Valerie gave him a gentle push. "Everyone is watching."

"I don't care." His lips found hers again for a quick kiss.

This time the staff clapped. There were even a few hoots.

He'd been more worried about Valerie than he realized. It wasn't until Mark had been caught that he recognized how much. Now he didn't care who knew it anymore. If Mark had harmed her, he didn't know what he would have done.

He looked at Valerie. Her eyes were wide, her cheeks flushed. She never looked more beautiful. He was in love with her. The realization should have scared him to death, but instead he felt alive again.

Dale cleared his throat. "The police are going to need statements from you two." He directed his attention to the crowd. "Everyone else please get back to work."

The staff members slowly exited the room.

Owen nudged Valerie out of the way as the guards lifted Mark into a chair.

"He'll be all right in a few minutes," Dale assured the guards. "Have the police come back here to get him." He turned to Owen and Valerie then smiled. "You two make a good team. Nice work. As soon as the police have finished with you, take off. I can handle anything else." He gave them each a knowing look. "Enjoy your evening."

Valerie's face pinkened again.

Owen stayed close to Valerie as she told the police what happened, then he had his turn. Dale assigned a nurse to sit with Mark as he came out of the drug.

"You ready to go?" Owen asked Valerie.

"Past. I'll get my purse."

On the drive home they said little. After his acceptance of his feelings for Valerie, he needed to take a moment to think about them. He wouldn't be surprised if Valerie sent him home. He had no doubt she would chastise him for kissing her. She'd been diligent about keep her distance. Would she listen or believe him when he told her how he felt?

He'd hurt her deeply with his rejection. How could he make that up to her? He had to find the right time to discuss it with her. Now wasn't it. They were emotionally drained. There would be a better opportunity.

A few minutes later he followed her into the condo.

Valerie dropped into a chair, leaned her head back and closed her eyes. "What a day."

"I couldn't agree more." Owen followed her example and flopped on the couch.

Neither of them talked for a few minutes then Valerie said, "You kissed me in front of everyone."

His chest tightened. Opening his eyes, he looked at Valerie. Hers remained closed. There was a tenseness to her despite her relaxed posture. "I did."

"Why?" She still didn't look at him. "I thought you didn't want anyone talking about you, us." She shrugged. "Then again there is no us."

"I want there to be an us," he said softly.

Valerie's eyes opened. "You do?"

"I do. I kissed you because I was relieved you were out of danger. I was proud of you. You helped catch a bad guy. I think you're wonderful. Strong, confident, smart. We make a good team, whether it's in the OR, catching criminals and when making love. I don't care who knows how I feel about you."

"But you didn't have to kiss me."

"I didn't plan it if that's what you're wanting to know. It was pure emotion on my part, and I'm not sorry I did it. You might not want to hear this or you might throw it back in my face and I won't blame you after the way I've treated you, but I kissed you because I realized I love you. I was so afraid for you when Mark went into your OR. Dale had to stop me from following Mark in, which might have tipped him off. I paced the unit floor until it was all over. I was terrified something would happen to you."

Valerie sat straighter, her head turned and she was listening intently. "What did you say a few words back?"

"That I was scared for you?"

She slowly shook her head. "No, just before that."

"That I love you."

"Yeah, that." A smile formed on her lips.

He moved so he could take one of her hands. "I do love you. I just hope I haven't destroyed what feelings you had for me."

Before he could take a breath, Valerie was in his arms giving him a tender kiss that had him daring to hope she might feel the same about him.

"I love you too."

He pulled her close and sealed the moment with another kiss. One that soon turned to passion. He nudged her away. "I have more to say before I can't stand it any longer and ask if I can take you to bed. It needs to be said. I want you to have no doubts about my feelings for you.

"I did you wrong the day after we made love. My only excuse is that I was running. I was running from my guilt, from my true feelings and my fear of how life had changed since you truly entered it. I think there must've been something more there even before we went to the wedding because you were the only person I considered taking with me. I think my feelings have run deep for you for a long time, and I just refused to open my eyes.

"I want you to know if you'll give me another chance that I'll never choose anyone over you. I'll never leave your side. You're the most important person in my life. In fact, you are my life. If I've learned anything in these last two miserable weeks of not having you in my arms, not kissing you, it is that I don't enjoy life without you. You brought me back to life just as surely as if you had resuscitated me.

"I've treated you badly. I know I don't deserve you, but I promise to always stand by you. I'll try to never let you down. If you'll give me another chance, I'll do my best to be the man you need. I do love you, and I always will."

Valerie cupped his cheek and kissed him softly.

"I've never heard a more perfect speech and I have one as well. Over the last few days you have stood by me. You disrupted your life to make sure I was safe. That's more than any other man has ever done. You've shown me more by your actions than anyone ever has in words what a special man you are. Even at the wedding, more than once you protected me, stood beside me. You are who I've been looking for all my life."

Owen pulled her into his lap and kissed her soundly.

"Do you remember back when you had us asking questions so we could get to know each other?"

Valerie nodded.

"I said I wanted to wait to ask you something because I didn't know what to ask. Well, I've thought of my question."

She grinned. "I already know your spirit animal."

"I'm not going to ask my question if you don't stop making fun of me."

Valerie straightened her face. "Go ahead. I'm listening."

"My question is, will you marry me?"

Her eyes widened, and her mouth dropped open. Her arms tightened around his neck. "Yes, my love. I can't think of anything I want more."

* * * * *

COMING SOON!

We really hope you enjoyed reading this book. If you're looking for more romance be sure to head to the shops when new books are available on

Thursday 28th September

To see which titles are coming soon, please visit
millsandboon.co.uk/nextmonth

MILLS & BOON

MILLS & BOON®

Coming next month

HER OFF-LIMITS SINGLE DAD
Marion Lennox

This was not sensible—not sensible in the least. There was no need at all for her to stay with Rob for a moment longer. She was this man's tenant and a colleague, and that was all. She lived at the far end of the house. She needed to keep some distance.

But distance had never been Jen's strong suit.

Maybe it was her childhood, absent parents who'd appeared sporadically, causing her to cling fiercely, to take what she could because she'd known they wouldn't be there the next day.

Maybe that was why she'd jumped into all sorts of disastrous relationships—okay, Darren hadn't been the first. Jump first, ask questions later. Take people at face value because looking forward didn't change a thing.

And here it was, happening again. This man had so much baggage—impossible baggage—yet here he was, looking down at her, smiling, and here was that longing again—for closeness, for warmth, for connection.

Her friend Frankie might have poured a bucket of cold water over her, she thought, demanding, "Will you ever learn?" But right now…

Right now Rob was reaching down to help her up. His

hands were strong and warm, and his smile was oh, so lovely.

Maybe this time…

What was she thinking? It was too soon—way, way too soon.

But that smile… She had no hope of fighting the way his smile made her feel.

And he tugged her a little too strongly, or maybe she rose a little too fast, and all of a sudden she was very, very close.

Here comes another catastrophe! She could almost hear Frankie's inevitable warning.

But Rob was right here, and she could feel his warmth, his strength… His lovely hands were steadying her, and he was still smiling.

She was lost.

Here I go again.

She could hear her brain almost sighing in exasperation, but did she care?

Not tonight. Not when he was so close.

So, she thought blindly as she felt the warmth of his chest, felt his hands steady her. Catastrophe, here I come.

Continue reading
HER OFF-LIMITS SINGLE DAD
Marion Lennox

Available next month
www.millsandboon.co.uk

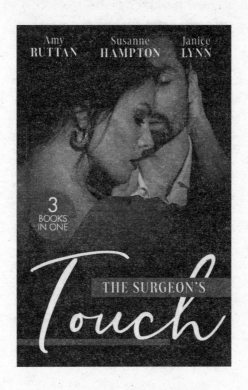

OUT NOW!

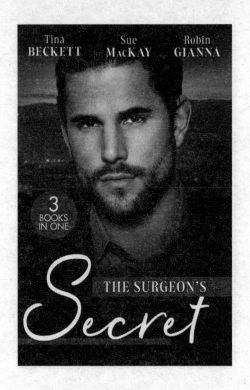

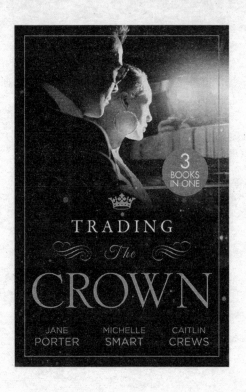

OUT NOW!

LET'S TALK
Romance

For exclusive extracts, competitions and special offers, find us online:

f MillsandBoon

𝕏 @MillsandBoon

◎ @MillsandBoonUK

♪ @MillsandBoonUK

Get in touch on 01413 063 232

MILLS & BOON

THE HEART OF ROMANCE

A ROMANCE FOR EVERY READER

MODERN

Prepare to be swept off your feet by sophisticated, sexy and seductive heroes, in some of the world's most glamourous and romantic locations, where power and passion collide.

HISTORICAL

Escape with historical heroes from time gone by. Whether your passion is for wicked Regency Rakes, muscled Vikings or rugged Highlanders, awaken the romance of the past.

MEDICAL

Set your pulse racing with dedicated, delectable doctors in the high-pressure world of medicine, where emotions run high and passion, comfort and love are the best medicine.

True Love

Celebrate true love with tender stories of heartfelt romance, from the rush of falling in love to the joy a new baby can bring, and a focus on the emotional heart of a relationship.

Desire

Indulge in secrets and scandal, intense drama and sizzling hot action with heroes who have it all: wealth, status, good looks…everything but the right woman.

HEROES

The excitement of a gripping thriller, with intense romance at its heart. Resourceful, true-to-life women and strong, fearless men face danger and desire - a killer combination!

To see which titles are coming soon, please visit

millsandboon.co.uk/nextmonth